You will have to read this novel for yourself to see how a brilliant writer has found the perfect form for evoking the effects of time and place and the forces of history and nature on the lives of human beings. As the title suggests, the movement of *Twister* is as inexorable as it is unpredictable. Genanne Walsh is a writer of extraordinary powers. The work of this novel is both raw and lush with poetry. Her characters live and breathe, and in their intersections, real truths are revealed.
**—Laura Kasischke, author of *Mind of Winter***

Genanne Walsh's *Twister* is a chronicle of a small town amid the calm before the storm—but so much more. This book digs beneath the surface of place to create a kind of *Spoon River Anthology* for our time replete with secrets, truths, startling reckonings—and very, very threatening weather. As fine a new novel as you will read this year.
**—Peter Orner, author of *Last Car Over the Sagamore Bridge***

Genanne Walsh's *Twister* is a gripping page-turner, but also has that much rarer quality of transcendent, almost preternatural empathy that very few works of fiction possess. *Twister* has it. Novels often get us to walk in someone else's shoes, but only rarely to climb into someone else's skin. Walsh miraculously climbs into the skin of not just one, but a dozen characters. When I finished *Twister*, I felt the way the Old Man in the novel felt about being struck by lightning: "It furrowed me into something new."
**—Robert Thomas, author of *Bridge***

# TWISTER

Genanne Walsh

www.blacklawrence.com

Executive Editor: Diane Goettel
Cover design: Janeen Jang / Amy Freels
Cover image: *Each Year We Pray* by Camille Seaman
Book design: Amy Freels


ISBN: 978-1-62557-937-9



Published 2015 by Black Lawrence Press.
Printed in the United States.

*For Lauren*

# Part I

I know what the wind knows.
Tearing across the prairie,

bits of grit riding its cold storm—
grit like coal dust, or like ashes:

*What's the difference?*
*There's enough love here.*

—Jane Mead

*

Sweeping over the Arctic Archipelago, puckering nipples and chapping faces across Nunavut: in Grise Fiord, Resolute, Gjoa Haven; crossing into Manitoba, freezing the top layers of Island Lake, Gods Lake, nameless ponds, dew crunching underfoot. The front gathers, pushes over Winnipeg, Grand Forks, Fargo, Lincoln, on it comes, barreling through tornado alley to meet its match: spring! A current weaves a lothario path across the Gulf of Mexico, up through Anguilla, Santo Domingo, Port de Paix, Nassau, bringing the scent of cinnamon, slums, and rotting magnolia leaves, trailing across tobacco farms, mighty rivers, strip malls, state colleges, Army barracks, drained wetlands, golf courses. Pushing west into dry Pacific air. Blowing across the southwest, arid and punishing—imagine dustbowls, cow skulls, locusts, parched earth—rolling off the Rockies, faster as it flows east. Sisters clash and mingle in the wide open skies of the continent's midpoint—dry meets damp, warmth amassed and shuddering into updrafts and squalls, rushed by the eager fingers of their cold northern lover. Thunderheads build, form, break apart, and build again, gathering strength unseen by those below. North, south, east, west, we'll put these people to the test. Havoc's in play, the winged creatures sense it, though even the crows don't know the scope of what's to come.

Hover at the midpoint. Turn the radio dial; hear snatches of the lives below. Listen.

Crows rustle on the wires over Main Street, over Mondragon's Emporium and Dunleavy's Fine Shoes (&Shoe Repair); over The Bluebird Café and the bank and the old town square. Black feathers lift and wheel past the liquor store and a shuttered B&B, past power lines, houses, cars, and churches, over the cemetery, streets giving way to fields, farms laid out in a neat expanse: the vast acreage of agribusiness, a few sturdy family farmers holding on, green squares of corn and soy bringing order; and in the center, down the old county road, not far south of Johnson's Creek and just past the Infamous Elm, Rose's overgrown reluctant acres.

One small, tangly patch, that land of hers, the well pulsing like a heart. *Listen.*

# Rose

Rose moved through the thickets with a sharp set of shears, pruning, smoking a cigar. Her dog, Fergus, dreamt and farted on the porch. All this growth and nothing to show for it. Lance would have been shocked. Her son was so good at making things grow—crops, blackberries, houseplants, hopes. There was nothing he couldn't coax into life. A good kid, her soldier boy. Smart in every sense of the word. Fergus thumped his tail. He always knew when she was thinking of his number one love.

"That's right," she said to Fergus. "Him." He scratched an ear in response. She had the sense of the sky pulling taut into a bow. No, she shook her head—a *bowl*. Overhead, a great bowl. Chipped at the edges but still functional.

Rose gave the stogie one final pull and coughed in a hard burst. Phlegm rose and Fergus lifted his head. She set her shears on the porch and peered into the well. Either the well was getting deeper or the sky darker; she couldn't see her reflection. There must be a scientific reason: cloud patterns, air molecules. Or no reason at all.

"Onward, into the void," she told Fergus. "Come on, let's check the mail." They walked down the long drive, gravel skittering, her anklebones clicking in protest.

"How did this happen to me?" she asked Fergus. There must be some mistake.

The well was getting deeper but the mailbox was smaller. Its little red flag was rusted upright, and faded letters spelled out her dead husband's name. *Theo*. She reached in to pull at the contents and could barely wrench her hand free. Nothing but junk. Last week there had been another letter from her stepsister, on prissy peach-colored paper and smelling of lilacs, with the careful spidery lettering of a serial killer. Rose hadn't read Stella's letter yet—it waited on the mantel for her to build a fire, so she could throw it in and watch the flames.

The mailbox held a catalog full of crap she didn't need. And more notices from the bank, the vultures. She tore the catalog and the bank's window envelope into strips and threw the pieces into the air. Shiny paper caught in the branches. Then the metal box vibrated a little—something inside wanted her attention. Fergus looked up the drive and whimpered low in his throat.

She shoved her hand into the mailbox once more and pulled out a flimsy pale blue airmail envelope that had been caught in the back seam. *Rose Red* looped across the paper, in elegant script. Next to her name was a sketch of a long-stemmed rose with a single thorn. There was no return address.

The bowl of the sky, paler than the envelope she held in her hands, contracted a bit. She cleared her throat. Her thumb was bloody, nicked in some way that escaped her, and she spread her fingers wide, considering. Something dark as pinesap had worked into her fingerprints and calluses, and her cuticles were a mess. She had no idea about the rest of her. All the mirrors in the house were covered.

In the parlor she set the new airmail envelope next to Stella's letter on the mantel, side by side. Just above hung a framed photo of her and Theo and Lance: Lance about four, skinny and stick-straight, grinning wide. Theo's left hand rested on Lance's shoulder, and the right dangled down by his side. Theo's eyes were open wide, giving him a look of quiet surprise, like a deer in headlights. What the hell had astonished Theo all the time? She'd never figured it out. Rose sat on Lance's other side, eyes squinting against the flashbulb with a fake, purse-lipped smile, looking like a stranger, someone she'd never want to know. Most of the pictures of Lance in the early days had Stella in them, so they weren't up. Rectangular outlines remained on the wall where Rose had taken them down. The phone rang as if from a distant room, or even further. She ignored it.

In the kitchen it was hard to find a clear space on the counter or in the fridge. She shoved some dishes aside and dropped meat scraps and yesterday's leftover oatmeal into a bowl for Fergus. "Eat up." Branches pattered at the window. She picked up a dish at random from the counter and went out to empty it into the compost pile.

A faint breeze gave her pause—not déjà vu, but a similar, physical feeling of almost-but-not-quite remembering something she'd forgotten. Crows swooped across the sky. Before she could start pruning, Fergus growled and barked down the driveway. His warnings had come in handy lately, giving her a few minutes to duck out on would-be company.

Today she wasn't swift enough and a familiar voice intruded. "Rose." Not from down the drive—he'd come from the east, directly through the fields. Her neighbor Brown, the young one, Perry. He stood embarrassed and determined, clean young face slipped over his father's, the Old Man's ears holding up shiny dark hair. Genetics. DNA. A crazy thing.

"Hello, Rose. How are you?"

"Fergus," she said. "Quiet." Fergus, proud of himself for giving a warning, settled into a spot on the porch to lick his balls.

Behind the young Brown she saw a flash of yellow in the hayloft window. The girl again, Sill, Perry's daughter, sneaking in where she wasn't wanted. Both of them—no, the whole damn Brown family—coming around individually and collectively. They didn't mean her well.

Perry shifted from one foot to the other and tried again. "How are you?" That question! She could live the rest of her life without hearing it.

Red blooms, white blooms, climbers, crawlers; heavily scented, with new buds always pushing up. They were as bad as weeds. Rose used to like them. Stella once put them in vases every morning. The trunks were young then, almost spindly. Now they were as thick as her leg. No more playing around—she took her shears and sent one flying. Take that!

"Have you thought about what I said?" he was asking. "Rose?" There was his Old Man, in the greedy eyegleam, apple not far from the tree.

"Perry." She knew how to handle him. "How is your father?"

The clean face reddened. A rough hand clenched the paper that he'd pulled from his pocket and then rolled up like a newspaper to swat a dog.

A few years ago Lance had set fire to a bag of steer manure—just for fun and high spirits—and left it smoldering. *Barnburner,* Old Man Brown had called her son, and threatened legal action even though the thing had only smoked, harmless. *Never,* she'd said to Lance. *Promise me, no matter what happens to me, you'll never let the Browns have this land.*

". . . My father," Perry was saying, "he's mellower, Rose, since the lightning. He was hit out on the east acres in '97. You remember?"

"Of course." The bowl flickered overhead, restless. She remembered. She shook her head, noticing a few new shoots already sprouting. Up in the hayloft, that yellow flash again. Fergus licked himself on the porch, rhythmic and soothing. Brown the Younger was still red, still talking, his voice lower now, like gravel. Did he know where his daughter was? People go missing all the time.

"I can offer you a fair price," he said. "And with Lance—" Fergus stopped licking and raised his head. Rose snatched the paper from Brown's hand and tossed it into the well. She turned and slammed into the house, Fergus close at her heels. Brown retreated.

Something clattered in the pantry, probably the mice trying to get to her bag of rolled oats. A shoot busily worked its way up the kitchen drainpipe, blooming in leggy insistence from the sink. She grabbed an old boot lying by the door and hurled it toward a gray mass—got you!—but missed, cracking open one of her jam jars. Goddamn it. Lance loved her preserves. He was always underfoot in the kitchen, the first place he came after school, eating her out of house and home. A hollow leg, that's what Theo used to say.

*Why did the chicken cross the road, Ma?* Not waiting for her to guess. *To lay it on the line*. He'd grabbed a thick slice of bread, knife dipping into the jam. She'd swatted the dishtowel at him and he swiveled out of the way, reporting that he'd seen Stella in town and then pausing for her reaction. His t-shirt had had a rip near the neck. Strange, the details you remember. What had she said to him that day?

She left the jam jar where it lay shattered, went to the mantel, and considered the airmail envelope—but instead picked up Stella's letter. The peach envelope, unstamped, had appeared in the mailbox like all the others from Stella. God, what a pain in the ass her stepsister was. Stella's spindly purple ink looked like crisscrossing lines on a map of underground streams. It took a while to decipher: *Dear Rose, I know you don't want to hear this, but I think about you and our Lance so often, and it is my deepest wish that you will let me come visit. Rose, we are still family, much as you might like to forget*—I have forgotten. I would. If you didn't keep reminding me—*We need to talk*—

Rose threw the crumpled letter into the cold fireplace and blew her nose into the hem of her skirt. An image came, burning into the back of her lids as she clamped them down: she and Stella sitting and rocking on a porch together, fingers busy making something, flying in a blur, a bright yarn stretched between them and mist rising through the branches above. *Stop it, Stella!*

Rose had a tall cup full of premium old pens on a shelf in the kitchen, with a few cheap ballpoints rolling around, leaking on everything. She took a ballpoint and a paper grocery bag and went to sit on the back porch, her feet propped on the rickety stairs, the brown paper crinkly on her knees.

*Listen, Stella. He's not yours anymore*—She wrote a few lines and scribbled them out, ink smearing, and started again an inch down. *Listen, Stella. I am much too busy to visit with you. My roses are shooting up gangbusters. Lots of pruning, like always. There's corn to manage and I don't have—Plus, the well is acting up, and Fergus needs his shots. A new well may need digging.*

*Stop bothering. However, have this jar of sour berry chutney, I found it in the pantry and thought of you.*

*Your stepsister, Rose.*

*P.S. Stop it, Stella.*

*P.P.S. The Browns are circling.*

A patch in back of the house still smelled like Stella. She'd seeped into the ground like spilled oil. Flowery perfume that cost too much, bought on credit. Dandelions dappled the green with splashes of bright yellow. They used to put Lance's little blow-up swimming pool in this spot and sit with their drinks and watch him splash around. The two of them, her and Stella, sunk in lawn chairs, watching Lance. Black hair with a straight part, red hair sticking up—that was them. White marble legs next to ruddy freckled legs, ice cubes clinking in old-fashioned glasses, lime wedges, red toenails, calluses. Sister sister, mother mother. Blood. But not quite. What were they? Lance: little birdwing boy, in the blue circle of his wading pool. Did he see it, splashing around in that plastic tub, his face already full of piss and vinegar—a fountain cherub come to life and making the most of it. *Look*, he'd yelled, *watch me*!

The softness of the air, the softness she saw in Stella's gaze, watching Lance, the softness in her own bones in that one lit moment. The pink and gold light of dusk fell, covering the branches and brambles, still manageable back then, covering them, their skin, eyes, hair. The grass under their bare feet reached up, soft and scratchy. "Fireflies," Stella said, running her finger along the rim of her thick-cut glass. *Watch me*! Lance spat upward like a fountain. They'd laughed hard, encouraging him. He pissed a loopy arc over the edge onto a blackberry bush and they were laughing too hard to stop him or say much other than, "Lance!" and "Boy, you'd better . . ." The light was too beautiful for anything more, and fading by the minute.

Rose remembered that day over others, over times they'd laughed harder or said more. Certain moments hold you in their palm. And later, when a different moment shakes you in its fist, it's that moment you were cupped in so gently that you think of. You have to bear them both. All the time between them falls away and they press together, intricate sketches on two sheets of onion paper held together up to the light. See what new shapes they make? See the people, now and then? Happy sad. Love hate. God shakes and tosses, yells, *Snake eyes*! It's just how it goes.

Rose touched her forehead. Enough of remembering. What had that ever gotten anyone? Several dozen freshly picked dandelions were in the apron spread across her lap. She began to knot the flowers into a chain. That far-off phone was ringing. *He's not yours anymore*.

The truck remembered the drive to town, even if Rose didn't. She'd done it a hundred times, a thousand—foot on the pedals, hands on the wheel. The dandelion chain dangled across her dash, and the paper bag letter to Stella waited in her pocket. She would deliver the flowers. Then she'd take the letter to Stella—why waste a stamp?—along with the jar of preserves that was now jammed against the seat seam under Fergus's butt.

The landscape didn't match the ache in her head; everything was flat and pale. "No way around but through," she told Fergus. He didn't hear—his head hung out the truck window. At the side of the road Old Man Brown's Infamous Elm tree loomed, the only thing in her field of vision that had any weight to it.

Some time later, Fergus's panting quickened as the truck slowed. Rose pulled off the interstate into an empty parking lot. Swaths of green dotted with white stones stretched out in unnatural perfection, and she felt a gut tug toward the overgrown thickets of home. As she cut the gas, the engine sputtered and sighed. Her breath caught. A flag on a pole hung slack in the windless air. The dandelion chain had slid off the dash onto the seat beside her. How dare she refer to those yellow weeds as flowers—what was wrong with her? Some sort of bird cawed.

Driving home after, Rose felt a niggling, a gnawing, as the buildings of town—Mondragon's, Dunleavy's Shoes (&Shoe Repair), liquor, bank, gas, The Bluebird Café, her father's decrepit shuttered B&B—erased themselves. Her wheels turned over and over, spooling everything behind them into grayness. She patted her empty pocket.

In Mondragon's she'd tucked the letter to Stella and the preserves onto a shelf next to a bag of rice. Stella had been nowhere in sight, but the husband had been there, all right. On the floor below the passenger seat was a shopping bag full of items that she didn't want and hadn't asked for. Ward Mondragon had insisted, and shoved the bag at her so urgently she'd had no choice but to take it. A man full of dough and confidence, he was kind to everyone because he could afford to be. He'd hung a framed photo of their empty-eyed president on the wall behind the register, a place of honor. "Please, Rose," he'd said, escorting her out of the store, leaning through the truck window and patting Fergus on the head. *Do you see the sky?* she'd meant to ask him, but Fergus had flattened his ears and looped his tail around his haunches. She'd started the engine. Ward Mondragon's panicked voice rumbled in her head; he used to know how to handle people in all sorts of weather.

"Stupid," she said to Fergus. "I shouldn't have gone." Fergus ignored her, head out the window, enjoying the loft of his ears.

The house was where she'd left it—scruffy, and fretful in its own way. She had the sense of a three-dimensional shape folding itself into something else. The truck engine still rumbled; the faulty gas line had kept going even after she turned off the key and slid out. Wait. Did she have the key? She looked at her empty hand and then down at her legs. Her knees were grass-stained. *Gravestained.* Two indentations pressed into freshly laid sod; that flimsy string of dandelions draped over a cold stone. She sank to her knees next to the truck, heaving one quick, hard cough—nothing came up. When had she last eaten? Fergus watched with interest, and she shoved him away. Cold spread out and radiated; her knees ground into dry gravel. Letters and numbers swam in front of her eyes, meaningless.

On the front porch she set down Ward's bag and opened the door. Somebody had been there. The air was different. Currents of it eddied and flowed in new directions, dust swirling in corners that Rose hadn't noticed, in the parlor, the old sewing room, even the staircase with its creaky boards. It wasn't Stella, she was almost certain. Stella wouldn't cover her tracks so well. The antique hand-shaped sconce on the wall near the cuckoo clock gave her the finger, or looked like it did.

The kitchen shocked her a bit, with its newly clean counters and sink. Her chair was pushed back from the table. A pencil rolled along the baseboard and dropped out of sight. She knew she should go collect the bag from the porch. But the front porch felt like another country. She had a feeling that as she walked through her house new rooms opened in front of her and the old ones closed off behind, locked forever.

"We're living in a funhouse," she told Fergus. He was next to the fridge, lapping from his water bowl. Rosehips pattered against the kitchen window. Under the sound of the ringing phone, she heard her own heartbeat. "Or a house of cards."

They were in the front yard again, pruning. Fergus thumped his tail. A prickling made her turn around. There he stood, as crooked and shadeless as his damn tree: Old Man Brown. Looming on her land, white-haired now, leaning on his cane. His eyes still wanted to eat the world.

*Don't say it,* she thought. But he did: "How are you?"

She clutched her shears and scanned the bushes for more blooms.

"Rose." He sank to one knee, sighing, "What's going on? You've gotta prepare yourself. I know what Perry's angling for. I'm here to tell you—"

*Don't talk to me about what to look out for, Old Man.*

". . . Hear me out. I know Perry will try again. He'll keep trying. He's like me, Rose. Like I was . . ."

"There's nothing—" her voice croaked and she stopped. Then started again. "There's nothing to be done, Sherwin."

The Old Man stood awkwardly and stepped forward. He held out a coin, glinty in the gray light. "Rosie, damn it all. Can't you tell there's weather coming?"

A faint reverberation came from the well. The bucket groaned and swung as Rose turned back to work, and the snip of her pruning shears matched it for rhythm. Out on the road, the leaves of the Infamous Elm fluttered.

Rose put some coffee on to brew, strong and muddy, in need of that zooming feeling. She filled a pot with water, set the flame on high, and dropped in three carrots and an onion. "It may boil down to something interesting," she said to Fergus. Her eyes stung. Fergus nosed the screen door leading to the backyard, asking to be let out. "Hold on," she breathed, then opened the door and watched as Fergus went under the blackberries and settled into a tight ball next to a small, mounded patch of dirt, nose resting on his tail.

"I have to lie down," she whispered. But Fergus was too far away under the brambles; his ears didn't even flicker. She swung the door open to call to him, and he stood and shook himself. Bramble shadows nipped at his paws as Fergus trotted toward her. The air was too still and the light was all wrong for early afternoon. Rose stepped onto the porch, peering overhead. "Do you know what's wrong?" she asked. Fergus circled around her and sat, unblinking.

Inside, carroty sludge burbled on the stove. Her head pounded. There was plenty of time before dinner. She took the blue airmail envelope from the mantel, traced her finger across its sketch of a single rose and thorn, and slipped it into her pocket. She went to lie down in the sewing room. A tall stack of canned corn hovered in the corner, and she peered behind it to find plant shoots creeping up the wall. Sneaky little bastards, always trying something new—she knocked over the cans and lopped at the shoots. She'd pry up floorboards, crawl into the back of closets, shake down the pantry. *Whatever it takes*. Fergus was curled up, asleep again, yelping softly. Such a deep sleep, it would be so good to surrender. She gave in and lay down, shadows fleeting across her eyelids.

*Rose, Rose, Rose*. She tossed and turned. Scratchy thorns pattered out odd rhythms on the window. She reached deep into her apron pocket and threw her pruning shears into the well, but when she leaned over to watch them fall, she heard another name: *Lance*.

Rose snapped awake with a coffee hangover, feet hanging off the edge of the twin bed. At some point the letter had fallen out of her pocket. Fergus had a paw on it. He watched Rose guardedly, his ears pointed toward the door, tail twitching. "Okay, okay." Rose grunted to her feet.

A thrumming came from the front of the house. The well was still going, with its blackness and strange noises and no frogs. The Brown girl yelled from her hayloft window. Rose had her shears in hand; the shoots called and swayed. "There's never an end to the work to be done," she told Fergus.

The Brown girl kept calling, wanting her to pay attention to paper airplanes that flew into the brambles, caught on thorns, and cluttered under Rose's feet. The girl was offering paper to Rose, as if Rose needed any more messages, ever. She picked them up, took the bucket down and peered over the edge of the well, leaning so far in she could feel the stones vibrating deep in her belly. The blackness felt dense. It wouldn't be that bad to just slide in. The darkness could hold her.

"Hey. Hey, Mrs. . . . Rose are you okay?" The girl yanked on her skirt until Rose hoisted herself up. Sill looked like the Old Man and Perry around the eyes, but was otherwise mousy and forgettable, soft chin and shaky hands. The girl pointed at the paper she'd flown at Rose—she wanted something, she trembled with want.

"Spit it out," Rose said. The sky rumbled.

The girl said something Rose couldn't hear, and her eyes were like eyes she'd known forever—searching and old, demanding what Rose couldn't give, posing a question she would not—

"A storm's coming," Rose snapped. "Get home." Words munched along the eaves of the house. Sodden clouds lumbered overhead. *(Whether the weather is hot, whether the weather is cold . . . )* As the girl's yellow t-shirt receded from view, the hayloft she spent so much time in leaned after her like a lover. *( . . . Whether you like it or not.)* There never was a less silly girl.

Rose waved the letter after her, shooing her off. The letter: there it was in her hand, with its light blue envelope. *Rose Red*. The only message that mattered. Fergus paced a circle on the porch. Rose threw it into the air and it came back on the wind, smack across her eyes. Okay, then. She sat on the porch steps and kissed the envelope's sealed flap. Here we go.

It opened under her fingers like a linen napkin at a dinner party. Everything fell quiet. She looked at the heading. It was dated a long time ago: months. She'd been warned about this, when they'd sent her his things. She'd been warned about a lot—the closed casket, the pieces of him, seams pulled apart never to be resewn. His things half-filled a duffel bag: fatigues, combat boots, some drawing pencils, a knife, strange binoculars that saw things blurry, letters from the Brown girl. Things from a man's world. But he wasn't a man. Just a boy.

*Dear Ma,*

*I hope you and Fergus are doing good. I am okay here in* ████████. *Things are hard sometimes and I wish I was home sometimes, but* ████████████████ *very important work, they say.* ██████████████ *then we had a meeting and I thought how funny that was. Funny strange, like you'd say. The food is crap and I still miss your cooking. Yesterday I ate* ██████████ *how do you like that? The guys in my squad call me* ██████. *There are* ████████████ *and* ████████████████████ ████████████████████████

*stuff you wouldn't believe, even though I'm sitting here writing it so you know it must be true. I'm thinking about the end of* ████████, *they say it's* ██████. *Have you seen Aunt Stella? If you do, Ma, tell her I have a new one, say that* ████████████████ *I hope to see you and the farm soon. Has Sill been visiting you? I sent her some emails that she says she'll pass on* ██████████████ *break down and get a computer? Well, I better go, we got* ███████ *before morning. Write soon and I'll get it sooner or later.*

*Love, Lance.*

Below his name he'd drawn a sketch of him and her, standing side by side in front of the porch. Her hair always looked wild in his drawings—but good, like real hair. He was good. The clouds, the rumbling at the edges. She couldn't hold it off. Stupidstupidstupid. Fergus poked her with his snout. *No.*

Rose slammed her back onto the porch, trembling and choking, her chest in a vise grip. The sun dropped from the sky and the only warmth came from Fergus's breath. Wind came ripping through the yard and Rose couldn't tell where her house ended and the storm began. Fergus scrambled backward and disappeared off the edge of the porch.

"Fergus. Fer-gus!" Wind tunneled through her chest and took her voice, whipped it up into the growing fury. Her yells disappeared in the voiceless roar. Things she'd screamed and things she should have screamed. *Lance*! She shifted weight onto her hands and knees, feeling the hard porch boards reach out for her, catch her skin and let go.

Something glanced off her back. The roof? *Oh, no, I'm not that easy*. Colors blurred past—odd shapes—furniture? animals? She held on to the screen door and couldn't get herself through, couldn't stop looking back. The sky was emerald. A clump of dirt blew into her face. *Ashes to ashes*, the wind screamed. *Lance*! The screen door buckled and shuddered under her fingers and then snapped; she was sucked backward with it. But the wide frame lodged momentarily between the posts on either side of the porch steps and Rose flung her right arm out to grab the porch beam, dragging herself toward it, clutching, trying to pull the wood into her chest. *Hold on, hold on*. The house trembled, wanting to let go, she could feel it talking to the storm.

Then a tremendous crack: wood split, the floor groaned. Something came at her—a hard, black shape—and darkness fell with quick, relentless grace.

*

Dust devils, cyclones, whirlwinds, waterspouts, twisters. Tornado. A modification of the Spanish word for thunderstorm: *tronada*.

A tornado begins most often with the *tronada*. Cumulonimbus clouds cluster. Warm updrafts cool in the atmosphere, water droplets and ice crystals form and fall; downdrafts are met by upstart updrafts. Air rushes in to fill the void. Nature becomes a vacuum, sweeping dirt into the vortex, growing darker and stronger, and spinning around its axis. The twister can travel anywhere.

The birds know first. They cluster unnaturally, stringing themselves along the power lines and flying in angular patterns. There is a more than usual darting to their movements, a quickening. Then insects disappear—dragonflies, bees, mosquitoes, ladybugs, spiders, cicadas, and weevils crawl for cover under leaves and into the rotting black logs out by Johnson's Creek. Voles burrow. Mice gather in their dark dens and fall into anxious dreams, kicking and biting in fitful sleep. Barn cats and house cats crouch in readiness, tails twitching.

Not all see it coming. The colorful denizens of a fish tank wind their way blissfully back and forth between the tines of the plastic merman's plastic trident. A worm in a supermarket pear shipped from Argentina eats a peaceful path through its mealy universe. This pear, long past its prime, sits atop Scottie Dunleavy's worktable in the small back room of Dunleavy's Fine Shoes (&Shoe Repair) on the almost forgotten end of Main Street, a few blocks down from the old town square.

Tornado. From the Latin *tonare*, meaning *to thunder*, which is also related to *astonish*, *detonate*, *stun*.

# Scottie Dunleavy

Loop around, again, to the morning of the storm.

*Here is the town, here are the people. Beyond are the farms, and the church with its steeple*. Scottie Dunleavy pressed his fingertips to the glass. He didn't care about churches or farms. Just watch what's right outside your window and you'll see more than most people ever will.

Across the street at Mondragon's Emporium, Ward Mondragon swept the porch with broad, distracted motions, not much dirt to pick up since he did the same thing every morning. Stella Mondragon's dark head moved among the shelves inside the store. Ward and Stella were the only signs of life from Scottie's front window. It was early. Mondragon's Emporium had been around even longer than Dunleavy's Fine Shoes (&Shoe Repair), and Ward was trying to keep up appearances. All of the Main Street shops had lost customers when the Discount SuperStore opened, though Mondragon's still took in business from people who didn't have time to drive twenty miles down the interstate for cheaper duct tape or flour. Ward bent to work some dirt into a dustpan and then set the broom by his door, turning to straighten the chairs that lined the porch, looking up and down the quiet street. Five years ago when Crown Co. opened a meatpacking plant on the edge of town, they'd waited for the promised influx of workers with wallets full of cash. They were still waiting.

After a while Ward went into his store and Stella came out with car keys and a cell phone in hand. Scottie stepped back nervously. Stella gave him funny looks. She spoke too slowly when she talked to him. Her eyes always found the spots on his clothes where he'd dribbled soup—he didn't have time to use the laundromat as often as he should. After his parents died and the house was lost, Scottie moved into the back stockroom of Dunleavy's Shoes with his cat, Dogberry, shoeboxes full of his mother's costume jewelry and his father's cufflinks, a cot, and paperwork charting the two-decade decline of the family business. His appearance rarely mattered. Dogberry didn't care. Ward didn't.

After Stella slammed her sedan door and started the engine, he stepped to the window. Stella, like most of them, thought he didn't see things simply because he looked at a slant. He did see things—he saw that Mondragon's was in trouble. And there was something unsettled about Ward's marriage to Stella. They never seemed to fight, but an air of struggle between them was palpable, and the conflict was about more than just the dead nephew. Stella had driven toward the old county road quite often in recent months, and there was only one place she could have been going: to her stepsister, Rose. Rose the estranged, Rose the thorn.

Ward reemerged from the Emporium and stood in the doorway watching his wife pull too quickly onto Main Street. His eyes met Scottie's. Ward waved and called something, gesturing into his store, and then he raised his arms toward the cloudless sky like a conductor before his orchestra. The sound of Stella's car engine filled the street and black feathers rustled overhead. Dogberry wound between his ankles. Time for breakfast.

At nine o'clock, as Scottie flipped the sign to *Open*, Nina Brown sailed by in her old tan station wagon. Nina was going to the bank, most likely, radio tuned to the Christian rock station, mind elsewhere, on her sullen husband or her irascible father-in-law, or their pale-faced teenage girl. Not so long ago, Nina's pregnant teenage belly had pulled Perry Brown out of the community college, where he'd been studying auto mechanics, and back to the Brown family farm. The Browns' place was big and sprawling, confident, encroaching on Rose's much smaller acreage. The Browns were the salt of the earth, people liked to say.

Nina Brown sailing by in her brown station wagon, cross hanging from the rearview. As she passed he saw them both clearly—the younger Nina and this current one, framed together in his store window. A quick snapshot. He watched Nina drive straight past the palimpsest of her scared, hopeful, pregnant former self, too busy now to stop and chat. The younger Nina pulled a blue jacket closer around her shoulders and her burgeoning belly. She checked her watch and looked overhead, and started walking east at a brisk clip. No fool, that one, even as a girl.

It wasn't only Nina he saw this way. The past and present often intersected outside his store window. Two cars rolling through an intersection: kids in the back waving and shrieking, oldsters in the opposite lane watching the horizon with tired eyes. One heading east, one heading west, sliding past, treating the whole journey like a jaunty straight line rather than a spiral. Don't they recognize themselves? Sometimes the past lingered while the present hurried by: the former selves pulled up to the curb in old junkers, got out, and stood along the street in ill-fitting coats, gathered at intersections, squinting and asking each other for cigarettes.

Scottie touched his fingertips to the window, and then dropped his hand. It was early yet, the sky clear. He suspected quite reasonably that he wouldn't have a single customer today. Out of habit, he checked the change drawer in the cash register and turned on the store's fluorescent overheads. He clicked on the radio and heard that silky-voiced buyer of wingtip shoes, former traveling salesman turned weatherman Ted Waite, talking about storm conditions. *A thunderstorm likely on the way, friends. Stay tuned and I'll have all the latest developments. We've got your back here at KA—*He clicked Ted off, uninterested.

In the stockroom Dogberry waited on the cot, sphinxlike. The shelves were stacked high and tilted inward toward a small clearing in the center where Scottie stood, sipping his coffee. Towers of shoeboxes teetered, arranged in an order that wouldn't make sense to anyone else. Some that dated back to 1964 should have been donated or sold for scrap long ago but here they stayed, little cardboard coffins. Tiny *x* and *o* ciphers marked their sides. Stacks of old newspapers and magazines sprouted under and around his cot, narrowing the pathways from shelving to sink. His worktable was an old door resting on two sawhorses. Next to his cot, a small trunk held clothes and books. A hot plate rested on a shelf right above it. Reconstructed bird and mouse skeletons perched between shoeboxes and along the metal shelving edges. Here, where there was no single place for a person's eye to rest, he was at peace, more or less.

On his worktable, a pear and his dirty soup bowl from dinner the night before sat atop a pile of outdated issues of *ARTnews*. There was one pair of leather shoes, Ward Mondragon's, that needed resoling. The table also held a bird skeleton, a rat skeleton, two pairs of sneakers, and a messy stack of index cards with Scottie's perfect, tiny block print running along the lines, occasionally veering off to form circles, loops, and animal forms.

He sat and worked for a while on the bird bones, using a tiny blade to separate the joints, brushing the individual segments clean, and taking care to set each piece in the correct spot on a waiting piece of paper, laying the segments out like a blueprint. He would refer to his bird book when he put the pieces back together. This bird, a red-wing, had flown into his net by Johnson's Creek forty-seven Sundays ago, time and date recorded on an index card. Now the bones were bleached clean, and so delicate he scarcely felt them between his fingers.

Dogberry leapt onto the table and perched with his front paws on a sliding fan of index cards, meowing. He was intrigued by Scottie's skeletons, and if he got the chance he'd bat them to the ground and pounce. "Red-winged Blackbird," Scottie said, shoving Dogberry to the floor. The cat, irritated, stalked around the crate that held Scottie's lamp and alarm clock. His tail gave the merest flick: *Caution*. *Look*.

When Scottie had heard the news that Rose's son Lance was killed in the war he'd had no reaction. Ward told him in a nervous whisper. Stella was all broken up at the loss of her nephew and home in bed, Ward said, and Rose, presumably flattened by grief, wasn't responding to their calls. Scottie listened and replied, "That's very sad," as he had been taught to do whenever someone died. Then he'd gone back to his store and sat on his cot. Vomit rose in his throat so quickly he didn't have time to make it to the sink. He was sick down the front of his shirt, stunned with the speed of it, bile seeping into the cloth. After a while he removed the shirt and washed his damp torso in the sink. He squeezed the soiled cloth into a ball and shoved it to the bottom of the trashcan. It was wasteful and unlike him, but he had to dispose of it.

He had watched for the boy's ghost since but had seen it only rarely. Through the town's intersections Lance slid, unmoored, shifting meaning, cueing one memory after another. *Lance*. Everyone knew him.

But what had Scottie known of him? Lance's feet were big. Rose had brought him in to buy sneakers about a year ago, the last time—

and one of the few times—Scottie had talked with him. He had written a message on the soles of the boy's new shoes, of course. That wasn't unusual. More unexpected was that Lance had seen one of Scottie's messages that no one else bothered to notice.

Now Lance was most apparent through the space he'd left behind. Sometimes he stood on Mondragon's porch, a too-bright glow coming off him. Nina Brown's daughter, Sill, almost ghostly herself, held constant vigil, and Lance trailed after her, occasionally reaching out to glance his hand across her shoulders. Scottie recognized him by the silky hair and the baseball cap and the way Lance seemed to lose texture based on where he stood, his outline fading into the old wood, or a street lamp, or a passing car.

Scottie imagined Lance, those long legs, that rectangle of a youth in the war and wearing Scottie's hidden message on his shoes—carrying the words into battle, into mess hall and tank and Humvee and dank prisons; into the morgue. Perhaps the sneakers were on his feet now, turning in the quiet earth. The boy wouldn't really have worn sneakers purchased at Dunleavy's to war. Scottie knew this. Yet it was the way he chose to remember Lance—it put the kid in context. Which, when you think of it, is the only way to understand anything.

Working, Scottie lost track of time. It was close to the lunch hour when the bell over the front door tinkled.

Louise Logan stood staring out his front window, clutching her purse to her body.

"Can I help you?"

She held her purse closer. "Hi, Scottie. Do you have sneakers?"

"Why, yes!" He saw what she'd been watching. Rose's blue truck was parked across the street and there were two heads inside Mondragon's, standing together in a center aisle. Rose shorter and lighter, moving in one direction and then another as Ward followed. Louise scarcely breathed, she was watching them so intently. She worked as a teller at the bank and made a point of knowing everybody's business.

"What, uh, what are you looking for exactly . . . uh?"

"Louise," she snapped, offended because she thought he'd forgotten her name. She picked up a pair of canvas Keds and told him her size.

In the back, he found the size and style she'd asked for, but in the wrong color. He paused and picked up his pen, pondering the message. Then he wrote: *How did I get here?* and, *Have you seen my lost youth?*

Louise sniffed as she sat on the bench, simultaneously thumping her handbag to the ground and kicking off her loafers. She held her hand out for the shoe, slid it onto her left foot, and looked down. He watched her register that the canvas was stained, perhaps from water damage, and the cardboard box was a bit misshapen. She did not notice his message, tiny print running in the grooves of both soles.

Her feet smelled—rank from the build-up of sweat inside her cheap leather shoes—Scottie backed toward the window, wondering if he still had a can of air freshener under the register. People like Louise were always pointing out other people's smells, completely oblivious to their own. She didn't even bother to tie the laces, just sat with her feet stretched out on the footstool and her eyes on the window. Rose and Ward came out of Mondragon's. Scottie and Louise dropped the pretense and gawked. Rose's shock of white hair made her almost unrecognizable, and Ward's big shoulders hunched as he leaned into her truck window—he looked as if he were pleading. Scottie touched his pants pocket nervously. Ward reached a bag through the truck's passenger window, and Rose's black dog pushed his nose into Ward's hand.

Scottie cleared his throat. "What do you think, Louise?"

"Hmmm," she glanced down. "I just don't know."

"Would you like to try on the other one?" He held out the shoe, looking somewhere to the left of her eyebrows.

"No. It fits, it's . . ." She peered at the scene on the street. "It's not quite right." Though their sons had been close, Scottie knew, Louise and Rose were not friends. Never had been.

He took the shoe she shelled from her foot, returning the pair sole to sole into the box, folding the tissue paper carefully over the canvas. Outside, Rose's truck engine ground and sputtered away. "Anything else?"

She said *No* and left without ceremony. He watched her cross the street to Mondragon's, probably to pump Ward for information. Louise had shrunk since she'd last come in, and not from weight loss. Ward too, for that matter. And Rose, from the glimpse he'd had—she was practically shriveled.

Scottie had never been in a war. No, no, no indeed. He'd have gotten out any way he could, if he hadn't been too young for Vietnam. A generation had forgotten what it was like—a generation spoon-fed glory tales of World War II, treated like children by politicians and pundits and the breakers of the news. And now they'd lost a child, Rose's child. It was stupid that the boy had gone there, to war, and stupid now to see people bemoaning it, acting dodgy, stopping by only to peep out his store windows, flabbergasted at its proximity. It wasn't a pretend war, though listening to some you might think it. *How could this happen? It can't be. It's so unfair. It makes no sense*. People were perpetually determined in their oblivion.

Soon Louise made her way down the street toward the bank, a small paper bag from Mondragon's in hand. Scottie knocked his knuckles against the shoebox under his arm. Even though Louise hadn't bought the shoes they belonged to her now, in a way that pleased him. His reconfigured bones were art, and the shoe repair was business. The sole messages he counted in another category entirely.

They were his tiny, secret protests, sent out into the world on the feet of his few customers, unknown to everyone except Scottie himself. When the idea first came to him, he'd clutched his pocketknife to calm himself. Since, he'd waited for an irate phone call, or a sullen demand for money back. But no one had ever brought back a shoe, and so he'd grown bolder, writing on the soles not only of the few shoes he sold, but also on his display items, and even along the dark stitching of the shoes he was asked to repair.

His long-term project was to write a message on each shoe in the store. He felt light at heart—light all over—as he made his tiny messages. Even if the shoes never sold and wound up in a landfill or on the feet of some charity case in Somalia or Bangladesh, his messages would remain.

A few years ago, in miniscule black print under the *Dunleavy's Fine Shoes (&Shoe Repair)* lettering on the front window, he'd etched, *You don't see what's right in front of you. The world makes fools of us all*. This proclamation was the only thing that kept him flipping the sign to *Open* some days.

The sky, he noticed now, was thickening. His stomach rumbled, so he went to the back and ate a can of creamed corn and cherry pie filling from a jar. He turned on the radio for company. "Be alert, folks," Ted Waite the weatherman said. *Don't take chances. That means you, too, Scottie*. The ants that nested in his walls' insulation trailed up the rim of the cherry jar, drawn from their storm shelter, made reckless by the sticky drippings.

They decided to board the shoestore window first. Ward's shirt-sleeves were rolled up his big forearms and his breath whistled a bit. He'd always been husky, but now he was downright fat. He took up too much room in Scottie's small space, standing by the window with a display brogue in his hand.

Scottie retrieved the plywood from the storeroom and lugged the boards to the front. "I'm working on resoling your shoes, Ward?" he offered, his inflection rising nervously.

"Great." Ward took some planks off Scottie's stack as they angled out the front door. He didn't ask when his shoes would be ready.

"I think they'll look good as new." Scottie set the wood under the window.

"I bet," Ward said. "Do you have an extra hammer?" He was thinking about the visit from Rose, Scottie knew, and by extension, about Stella.

Scottie went to the back for his toolbox, wishing he had finished the resoling project so he'd have something definitive to hand Ward. Instead, he gave him his smaller hammer and a few nails.

"Thanks." Ward lifted a board and set it across the window frame. "How long has it been since we've had an alert over this many counties?"

Scottie placed a nail. "Eight years." The effort of talking and pounding was too much. His hammer glanced off his thumb and he yelped.

"You okay?" Ward asked. Scottie didn't answer, just sucked on his finger for a moment and returned to the task at hand. Ward didn't really care how much time had elapsed since the last big storm warning, he was just trying to calm Scottie down. That was the problem with Ward, the closest thing he had to a friend—with one soothing word, he could remind Scottie all over again of his place in the world. The air that had felt heavy and close suddenly seemed thin, and the sky had a sickly tinge.

They finished and went to Ward's store. Scottie wandered in the aisles while Ward went to the back for the boards and tools. Pausing in an aisle far from the stockroom door, Scottie pulled out his pocketknife and made a tiny nick in a five-pound bag of sugar. His heartbeat slowed. The radio blared the angry voice of an a.m. talk show host, and Ward dropped something heavy in the back. Scottie ambled down the aisle, picked up a small, unlabeled jar, jam of some sort, and then noticed there was a note tucked under it. A message scrawled on a piece of brown paper, signed by Rose. He tucked the paper into his pocket. His hands were moving, but his mind was on the overwhelming details of the store: the too-loud radio, the tired-looking merchandise on the shelves, the photos of Ward's parents and grandparents on the wall near the stockroom door.

He touched a bag of rice, wondering what to do about the note, which wasn't his. But now it was in his pocket. He would take it out and hand it to Ward, who obviously hadn't seen Rose set it down while she was in the store. Relieved at this decision, he made one more cut, the bottom corner of a bag of cornmeal, and was setting it back into place when Ward asked him what he was doing. *Just relieving a bit of pressure. Can't you feel it?* Scottie's head felt large and square, too big for his body. He was stammering a non-answer when the phone rang. Stella, just in the nick of time, diverting Ward's attention.

Scottie counted each step across the street to his front door. *Eleven.* His sleeves had unrolled, and they swung past his hands. He had played the Scarecrow once, in a middle school production of *The Wizard of Oz*. His mother had altered one of his father's old suits, took in the arms and legs, and added rough patches and bits of straw. He'd sung and danced, pointing at his head and saying, "If I only had a brain." He was a mediocre singer, and not much better as a dancer. But in becoming someone else, and having it acknowledged and applauded, Scottie had lost that feeling of displacement that he carried with him. As he flapped awkwardly, and sang, and pointed at his head with a goofy expression, he forgot how his clothes were separate from his body, his bones separate from his vocal cords. It all worked together, for a purpose—the message he conveyed was straightforward and disturbing and yet the audience was charmed. *I am missing something. I am not whole*. Bravo! He had swung his arms wide across his body as he'd bowed, letting the loose cuffs of his oversized shirtsleeves fling into the air. Bravo! The parents and teachers and siblings had given the performers an ovation at the end of the show.

He turned to face Mondragon's. The power lines hummed. His young Scarecrow self stood catty-corner across the street, in the shadow of the old bank building. Scottie spread his arms and bowed. His ghost bowed back, and then stepped out of sight around the corner.

Inside, the boards across the windows made his place dim and close. A semblance of night had entered the store, and in the darkness the shoes lined his dusty shelves like a bodiless, expectant army. Scottie flipped the sign to *Closed* and headed straight to the back. He flicked on the overhead light in his stockroom and it fell in a warm, yellow circle onto his table and cot. Shoeboxes rose darkly around him, and his tiny skeleton figures seemed one beat from animating, circling overhead, and demanding flesh.

He sat at his worktable and made tiny cracks, crevices in Ward's shoe sole, wondering what message to hide within. He had to think about what to say when Ward asked again about the cutting. Ward *would* ask, when enough time had passed, his voice even and full of regret, a resigned downward slope to his shoulders. Can't you feel your stuckness, Ward?

The note. He'd forgotten to give it to Ward. He pulled it from his pocket and reread it: Rose's handwriting sprawled, as many lines scribbled out as were left readable. They described a few domestic details of her life on the farm, and no mention of Lance, all in a snotty tone addressed to Stella. *P.S.* she'd written. *The Browns are circling.* The Browns—they must be doing an interesting dance, sussing out whether Rose's land was up for grabs. With the note, she was pushing Stella away and also pulling her closer. He shoved the paper under a stack of magazines, wanting to be done with these people, his neighbors and their complications.

Scottie attached sturdy new leather soles to Ward's oxfords and wrote in tiny perfect script along the seams. On the right, *Who are you really?* On the left, *Wouldn't you like to know*? He pushed back from the table, regarding his work. Dogberry's eyes grew wider and even more golden. All of it—the shoes, the bones, the tiny slices he made at Mondragon's—he was a master of the microcosm, imperceptible seismic events centering on the same question: how small could his impact be yet still be felt?

He pressed his palm into the worktable and looked at the veins on the back of his hand. If he had once been primarily made of water, now an element with less weight composed him. "Dust," he whispered. "I'm a fool too." There was more work to do but he could not focus. He set Ward's shoes onto a shelf.

"Well," he said, and Dogberry, hackles raised, arched his back and hissed in a kind of triumph. The overhead light swung gently in the cloistered room.

The clock read 3:15. Scottie had never switched off the transistor radio, and he heard, faintly, Ted Waite talking about a tornado, pace urgent, reciting names of alerted counties. The weather felt far away inside this quiet, though he knew it wasn't. Elements felt different: dust and decaying leather, slackening skin and mammal odors, the sharp clean scent of his indelible ink, and papery air. Now outside pressed in—the atmosphere was heavy and his skin, save for his lips, felt plush. Dogberry's scratch on the back of his hand had faded to a dull pink. He warmed a can of greasy noodles on the hotplate and quickly ate, rubbing his lips together to feel the soothing oil work its way into the crevices.

He picked up the cleaned blackbird bones, wanting to etch sentences onto the white calcium. There wouldn't be room, of course. So instead he wrote *sunken* on one wing, *waiting* on the other. Then he reset the pieces in perfect formation and pinned them together. He would add this to the flock perched on his shelves, skeletons with secrets embedded in their bones. Eventually he would bury them all.

He wondered what Rose's boy, Lance, would have thought that day last year if he'd stumbled upon this message instead of the tiny one that Scottie had etched under the sign on the front window. *The world makes fools of us all.* Wishing that the boy had spotted one of his more elaborate creations was a kind of weakness and it unsettled him, like hearing the Scarecrow applause. Lance's ghost had not shown himself earlier today when Rose went into Mondragon's. Scottie had chalked this up to the weather, but now he wondered if it was due to some greater failure on his part. He could have looked harder for the boy, after all. He could have beckoned.

"Ask me about my winnowing shot at happiness," Scottie whispered. "I am a fuckwad." Dogberry arched his back and jumped onto Scottie's table, knocking the reconstructed blackbird bones flat. It was too quiet. The light flickered overhead. A great rumbling drowned out the voice of Ted Waite on the radio, and the light clicked out with a definitive pop. Dogberry leapt to the floor with a low growl. "Time to flee," Scottie said, grabbing the cat as he bent to yank up the trap door in the floor. He chucked Dogberry, still yowling, down the hole, pulled a battery-operated lantern from the shelf over his cot, and followed.

Above them, all of them, out in the world, the storm drew into a fist.

*

Leaves flutter and upturn. Branches gather toward their trunks. Trees reach further into the ground seeking anchor, their roots giving off a slow knell, a frequency felt by the earthworms—not a warning, an acknowledgement: *something is coming.*

Stalwart birches planted as windbreaks around farmhouses stand like pale soldiers. Wildflowers clasp their thin petals shut. The well-kept kitchen gardens of farmers' wives pause their fecund celebration: Early Girl tomatoes, sweet peas, and spinach shoots curl their heads toward the earth.

Prairie grasses, where they're left, undulate, though there is not yet wind to move them. The settlers had scrabbled life out of the land in bad years and walked through seas of golden wheat in the plum years. But they never truly claimed it—and sensing this, they cleared and plowed more vigorously, wore themselves out and died young. Before the great-great-grandparents came, before stakes went into the ground and lines were drawn and feuds begun and forgotten, this land and the people on it were all of a piece. So vast it terrified the new ones in their tiny wagons, clutching colicky babies and leather-bound Bibles. Some descendants feel it underfoot like a breathing thing, roads and borders mere scars crisscrossing thick hide.

Abutting Rose's place, Perry Brown's house stands proud on its hill. His rocky untilled acre is solid and unmoved, and he feels the weight of one stone more than any other. Two limbs of the Infamous Elm rub together, giving off an imperceptible sigh, and corn prepares itself to lie flat in great waves.

# Perry Brown

On the morning of the storm Perry woke at 4:00 a.m. as if to the click of a light. He made a fist and rubbed at a sore spot on his knuckle, and then swung his feet down to the rag rug. Nina rolled over in sleep. It was a morning like any other: the cold splash of water on his face and the first heavy yellow piss of the day. Then into jeans and a t-shirt. His shoulder brushed the plaster wall on the stairwell and steps creaked underfoot. He wasn't the first one up—that honor went to the Old Man, Perry's father, a rattling cough downstairs in the back of the house.

In the kitchen, Perry ate rolled oats with raisins and milk, his spoon scraping the bowl for the dried fruit and his jaw aching a bit from chewing. The radio gave off a soft crackle—"Unseasonable cold front moving down from Canada . . ." according to Ted Waite, the announcer. There was an advertisement for a cell phone service, a news blip on the faraway war. The numbers of the dead. The number of raisins in his bowl. "Squalls possible tomorrow but it's looking clear today, folks," Ted Waite said, friendly as ever. "Keep on your toes, keep on truckin' . . ."

"Storm's coming," the Old Man said, shuffling into the kitchen.

"The radio says tomorrow," Perry countered.

His father muttered something, picked up his "#1 Grandpa" coffee cup, filled it with black, and stood at the counter to prepare his usual bowl of instant oatmeal. The cane was slung over his forearm—the Old Man used it more and more these days. He was supposed to let Perry take on more decision-making power, a natural generational progression, but his father was ornery, still trying to run what he could no longer work. He'd recorded every crop they had planted and harvested since 1957. Read like the Bible, consulted like an oracle: ledgers stacked on his bedside table and pulled out whenever Perry talked about trying something new. *Not everything new is radical, not everything radical is new,* Nina had whispered across the pillow last night.

The Old Man sat, spooned oatmeal into his mouth, and coughed. Tiny bits of oats dotted the table between them. Without Nina's presence, the less they said to each other the better. Perry pushed his chair away from the table and put the cereal bowl in the sink. He went to the parlor and pulled the old Webster's dictionary from the shelf. After Rose's last rebuff, he had pressed his copy of the unsigned lease between the pages—in the "P" section, "predispose" to "pregnant." He put the folded contract into his pocket and walked back to the kitchen to pour a glass of juice for his father. Then he went to the mudroom for his boots and headed down to the barn, tongue working a shred of raisin still stuck between his molars.

A crow swooped overhead with a baby gopher dangling from its beak. The bird perched on the eave of the barn, holding the motionless body as if waiting for applause. Then it set the rodent down and the thing scurried into action, running west along the roof in a mad dash. The bird shook its feathers leisurely, spread its wings and cawed, and then launched into the air, plucking the gopher up again. *There it is,* Perry thought, *in a nutshell.*

The raisin was stubborn between Perry's teeth, and he pressed it with his tongue as he rode out to the east fields to clear rocks. He had been paying particular attention to Rose's adjacent acreage ever since the day three months before when Nina told him, her voice crackly: "Jim Culp drove out to see Rose and Sill followed him out there and made him tell her too. Lance is dead. My God, Perry, the boy is killed. What's Rose going to do?"

It was natural for the Browns to acquire Rose's land now. It would be practically negligent not to. *Grow or die*, was one of the Old Man's pearls of wisdom, imparted, in the old days, with a rare grin. Perry wanted Rose's land but the want came from his head, not his gut. That's where he and the Old Man differed. That, Nina said, was Perry's strength.

The corn was growing well. He passed it by, moving on to the untilled acres, and then cut the tractor engine and stepped down. There was no sign of life from Rose's place. Perry stuck his index finger in his mouth, pulled out the raisin shred with a fingernail, and flicked it away. His mouth tasted metallic. They'd gone to Lance's funeral: a folded flag, buttons on a uniform, a crisp salute. What was there in those things for a mind to latch onto? The whole town had turned out to pay respects, except for Rose herself. They'd tried to visit her afterward but she wouldn't speak to them. Was busy, she said. Pruning.

The Brown land that abutted Rose's was untilled, an old pasture that hadn't yet been made into something new. Perry had been slowly clearing rocks and brambles from a portion of it, without machines. He'd come to look forward to the time, just an hour or two most mornings, spent rolling and lifting rocks, digging up stubborn roots, watching the rich soil revealed bit by bit. He was creating a dividing line of sorts between the acre he wanted to reclaim for pasture and the rocky piece that he'd leave be. Nina had scolded him for not wearing gloves—he'd dinged his hands more than once. He always felt best when he climbed off the tractor and worked the land directly. Now he surveyed his progress and bent to hoist a mid-size stone, clenching the muscles in his legs and back. He crab-walked with it to the edge of the pasture and settled it into line.

Perry didn't fool himself that gaining a hold over Rose's land would bring him peace. What it would bring was authority, a wedge in his father's grip on things. He had a plan. Rose would lease him her place at a fair price. At the dinner table, he would hold up the contract and say, "It's ours now. I have ideas—" and the Old Man would set down his fork, acknowledging the inevitable handover of power. Sweat soaked the back of Perry's shirt. His segmented dividing line grew rock by rock, and as he worked, he kept Rose's property in his peripheral vision. The air was soft. A tickle of extra humidity caressed his skin—so much for the promised cold front. If the Old Man was right about the weather, he'd be sure to remind Perry of it over dinner. And Perry would sit there and feel the tilt of their elevated house and the weight of the unclaimed land.

The folded contract felt stiff in his pocket, and his knuckle was bleeding a bit. Perry paused to rest, dragging the back of his hand down the leg of his jeans, and then without thinking too hard about it he hoisted himself to his feet. His pasture gave way to hers, and soon enough he walked through the thicket that led to her front yard.

She stood on the porch as if expecting him, holding a casserole dish in one hand. Tinfoil dangled from one corner, juices dribbled out the side and spattered to the ground. There was a smell of rot. Lance's dog, Fergus, growled a few times then wagged his tail. Perry cleared his throat but she didn't look up, just tossed the dish onto some sort of compost heap.

"Rose, how are you?" She didn't acknowledge him. "Rose?" Her hair hadn't just gone white, it had changed texture; tendrils strayed up to the sky.

"I just thought I'd . . . Are you okay?" Her shoulders curved inward. She grabbed a pair of pruning shears from the porch step and walked to her overgrown plants. He swung his arms out in a fake relaxed semicircle, sore knuckle landing in his opposite palm, some part of him still thinking this might go well. "Rose—" he started. "Rose, will you please just think about my offer? Me leasing from you is the best thing for both of us."

She ran her thumb along the handle of the pruning shears and fixed her eyes behind him, on the hayloft. *Your place was a refuge for me once,* he thought. *But maybe you never knew it.* "Have you thought about what I said last month? I want to make it easier on you, Rose. It'll help you, it'll help me. Please." He reached toward his pocket.

"How is your father?" she asked, eyes sliding past his. She couldn't stand the Old Man. Rose without family, standing among the brambles with long shears, looking for all the world like someone who shouldn't hold sharp objects. *She'll turn them on me,* ran through his mind before the other: *She'll turn them on herself.*

"He's fine, Rose. He's just slowing down . . ." Perry pulled out the lease. "I brought this for you just to read over . . . just to think about." He paused. "With Lance—" Her eyes went sharp, her mouth twisted. She came at him, hair flying, a great rushing of air and the paper was gone. It took everything he had not to fall back. The dog was at her side, his eyes yellow, tail pointing upward. Hairs rose on the back of Perry's neck. He looked over his shoulder and took a deep breath. "Keep it up, Rose, and the bank will take this place."

Her face crumpled, and her fingers twisted the fabric of her skirt. He felt like a kid seeing an adult, the person supposedly in charge, collapsed. Something splashed in the well. How had it come to this? Rose batty, older than her years, and him clutching papers in a grabby fist. Both of them not their true selves. Or perhaps these were the selves they'd been working toward. Fergus scratched his ear roughly and whimpered in a kind of sensual relief.

"I'm sorry. I'm not trying to . . ." Perry stuttered. "I only want . . ." Even as he spoke he backed toward the property line. She seemed to have already forgotten him. The screen door screeched shut.

"Rose," Perry begged, too quiet for her to hear. His breath came fast as he retraced his steps. He passed the clearing project and his work seemed negligible, a new line of rocks dividing nothing from nothing. The tractor hunkered where he'd left it on the edge of a row of corn, and he climbed up. He had a couple of hours until lunch and work would calm him. Yet he sat for a while, unmoving, his mind empty of everything—want, fear, care, love. The bloody spot on his knuckle dried to form a thin protective crust.

Then he turned to the county road, hearing it before he saw it: Rose's blue beater of a truck sputtered toward town.

Every day at noon the Old Man pinpointed Perry's location and drove out to deliver lunch and tell him how he should be doing things, tossing the paper lunch sack up to Perry's waiting hands. Today the bag held a ham sandwich and an apple, as it always did. Nina liked consistency. Perry started with the fruit, chewing while the Old Man surveyed the fields.

As his father held forth on how the corn was doing, Perry scanned the horizon. The apple skin was tough. "Nina home?"

The Old Man shrugged. "She let Sill beg off school again today. The kid's taking advantage."

"She's grieving." His daughter wasn't ready to let the boy go.

The Old Man bent to inspect the roots of a corn plant. Then he straightened and raised his palm to the air. "The weather is worse. I told you there's a storm coming. You can't plan to be out much longer."

"I heard you," Perry said.

"The warnings are on the news."

"I know." Perry didn't know, and how would he? The radio on his tractor was silent. But this was often the stance that he took with the Old Man—agreeing without agreement, a way to tamp down the barrage.

"Don't waste time dithering. If you want to keep working, there's plenty up closer to the house you can do."

Perry moved on to the sandwich. The Old Man hadn't seen him coming from the direction of Rose's place. A few years ago his father had coveted Rose's land and tried to buy it, but he'd since done an about-face. Perry looked toward home. A swatch of pink moved through the green below the house at a quick clip. As the figure reached the clearing at the bottom of the hill he could see that it was Nina, carrying a bag and wearing a blue kerchief on her head. She took the slope in long strides, rounding toward the back door and moving out of view.

The Old Man was still talking about fertilizer. Perry had barely tasted his sandwich. He considered the piece of crust in his hand, and swallowed. He could bring up his plans again—it had become a monthly ritual. *When do I get to try my ideas? When will you let me take a shot?* But he didn't trust his voice. Perry watched the corn grow and tuned out whatever his father was saying. He folded the empty lunch bag and slid it into his back pocket as the Old Man stalked to his truck.

Perry worked until mid-afternoon and then cut the engine, wiping his forehead and glancing toward the house. He wasn't ready to face them yet. If the light seemed muted, it matched his thoughts. He was near the untilled land again—not something he'd planned, but as he leapt to the ground the earth met his feet, solid and reassuring. He took a few steps and kicked a small rock to reveal the hard-packed, thirsty soil underneath. Then he crossed over to the fallow patch and found his stone, knelt, and rolled it aside. Perry stretched his body across the ground and whispered into the hole: *I will hold the land any way I can.*

When Perry was a boy, his father told him that to get rid of bad dreams and sadness you whisper them into a hole in the ground.

This was advice about his newly-dead mother after the Old Man grew tired of being waked by Perry's sobs. Perry had come to this spot and dug a hole, whispering his mother into it as she had become, unrecognizable as the illness progressed—sharp cheekbones and undereye bruises that moved further and further down her face—then whispered in all the things he'd loved about her too. He'd covered the hole with a sizable stone. His father had meant the advice as comfort to a grieving child, but Perry never outgrew the habit. Whenever the Old Man cussed about these rocky acres, in his head Perry saw just one stone, his stone: rough and flat and unremarkable. This piece of land he'd never clear.

A chill came over him. He pressed harder into the dirt and whispered: *Forgive me.* And: *I should've done more for Lance.* And: *Time to shake it up or give up once and for all.* If the Old Man—or Nina, or anyone else for that matter—saw him lying here they'd assume he'd gone the way of Theo, or just lost his marbles.

One final whispered vow: *I won't repeat the Old Man's mistakes. I might make new ones, but they'll be mine.* Then he hoisted himself off his belly, rolled the stone into place, and smacked the dust off his shirt and jeans. He pushed his chest forward, loosening his shoulders, and wiped a sleeve across his mouth. It smelled dry and clean as bones. He bounced on his toes to get his blood moving again and turned toward home.

By the time he pulled up near the barn the air prickled. The house at the top of the hill looked angular and exposed—it was time to repaint again. He rounded the barn, unlatching the doors to swing them wide. No barn cats to be seen. Perry picked up a can of oil and went back out to the tractor. The Old Man must have been watching for him—he humped down the hill, moving fast.

Perry took a breath, still smelling the untilled dirt. "Nina inside?"

The Old Man affirmed that she was, his eyes rheumy. Perry thought of Lance's dog, Fergus, sitting at Rose's side, thumping his tail and waiting for him to make a move.

He cleared his throat. "We need to talk about my ideas . . ." The Old Man tightened his fist on the cane. Perry's fingers crept up to fiddle with the button on his empty shirt pocket. He made himself drop his hand before he spoke again. "You know what I mean. I've proved myself. I want to try hogs."

"Hogs! They'll break your back."

"They didn't break your father's." Leaves rustled. Perry felt a caress of wind at his neck, egging him on.

The Old Man picked up a fistful of dirt and sniffed it. "Pigs are too much, whatever they're worth. You've got to worry about vet bills, parasites, blocked birth canals. You don't want it."

"I want to turn Rose's southern acres and some of our fallow piece into pastures. We need to face facts, we'll never get enough land to beat the suits, they'll always win at that game. But if we can focus . . . people will pay good money for organic—"

"Where's Rose gonna go, if you buy her out?"

Not the question Perry expected. He shrugged. "Stella's. She's got that big place in town now. The farm is too much for Rose."

"Stella!" The Old Man winced. "Rose would peel off her own skin before going there."

"What do you care?" What *did* he care? The Old Man kept talking, pissing on Perry's ideas. Perry braced instinctively for a backhand: a blow that could've come any time from the year Perry was old enough to stand for a beating to the year he graduated high school. His heel ground into the dirt. "I've earned this. I've put in my time."

The Old Man let go the fistful of soil and swiped his palm against his blue pants. "You want it so bad, take over. See if I stop you." A long powdery stain on the Old Man's right thigh was all that was left of his handful. Perry turned to the barn. The cracked voice pulled him back again: "Put the tractor in the shed."

"I'll do it after supper."

"Don't be a fool, boy. The storm is coming." The Old Man reached out and clamped his shoulder. "Look at the goddamn sky."

It was purplish green overhead, almost camouflage. Wind bent the border of trees along the side of the house. Perry shook his head, making room for the lowering clouds.

"I'll tell her to get the house ready." His father swung round, hobbling up the Brown hill.

Perry jogged toward the tractor, toes pressing uncomfortably against hard leather. Then he stopped. "Where's Sill?" he yelled.

The Old Man yelled back, ". . . find her."

Perry angled the tractor neatly into the shed, lashed down the tools, left the doors and windows swinging wide so the wind could find an exit, and then went to check on the barn. The barn cats' silence was nudged out by the rising wind, blowing the sky along darkly. His father hadn't even paused to gloat. Clouds careened past the door. "Twister season," the radioman had warned, vowels shortened and run together in that put-on drawl.

He circled the barn's exterior, scanning for things he'd missed. Hooves galloped along the edges of the sky. An image of the hole flashed before him: his stone flipped and split, the rent in the earth matched by the gash of a funnel cloud, his secrets sucked up and scattered. He trotted up the hill and around to the back of the house, arms swinging at his sides as he ran over the emergency list in his head: blankets, batteries, first aid kit, canned food, water, flashlights, radio. Nina had taken the wash off the line and picked up any garden tools. The windows were open, yellow checked curtains blowing into his father's bedroom.

She was in the kitchen with the Old Man, fiddling with the radio. "Tornado advisory in the following counties . . ." Nina looked up when Perry entered and said, "It's bad," just as the Old Man barked, "It's coming near, all right," with a strange tone in his voice, almost satisfaction.

"Where's Sill?" His daughter's nickname sounded hollow. He'd been negligent. It was time to tell Sill about the stone, about laying her grief to rest. She needed to know, he needed to help her.

"She probably took shelter with Rose," Nina said, reassuring herself. "She's been spending a lot of time over there."

"Of course she's at Rose's," the Old Man spat.

His father went down the hall and Nina stepped closer. "Rose said, *No*, and so did the Old Man," Perry told her.

She flicked her braid back and took a breath. He could have leavened it, mentioned that the Old Man had left him an opening: *See if I stop you*. But it was easier to keep it black-and-white with Nina. There were only so many expectations he could disappoint in any given day. Two spots of color appeared on her neck and she said something snappish about giving up. She was worried, he knew, more than angry. About him, and about Sill. He poked her gently in the shoulder as the Old Man clattered back into the kitchen.

"I'm trying," Perry said. Neither of them answered him. The kitchen lights flickered.

Perry picked up the phone to call over to Rose's and then set it back down—a busy signal, the lines were overloaded. Sill knew how to take shelter. "Let's go," he said, and they all three walked out the front door. Nina held the Old Man by the elbow, and Perry veered off to do another sweep around the house. The stiff chicken wire around Nina's vegetable garden whipped in the wind. He was standing on the bluff at the east side of the house when a tree branch smacked him across the kidneys. Hard and quick, it knocked the air out of his lungs and sent him down on one knee. He staggered to his feet and ran to the front of the house just in time to see Nina and the Old Man tumbling down the final third of the hill, the Old Man crumpling and Nina dragged along after, rolling, flashes of skin, her hand locked onto his elbow.

He reached them soon after they hit the bottom. Nina was already on her hands and knees, struggling to stand. The Old Man's legs flailed. He'd lost his cane and Perry scrambled for it, shoving it into his father's hand. He grabbed them each by the arm and pulled, yelping as the muscles tightened in his lower back. The wind caught his cry and threw it back on them.

"Sill!" Nina turned toward the house.

"No," Perry yelled, "That was me." But she trotted back up the hill, waving her arm behind her, and shooing the men toward the shelter. "You heard *me*." Perry tried to make her understand.

Nina was too far off to hear. The Old Man's sinewy arm locked around his neck. Something was wrong with his father, as if all his strength had been stored up in that wayward cane. Perry swung his arm around him and they turned to the cellar, just ten feet away. When he looked back again Nina was by the porch standing face to face with Sill. Right there, the only things he loved. He waved his free arm at them and yelled but his father crumpled a few more inches and he had to turn, he couldn't wait. The sky was an ocean, brackish and churning.

Everything was wrong. Sill and Nina left unsheltered, the Old Man shriveled at his side. Perry's back throbbed. He fumbled to swing the trap door open, pulling it hard against the thick wind, and the Old Man slid awkwardly down the ladder. Perry turned to look at his wife and daughter but there was too much in the air—pieces of wood, grit, rock—and he had to cast down his eyes. He'd settle the Old Man and go back up for them. The trap door tore from his hand and slammed down as he followed his father into the dark.

*

People speak of the quality of the light. Not the dark greenish sky of extremity but its precursor: slightly overcast but bringing a clarity that makes everything—trees, houses, sidewalk cracks, cars lined in a parking lot—eerily distinct, strangely beautiful.

Some liken it to the light during a partial eclipse. The degree of brightness changes. As if the diffuse light of the sun gives way and the moon takes over, no matter the time of day. A cooler eye, sharper outlines. Images imprint and linger on the retina. A mundane afternoon feels like eight o'clock on a summer evening and, a switch flipped, you crave an ice pop. *Twister weather,* the old ones say, meaning, perhaps, *twister light*—but they're proven wrong as many times as right.

Citizens with experience might begin to assess the proximity of shelter. But many do not. It is, some say, intoxicating to feel newness in a world you think you know so well, to be reminded of its otherness. An average middle-aged woman will see a shadow cast by a power line on Main Street and think of her long-lost father: young, mowing the backyard in a white t-shirt, so alive that each blade of grass vies for attention while beyond, a mile away, noted but judged no immediate threat, a funnel cloud meanders gracefully through an empty field.

Of course reason prevails. Minds turn to the quiet spaces that usually sit forgotten. Many people nowadays do not have storm shelters. A basement will do very nicely; or bathtubs, interior closets. These spaces take an imperceptible inhale of possibility. Before the day is out Louise Logan and two other bank employees will shelter surrounded by safety deposit boxes in the hushed cloistered space of the vault. Portentous, padded with valuables and legal documents and lit by long white fluorescent bars, the vault is a church of secrets.

# Louise Logan

Louise pulled into the parking lot that morning at the same time as her coworker Dayana—8:25, just ten minutes after their boss. Dayana waved and cut the engine, and then slid out of her car holding an enormous travel coffee mug. She jutted her hip in its figure-molding skirt, hiked a knockoff designer bag over her shoulder, and leaned over to lock her car door. Louise knew that if the big bosses decided to save money by cutting a teller they'd most likely keep Dayana, twenty years younger, and cheaper in every way. Louise bared her teeth into the rearview to check for lipstick smears and chided herself. Dayana couldn't help it. What did seniority and experience count for these days?

She took a breath and stepped out of the car, adjusting the waistband of her A-line skirt. They walked together to the glass door, waiting for their boss to let them in. "Bill's cake is in my backseat," Louise said to Dayana. "I'll leave it there for now."

"Oh damn!" Dayana smacked her purple faux leather bag with her free hand. "The birthday card's in my other purse."

"No big deal," Louise said. They could do without, or make one.

"I don't know where my brain is. The barometric pressure or something."

Bill appeared through the glass, greeting them as he swung the door back and ushered them in. Louise had overheard him talking about plans to install another ATM. Their jobs, their very relevance, were in jeopardy. She went straight to her station and set to work—she was good at what she did, might as well remind him of that.

Louise moved through tasks she knew by heart. She tore open the plastic shrink wrap around a roll of pennies, careful not to chip her nail polish, wound the pen chain at her teller window into a neat spiral, and checked her inventory of receipt slips and lollipops. Outside the thick glass, a few cars made their way down the street. They'd probably get a handful of customers before noon, nothing earthshaking. Either one of them could handle it alone. Dayana, too, was looking busy.

In his office, Bill rocked gently in his chair as he looked over a sheaf of paper, his own busywork. *A glass house,* Louise thought, *home is where the . . .*

"One minute," Dayana said.

Louise flicked on the overhead lights as she went to unlock the door. "Hello, World!" she announced in her best Broadway voice. On the street, Stella Mondragon's champagne-colored sedan came into view. Stella was a fast, loose driver. She liked to go top speed even on poky Main Street, and she hit the brakes abruptly at stop signs as if she had no idea they were coming. The car jerked to a halt at the intersection in front of the bank. Stella's hair was dark and shoulder length, her skin powdered. She wore plum lipstick, and a sparkly, too-youthful barrette held the hair over her left temple. Her face looked distracted, even harried; she scratched her scalp with one finger, gave a cursory check for oncoming traffic, and sailed on.

Louise's fingers unclenched from the door handle—she'd been readying herself to face Stella—and she flipped the sign to *Open*. "Not a soul," she said, reading Dayana's questioning eyebrow. Dayana had seen her notice someone, and was probably expecting a catty comment. Though Louise was a perfectly competent bank teller, she was an *artist* when it came to knowing, understanding, and disseminating other people's secrets. Some people looked down on it, called it gossip. She called it public service. What knits a random group of people together? What makes a town a community? Knowledge—shared knowledge—of what makes people tick, and what they've overcome and struggled with and succumbed to. Especially what they've succumbed to.

Soon a few customers came in and she and Dayana took turns providing the kind of customer service the Corporate Office couldn't teach, no matter how many badly acted training videos and PowerPoint presentations Bill foisted on them. Louise was finishing up a deposit transaction when Nina Brown stepped to her window: tall and thin, with a long face to match the rest of her. She wore a gold cross around her neck, and a light pink sweatshirt with a calico heart on the chest. Nina's hairstyle hadn't changed since she was a girl—brown braid, tendrils held back at the temples with two serviceable black barrettes. Her hands were red and the skin along her nose was dry, as if she'd run out of moisturizer two weeks before and hadn't made time to restock. Louise filled her lungs and smiled. They went to the same church, First Methodist. Even in a house of worship Nina seemed rushed, on her way to the next appointment—though so far as Louise could tell she spent most of her days on the Brown farm, shuttling between the house and the garden, usually only coming into town for Sunday and Wednesday services. She lived with her quiet teenage daughter and equally taciturn husband, Perry. And Perry's father—Louise straightened her shoulders in sympathy at the thought of that flinty bastard.

"Nina, good to see you. How's life?" Louise shut the cash drawer and gripped the counter.

Nina smiled, crinkling the eczema along her nose, and handed Louise a withdrawal slip. "Good, good. Fine. Yourself?" Nina was pleasant as pie, but she'd stretch on a rack before volunteering personal information.

"Same as ever." Their conversation could have trudged along the expected track, but then, as if she were standing to the side and watching the words float up and dissolve into the air, Louise heard herself ask, "Have you seen Rose lately?"

Nina paused. "Rose?" She pulled a pack of gum out of her pocket.

"Yes." Louise punched a code and opened the cash drawer. "How is she holding up?"

"Funny you should ask. We visited after the funeral and she wouldn't . . . she's not ready to talk."

"God bless her," Louise said automatically, picking up a stack of bills. "I saw Stella this morning, maybe that's why I . . . How's your girl, by the way? Good grades?"

"Decent. Could be better. And Ben? How's he liking college?" Nina stuck the pack of gum back into her purse without offering a piece to Louise. Then she thought better of it, retrieved the gum, and held it out.

"No, thanks, I'm trying to be sugar-free . . . Benji's great! Having the time of his life, but he took the news about Lance hard, of course. They were so close." This was largely speculation. Benji was only four hours away, and his reluctance to come home for weekends had stung. He wanted nothing to do with his parents, it seemed. Louise sighed and shut the cash drawer. "It's a shame, that's what it is. It weighs on a person. I still don't understand it. Lance was . . ."

"Yes," Nina said.

Louise handed her a receipt and eighty dollars in cash. They were both uncomfortable now; it was time to end it.

"Where does it all go?" Nina shoved the money into her jeans pocket.

Louise pressed on. "Will you give Rose my sympathies when you see her?"

"I will," Nina said. "You know how prickly she is . . ." She paused, her fingers on the edge of the laminate counter, mirroring Louise's, and her lips pulled into a frown, emphasizing the flaky skin around her mouth. Louise wanted to reach for the bottle of lotion she kept in her drawer and pat it all over Nina's face. "She's acting . . . she might not want . . ." Nina shook her head.

Bill walked from the corridor that led from his office onto the larger floor, headed in their direction. Louise leaned over and grasped Nina's sleeve. "Maybe you should go see her?" she whispered. "Just to check up?"

Nina blinked. "That's just what I was thinking." She looked down at Louise's fingers on her cuff and pushed her gum from one cheek to the other.

"All righty." Louise let go of the sleeve and brightened her voice, pitching it toward the manager. "Thanks again, you have a great day!"

*Weird*, she thought, watching Nina through the glass as she walked to her station wagon. Bill, asking if she'd seen yesterday's receipts, interrupted her thoughts. "I gave them to you," Louise said.

"I know." Bill held out the crumpled bundle. "But the report says you missed one." Dayana pulled a sympathetic face behind his back.

They found the lost slip caught in a tiny hollow at the back of her drawer. "It could happen to anyone," Louise said. She had to say it, because no one else would.

If Louise were to come face to face with Rose, what would she say? It would most certainly be a question: *How are you? Is there a thing in this world that's understandable?* She shook her head. Really, what she would most likely ask is: *How can I help you today? Withdrawal or deposit? Would you like to find out more about our CD interest rates, Rose?*

All of this was speculation because if Rose came into the bank she'd pick Dayana's window. This in spite of the fact that Lance and Ben had been best friends, playing junior varsity football together, not to mention countless Scouting trips. Rose never banked with

Louise—not for years, ever since Louise had let slip that she knew the reason for Rose's rift with Stella, that tawdry triangle. In spite of their sons' friendship, their paths scarcely crossed—a mutually agreed upon avoidance. The weekend after news about Lance's death had broken, she'd made a pot of stew and picked a bouquet of Lazy Susans and delivered them out to church; Pastor Bowen was going to pay Rose a visit. She didn't deliver them herself. A visit from her would be unwelcome.

Louise looked over at Dayana, who felt her eyes and glanced up.

"I'm not myself," Louise said.

"Colitis acting up again?"

Louise flushed and looked toward Bill's office door. "No. I'm okay." She took a breath. "I can run over to Mondragon's during my break and pick up a birthday card."

"You sure?"

"The walk would do me good." It was a ten minute walk down a stretch of old Main Street to the one store, aside from The Bluebird Café and Rikker's Liquors, that still seemed moderately successful. She could stop in at The Bluebird and get herself a sweet coffee drink, and then go see what Ward Mondragon was up to.

Before heading to Mondragon's, Louise went around back to the employee parking spots and pulled the cake from her car's backseat. It was a small square with white icing and blue cursive: *Happy Birthday, Bill!* When she'd placed the order she had asked them to make dollar signs and stars, but the message had been lost and there was a large clump of clumsy green frosting carnations right next to Bill's name. She'd complained at the store and the sullen baker had added a few stars. Now the cake just looked cluttered and gloopy. She sighed. Bill wouldn't care, and Dayana would scarcely notice. Louise took the box inside and set it on the counter behind her station.

She didn't wear a jacket, just slung her purse over her arm and started walking. The sky was close to the earth, light filtering through the clouds in a gauzy haze. Louise passed The Bluebird without going in, waving to Emma Templeton through the window. She'd stop for a coffee on the way back.

Half a block on she heard an engine, and a tingling in her fingers told her not to turn around. From the corner of her eye she saw an old blue pickup. *Rose.* It had to be. As if she'd been summoned up from that awkward conversation with Nina Brown. Just feet away, the truck chugged past at a steady pace. Louise couldn't help it—she looked at the woman behind the wheel. Rose's hair was snowier than Louise's mother's, like a flash of something electric had passed through her and left a tip of ash. But her face—the nose that belonged on a statue, the square jaw, the mouth as set as ever—at least in profile, she was herself. Lance's black dog sat in the passenger seat, his head hanging out the window. He smiled in Louise's direction, baring yellow fangs. She stepped back, undefended.

The truck continued past, no indication that Louise's presence had registered. She would bet her wedding china that they were headed to the same place—it would be just her luck. Her hand lit on her cell phone without thought and she pulled it out of her bag, checking the blank screen, empty of incoming calls. Well, she could make an outgoing.

She had learned to let it ring a long time. With each ring she pictured her mother moving a step closer to the phone table. The door to her room would be open, attendants and other residents moving along the polished industrial floors in the hallway. Her mother would be wearing slacks and lipstick and wide-soled leather shoes.

"Hi, Mother!" she said brightly, as soon as the receiver clicked.

"Hello?" The voice was thin and wavering. "Hello?"

"It's just me, Mother." Louise was out of breath. She stopped walking and stood against a shuttered storefront. The clock above the old town hall was broken—it read 7:20 and she had a momentary panic, as if she'd entered a time warp and leapt hours into the past.

"What is it? What's happened?"

*God,* Louise thought, *everything is an emergency—and I never gave her an ounce of trouble, not once.*

"Nothing. It's fine. I'm just on my work break and I'm walking over to Mondragon's to get a birthday card for Bill."

"Oh." Her mother inhaled and coughed. For the second time that day, Louise felt dismissed.

"Mother, Rose just passed me on the street."

"Who?"

"*Rose.* The one who—"

"The Anderson place? The old boarding house? *That* girl?"

"Yes."

"That family never had what it takes."

"No."

"Anywhere they went, and it wasn't just here. No sense of place."

"Right. Her—"

"And the father! You know, he tried to talk me and Edna and some others into a fishy real estate deal. It was some sort of . . . what do you call it? . . . Pyramid. A pyramid scheme. He was as slick as they come. And his wife? Ha! Prancing around in four-inch heels and French perfume . . . you could hear the little gin bottles clacking around in her purse. Once even at the post office . . ." Her mother's voice was stronger now, full of indignation, as if other people's bad choices hurt her deeply.

Rose's truck had given off a cloud of exhaust. Louise breathed a lungful of carbon monoxide, feeling calmer. Her mother could go on, and would, with minimal prodding.

". . . The girls were pretty, though. What was the other one's name? Stella. She had princessy ways, sticking out her finger when she drank tea like she was seeing whether she could hook a man on it . . . Once at a social I heard the mother telling the girls to act like they owned the place, building them up, you know, elevating their expectations—and of course they weren't godly in the slightest, they just came to church on special occasions. What an inheritance: bad advice and bills!"

Louise straightened her shoulders and began walking, slowly this time. If there were any place other than Mondragon's to buy a card she'd give up on that store. She pulled the phone a little closer to her mouth. "Her son died. Rose's son died, Mother, remember? Just a few months ago. In the war."

"He died? Well . . . that's a shame. Really. What war?"

"Mother."

Silence. The clock in the tower clicked its long hand forward a notch, and then back again. 7:20. A sedan drove by, the acquaintance behind the wheel raising a hand in effortless greeting. Louise waved back.

She shouldn't have brought up the recent past, which was becoming foggier and foggier for her mother. Next visit, Louise would be sure to remind her that Benji had promised he would come home next month for Dave's birthday, his first trip home since Lance's funeral.

"How's your day, Mother? Do you need me to bring you anything tomorrow?"

"I'm eating a sandwich," her mother said. Louise added that to her picture: brown slacks, black shoes, pink lipstick, tuna on wheat, left hand pressing the red receiver to her ear, a look of impatience on her face and a few crumbs dotting the dry corners of her mouth.

"I'm sorry," Louise said.

"What for?"

"Interrupting." She was moments from Mondragon's and had to make a decision or she'd wind up face to face with Rose. Louise paused again, stopping under the awning of what had once been a dress shop. "I interrupted your lunch." They had plenty to say face to face—her mother held court and Louise courted. But now she wasn't sure where to focus her attention. Her mind felt as shuttered as the window at her back.

They were both relieved to hang up. As Louise stepped across an intersection she could see the ramshackle white clapboard on the corner down the block, the old Anderson's B&B. The empty building looked even more run-down than it had when Rose and Stella and their parents had lived there. A dump, home to hapless travelers and wayward types, the down on their luck. The carpet on the stairs had been a threadbare crimson, a sign of better times, and the one time Louise had climbed those stairs her toe caught on a piece of buckled rug at the top—she'd pitched forward clumsily.

Louise had a sudden wish for winter—the punishing cold would clear her head. She shoved the phone into her purse, taking care to watch her step on the uneven sidewalk. Up ahead, just as she'd figured, Rose's truck was parked in front of Mondragon's. Louise crossed the street and ducked into Dunleavy's Fine Shoes (&Shoe Repair), the sad, dusty little place directly across from Ward's store. Scottie Dunleavy had run the shop into the ground. The bell tinkled above the door, but there was no sign of life. Through Scottie's window she could see two people inside Mondragon's: Rose moving in one direction and then another, Ward following at his respectable, polite pace.

"Can I help you?"

Louise turned. Scottie lurked over by the men's dress shoes, his eyes not quite meeting hers. His hair was lank and gray, and his gauntness made him look taller than he was. There was a long, ugly red scratch on his forearm. He was clearly searching for her name, though he should know it. Scottie had always been a strange one, spiraling further down since his parents' death. A tabby cat walked out from the back, sat at Scottie's feet, and yawned. Louise cast a glance at the street. Rose's truck was still there.

They had a stilted exchange about the type of shoe she was looking for, and Scottie slid away. Louise kept watch out the window so intently that she didn't hear him return. She didn't care what Scottie thought of her behavior. In the old days she would have—the Dunleavys were chic and fashionable; the most sophisticated couple in town, Louise's mother had always said. Scottie took after the men on his mother's side of the family, unfortunately. You could see his high-strung, seedy grandfather just in the way Scottie's fingers shook as he held the shoebox. Blood will out.

The shoe he brought her had a dark stain on the canvas. She tried it on out of politeness, keeping an eye on the window as she sat on a bench to slip off her loafer. Scottie hovered a bit too close. Rose's truck pulled away, finally, and Ward stood on his porch, patting his belly nervously. Good to know she wasn't the only one who found Rose unsettling.

"What do you think?" Scottie asked, and she looked up, surprised. But he was only asking about the shoe she had set back into its tired box.

"Not quite right."

In Mondragon's, Ward greeted her and Louise plucked the first birthday card she saw from the rack, slapping it on the counter. A framed photograph of the President hung above Ward's back counter, eyes gazing over their heads into nothingness, the man's thin lips pulled back in a smile-grimace, a look that Louise recognized: *I'd rather be elsewhere*. Next to the President was a plaque that Ward had been awarded by the Chamber of Commerce: Small Businessman of the Year, dated fifteen years before.

Normally, she would have tried to get information from Ward, coming in at an angle and coaxing it out of him. *Was that Rose I saw leaving? She looked so spent, didn't she? It must be so hard for you and Stella . . .* But she felt too flustered to pull it off today. Something in the way Ward slowly counted change into her palm made her hold her tongue. They exchanged a bit of halting small talk, and he reached for the phone before she made it all the way out the door.

Louise retraced her steps to the bank, eyes on her feet in their scuffed loafers, moving faster now. She felt but didn't see the abandoned Anderson's B&B as she passed. She could pace out all of Main Street if she wanted, and know where she was by feel and the cracks in the sidewalk. *I might as well be blind*, Louise thought. The horrible crows that had driven out the songbirds flapped overhead, and shadows stretched along the cement. She checked her watch—Bill and Dayana would be wondering where she was; there was no time to stop for coffee.

"My hair's extra frizzy, is yours?" Dayana called as Louise swung open the door. An empty Cup o' Noodles rested on the counter behind Dayana's station. Though they weren't supposed to eat at their windows, they both routinely broke that rule.

"Got it," Louise said, patting her purse, a weak smile creeping across her face.

"You're the best." Dayana didn't seem to notice Louise's state. She shot a look at the back office, lowering her voice. "Bill wants to have meetings with each of us late tomorrow. You at 4:30, me at 5:00."

"About?"

Dayana shrugged. They both knew: cuts, efficiencies, belt-tightening measures. The corporate office sent new memos every week. Dayana had the bilingual advantage, handling all their Spanish-speaking customers, and she could probably take on Louise's workload without breaking a sweat.

Louise felt her face redden and shook her head, annoyed. She slammed her purse into the cabinet under the counter. They signed the card to Bill and decided they'd give him the cake mid-afternoon, during the usual customer lull. It was slow even now. Dayana had tuned the radio to the weather station at Bill's request, and the slickest of the newsmen was on, pleased with himself as he nattered on about storm conditions—his voice was vaguely familiar.

For a couple of hours they looked busy and the sky thickened. The radioman mentioned storm conditions and alerts. One or two customers came in. Tom Muldoon was the last, his craggy face more creviced than ever; his eyes darted to Dayana's cleavage as he stepped up to the counter. So predictable. Bill sat and swiveled on his office chair, building and then disassembling a tower of paperclips on his magnetized desk toy. Louise could still feel the path she'd walked on her lunch break, dull vibrations in the soles of her feet, and the faint shame she'd felt as she passed the old Anderson place.

"Yipes," Dayana said, pointing at the plate glass. The sky outside, even considering the dim panes, was disturbingly dark. *Bruised,* Louise thought. Bill should have called the maintenance guy and had him board the windows. The clock on the wall read 3:15.

"You'd think it was closing time. Tell Bill to go ahead and open the vault," she said to Dayana, "I'll do the door and the lights." A storm siren started to blare. Bill rummaged in the tiny employee kitchen next to his office, looking for the emergency kit—tardy in following protocol but of course he'd get away with it.

The birthday cake waited on the back counter. Louise opened the lid of the cardboard box, wondering if she should bring it into the vault and present it to Bill. It would give them all something to talk about: that time they celebrated Bill's birthday surrounded by safety deposit boxes while the world spun outside. The green frosting was too bright, likely left over from St. Patrick's Day. She went to the front door and flipped the sign to *Closed*, sliding the bolt. There was no one to lock it against; the street was empty. On the corner up ahead, the streetlight turned from yellow to red, directing a nonexistent flow of traffic. Anyone in his right mind out there now would floor it through a red light.

In the back, Bill said something that made Dayana laugh. They got along pretty well, those two. Louise pressed her forehead against the glass. She shivered for no good reason, and thought of a soup she'd eaten at The Bluebird months before, a wonder of chicken and rice that had warmed her from the inside out. "I wish I were . . ." She closed her eyes. The thick pane wasn't entirely still, and she wondered whether its faint vibrations were from the air pressure outside or from her own breath.

*If I had the guts I'd say something to Rose. Her hair was a shock of white. It doesn't seem possible, but I saw it. I'd walk right up to that truck, not shrink past. I'd walk up, rap on the hood, and make her eyes focus on something. Rose, I'd say. Rose, I know you thought you were special. But none of us are. He was a beautiful boy . . . If it were my son . . . But what you make of it is your choice*—She shuddered and opened her eyes. The sky to the east was churning, a wall of gray. A finger dipped out of the clouds and her stomach lurched.

"Come *on*, Louise," Bill called, and she hurried to her station, pulling her purse from its spot under the cubby.

She took one more look at the cake and picked up the heavy, multidocument stapler from the back counter, hoisting it six inches above the open box. If she let go, it would make contact with a soft slurp and lodge in the thick frosting at an angle, bisecting the lettering. The storm siren urged her on. That's all the ugliness needed, to be rearranged. She set the stapler down and left the cake untouched, flicking off the lights as she went to the back.

*

Streams, swimming pools, reservoirs, creeks—water senses water. Molecules pull taut and ripple gently. Submerged rocks settle themselves and pebbles clack. In clear currents and brown standing water, in farm runoff and underground streams, microscopic life teems unabated. Surfaces swell and vibrate under the weight of bugs, twigs, and lapping tongues. Leaves fall, swirling into tiny eddies.

Patterns become insistent. When the sediment at the creek's bottom is disturbed it surges, spreading outward—darkness at the center, lightening further out, with mottled, constantly moving layers. And the colors: browns and grays and blacks—but also, depending on the sun, shot through with blues, greens, even pinks and reds. What had seemed flat and negotiable becomes elemental—a witch's cauldron; primordial soup; the end of things, or the beginning. A chucked pebble or fallen tree branch sets off a submerged implosion that replicates in miniature the supercell storm cloud gathering overhead—billowing darkness, the light refracting, its churning restlessness. Elements rearrange themselves, breaking open and reconfiguring, feeling a pressure that tugs toward the center. Gravity loosens its grip.

At Johnson's Creek a waterbug launches into the air, leaving a fleeting concentric footprint behind. A rotting log collapses neatly into itself, and a small bird net flaps empty. No footfalls here today. The memory of footfalls: women and children sitting on a bank, neighborly voices, calls and laughter. Only vibrations now, and that pull toward the heart of things. And waiting.

When Nina Brown steps into her kitchen garden to turn on the hose, beads of water arc and fall—and even these tiny bodies feel the call skyward.

# Nina Brown

It was a three-minute drive to the neighboring farm, and a thirty-minute walk. Nina walked. She wanted time to figure out how to handle Rose.

At the bank earlier that morning, when Louise Logan had asked after Rose, Nina hadn't known how to answer. She had seen her neighbor only once, right after the news about Lance, in a stilted visit to deliver flowers and meatloaf. Since then Rose had shut herself off—and the short, shameful answer was that Nina didn't know how she was.

Warmth from the black macadam drifted up her pant legs. Canned pears and seven single-serving plastic containers of bean chili thunked against the small of her back, shifting in her tote bag. The mid-morning sky was bright, a few cirrus clouds belying the storm condition notices. Storm-warners, doomsayers, people who held sway over your life with words words words, never actions. They'd been wrong before—but they'd been right sometimes, too. Nina pulled the tote closer, and pears sloshed in their syrup. Yellow wildflowers sprouted in the spring grass by the edge of the road, turning up their faces like little portents of happiness.

It stuck in Nina's craw that Louise Logan, of all people, had guilted her into visiting. Louise, with her dyed chestnut pageboy swishing around a jawline that didn't need accentuating, and her wet, bright eyes watching too intently. She reminded Nina of a vole—something that tunneled, that sat perfectly still, jaw working and working, looking behind you to see what else was there, and then darting under for reasons known only to her. Now here Nina was, sent on a mission by a woman she didn't like, to check up on a woman who didn't like *her*.

A mailbox rose up, rusty along the seams, its flag stuck into an upright position. Rose's driveway was narrower than she remembered. It looked spat out from among the tangly branches like a half-digested chickenbone. Nina stepped up the driveway, making a mental list of chores she could ask the Old Man to do at home, to keep him busy and out of Perry's hair. The less those two crossed paths the better. Could she send him over here to repaint Rose's mailbox? She ruled out that idea—he hadn't come to Rose's place in years.

The house appeared around a final bend. Its shingles and tilting chimney were jagged against the sky, and the whole place looked like it could give you a black eye. A crow cawed, flying in an ungainly path toward the barn. Nina crossed the creaky porch to the front door and knocked, but there was no answer so she went around back. Curls of peeling paint sprinkled the porch floor.

"Rose," she called, rapping on the screen door. "You home?" She looked around the yard. No sign of life. She peered through the screen into the kitchen to call again. A putrid smell came from inside. She set the tote bag at her feet, wondering where to leave it. It would be fine on the porch for an hour or two. But where was Rose? And what was that smell? What if Rose had—.

Nina pushed the screen open. "Hello?"

The source of the stink was clear as soon as she entered: the trashcan overflowed, and dirty dishes cluttered the counters and table. Nina made a spot for her bag and pulled out the items that needed to go into the refrigerator. She opened the fridge door and stood, honest to God stunned. It was a tinfoil shrine. At least ten casserole dishes, untouched, in varying stages of moldy putrescence. A gallon of chunky milk. Something furry in a produce bag. On the door, lidless slimy jam and pickle jars, and one pristine stick of butter.

Here was the answer to Louise's question. *Lord, Rose. Rose, you're what, ten years older than me? You can't be losing it, you just can't, you have to pull it together.* She shut the fridge door and went to the living room, calling Rose's name.

Nina walked quietly through the rest of the house, as if to lessen the impact of her intrusion. Upstairs, she paused outside the shut door that had been Lance's room. Touched the wood. Then moved on. Rose's bedroom was empty. Down the back staircase, the sewing room had a twin bed that looked like it had recently held a body; cans of corn were stacked in a pyramid in the corner. The dusty parlor was strangely warm, and she paused in front of the mantel. Five black feathers fanned out above the fireplace with a thorny branch of dried rosehips—the makings of some decorative arrangement in the underworld.

A family photo hung crooked above the mantel: Rose and her late husband Theo sat on either side of Lance. The boy looked like an imp, a sprite—a spirit that hadn't left him even after he was a lanky teen, knocking on her back door to take a walk with Sill. In the photo he was about four, his face screwed into a toothy smile, brown hair falling into his eyes. On Lance's right, Theo leaned back as if anticipating a blinding flash. Rose looked solid, her hands folded in her lap, staring straight into the camera like she could bore through and touch the other side.

A presence seemed to breathe into the house—was that the screen door whining? Nina put a hand to her throat and turned around. "Rose?" *How will she bear it?* she had asked Perry when the news had broken. If she walked to the backyard she'd surely find that spirited little boy from the photo sitting in the dirt with Sill and a hose, making mudpies.

Nina hurried back to Rose's kitchen. The screen door wasn't quite shut, so she pulled it tight in its frame. On the fridge door two strawberry-shaped magnets held a sheet of paper, folded in half. A faint etching of black ink pressed through the white sheet. Nina unclipped it and unfolded the page. Now she was just snooping. Louise Logan would be proud. She ignored her trembling fingers. Her daughter's name ran bold and black across the top of the paper—it was an email that Sill had printed out, dated five months back. The subject line read "For my mom."

*Dear Ma—My best girl says she'll pass this message on to you. I haven't had time to write a paper letter. How are you? The food here is terrific (not!) as ever and it's been real hot. I wish I could time travel back for the weekend for some good food. Damn that I don't have super powers—ha, ha. Don't worry about me, we are careful. How is Fergus? I'll write more next week. Maybe even pick up a real pen? Better go, there's a country that needs saving (oh boy). Love, Lance.*

Nina refolded the paper and returned it to its place on the fridge. Sill had never told her she relayed emails to Rose, but it made sense. Her daughter was locked now in a dance with Rose that Nina couldn't follow. Sill had been as in love as a girl could be at sixteen. Nina remembered her own youthful passion with Perry, wrenching and electric, and cursed Lance for mixing it up with Sill before heading off to war. Then, just as fast, she grabbed the cross around her neck and offered up a quick plea for forgiveness. And for Rose—a prayer for her too, not that she'd want Nina's prayers.

All told, Nina was in Rose's empty house for almost two hours. She lugged out the trash, filled the sink with soapy water and washed the dishes stacked in it, then the pots lining the counters. Holding her nose, she emptied everything from the fridge—pouring liquids down the drain, scraping solids into the garbage can, and took out the trash again. She scoured every casserole dish and scrubbed the fridge shelves, and then found some baking soda to set inside it. She washed Fergus's food bowl, filled his water dish, and swept the floor. Then she set her chili in the sparkling fridge, leaving the canned pears on the table, and took a piece of paper from the shelf under the phone.

*Dear Rose,*

*I stopped by today and I apologize for letting myself in, but I brought some chili that had to go into the fridge. I also brought some fruit I canned. We had too much. I hope you enjoy it. I was very sorry to miss you.*

*Rose, I am so sorry for what has happened. I pray for Lance every day. ~~Sill cries in her room—Sill is heartbroken~~ Sill misses him too.*

She sat, staring out the window. What more was there to say?

*I'm sorry we aren't closer, Rose, the way we used to be. ~~I have no good excuse, other than—Can you ever—Just because I have their name doesn't mean I'm like them.~~ Will you please call me to let me know you got this?*

*Yours truly,*

Just as she was going to make a clean copy and sign her name, an engine rumbled into the yard. Rose's truck. Nina knew the sound of that old junker. Stupidly, she hadn't checked the side of the house where it was usually parked. Rose had just gone to town, out driving, running errands like any normal person—she didn't want Nina's charity.

Nina leaped up from the table. Her chair clattered onto the floor, note fluttering after it. The pen she'd found in a drawer near the phone rolled off the table toward a crack by the baseboards. She grabbed her tote bag and rushed out the back door, rounding the house and cutting through shrubs toward the low wall that separated the yard from the fields. Then she chucked the bag over the wall and scrambled after it into the corn. Behind her, the hayloft leaned at a funny angle and a bird minced from one corner of the eaves to another.

Nina half-jogged home, only pausing when she hit the base of the hill. The Brown house was the only place for miles with a view—a sloping elevation starting just past the old carriage barn and leveling off twenty feet above ground. Who had the luxury, in the old days, of using horses for any purpose other than working the fields? For that was how Perry's great-grandfather, Elias Brown, had done it: hitched up the horses to push dirt into this homemade hill. Then he packed it down hard. Earth heaped as a pedestal, out of hubris or spiritual symbolism or just a desire to look down at the neighbors. The house appeared reproachful to Nina. She felt utterly ridiculous, dodging Rose like that. It was cowardly. She took a breath, not ready to go inside. The Old Man would be there and Sill wouldn't. Nina walked into the yard, stepped into her garden shed and clicked the latch tight.

The shed smelled of good, clean dirt. It was the one place entirely her own—her labels on the neatly ordered shelves, her carefully chosen seed packets sealed in airtight plastic containers. Perry and his Old Man argued about how to handle their hundreds of acres, but the vegetables that they ate most every night—those were *hers*. Nina puttered to collect herself, letting her sweat cool and dry. She pulled a container of seed packets from the shelf and flipped through, planning what to sow once the rabbit fence was fixed, feeling steadied by each decision she made.

Slipping a seed packet into her pocket, she picked up a trowel and went to the garden. The southeast corner of the fence had succumbed to the thumping feet of hungry rabbits. Nina's carrots and crunchy romaine were the first to go. Now they'd had most of her baby spinach and lemon cucumbers. She pulled the damaged plants, tossing them into a bucket. Then she sat in the cleared space. It was still humid, and the sky felt a shade less bright. The few sprouts the rabbits had left behind bent toward the dirt—a sign of threatening weather. Nina crouched to look at the indentation her butt had made. She poked a dozen holes into each moon shape, sprinkling in some arugula seeds and patting the dirt back into place, and then pulled out the hose to soak the soil. Arugula was peppery and bitter. Perry and the Old Man pushed it around on their plates, but she and Sill liked it, and best of all, it grew like a weed—the rabbits let it be.

In the laundry room, she slung her braid away from her hot neck, peeled off her dirty sweatshirt, and washed her hands and face. The lunch hour had come and gone. She strode to the kitchen, pulled out the orange juice and paused, listening for sounds upstairs. Nothing. She took a long drink, cold and sweet from the carton.

The downstairs bathroom door bashed against the wall. "Storm's coming," the Old Man said, shuffling in.

"Zipper," she replied, setting the carton back on its shelf. Ever since he'd been struck by lightning out near the Infamous Elm, he'd been slipping—he had walked out of the bathroom once with his pecker still hanging out of his pants. But aside from that one thing, she didn't mind the change. He was humbler now, and didn't act like he owned the world.

"Seen Sill?" she asked. Sill had claimed cramps this morning and begged Nina to let her call in sick to school. Nina had agreed, though that excuse, like all the others, was wearing thin. At first she had indulged Sill's grief, but her daughter had to learn how to stand against it and keep going—and if that meant Nina being brusque or cold, well, so be it.

The Old Man shook his head, clacking his cane against the table legs as he settled into a chair, and gave a phlegmy cough. "I can feel it coming."

She'd had enough of kitchens for one day. Nina went up to the second floor without another word to her father-in-law. As she'd expected, Sill wasn't in her room. There had been no sign of her at Rose's; maybe they'd gone to town together. Nina sat on Sill's bed, running her hand over the pink-flowered comforter cover.

*How will she bear it?* she'd whispered to Perry, meaning Rose of course—but she'd meant Sill too. On a corkboard above Sill's dresser was a photo of Lance. He leaned his back against a tree trunk and looked into the camera with his head tilted. The expression in his eyes—a soft velvety brown—was blatantly seductive. Looking at it now, Nina knew: *They slept together.* That bolt of knowledge made her scan his face for deceit, but she saw just a boy, looking seductively at *her,* Nina, with a question in his eyes that she couldn't decipher. Thank God Sill hadn't gotten pregnant. She pulled the comforter cover into her fist and smoothed it out again.

It would be necessary for Perry to take over Rose's land—what she'd seen today made that clear. If the Browns didn't get it, the bank would. Perry would require Nina's firm hand on his shoulder to see it through, just as he needed her encouragement to stand up to the Old Man. She took a breath before she stood, and then fluffed Sill's pillows.

Downstairs the Old Man still sat in the kitchen, listening to the radio. The weatherman, Ted Waite, recited a list of the counties on alert. Perry had known the man a bit, years before, when he went by "Eddie" and sauntered through town picking up girls. Nina thought the radioman still sounded like a philanderer, even now, with that wide, shallow smile in his voice. She turned the volume down.

"How about fixing Sill's bike? The front wheel has some bent spokes." She was usually able to get the Old Man to do things for her, though she didn't push. First she'd ask him to do the bike, and if he balked at that she'd move onto the thing she really wanted—the rabbit fence. She'd learned how to handle her father-in-law through trial and error, and unlike Perry, she didn't take one stone for a whole wall.

He stuck his pinky finger into his ear and then withdrew it for inspection. "I'll take a look."

"That'd be great." She opened the dishwasher and started unloading.

"Not today."

"Okay, whenever you can." Perry planned to ask his father again about his idea to try some livestock. She'd urged him to—it was past time that he took over officially, and the way his father was stringing him along would only bring about more bitterness. The Old Man coughed. He'd sit there for hours, rattling the newspaper and working his post-nasal drip. If she turned around now, she'd hurl something, or scream.

"We've gotta get ready," he said.

Toast crumbs littered the sink. She rinsed them down the drain and wiped her hands on a dishtowel. "I know." She had the storm routine down pat—they'd done it often enough, when tornadoes had cut close, but ultimately passed them by. Nina would open windows to give the wind leeway. Then she'd help the Old Man to the root cellar and they'd sit, breathing the dank air until the battery-operated radio gave the all clear.

The confident voice on the radio faded out and a jingle for an auto body chain came on, offering an oil change and brake check special. For no reason at all, the neat pyramid of canned corn she'd seen in Rose's sewing room popped into her head: the only tidy thing in the whole house.

"Sherwin, I went to Rose's this morning."

The Old Man set down the paper, waiting.

"She wasn't there. The place isn't . . . she's not . . . I cleaned the fridge." Sill would be with Rose now, maybe eating lunch—did they sit and talk and cry about Lance?

The Old Man brushed his hand over his head and touched the tobacco tin in his left shirt pocket. He had done his part to ruin the friendship between their two families. She'd never asked what his regrets were. When Theo died and Rose was alone with her boy and a mortgage, the writing was on the wall, even if Rose wouldn't admit it. The Old Man had started going over there to talk Rose into leasing some acreage, and it was more than just looking out for widows and orphans. Nina suspected that he went to court her. That was a sore point with Perry, so she never mentioned it. One day the Old Man came back, his shoulders stiffer than usual. *I'm done trying to help that crazy witch,* he'd said. And that was that—three generations of complicated neighborly history officially unraveled.

He didn't look stiff now. He'd shrunk a little at her words and slumped in his chair. But soon he rallied, picked up the paper, shook it, set it back down and pointed to the radio. "You'd better get the clothes off the line."

"I think Sill talks to her." Nina's eyes stung. "She won't talk to me, you know. My own daughter." Her voice seemed too loud, and she blinked. She pulled the dishtowel off her shoulder and turned to swipe it along the counter by the sink, collecting more crumbs. "I'm going to make coffee. Do you want some?" They both needed something bracing. He loved her coffee, and he'd take it as it was meant—a peace offering.

The Old Man shook the newspaper again. "No, thanks."

She opened the coffee canister and measured out a quarter pot's worth. The smell made the kitchen brighter. "Oh, what the heck," he said. "Okay." So Nina kept going, counting out a full pot at twelve heaping scoops. She liked it strong, and so did he.

"She'll come around," the Old Man said to Nina's back. "The girl won't find what she needs over there."

Nina drew a breath, sliding her shoulder blades down her back. "I just can't believe he's dead. That it happened. Do you remember that time at the creek when the kids were little and Lance almost drowned? He was only four. He *did* drown. I think his heart stopped. Remember? I can't stop thinking about that day. Sill doesn't remember anything about it . . . but why would she? None of us spoke of it after."

She couldn't tell if he was listening. He tapped his fingers against his chest, a nervous tic for as long as she'd known him, which was almost half of her life. When the smell of brewed coffee filled the room, she poured them each a mug. Ted Waite was back on the radio, talking about being alert, being careful. The Old Man shoved his chair back from the table as she set the mug in front of him.

"Sherwin, why didn't we ever speak of what happened? At the creek, I mean. I don't understand. It was so . . . was it out of respect for Rose, or some sort of, I don't know, some sense of shame that we let it happen in the first place? Or fear? Was it too close for comfort?"

She slurped at the coffee and stood with one hand clasped behind her neck. Though she'd been horrified that Lance was killed fighting in that strangely muffled, faraway war, a part of her was not surprised. Rose had snatched him from the maw when he was a child, but all she'd done was buy some extra time. They were followed by a shadow. Nina believed this with a conviction as strong as any she had, and her convictions, though they'd narrowed over the years, had deepened apace. But she'd never say aloud what she thought about Rose to anyone, even the Old Man. She knew how it would sound.

Her questions sank into silence. The Old Man cleared a gob of phlegm from his throat, spat into a paper napkin, and took a sip of coffee. Perry would be amazed to hear her speak like this to his father. Her husband thought, because she was pushing him to take over, that she resented the Old Man as much as he did. Well, she didn't have a buffer, like Perry did. She *was* the buffer. And most days, she and Perry passed like ships—with him, it was all logistics and whispered dethronings. But the Old Man was around and underfoot, peppering her day with conversation. They talked more than Perry would ever know. Both men would be shocked at the way she talked to the other. Constant daily betrayals.

"I had a friend in Korea," he told her. "Joe Carnahan." Not again. Another one of his rambling war stories. She stared into the black brew in her mug. "Got shot up outside of Pusan. He was a good guy. For more than a week I thought he was dead. Where do people get buried in a place like that? I mean, in New York City. That's where he was from. It's all I thought about. But it turned out he'd lost a leg and they shipped him home." He'd never heard from Joe again. That's how war was. People who were like your own flesh, then an empty space, and it all kept going. The names changed, but the purpose didn't. They were Americans, that was all they were. "Common ground," he said. "That's what we fight for."

She put her empty mug into the dishwasher and shut the door with a click.

The Old Man had trailed off. Ordinarily, she would say something about sacrifice or bravery or how the world used to be, but he didn't seem to be waiting for that. He looked at his fingertips, pushing them together in a steeple shape. Perry and his Old Man would duke it out until the Old Man finally relented and let Perry make some decisions, and it would be up to her, Nina, to referee, to make sure it didn't implode, or (and here's where the tricky part came in) that it *did*. A necessary tumult before resolution.

"More coffee?" she asked, feeling her failure in the question. She would make a special trip this week to talk to Pastor Bowen. And she'd take Sill with her.

The Old Man stood, a struggle in the way he pushed himself against the wood table. His bones were worrying him. He crumpled the snotty napkin onto his dirty plate and pushed it, not unkindly, onto the counter next to Nina. Then he told her it was pointless to dwell on the past, reminded her about the sheets on the line, and limped out the door, probably to corral his son.

Wind pushed at the kitchen curtains. Nina grabbed the laundry basket from its spot near the back door and stepped outside.

She felt a sheet, pulled a handful to her nose, and deemed it dry enough. Light blue cloth slid off the line into her plastic basket, and a queen-sized vista opened in front of her where there had been percale. The same view she'd seen while gardening and hanging laundry for the past seventeen years: the downslope with its scratchy grass, the start of the fields, the big sky. There was the storm, all right. A heavy bank of clouds in the west, miles away.

She felt a prick in the air, a twingy feeling on her forearms and the back of her neck. The storm front cued in the rest of her senses. A breeze brought a smell of manure and minerals on a whiff of super-oxygenated air. Perry's tractor grew louder—he must be pulling it up near the shed. Once he cut the engine an expectant silence fell. She pictured him sitting in the high seat, not yet moving, listening for her as she listened for him. Here we go again, stumbling through the motions and then pulling up, startled, to find ourselves in the thick of it. In the thickets.

If someone asked her whether she knew what to do in the event of an emergency she would laugh and say *of course*. But that's not what Louise Logan asked her, or Rose or Sill. *How will we bear it?* On the horizon heavy clouds dipped low toward the ground, and then dipped again. She saw a little upside-down peak form, an exploratory finger, soon sucked back into the larger mass. It emerged again, and then again, larger each time until the peak became a funnel, dipping down, swirling back into itself. She'd often seen them from a distance. Once she'd watched two funnels emerge from the same cloud, a dark ribbon and its shadow, twisting together, receding from view. This one wasn't receding, it was heading toward them—far enough away, but growing. A blurry gray-black, churning and strengthening.

Nina felt a pang in her stomach—she'd completely forgotten to eat lunch. There was something about the shape's quickness, the darting of it, that reminded her of a child at play. What if Sill wasn't with Rose? What if she was somewhere else, in the path and unprotected? Nina ran into the kitchen. The Old Man had the back panel off the transistor radio and was rummaging in the drawer for batteries. Perry came through the front door just as she set down the basket and turned to the phone. Here he was, finally, her husband, his eyes squinty and his face red. He asked for Sill. "She's with Rose," Nina said, and Perry nodded. The phone line was dead. His hands dangled at his sides as they always did when he was indoors, knobby and rough.

"Sill's gotta be with Rose," Nina repeated. The Old Man agreed, though she had no idea how he would know—he scarcely acknowledged his granddaughter most days. Perry looked at them both blankly, and the Old Man headed to the bathroom, grabbing his belt buckle as he went down the hall.

She knew what Perry would say before his words came. He rubbed a palm against the leg of his dirty jeans. "Rose said 'No.'"

Nina took a breath. "As long as the Old Man has a grip, we'll never—" She could finish that sentence, and had, a hundred different ways: threats, warnings, pleas, predictions. The skin of her neck felt crepey, still warm from her run through the fields. She pictured Sill and Rose, crouched together in that tiny sewing room, whispering, backs curved around their memories of Lance. Down the hall, the bathroom door handle smacked against the wall. Nina shrugged. "Let him have the place. Better yet, let the storm take it."

A far-off storm siren wailed just as the Old Man clattered back into the kitchen. Nina brushed a hand over her face and grabbed his elbow. Perry took his father's other side and the three of them angled awkwardly toward the front door, a six-legged beast—seven, if you counted the Old Man's cane.

As she swung the front door wide the wind stirred her braid and lifted her shirttails—they stepped into an ocean of noise, that first lick of wind promising salvation. *Lift me up and take me out of here.* "We've got it," Nina yelled across the Old Man to Perry. "Go do one more check for Sill."

Perry turned toward the back of the house.

"He'd better move his ass," the Old Man said, and started down the sloping hill to the storm cellar. He was moving too fast and wobbled, flailing his cane. She lunged for him and grabbed his arm but he shook her off, impatient as a kid. It struck her, as it often had, that he wasn't holding control of the land to punish them: he was holding on as a boy holds onto his favorite toy—a prehensile greed, that aversion to sharing that most of us unlearn, or pretend to. She kept pace and grabbed his elbow. He tried to shake free again and she needed to say something sharp, pull him into line, but instead she shook him right back, pulling his elbow toward her and then shoving. He crumpled, his hand latching onto her wrist. They fell together, rolling down the slope. The Old Man gripped so hard the bones in her wrist shifted. A pebble bounced off her cheek, and she clamped her eyes shut. The air rushed by, fabric tore, someone yelled, an elbow clocked her in the head.

They rolled to a stop, and by the time she'd disentangled her limbs and struggled to her knees Perry was there, yanking her to her feet. The Old Man still held her wrist and she grabbed him with her other hand and helped Perry pull him up. His eyes blazed as she unpeeled his fingers. "Take him," she said, her breath snagging.

Up the slope, a yellow t-shirt. "There's Sill," she yelped. Scrambling up the hill, she heard Perry yell something she couldn't catch.

Nina fell onto her hands once, the whole sky crunched, and at last she stood face to face with her daughter.

Sill's eyes were bruises. Nina put her hands on her daughter's shoulders. There was blood on the yellow shirt—one of them was bleeding. They had to get to the cellar. "Come on." Nina grabbed Sill's hands and backed down the hill. *You aren't lost, you're here with me—it may not be what you want but this is home. We—*

Screaming wind blew Sill's hair up and back, and her lips moved too fast, something about an album . . . *lost . . . trying to find . . .* Then Sill broke away and ran in the wrong direction. There was nothing to do but follow.

*

Time buckles. An hour passes in what feels like a minute, a minute catches and pulls itself out of the weave, stretches into two minutes, ten, an hour, taking on a quality of endlessness, of suspension. This generally occurs during moments of great emotion. Acts of God, battles at long last begun, knife fights, first kisses, drownings.

The body knows before the mind, and begins preparing. A temperature rises a degree or two, a heartbeat quickens. When the event itself begins, the body hurls in and the mind, left behind, is becalmed, still at the crest of the wave while the flesh swoops down to the watery depths. The merchant Ward Mondragon checks his storm supplies and readies himself as best he can, and if you ask him later how long it took, the waiting, the readying, he will surely overestimate. The actions he can control will take on greater heft, while the moment he loses his grip—the struggle finally acknowledged, the boards of his store splintering—will tighten and shrink, becoming manageable in memory.

In the telling the mind rearranges, the residual feeling of suspension spurring a need to tighten the loops. The body still knows the truth, of course. Look at the shaking hands and the dark circles under the armpits.

*Becalmed. Be calm.*

# Ward Mondragon

Ten o'clock, and no customers yet. The radio was Ward Mondragon's only company. *Better safe than sorry*, Ted Waite the newsman purred, warning of storm conditions.

The phone rang, but when Ward picked it up he heard only a dial tone. The receiver smelled faintly of Stella's perfume, citrusy and light. His wife had gone to set their house in order. She'd said she'd call when she got home, but he hadn't yet heard a peep. Stella was avoiding him. A high-pitched tone sounded in his head after the receiver clicked back into place, an incessant humming, not tinnitus. *Stress*, Dr. Willis had said, patting Ward's shoulder and telling him to lose weight and take a week's vacation with that knockout wife of his.

*Keep an eye out, folks*. Ted Waite had always had an unsettling smirk in his voice. Ward switched the dial to his favorite a.m. talk show and set to his usual mid-morning routine, checking the shelves to see if anything had been tampered with. The petty vandalism had started about a year ago: bags of rice cut precisely in the lower corner to facilitate a slow and steady leak. Or fruit tins punctured, treacly syrup pooling on the shelf. Boxes of small nails and staples cut along the bottom so the first person to lift them would scatter sharp metal across the floor. Cans of scouring powder X'ed across the face. Shoelaces severed; candles snapped in two. Nothing pricey was damaged—he kept alcohol and power tools safe in view by the register. Ward suspected it was teenagers. If Stella's nephew hadn't been gone, Lance would have been Ward's prime suspect.

As Ward worked the talk show host's deep baritone filled the store, bringing, as it always did, a feeling of crackling energy. Unlike the smoothness of Ted Waite's carefully phrased news and weather updates, this man was staccato. The host could expound at length about anything, but his favorite topics involved what he called the "amoral, lily-livered leeches" that used and abused the goodwill of hard-working Americans. He was charismatic and combative. Stella hated him. Today he railed about illegal immigrants. Lulled by the familiar cadence of umbrage, Ward listened as he worked. He'd tried to explain the man's allure to Stella, to no avail. The talk show host was a showman—someone to be entertained by but kept squarely in your sights, like a bully at the back of the school bus.

No sign of the vandal's work on the store shelves today, so Ward set to polishing the counter to a gleam. The phone rang again, and he straightened his shoulders as he answered, ready to talk to his wife.

"Ward." It wasn't Stella.

"Emma? How are you?"

"Slow today. Did you place the order yet?"

"Ah, no. I've been busy . . ."

Above the phone he'd stuck a post-it with a scrawled phone number for the Chicago Engraving Company. Ward had been charged with ordering a memorial plaque. Emma Templeton had collected money from "town leaders," including Ward himself, and his job was to interface with the engravers.

"It's on my stack for this week's ordering. But I can call today, Emma."

"Well, I had a thought about wording, if you haven't placed it yet. 'Heroes are never forgotten.' Period. What do you think?"

"It's beautiful. Remind me, what was it before?" He had, in a drawer by the register, the wording that she'd given him a few weeks ago. It wasn't like him to let an order languish.

"It was, heroes, comma, never forgotten."

"Ah."

"I just worry that it's too . . . commas can get lost, they're so small."

"Lost?"

"Yes. Use *are*. 'Heroes Are Never Forgotten.' All caps. And all the rest is the same."

"Right."

"Thank you for doing this, and for your donation," she said, hastening to add, "And Stella's too."

"Of course. We wouldn't . . ."

*Why not wait 'til the war is over,* he'd asked Emma when she'd first come to him, *and then do all the names at once?* That was how his father had handled previous wars. It was how you knew what size plaque you needed, and how big or small to make the letters. But Emma's grandson was over there, and her reasons for jumping the gun were clear enough: don't let what's befallen Rose happen to me. Engrave the dead and set them firm, unchangeable.

"It's so muggy . . ." She sighed. "Are you feeling it?" A black pickup truck with flame detailing drove down the street, heading west. The truck disappeared from view and after a moment he could hear it over the phone, passing Emma in her Bluebird Café three blocks down.

"I'll get it done," he said.

"If you have time, swing by for a coffee. I'm brewing a fantastic Guatemalan blend."

"Sounds great."

"Damn right," she agreed. "Adios."

He'd never seen the point of telling Emma that he preferred his coffee freeze-dried, from a can. But her café, with its new espresso machine and Greek salads, had adapted nimbly to changing times. The Bluebird certainly brought in more customers than he managed—his business lost ground every month. A slow erosion rather than the sudden, dramatic demise predicted by some of his fellow merchants when the Discount SuperStore opened twenty miles away. Ward knew that plenty of his friends and customers shopped there, guilty, but doing it just the same. Their guilt brought them back to him when they needed a small item or a special order, but the money came in dribbles rather than the steady flow of the store's heyday.

He pulled the order slip from the drawer and filled in the new wording for Emma's war memorial plaque. Brief and to the point. Nouns, verbs, a beginning date. There was not yet an end.

After Lance's funeral, Stella had gone out to Rose's farm. *Too much history there,* he thought, *it won't go well*. And it didn't. It didn't go, period. No answer to the knock, Stella told him, and no response to the note left with a casserole on Rose's doorstep. Now that he was married to Stella he was related, in a strange way, to Rose, and to her loss. Related most of all to the grudge between Stella and Rose. Lots of marriages and a couple of divorces, and he, as the boy's step-uncle and the most approachable member of the family, received condolences. *Give my regards to Stella . . . Have you seen Rose? Will you tell her she's in our prayers?* He would, he said. But he never saw Rose. And any mention of it would just upset his wife.

Lance's death had brought the war home, and Ward had expected the resulting upsurge of patriotism from the town. Yellow ribbons and flags at half-mast. Many people, including Ward, had supported the invasion, understanding the responsibility, the burden, that came with strength. But he was surprised by the whispering: across his counter, over the phone, in the back booths at The Bluebird. More than sadness there was anxiety, and indignation. And a whiff of something he couldn't quite name. Homesickness, or heartsickness. He thought of the pungent smell of the liver Stella had made for dinner the night before. Pale and bloodless—neither of them liked liver.

Ward traced his fingers across the order slip, pulled the post-it from its place above the phone, and dialed the number for the engraving company.

"Chicago Engraving, how may I help you?" The woman's voice was friendly, with a husky smoker's lilt. Ward exhaled.

"Hello?" she asked. On second thought, the voice was impatient; she had other things she'd rather be doing.

As did he. The sky looked like an eggshell, and he had to keep the phone lines clear.

"Wrong number." He set the receiver down. Friday would be a better day to call, the usual day he placed special orders. His father had taught him that it was best to stick to a schedule, lest little tasks take over a life.

The air felt thicker—Emma was right. Ward turned the radio dial back to Ted Waite's news station, but heard only the usual advertising chatter. Two at a time, he brought in the chairs from the porch and stacked them against the long counter behind the register. He'd swept first thing in the morning, but it wouldn't hurt to tidy up the empty porch. Under his broom, dust motes kicked up and idled above the wood. A rusty blue truck sputtered closer and came to a lurching stop. The engine kept coughing even after she cut the ignition.

*So she still drives it, then*. Rose hadn't once come into the store during the five years he'd been married to Stella. It was as if anything associated with her stepsister had been swallowed by the earth. Ward set his broom down.

She jumped out of the truck and swatted dust off her cotton print skirt. It wasn't completely laughable for him to think, *Stella's notes have worked, she's come to seek comfort.* In those brisk movements, she was still Rose. But her dress looked like she'd been digging ditches in it, and her hair was a shock of frizzy premature white.

Her eyes rested on his for a moment and then slid past. "Rose," he tried. "Please come in." He arced his arm toward the open door and stepped back.

Still she hesitated.

"She's not here," he said. "But please come."

As she stepped over the threshold he noticed grass stains on her knees. Her neck was dirty. If Stella were there, she would grab Rose by the shoulders and say, "Rose! Are you all right? How are you coping? What do you need?" But Ward felt shy. He ushered her through the store with sweeping gestures, pointing toward the rice, flour, neatly stacked cans.

"We've rearranged things a bit, since . . . Here are the dry goods, there's the Campbell's and whatnot, and over there are the tools . . ." She ran her index finger slowly along one shelf and he wondered for a split second if she were the vandal. But he quickly dismissed the thought—there was no way she'd enter the store unnoticed. *Who's been taking care of you,* he wondered, *since you won't let Stella do it?*

*Listen up, folks,* Ted Waite said, and Ward looked to the radio, startled.

"Oh," he said. "Rose, have you been listening to the news about the weather? They might issue a storm warning, you should be ready. We should all—"

"Do you have split peas?"

He brought her a bag of peas and she took them, eyes resting on her hands.

"Rose," he began, "we're all very—" She stepped back, knocking a stack of boxed safety pins to the floor, silver scattering like a school of tiny fishes. Then it was a race to the counter. She pulled two crumpled dollar bills from a fold of her dress and threw them down.

"Wait," he puffed. "I have to . . ." He grabbed a plastic shopping bag and hurried through the aisles, hands fumbling, feet sliding once on the damned pins. *Provisions*, he thought, as if she were the soldier, choosing food that would keep for a long time, throwing items into the bag. By the time he was done she was out the door, split peas in hand.

She seemed to have forgotten him as he followed her, simply climbed into the truck and slammed the door shut. Her black dog sat in the passenger seat. Ward leaned in the rolled-down window and set the bag of food on the floor below the dog. Rose had left the keys in the ignition and gunned the engine to a start.

"Good boy," Ward said, patting the dog's head.

Rose started at that—her eyes locked in, hearing those words in a different way from all the others. She opened her mouth. Then closed it. His heart thumped. Her mouth opened again, twisted and the words came with a grinding effort. "I went to his grave."

His eyes dropped to the grass stains on her knees. He filled his stomach with a swell of air. "Rose, I am so—" he choked, but she quickly shifted into reverse and he had to step back or be pulled along with the truck.

She was gone.

He returned to his space behind the register, ears humming, palms falling into their natural resting place, trying to steady himself before calling Stella. You see your customers in all kinds of moods, all through the years. Still, it's not often that you see them the way he saw Rose in that split second, stripped bare, facing the void. And the way she saw him. That part he couldn't tell Stella because that part had no words.

*Hey, singles*, the radio chirped. *Are you tired of being lonely? Other quality singles are waiting for you . . .*

Quick steps announced another customer before he could pick up the phone, and Louise Logan stepped into the store. So much for a slow day. They exchanged greetings and she walked directly to a rack of cards. Louise always knew exactly what she wanted and where to find it. She picked up a birthday card, flipped it open and deemed it fine—he could tell by the way her fingers loosened on the purse. Something had made her a bit overheated, and damp tendrils of chestnut hair were plastered to her temples.

At the counter, she peered toward the back room, obviously wondering if Stella was around, though she didn't ask. "Quietest storm season in quite a while, isn't it, Ward?" She tilted her head toward his radio. He waited for it. Then she rapped knuckles against the wood counter. Her fingernails, he noticed, were carefully manicured with tiny flower appliqués.

He smiled and nodded, dropping change into her palm and sliding the bagged card over the counter. "Let's keep it that way."

On the third Tuesday of every month Ward drove to a retail supply store in the city, to stock up on bags and register tape and things of that nature. Orders could be delivered to his door with the click of a computer button, yet the trip was a tradition he would not relinquish. He started his car engine to warm at 5:00 a.m. every third Tuesday. And the Monday prior he'd go to the bank, step up to Louise's window and she'd count out his travel money: ten crisp twenty dollar bills. She so liked knowing his routine that most times she'd have her hand on the stack of twenties before he gave her the withdrawal slip.

Louise didn't pick up the bag that held her card. Instead, she rotated the spinning display of novelty magnets that sat on the counter next to the register. Stella had ordered them last year: colorful 50s-era pictures of women with fancy outfits and funny sayings. Once that counter space had been reserved for a little spinning rack of buttons. He'd restocked it every Monday after school, his first job in the store. Bone and mother of pearl and plastic in every color. When he'd spun the rack they clacked against each other pleasingly. Spin fast enough and whorls of color would blur and lengthen before his eyes, buttons flying in all directions. His mother caught him at it, and he learned that even his favorite things could be treacherous if he wasn't careful. Nobody sewed anymore. The button rack was long gone by the time Stella ordered these magnets, and they apparently missed the mark as impulse items. Louise picked up one bearing a beaming lady with a beehive and the words, *I am only as strong as the coffee I drink and the hairspray I use*. She didn't crack a smile, just set the magnet back into place.

"See you Monday?" she asked.

"See you then," he confirmed. Like his visit to the bank, his route to the city was set, clear in his mind as lines on the map. Her eyes searched his. A warmth spread across his chest and he felt himself blushing.

As soon as Louise left he called Stella again, leaving a long-winded message, all the while imagining her sitting in the study next to the phone, listening with a pale face as he stumbled over his words. *Give me a ring, Stella. Have you been listening to the radio? I've got something to tell you, something important. Honey, are you okay?*... The machine hung up on him, and he went to look at the sky.

Louise had passed out of view. No cars drove by, no sign of life on the street. Everything that had formed him stretched out from this tired, forgiving line of sight. His body, big as it was, felt flimsy.

"Ward?" Scottie Dunleavy poked his head in the door but remained on the porch.

"Yes, I've been listening," Ward said. The warnings had picked up, and so had business. A handful of customers had stopped in, most of them swing shift workers from the Crown Co. meatpacking plant, to stock up on batteries and bottled water. Now it was near two o'clock, past time for his afternoon snack.

"Help with mine first and then we'll do yours?" Scottie asked. They weren't hesitant to board the windows—both had learned the hard way, shelling out for expensive plate glass over the years. Ward followed Scottie into the street, empty of traffic, a few storefronts closed up already. *Ghost town,* he thought, but didn't say.

Dunleavy's smelled gamy. "You ever clean the catbox, Scottie?" His friend had issues, folks liked to say, though he was steady enough most days.

"Sure, sure," Scottie replied, heading to the back supply room to get the boards. Scottie's store was a quarter the size of Ward's. Four long shelves ran the length of the space. Men's shoes on the left, women's on the right, arranged by size and covered with a thin layer of dust. Scottie, like Ward, had inherited his parents' business, but nobody bought fine leather shoes these days—people wanted sneakers with thick rubber soles and made-in-China mules, cheap enough to toss aside six months later. In a show of initiative that had surprised Ward, Scottie had taken a correspondence course and become a certified cobbler, sending repair samples back and forth in the mail to an outfit in Philadelphia. The word *cobbler* made Ward think of little elves working industriously in the dead of night, and enchanted princesses with worn dance slippers. If anyone needed help from elves, it was Scottie Dunleavy.

Scottie brought the boards to the front and they hitched them into the grooves left over from last year, making quick work of pounding the nails. Once the boards were in place Scottie said, "Now yours." Walking into the street, Ward took a good look at his place from an angle he didn't see every day: long porch with cement bolsters to keep it from sagging, picture window with the *Mondragon's Emporium* sign in old-fashioned lettering, and visible through it, a rack of neglected rental movies. All the way across the street Scottie kept a few feet behind, limping and smelling like his store: dusty with a hint of piss.

The sky was still clear, but the light had thinned. "Look there," Scottie said, pointing west, and they saw movement miles away, darkness gathering. "It could head anywhere," Scottie said. "It could get sucked back into the sky, or it could bounce off us like a cueball."

Inside, Ward moved quickly to the storeroom for boards and nails. When he returned to the floor, he found Scottie in the food and sundries aisle, facing blankly toward the window while his hands fumbled along a shelf. He sliced into the bottom of a cornmeal bag and set it down.

"Scottie?"

Scottie jumped, his knife dropping to the ground. "I've already got a hammer."

"I know. What are you doing?"

"Doing . . ."

"To the cornmeal. What are you doing to that bag? Look—" the phone rang and Ward veered off to answer. "Hello?"

"You okay there?"

"Stella!" He was surprised to hear himself panting, out of breath. "Where have you been? I've been calling, didn't you hear the phone?"

"Oh," she said vaguely, "getting things ready. I heard the weather report."

He pressed his fist hard into his solar plexus and gave a little cough. Scottie stood in the aisle, hands hanging by his sides. "Honey, I saw Rose. She came into the store."

"*What*? Tell me."

"That's why I've been calling." He let her hear the pique in his voice. Ward spoke quickly, filling her in. "She isn't right, Stella. It's not just . . . she seems . . . we're going to have to do something."

"I'm driving out there," Stella said. "She's going to have to open the door."

After a yawning silence he said, "Don't drive out there. *Don't*. Honey . . . listen to the weather report," he coaxed. "Sit tight for now, we can go out tonight, as soon as I get home, I promise." He slowed his tone and rolled the words off his tongue. "Okay? Honey?"

Something clattered. From the corner of his eye, Ward watched Scottie step back, hands raised in a gesture of innocence. Stella didn't bother to respond.

"Stella? Stella, wait, okay? Just wait until the weather's clear and we have time to—"

"Did you board the windows?"

"Scottie's here, he's going to help me." He looked directly at Scottie, trying to reassure the both of them. "Honey, Rose has supplies. I gave her food. Just let her be for now."

He heard a rustling over the phone, as if she were moving around. He'd pictured her in their kitchen, but maybe she was in the study. Or the bedroom. She could be anywhere.

"Stella, you aren't responsible."

Silence. Finally she said, "All right."

"Get to the cellar. Take the radio and a magazine and just relax."

She breathed heavily into the receiver. "It's not a fucking visit to the spa, Ward."

"Pretend it is," he said. She hung up.

Scottie had moved closer to the door, looking ready to bolt; there were small rips on his pant cuffs. "It's going under," Ward told him. "The business, I mean."

Scottie nodded. Without another word, they set the boards into place. Scottie started to pound the nails in, but Ward told him he could manage that part himself. His friend stepped back, bobbing his head around in approximation of agreement, or apology. As soon as he left, Ward went back to the phone to call home. No answer.

Frustrated, he turned the radio dial back to the talk show; it was national, there would be no worrisome mention of storms. Illegals were still the focus, and now the host was reading email questions from his audience. "You, my friend, are no Einstein," the man said, and Ward laughed. Everything about the host—his nasty humor, the bright, hard thrust of his words—was so far from Ward's experience of being that he felt a pleasing disassociation. Just for a moment it seemed far-fetched that he and this man came from the same race and generation, let alone the same political bent. *Who isn't foreign, really?*

It was true, what he'd told Scottie. The store would have to close in a little less than a year. He had mapped it all out on spreadsheets the way he'd learned in business class, and even so it had taken a while for him to grasp. The Mondragons had always done well. But the free market had failed him. A better explanation than the alternative: he had failed. Ward would mourn the loss of his inheritance. Though lately he felt that he'd been mourning so incrementally, he couldn't muster the requisite passion. He hadn't told Stella yet. She wouldn't take it well.

He went to the small fridge in the storeroom, pulled out a cold bottle, and took a long swig of sweet tea, humming lightly. Stella wouldn't stay at home, and perhaps she hadn't even been home when she'd called. Ward arrived at that knowing the same way he arrived at all hard truths: placid on the surface, but a churning deep in his gut. He looked at the phone. Of course she'd go to Rose. It was all she'd been doing, in one way or another, for the past three months. She didn't care about the weather, or the house, or what he'd asked of her. She had to get to Rose. What she'd do when she got there, he doubted she'd thought through. He wiped his forearm across his brow—setting up the planks had made him sweaty—then took another long pull at the tea and ran a palm over his belly. Ward picked up the receiver and held the cool plastic against his chin, expelling shallow breaths. The talk show host's epithet sprang to mind: *lily-livered*.

Ward set the phone down, switched back to the weather station and turned the volume higher. Ted Waite's voice was a welcome intrusion, running over a list of phone numbers to call in the event of an emergency. He had run into Eddie Waite in the city years ago—back when Eddie and Stella were still married, before the man had started going by "Ted." Ward had been walking with a man that he knew, rounding the corner, eyes cast downward and shoulders hunched against a sharp autumn wind, when something made him glance up. There was Eddie, greeting Ward with a wry, knowing wink. Eddie had nodded and kept walking. To this day, Ward was ashamed of the hot flush that had spread across his face and down his neck. As if Eddie's wink had leveled a lewd accusation and precluded Ward's defense: men catting about in the big city. Most any other neighbor would have stopped to chat and asked after his wife.

*Here we go, folks,* Ted said now, chummily, and launched into a litany of alerted counties.

Each time Ward descended the stairs to the dark cellar, his childhood nerve-endings sparked. But as soon as his hand hit the light switch at the base of the stairs the thrilling fears of his past receded, leaving dusty outlines and the disappointing present: stacked file boxes, extra display shelving, cases of old merchandise that he would never sell. His grandfather's uncomfortable burl walnut desk lived here with its matching, too-small chair.

Ward hadn't yet nailed the boards that he and Scottie had set up. He could picture, exactly, the box of nails that he would use: freshly opened, unsellable, Scottie's cryptic *X* scratched across the lid. He should check the box of emergency supplies in the corner and get back upstairs. Instead, he took an unmarked file box from a shelf. One folder inside charted the steady decline of Mondragon's Emporium profits—that wasn't the one he was after. He took out a purple file folder and set it on a box of Fourth of July decorations, flipping it open to scan through. His finger ran across fine print and paused. Ward pulled out the chair and sat at the desk. In the dim light, the white photocopies looked like parchment. He went to the emergency supplies box and pulled out a battery-powered lantern. Crisp white fluorescence suffused the desk. *Indemnity*, he read. *Deductible... liability... waiver.* His breath rustled the papers, and he closed the file.

The ringing in his ears could mislead him sometimes, and for a moment he thought he heard the phone above in the empty store, or perhaps a voice calling to him—maybe Stella? There was a direct line between his early memory of Stella and the woman she was today. The slimness, dark hair, pale skin. Now her flirtiness was aimed, intentional, and much more rare. Age was visible, of course. She put something called "youth serum" on her face each night and limited portions to keep her figure. More flinty than flirty. Yet, he could look into her eyes and see that girl—eagerness, dreams, foolishness, love—all still there. He felt it just as he felt his own young self, solid as bone under the upholstery of years. It's why he'd married her.

He walked to the foot of the stairs to listen. Ted Waite's voice threaded through the empty aisles above. Ward shoved the chair flush against the desk edge and took a quick stock of his emergency box: gauze and antibiotic ointment, canned goods and water; a half-full bottle of Stella's Valium. He unscrewed the childproof cap and downed one for good measure.

A siren started. He threw tarps over the shelves closest to the front window, locked the display cases, and then picked up the phone once more. The line was dead. His cash box sat in a cubby under the register; Ward was moving toward it when the whooshing sound outside changed to galloping horses, drawing him back to the window.

He had left a gap of several inches between two boards across the widest pane of glass. The darkness he and Scottie had seen far away was on them now. A lawn chair blew down the street, followed by several buckets held together with string, and a tricycle. Then a lull. Across the street, Dunleavy's was boarded up tight as a drum, looking abandoned. Scottie would most likely pull it out. He'd keep his business going long after Ward was closed up and gone. *He's a camouflage artist, that Scottie. How easy and tempting it is, to underestimate others—* Something heavy smashed onto his porch with a huge crack. The walls shook.

Ward jumped back and fell, knocking into the rental videos. Boards shifted under him, plate glass trembled, and merchandise spilled to the ground. He turned and crawled toward the counter. The window cracked and fell from its frame, unfastened boards tossed aside like toothpicks. Screaming wind shoved at his back, driving into the store, plowing glass shards through the air. He scrambled to the counter, pulled himself heavily across the top to the other side, grabbed the cash box and sank down, wedged between the counter and three liquor crates, his head on the rubber mat Stella had set down for a shock absorber.

The metal cash box pressed so tight against his chest, it would leave a triangular indentation in the tender flesh between his armpit and breast—it contained sixty-four dollars and change. He held it because he couldn't hold the wide counter or the sagging porch or the plate glass. Even in pieces, it was his. The radio fell off the shelf above and bashed his shin, voices drowned out, green power eye still lit. A waterfall drummed against the counter and it shook but did not give. Wood vibrated against his head, novelty magnets scattered across his feet. His ears popped. He curled tighter around the cash box and felt the change inside shift. The smaller he could make himself, the better it would be. This box might as well hold buttons, for all the good it would do. *Buttons, a hank of ribbon, a train ticket.* He could start over. He could be new.

*

Don't forget the dogs.

The cats may sense it sooner, but the dogs try to give warning. In the kennel on the outskirts of town, a stray shepherd mix paces the perimeter of her cement floor. There is no window. Exterior scents waft under the doorjamb from the veterinary clinic down the hall: the sour lemon scent of the vet, the vet's menstruating assistant, the breakfast on their breath, antiseptic, an infected tumor in the mouth of the dog who has been brought here to die; the storage bin full of dry kibble; and then beyond that: parking lot, cars, fresh markings in the yard, a banana peel. She pauses, nostrils fluttering and head raised. There it is: extra ozone, warm air rising, cinnamon, the beginning of something. She whimpers, scratches at the drain in the center of her small room, and squats to pee. A whine rises in the back of her throat. In the clinic down the hall, the dog with the tumor flicks his ear. He has caught her anxiety, though he is too spent to give a warning himself, just a soft groan as the vet injects a sedative into the vein.

Elsewhere, in a tidy backyard, a Labradoodle who spends most of his time alone is gathering toys—balls, squeakies, chew sticks, stuffed hedgehog—and stacking them on the Adirondack chair that sits on the patio. Farm dogs slink through barn shadows and dig up long-buried bones. A collie-boxer mix catches each of her pups by the scruff of the neck, one by one, and deposits them into an empty cardboard box underneath a doublewide in the trailer park.

Almost as one, noses raise, breath huffs. Then in the kennel, the shepherd lifts her whine to a howl; she is joined by dogs in the adjoining rooms, voices rising but not yet carrying because there is not yet wind. *Take care,* she says.

Fergus watches Rose hack at the brambles. His primary love is gone, and though snatches of the boy's scent remain, they lessen by the day. This confused Fergus for a long time, but he has learned to incorporate the absence as part of his world. He has a job to do. The woman is his secondary but he must watch over her while they wait together for the boy to return. His nostrils work. He thwacks his tail. *Take care.*

An old man tosses in his sleep, feeling what's to come in flashes that he will not remember on waking: a tin cup, an ancient tree giving way under an axe, wagons circled around a campfire; bright, rabid eyes watching from the shadows.

# The Old Man

The morning of the storm the Old Man's tricky pelvis gave him more trouble than usual. Pain traveled from his tailbone outward. Before he rose from bed, he lay for a moment and looked at the Almanac and the planting ledgers stacked on the bedstand. As he stood to grab his cane and head down the hall, the bone feeling subsided a bit. His right knee was hurting too, and he tried not to limp as he walked into the kitchen and saw Perry, head down, spooning cereal out of a bowl. "There's weather on the way," he told his son by way of greeting.

Perry nodded, and the Old Man was grateful not to hear him, not yet. Perry's voice strangled in his windpipe whenever they spoke. It was involuntary, along with the red splotches on his temples and the way his fists opened and closed loosely. The Old Man was fine with the silence—it was like hip pain after the early morning sharpness had dulled, nonspecific and radiating. Then Perry ruined it, saying, "The radio says no rain 'til tomorrow . . ." His son listened to the idiot who read the news, ignoring his own senses. The Old Man grunted, not dignifying the comment with a response. He fixed a bowl of oatmeal and sat.

He knew storms. He'd been struck by lightning some years back. A freak of nature announced through the coins in his pocket, turning them so hot that when he'd reached for them on instinct, he'd burned his fingers. The lightning-struck change included two quarters, three dimes, a few pennies, and a lucky Indian head nickel. He still had that lightning-bolted Indian head. Lucky, unlucky, who knew? He just liked to keep it in his pocket: discolored and with roughened edges, a reminder of where he'd been.

"Price of corn at X," the glib-folksy reporter announced. "Price of soy at Y." Perry ducked his head in that half-glad, half-shamed way he'd greeted the world for as long as the Old Man could remember, his eyes on the radio as if he were watching the announcer's face.

*You're my best thing,* the Old Man thought, and a bit of dehydrated apple hit the back of his throat. He coughed. "Turn it up," he told Perry, and his son complied.

There would come a time when Perry wouldn't comply, not for anything. The Old Man could feel it bearing down like wind. He coughed again, and shivered. Perry stood and left the room without a word. But in a few minutes he returned. "Want some juice?"

The Old Man glared. "Yeah." His acceptance registered in Perry's shoulders as he stood in front of the fridge—a slight loosening. Perry poured orange juice into a jelly glass, handed it to his father, and then took a swig from the carton.

"Clear skies," said the radioman.

"Bullshit," the Old Man replied. There was an ad for a truck sale, a fast food joint, motor oil. The Old Man spooned oatmeal out of his bowl, looked up and his son was gone, out to the barn.

He grabbed his cane from its resting spot, hoisted himself up, picked up the glass of juice and limped down the hall to his bedroom at the back of the house. Who says old people are slow? The weight of seven decades hurtled him forward like a cannonball. Overhead, the grandkid was pacing again. Her room was right above his and he heard her at all hours, walking a path from her dresser to the closet: a knock on the jamb, a whisper and then back again. It was some sort of spooky séance, she was trying to bring her dead boyfriend back. The routine was too personal and embarrassing for him to acknowledge, which was the way he felt about her in general. Sill sprouted up between the floorboards like a pale little mushroom—unassuming and hard to identify, easily trod on but potentially fatal. She reminded him of her grandmother, his dead wife, Mae.

He'd mention the pacing to Nina, when the time was right. She'd let the girl have too much leeway since Rose's boy died, out of pity or fear or both. Ever since Lance had been killed the Old Man felt a white-hot rage, not sure where it was aimed. At the kid for dying? At Perry for not fighting? At the politicians he'd voted for who seemed intent on mangling everything? At Rose, for losing yet again? She'd lost and lost, that Rose, but didn't have the good grace to accept defeat. He sat on the edge of his twin bed. Relegated to a monk's mattress, a room off the kitchen in his own house. As the bedsprings squeaked, the tread above stopped. He cleared his throat. Silence. He sipped the juice.

He would eventually concede, let Perry make the changes he wanted. He knew that. Perry didn't seem to, and it made the Old Man less inclined to budge: an opponent who doesn't know the rules of the game. He looked at his scarred fingertips, curled around the jelly glass. His cane slid down the wall and clattered to the floor. For Christmas a year ago they had given him a television with a remote control. He flicked on the news. The idiot box blared a terrible morning show—it irked him that he knew the name of the woman who hosted.

He turned off the television, laid his folded handkerchief over his eyes and stretched out. Joint pressure was wearing him down. He'd need to talk to the doc, he supposed. A soft breeze nudged through the window, so light that the curtains moved against the metal blinds with the merest swish. He could hear, in the distance, the engine of his son at work. Perry didn't know what was coming. The Old Man pressed a hand to his shoulder and breathed.

He'd taken a bullet in the shoulder outside Pusan, and when they were wheeling him into the bright OR to dig it out, he told them he didn't want gas. The doc didn't answer or laugh at him, just held him down on one side and jerked his head at the medic to hold him on the other. They put the mask over his mouth and nose and the doc held his eyes as the gas did its work, light gleaming off his glasses. In dreams the Old Man still saw the surgical mask and that impassive bottomless white glance. That image became the face of his war—the face of all wars, even this new one: the glaring glasses, the mask. He figured he was lucky. For other guys, the face of war was someone they shot or the face of the man who shot them. Burned babies, maimed women, the mangled limbs of a dead buddy. The doc was a decent alternative, though even in sleep the Old Man's heart sped and he panicked before the inevitable descent. He stood at the edge of a great precipice and stared into the implacable glare—but then he rolled further into blackness, a tuck and fall right off the edge into something irrecoverable. He never remembered his dreams, except for the glasses; nothing else pierced through.

He'd decided, long ago, to be grateful for that.

He woke with a start, the soft light of full morning filtering through checked curtains. Almost nine o'clock. Nina would have been up for a few hours, she would have made him fresh coffee. She knew that he slept after breakfast every morning, but she could be counted on not to mention it to Perry. He didn't often talk with his son or his granddaughter, but with Nina he could hold a conversation.

He'd dribbled a bit of oatmeal down his shirt so he pulled it off and put on another of almost identical worn blue cotton. All of his heart-side shirt pockets had a whitish ring, threads worn thin from the ever-present tin of tobacco. Rose had traced that circle once, rivaling the lightning for electricity. She'd traced it and then tapped the center hard as if to crack him. "The last thing I need is your ideas," she'd said, and turned her back.

Nina wasn't in the kitchen, though Mae's old *Complete Guide to Home Canning and Preserving* book was fanned out on the table, dog-eared and syrup-smattered. Nina had been canning almost nonstop the past few months. She was a hard worker, his daughter-in-law, though in general her cooking ran to twenty-minute dinner recipes and cake from a box. A note pressed to the counter by the coffee pot read, "*Gone to the bank—N.*"

He took a swig of coffee, only to find the brew bitter and cold—Perry's crack-of-dawn dregs. Nina had left him with old coffee. Was it punishment or forgetfulness? Either was likely. Maybe it was both.

A crow sat on the eaves of the house, cawing like a crying baby. The Old Man went to stand in front of the bathroom mirror and surveyed the patchy hairs on his chin and cheeks, sticking his tongue into his upper lip to pull the flesh taut. His eyes gleamed in the grayish light that filtered through the window. The air had the feel of an older, more worn day. Storm weather messed with the passage of time. He splashed his face and then grabbed the can of shaving cream from the shelf over the sink. His hand, in the mirror, looked like a stranger's.

The Old Man set the shaving cream down and studied his finger pads. The lightning scars were raised and clear, though it was five years now since he'd been struck. One of the strangest things that had ever happened to him, and only the fourth time his name had appeared in the local paper. The first was to declare his birth, the second his return from Korea, the third his marriage, and the fourth a full-column clarion call announcing that he was a dipfuck who didn't know enough to come in out of the rain. A reporter had asked him if he remembered anything about the event and he'd said, "What's to remember?"

Steps creaked overhead, and Sill's sneaker tread came down the stairs. So the grandkid wasn't at school again today. Nina was much too lenient with her. Sill would be in the kitchen, foraging for peanut butter. He dried his unshaved face and swung the bathroom door open hard so she'd know he was on his way. His right knee twisted awkwardly when he hurried into the hall, flaring the arthritic joint.

By the time he got to the kitchen, a yellow t-shirt and Sill's wheat-colored hair passed across the window, moving quickly out of view. She was heading east on her bike—in the direction of the Infamous Elm and Rose's land. If Rose's boy, Lance, were still here, the Old Man would assume she was going on a tryst. He bent and rubbed the flesh around his kneecap, heart racing, not sure what he'd have said to Sill if she'd waited for him. *There are things you think you can't get through—but you look up one day and years have passed and you're still kicking.*

The radio droned softly on the shelf above the kitchen counter. His cane thumped along with him down the hall and he stepped out the back door, pausing as he always did to survey the view—the quiet county road and solid old house at his back, his own land surrounding him. The whale on the vane at the top of the house faced due south. Any one vantage point has its limitations. At least this was a pretty decent vista.

He walked down the long slope into the fields, moving a bit more smoothly now, his hip loosening. Corntips stretched out in neat rows. No sign of Sill. The air was unusually soft—a pinkish glow on everything and the sky so big it dwarfed the world beneath it. He took a breath and crouched, hearing his sore knee pop, to run his hand just over the tips of the green. A pulse emanated from some place deep in the center and carried up through the corn into his own veins. He was tiny under the dome, a speck in the fields, listening for a pulse that was and wasn't his own. They had a while before the weather worsened. When he took Perry lunch, he'd warn him again. He wondered if he should also warn Rose, or try to.

The Old Man grabbed some dirt and lifted it to his tongue: low nitrogen. And a tiny beetle.

*Cah!* From the roof, the crow started up again.

He spent the rest of the morning in the barn, building portable screens for Nina's kitchen garden. She had complained about how the birds and rabbits were munching her sprouts and had shown him a picture from a gardening catalog. He took pleasure in watching an idea take form under his hands: measuring a frame, sawing, inserting screws. When he ran out of screen mesh, he stopped; he'd have to order more at Mondragon's. Still for the first time in a couple of hours, he noticed the absence of Perry's tractor engine and for a moment thought he'd missed lunch—but his stomach rumbled. His body knew when he was expected.

A quarter to noon. Nina's station wagon was parked in its usual spot in front of the house, but the kitchen was empty. Nobody had bothered to turn off the radio, and the newsman was starting to take the weather seriously, his voice flowing in a quicker tempo: *Keep an eye out, folks.*

He slung his cane over his arm, re-tucked his shirt into his trousers, grabbed his son's bag lunch from the top shelf of the fridge, and headed out. Perry's tractor was going again, kicking up dust. The Old Man climbed into his truck and headed down the drive and onto the county road until he came to a good place to pull off and head in. Perry cut the engine as soon as he saw him, with a smoothness that could be mistaken for obedience.

"Here ya," he told his son, tossing up the sack.

Perry dug into the bag without looking and took out the apple. After a few bites he said, "Thanks."

"The storm's coming. You can't plan to be out here much longer."

Perry chewed his apple and hedged. Probably out of spite, he wouldn't show the proper concern. He wouldn't until the Old Man gave him an answer to his latest ideas about the land, the next round of *no*. The Old Man took a step backward and inspected the rows. "The rootworm beetle's making a comeback," he said, rubbing a stalk between two fingers. "We had them in '84, before they made the resistant corn, and it wasn't pretty." Perry moved on to his ham sandwich and ate silently, then started up the tractor and worked it steadily down a row.

What was his son's next move? Take over Rose's land, probably. The Infamous Elm swayed at the side of the road. His knee pulsed. Overhead, the sky was a bleached saucer.

Rose was on her porch, head tilted, listening to something he couldn't hear. He cleared his throat to announce himself and the dog barked belatedly. She kept her back to him. Rosehips bobbed on the highest branches of her overgrown bushes. A window banged. He caught movement out of the corner of his eye, a blur of light hair, but when he turned to the hayloft it looked empty as ever.

"Rose." The old cuckoo clock in the parlor gave a warble. She stomped her foot and it halted abruptly. He had that old sense that if she wanted, she could stop time. But her color was wrong—as if her red hair had been pulled out by its roots and replaced with white straw. Her eyes were the same shade, though instead of searching his, they darted past.

*Holy hell*, he thought. "Rose, how are you doing?"

Her foot knocked against a plastic shopping bag that she'd set on the porch. A can of tuna rolled out, heading along the downward slope of the uneven foundation, and dropped off the edge of the porch onto a mound of mulch. Without a word, she bent to pick up some shears and walked past him into the yard, shuffling in oversized muckboots as she moved between the brambles.

She'd been busy, he'd give her that. Cut branches lay scattered. He picked one up and held it out in supplication. Without really thinking about what he was doing, he sank to one knee like a suitor. She didn't look at him, just kept hacking at those bushes, and it wasn't the right time of year to prune.

"Hear me out. Perry's trying to pull an end run, even though he knows I'm against it. I heard him and Nina talking. He's going to come make you an offer, if he hasn't already. But you can't sell him this place, you have to hang on."

She didn't give a sign, nothing. He touched his tobacco tin.

"Rose you've gotta hold onto what's yours." Who was he trying to help, himself or her? Was there a difference? If Perry got Rose's land, it was over for both of them. Anything they mattered for wouldn't matter then.

"Just trust me on this. You've forgiven me, Rose, don't act like you haven't. We're on the same side now." His sore knee pressed into the dirt. He was begging something of a woman so addled by grief she didn't know how to cut her way out of it.

*Keep going.* "Rose, listen. Don't let it go. Rosie." He waited. He wanted to stand up but was afraid of how long it would take. "Unlike me, you're still young, or young enough. I can still see it . . ."

She pulled a branch down and snipped through. The trunk trembled.

"Rose, I know you think you hate me. But I'm not the same . . ." Her dog lifted his head and sniffed at the air. *Yep*, the Old Man thought, *he knows what's coming*. His fingertips tingled. A thorn pressed into the base of his thumb and his heart hammered against the tin in his pocket. She turned to look at him, finally, and her eyes caught on his.

He tried another tack. "You weren't there when I was hit by lightning. I was near the old elm, the one Stella made infamous . . ." She stiffened at her stepsister's name, which struck him as a good sign. A reaction. Normally he would never bring up that old betrayal, or his role as witness to it. He paused, waiting for her to look at him again. "I hate the way that goddamn tree got scarred. But give me a chance to . . . I was near the elm. I'd gone out to the east field to check on a fence and the weather changed. I didn't have the truck, I had to hoof it and the rain came fast, everything was lit. My scalp tingled, my skin was on fire. I was thrown, I guess about twenty feet . . ." It had changed him in a way he was still figuring out. He'd never told anyone what it had felt like, but when he had imagined trying it had been her, Rose, who'd listened.

Another pause. There were no signs she'd heard him, just his own breathing and the trickle of tobacco juice down the back of his throat.

"Rose, I survived it. I'm still here." He pulled the Indian head nickel out of his pocket and held it out to her. "This was with me then, and now it's yours. For luck."

Her voice came out cold and a little reedy. "There's nothing you can do, Sherwin."

He cleared his throat and spat. Then he dropped the branch, struggling to his feet. "Dammit. Can't you see there's weather coming?"

She clomped up the stairs and slammed the door behind her. He followed her as far as the jamb and peered through the window into the empty parlor. A gray blanket covered the couch. He set his nickel on the windowsill and retreated.

Back in the truck, wind whistled past his ears.

Gravel pitted under the wheels as he hit the brakes, halting on his own land again, where things made sense, truck idling, a new plug of tobacco in his cheek. He pounded the steering wheel with the heels of his hands. *Fine, then. So be it.*

The Old Man rolled the window all the way down and smelled his crops and fertilizer. It was past time to dust for beetles.

He was in the bathroom trying to take a leak when the screen door at the back of the house screamed open. Nina's tread moved down the hall from the back porch. *Finally.* In his eagerness to talk to her, he flung back the bathroom door so hard it shook the wall. His daughter-in-law stood in front of the open fridge, drinking orange juice out of the carton. Nina was taller than he liked in a woman and had almost no curves; she left her long hair in an unbecoming braid and didn't fuss with her clothes. One of those plain women you barely notice for years on end, until they take your breath away with some miracle of sense and purpose. She was, these days, more like his child than Perry—a forthright presence, a person who had the sense to come in out of a storm.

"There's weather—" he started, and her shoulders rose in that "I know already" circle.

She swallowed audibly. "Seen Sill?" He shook his head. Nina went upstairs to check for herself. He sat at the kitchen table and picked up the newspaper. Words flew across his eyes and meant nothing. The radioman came back on, late to the game with his warnings.

When Nina came back into the kitchen she was in more of a talking mood. She asked him to fix Sill's bike and he agreed. Nina still found him useful, at least. There was something harried in the way she pulled the dishes out of the machine and clattered them into their places in the cupboards. His dirty lunch plate was still on the kitchen table and he looked at it, inspecting the cracks in the glaze. She was hard on things. *Poor Perry,* he thought, not for the first time. No wonder his son seemed so confused, ricocheting from one idea about how to increase profits to another. The Old Man blew aside his sandwich crumbs so he could see the cracks more clearly—tiny fissures all over the round white disc.

Nina said she'd paid a visit to Rose, and he stiffened. They must have just missed each other. Now she was chewing over an old memory of Lance as a little boy. It struck him, not for the first time, that nobody likes to talk about soldiers directly—what they have to do, what's expected, why they're gone in the first place. How they die. He tried to correct this, reminding her about his Korea buddy, Joe Carnahan, and how he'd lost his leg. But Nina didn't even pretend to listen, just leaned against the counter and stared at the floor.

He reached for his pocket, where the lucky nickel wasn't, and stood to set his dirty plate on the counter. "There's no point in working over the past," he said. "For any of us. Talking about it won't help Rose. You just have to give her time. Let her be. Give her—" He'd thought there was a chance Nina would listen to him, a chance that he could still influence the way things were done, but something hard settled in her eyes—knowledge worn down by time. A great wave of weariness passed over him.

"Get the clothes off the line," he reminded her, backing toward the door.

He didn't blame Nina and Perry for being opportunistic about Rose's land. That's how it worked. It's how he'd got the best price for livestock when it became clear the hogs were a backbreaker and he had to unload them. It's how he'd acquired an extra two hundred acres when everybody else was selling to the banks. It's how, when he got wind that Rose was in trouble after Theo had died, he'd tried to play his cards so he could pick up three hundred adjacent acres. It hadn't turned out the way he'd expected. Maybe it wouldn't for Perry and Nina either.

On the porch, he filled his lungs with air and exhaled hard, using extra effort. The weather made the air heavy. Perry had come in from the fields at last and was down by the barn, wandering around with a can of oil in his hand. Even from where he stood, the Old Man could see an inch of brown paper sticking over Perry's back pocket. His empty lunch bag—Perry would reuse the same one all week, retiring it when the seams got fuzzy and split at the corners.

"Got that habit from me," he whispered, and walked down the hill. The sky was too close. *Here it comes.* He kept waiting for his son to see it. *Look up*, he thought, and as he drew near Perry he kicked the ground. Dust puffed up in slow motion—the air was swollen, pressing everything down. Even Perry looked dusty, like he'd been rolling around in the dirt instead of sitting on a tractor all day.

Perry asked again about the ideas he had, made his pitch for improving the farm. The Old Man bent to grab a fistful of dirt so his son wouldn't see his face. Not long ago, he would have welcomed this conversation, welcomed the chance to stomp down that ambition for one more season and then watch it sprout again—his son, his proudest accomplishment, his obliterator. But he took no satisfaction in any of it now. He said what Perry expected him to and trailed off.

They were neither of them paying attention to this dance anymore, not really. He let the dirt drop from his fist. He reached out to grab his son's shoulder and shook. He said, "Look at the goddamn sky."

The wind picked up, ushering them as they hurried back and forth. Perry stood in the kitchen doorway, breathing heavily; he asked Nina about Sill and they reassured each other, saying that she had to be at Rose's.

"Of course she's at Rose's," the Old Man barked. She was a sad kid but not a stupid kid—she knew enough to take shelter during a storm. He hobbled down the hall to the bathroom and when he returned, some furtive communication had passed between Perry and his wife. He glimpsed again a distance in Nina's eyes when she looked at him. She held out her arm and he took her elbow.

Miles away, a siren started. The radioman droned the names of affected counties. They angled out the door and stiffened at the thickness of the air. To the west, the sky churned. "It's coming," Nina said, and squeezed his arm.

"I'll do one more sweep to see if—" Perry trotted around the house to look for Sill. *The kid had better get out of the hayloft,* the Old Man thought. She'll get in Rose's root cellar. Will she be able to get Rose down there with her?

*I've wrecked it,* he started to say, but it came out more like, "Perry'd better move his ass." Nina shook his arm, and he yanked out of her grasp, wanting her to look at him. But he teetered and she reached out too hard to grab him, and then they were reeling together and falling down the hill. Her fingers dug into his arm, his cane clocked him in the shins and he lost his grip. The ground smashed his hips hard. He gave in to gravity: his achy pelvis, the lump in his shin, grit in his eyes, his teeth on his tongue, soft brain rattling around in his skull, and Nina's dug-in fingernails. They rolled to a stop near the root cellar, the sky spinning.

Perry came out of nowhere and hauled them to their feet. "Can you walk?"

Words hit the dirt in his mouth and came out muddy. "Gah," he spat.

Perry had the cane, and shoved it into his hand. He tried to straighten himself. Nina yelled something, but the wind snatched it. His son's shirt billowed away from his back, and above them the house hunkered under the low churning sky. *We're screwed now,* the Old Man thought, *the storm will take the roof, and could take more.* It wasn't his head that knew this, it was the scars on his fingers, it was his tricky hip. The knowledge lodged itself in his secret places.

Nina ran up the hill toward the house. She was favoring an ankle, must have hurt it during the fall. "Where's she—" the Old Man started, but Perry grabbed him by the shoulder and together they heaved open the cellar door.

Perry held the door while the Old Man descended—he went by feel, there was no light, and the wooden steps were rough under his fingers. The ladder led five feet down into the dark. A familiar smell hit him: must and kerosene and sweetrot. The cessation of the wind was a vacuum, pulling gravity away so he could stand straighter; the howling dimmed enough to hear his son's boots slide heavily down the rungs, and the door banged shut as soon as Perry let go of the handle.

In the sudden quiet the Old Man grabbed his son to steady himself and then backed up until his heels hit something. His whole body hurt. Perry fidgeted next to him, waiting for his eyes to adjust. The Old Man's fingers found the shelf, a paperback, a tin can, smooth glass with a ridged base, and then a metal cylinder that he knew to be the flashlight. It sounded as though someone were throwing clods of dirt at the trap door. It was suddenly very important that there be light, and he fumbled for the switch without having a good grip, knocking the flashlight off the shelf. It spun briefly and clunked to a stop.

"Aw, no," the Old Man said.

"Was that the flashlight?" Perry asked. "Sit on the cot, I'll find it." His son swung him around and as they moved a small susurration let loose pockets of grit blown into the folds of their clothes. The Old Man felt the cot behind his knees and sank to a seat with an involuntary groan. His knee throbbed. Something was wrong with his left hip. A beam of light sliced on, illuminating his son's hand and the dusty Army blanket.

"Needs new batteries," Perry said. He pointed the light at the dented old supply trunk, where packs of batteries lay arranged by size.

The Old Man grabbed his son's arm. "Why'd she go back?" he asked.

"She saw Sill. I've gotta find . . . can you get the batteries?" The light caught the wall across from them and an eyelash blinked.

The Old Man leaned forward, struggling to focus, but Perry was moving the beam too fast. "Sill's with Rose," he told his son, rubbing his knuckles over his eyelids. "I saw her over there earlier."

"You did?" Perry asked.

"I warned you this was coming." The Old Man grabbed his son's wrist and angled the beam back toward the dark blinking wall—the eyelash was still there. Perry handed him the flashlight and moved to the ladder.

"Yeah, you did," Perry said. Something glanced off the trap door. The Old Man felt for his cane. In the beam of light the eyelash was revealed to be a centipede, legs working. "You okay?" Perry asked, feet already on the rungs.

The Old Man waved his hand. "Wait it out," he told his son. "Don't be an idiot. Nina knows how to take cover."

"Can't." Perry climbed. A groaning came from above them, the sound of wood planks bending against the grain.

"Hear that?" the Old Man wheezed. "Hear that?"

"I'm not deaf, Dad," Perry said. He put both hands against the trap door and heaved it open. Wind tore through the pages of the book on the shelf.

"No, Perry! You hear me?" The door smacked shut overhead.

He breathed in the soft smell of apples. He raised a shaky hand to touch the tobacco tin in his pocket, but it was lost. His blood thought he was still falling and rocketed helter-skelter through his veins. He touched his fingers higher, into the hollow just below his left shoulder where the doc had dug out the bullet. It was the one wound that never gave him any trouble: just a small round scar.

"Slow down," he said to his blood, pressing his shoulder. "Go easy." That's what he should have said to Perry, not the other thing.

He heard a high-pitched whine, and could tell it was coming from inside his head because of the way it followed his heartbeat. Had Perry made it to the house? His shadow stretched across the wall, chased by the flashlight. The centipede was prehistoric looking. He shivered, wishing he had a shovel with a sharp edge. "I know you," he said, not sure whether he was talking to himself, the insect, his son, his land. He picked up his cane, leaned forward awkwardly and jabbed it into the wall until the thing scuttled away.

He should put new batteries in the flashlight before the beam faded further, but the supply trunk receded across a chasm of dark packed earth. He had to take stock of his bones. He leaned back, hoisted his legs onto the cot, and touched his hip gingerly. His knee had gone numb. If Perry hadn't been right behind him, he might not have made it down the ladder. *Perry.* The Old Man had offered a thorny stem and told Rose things he had no business saying out loud to anyone, not about his own son. She'd rattled him, made him want to say things he barely owned. Rose: her eyes shadowed and unfocused, slicing the rosehips off in messy square cuts, hacking at limbs haphazardly, with no thought to next year's growth. *Rose, where are you? You've always been so alive. I won't take it.*

"You weren't there," he said aloud. His voice had a pleasing fullness in the dark space. Hail hit the door. The flashlight beam flickered and dimmed. He switched it off to save the batteries, and the darkness was total, deeper than it had been when Perry shared it. He could feel the centipede travel on its path; he could hear the earth breathe. A weight sank onto the cot and he reached out his hand, but there was no hand reaching for him. Still, he spoke to her.

"You weren't there today, Rose, not really. It's the shock, but you can come back from it." He touched his fingers to his throat to feel the pulse, still hammering. Perry had made it to the house, there could be no question. But what would happen to the house? The storm whined, or maybe it was his blood. Rose was waiting for him to finish. He reached his hand toward the foot of the cot. The storm roared overhead; something large careened against the door and jolted off. A coldness clasped him, and his breath rattled.

"I was trying to tell you . . . the lightning. I was slower than I should've been, I didn't hustle like I knew I had to. But that rain smell came off the ground and I remembered why I'm here, what we're made for. Dirt turned to mud, Rose, and rain . . . how can these things bring joy to a body? Repeat this to a soul and I'll deny it. But listen. Time felt thick. The corn turned so bright! The cracks in the sky were harsh in that way that makes your blood move sharp, and the elm leaves turned skyward. Everything was lit with a pale green fire and I was a stalk in the field. I heard it before I felt it, my guts vibrated—my fingers gave off smoke and I was pushed further than I thought possible. It furrowed me into something new."

His words were round and untethered in the quiet. He could get through to her. She didn't expect to see new growth in the spring. That was her problem and if he could find that thought and extract it like the surgeon had extracted his one piddly bullet, she might be saved. His fingers worked at the dusty blanket. His heart skipped, and then slowed. The storm would sort itself out.

*Where were you, then? None of my business, I know that's what you'd say. I'm circling around something here and I need to say it true. But I can't . . . I don't know what it is. Fresh made mud, Rose. Upturned green. When I came to, the land under my back was hard and unforgiving and mine, my inheritance. That's what I mean. Not the things but that feeling. That feeling I had is all I know.*

He no longer tasted mud or heard the whine. A stone slid from one side of his mind to the other. A gleam moved toward him through the darkness. He was fairly sure his eyes were open as he saw the surgeon's masked face, glasses flashing white. *Not yet.* He wanted to speak a few more heartbeats, telling the earth what it already knew. His body jerked like a falling sleeper.

*

A hum comes over the wires, a message from the meteorologists who are miles away watching color patterns swirl and break apart on the Pulse-Doppler radar. Yellow, green, red, blue, black—pixels in all colors of the rainbow. *It is beautiful*, they think. Kaleidoscopic. Majestic. Aloud, one will begin the alert sequence: rapid air movement, supercell gathering into a wall, affected counties. The alert becomes an all-out warning because science makes it so.

Emails, text messages, faxes, phone calls; printers spit out paper with bold captions. An intern hands a radioman a piece of paper and points to a message blinking on the computer screen in front of him; he pulls his chair closer to the microphone and prepares to read. One county on the list is more familiar to him than the others, but Ted Waite is a professional and does not pause.

Weather Channel, cable access, amplitude modulation, frequency modulation. The warning follows proper notification procedures. A secretary picks up the phone to call her boss in the mayor's office, panicky that she has forgotten something important in the protocol. Another staffer in another office runs down the hall to make sure the safety officer, who has been having troubles at home, is at his desk. Storm chasers who have been following the alerts pile into cars and floor it, determined to see for themselves: *this time oh yeah this one*.

Sitting at his desk holding a cup of cold coffee, Ted Waite watches the cloud front grow wider on his screen, brilliant green overtaken by a thickening yellow, with a deep crimson pulsing at the center. The hum rises to a chorus—whirrs, beeps, clicks. He leans into the mic. *Take shelter, hold tight*.

Not everyone has a radio. In Rose's hayloft, a farmer's daughter holds tight to other things entirely: the mutterings of a lost woman, adults coming and going, the clink of dog tags, a locket. A red folder leaning against the barn wall.

# Sill

Sylvie rode her dirt bike through the corn, a path known by heart, careful not to ding the plants with her handlebars. Before the stone wall she hopped off, pushed for a few feet, and then shoved the bike behind some brambles and hoisted herself over. She scrambled through the thorny branches and scuttled low along the edge of Rose's yard into the barn and up the ladder to the hayloft. Morning sunlight poured into the loft, softened by the haydust. A huge rush to get to this stillness.

Through the window Rose's house leaned forward, wanting to tell a secret. Lance's mother spent her days hacking at bushes and making herself scarce when anyone tried to visit. She was more than sad; there was an extra weight in there. As Sylvie had heard her dad put it, Rose was acting out of it—but that wasn't exactly true. Rose was inside, far in, too far to come out and pay them mind. Sylvie knew because she spent most of her time here. She'd tried to talk to her early on—had walked right up to Rose and said, *I want to see his room again. I need that picture he drew for me.* But Rose's eyes refused to focus. She seemed to not remember Sylvie's name—her, Sylvie! Rose's neighbor for her entire life.

Lance was dead. And his mother muttered to the empty house, slicing the branches until even the strongest, oldest ones turned brown. Sylvie watched it all from up in the hayloft. Her parents thought she was in her room or at school, if they thought of her at all. Lance was dead—and details that she'd known like her own skin were fading: the exact shade of his brown eyes. Red scratches rose on her forearms from shoving through the thickets. She liked them, they brought clarity. They got there because she was trying to understand things. Every time she clambered over the stone wall and pushed through the brambles his face flashed before her—then gone.

A familiar voice below: Dad talking to Rose in the yard, holding a rolled-up piece of paper. He looked younger and smaller from her vantage point through the high window, and he was asking for something but Rose was having none of it. Sylvie knew how Rose made him feel. He wanted to lease Rose's land because it hadn't been worked much in recent years. The soil was rich and they could transition it more easily to organic. He'd mapped it out at the dining room table, talking softly with her mother. Sylvie and her granddad had sat in the living room, watching an old war movie but also eavesdropping. *Farmer's markets,* they'd heard. *Sell direct to city people. Everything old is new again.* In the movie, the girl cried for her soldier and looked beautiful in black and white: hair combed and lipstick and high heels; the soldier came home, wounded, and the girl nursed him back to health. Sylvie felt her granddad's glare. He didn't approve of much, but he cared about everything. When her parents came into the living room, Granddad pointed at the television, voice rattling with unspit loogies. *A good war. A just war.* Her father popped a beer open and said, *I know,* like he'd heard it all before. *Turn it off,* her mother said. Then they were all looking at her.

Now her father retreated over Rose's stone wall, shoulders up around his ears, and she waited for him to notice her bike. Not a flicker. She wasn't surprised. For a second she thought she should call to him. *But I don't want him to get what he wants, either.* Her granddad said once that Rose's land was cursed. People crushed and splintered and lost. *Superstition is from the Devil,* her mother said. And Granddad replied, *Sometimes the Devil bears listening to.*

Rose stomped into the house, her hair, her whole outline, vibrating like the weather vane on top of the barn. Down below, Fergus whimpered at the foot of the ladder. He liked to come visit. Being the only one she talked to, Fergus knew Rose was off her rocker before anyone else. Sylvie had cheese slices for him so he wouldn't bark. Gradually, she'd brought over things to make the hayloft hers. First, a pillow and a wool blanket. Then a change of clothes. Some books and a journal. Snacks. Gum. Water. A flashlight because her granddad had told her to always have one around, and a milk crate to hold her things. It was nice to see how little she actually needed.

Fergus put his paws on the bottom rung of the ladder, and Sylvie unwrapped a cheese slice and dropped it down. School was a problem. Some days, like today, her mother gave permission not to go. Other days they didn't know about. She had intercepted two letters addressed to her parents, warnings about absences. But she did her work; they couldn't say she didn't. The books and notebooks she needed sat in the crate. Ben Culp, Lance's best friend, gave her the assignments she missed. Ben C. was supposed to graduate and sign up with Lance, but he'd flunked twice and his parents wouldn't let him go without a diploma. Sylvie wondered if he was as bad at English as he said, or if it had to do with not wanting to sign up. Lance's other best friend, Ben Logan, was in his second year at State. She talked to the Bens sometimes, and sometimes it helped. Other times she could barely stand to think of them.

Lance had told her she was his best girl, the only one. Though after he died Amanda Vega cried every day—sat in class with black streaks down her face, and didn't even wipe them away. So Sylvie stopped going to school, until it went on too long and they made her go back. *No more excuses,* her mother said, palm hot on her back as she shoved her out the front door. *You have to buck up, Sill.* Her mother didn't say her real name often. Sylvie could count the days since someone had spoken her real name: six. Nicknames didn't count; Sill didn't count. Lance didn't call her Sill.

Fergus had swallowed the cheese slice in a gulp and lingered, waiting to see if another might be coming. Now he wheeled around and trotted away. Rose was on the move—a sputtering rumble started up from the driveway. She hadn't driven anywhere since Lance had died, but now she had the truck going. Sylvie went to the window. Fergus put his paws on the truck handle and barked and barked until Rose leaned over to open the passenger door. He scrambled in, expending a lot of effort to get his legs up on the high seat. Rose started backing out even though the door swung wide.

"Hey," Sylvie started. The word came out croaky. "Hey, don't—" There was no way Rose could hear from this distance and over the rattling engine, but after another moment of backing up she stopped the truck and leaned over to close the door.

*Hey, don't do that, you'll lose your dog,* is what Sylvie was going to say. *You can't afford to lose anything else, Rose.* If she'd shouted down from the hayloft, Rose might have taken it for the voice of God.

*She doesn't believe in God,* Lance had told her once. *Do you?* she'd asked, though if he were damned to Hell it wouldn't change how she felt. The light from the haywell made his hair dusty-shiny. They'd sit here in this hay, running fingers along each other's thumbpads. Her thumb along his thumbpad—why did it feel so good? She had willed herself tiny so she could explore it like new land; hike along, plant a flag. Fergus whining below, their shoulders shaking, the sweet powdery hay smell in their mouths.

She touched her arm, pressing hard on the scratches the brambles had given her. *Pay attention.*

When the dust from the truck settled Sylvie stood, blood tingling, sluggish in her ankles and calves. As she slid down the ladder the sharp prickle grew bearable. She figured she had maybe an hour before Rose returned. By the time she reached the back door her legs felt almost normal, so she did a little stomp and sway there on the porch, looking out over the backyard. They'd played there together so often as kids that it was hard to see the yard now as changed. But it *was* changed, mostly the light and the shadows.

The bushes had some starter berries on them, and for old time's sake Sylvie stepped down the stairs and ate a few—gritty and sour. Under some low branches she saw a small mound of dirt like someone had buried a baby doll, or Fergus had taken extra care with one of his soup bones. She gave it a little pat with the sole of her sneaker and then went into the messy kitchen. Plates and dishes were stacked all over, and a crusty pot sat on the stove. Sylvie touched the table as she walked by and her fingers pulled through a sticky patch of honey or syrup.

She stopped in the parlor. Quieter, that was all. Sylvie had been there the day Jim Culp came to sign Lance up. Had stood right outside this door, pressed into the ugly old wallpaper, not ashamed to be eavesdropping. She could see them reflected in the mirror that hung on the wall, sitting on Lance's grandmother's silkprint sofa. Rose and Lance and Jim Culp in his crisp uniform. A plate of untouched cookies on the end table. *What's to fear?* Rose asked, and the recruiter replied, watching Lance, *You'll see the world, and they'll pay for school*. Fergus had sniffed at Sylvie's empty pockets and then wandered into the room to be near the cookies. Lance had wet his hair down, and Rose's hands smoothed the skirt across her lap over and over again.

That afternoon Sylvie had snuck upstairs the way he had showed her and now, even though she might forget the exact color of his eyes, her feet remembered. Hug the wall to the left at the bottom of the staircase, but then, before you push off the first stair, slide all the way to the right, toes spreading inside sneakers. Blood sounded in her ears, and she took three deep breaths before starting to climb. She skipped the fourth step and the seventh, because they creaked no matter where you put weight. Almost at the landing, she grabbed the handrail and hop-skipped fast across the squeaky board in front of his bedroom.

*Made it.* A bubble of happiness swelled in her chest. His bedroom door was shut, and like the backyard, it felt stark just in the fact of itself. Stained walnut. She opened it fast and stepped in, pushing it closed behind her. Everything inside was the same: his extra long twin bed covered with a blue blanket, the poster of the blonde bikini beer goddess on the wall, and the football trophy in the corner on a stack of books. It had worked. His face swam before her, eyes exactly right, nothing misremembered. But the happy bubble popped—the feeling had come from habit, like her feet sliding over the boards. Curtains billowed. Sylvie wondered if the dirty magazine was under the mattress or if he'd had the sense to get rid of it before he'd left. She didn't feel like lifting the bed to check.

Lance had drawn pictures, good ones. Fergus scratching himself, Sylvie's granddad looking skinny as his cane, crows lining the wires on the county road. Sylvie, sitting by the well: *Look to the left,* he'd said, and the sound of his pencil was all she'd heard for a good long stretch. When he'd showed her the drawing, it looked like her the way the drawn well stones looked like stones—familiar and not familiar, recognizable but also strange. Looking, you didn't even notice the college ruled lines of the paper. He'd set the notebook down and chucked a pebble into the well, putting his fingers to his lips and whispering, *Listen.* They'd leaned their heads against the stones and closed their eyes. A frog croaked and jumped, water lapped; small sounds rose, echoing louder like a train through a dark tunnel; little chimes of sound grew rounder until the stones vibrated against their skulls. With a memory like that, how could she help but love him?

Rose saved his drawings. She must have. Sylvie wanted that one back.

He'd kept his portfolio and art supplies in the top dresser drawer, but when she opened it she found only half of a busted pair of scissors and a few spools of thread. A quick search of the other drawers revealed nothing. In the corner, his overdue library books: *Of Mice and Men*, *Woodworking for Idiots*, a biography of Sandy Koufax, a book of Marc Chagall's paintings. Never to be seen inside the four square walls of the county library again.

His clothes hung neatly in the closet. The upper shelf held random sports equipment and old yearbooks. She pulled a small box from the corner. *Letters* written across the cardboard in Rose's hand. Sylvie sank to the floor, her back against the closet doorjamb, flipping through old envelopes and pulling some open. Most were from people Sylvie didn't know. A few were addressed to Rose from her dead husband, dated back when Sylvie and Lance were little kids. A postcard from Stella with a photo of Miami, mentioning her honeymoon and some man named Eddie. There was one that looked newer: peach colored stationery still lush under the fingers, a messy script scrolling across the front of the envelope. The paper inside didn't match the creamy exterior. It was crinkled and creased, one corner blackened. A brief note from Stella, dated almost two years ago, offering to help pay for Lance's college tuition. Sylvie took a breath and reread it.

His pretty, friendly Aunt Stella—who always greeted them warmly in Mondragon's, who always had a special word for Sylvie. She could have saved him. He could have been at State right now with Ben Logan, just a few hours away and home on the weekends. Sylvie sat staring into the deep closet, her head blank. Quiet lay over the room.

After a while she stood, slid the folded letter into her pocket, and rummaged through the rest of the closet for his drawings. Nothing. She could look for his art in Rose's room; she wanted to find something valuable to Rose and take it. Sylvie opened his nightstand drawer but it held only a ChapStick and some old Scout patches. A voice called below—she shut the drawer so fast it gave a clap. Then no sound. Air vibrated, and a screen door banged. Footsteps came toward the stairs in the foyer. Sylvie's skin jumped. She slid the drawer open and picked up the ChapStick, pocketing it.

A nervous voice called, "Hello, Rose? Rose, are you up there?" It wasn't Rose home early. It was Sylvie's mother.

As Nina climbed the stairs, Sylvie crossed the room and pressed into the wall behind the shut door. If it swung open she wouldn't be seen right away. She wouldn't be in trouble, anyway—barely anything got her in trouble these days. But still. It was his room, in Rose's house, and she was trespassing. The beer goddess on the poster was in cahoots, still as Sylvie, who was listening to her mother breathe on the other side of the door. Her pulse was fast, as if Rose herself were out there. She reached fingertips across her chest and touched the wood panel. *She won't come in. I don't know why she's here, but it's not for this room.*

Her mother stood for a minute. Then she sighed, shifting her weight. From where her footsteps traveled next, Sylvie knew she was peering in at Rose's empty bedroom, glancing at the rusty drip stains in the bathroom sink. Nina went down the front stairs, and as soon as Sylvie heard the fourth step creak she opened the door, moving quickly down the hall toward the rear staircase. Then she took a few steps backward and pivoted, entering Rose's bedroom. A jewelry box sat on the dresser, covered in a film of dust. Not much inside: some old hairpins, a worn wedding band, and a locket on a chain. The locket was big, made of real gold with filigreed edges—clearly the only thing of value. It held a faded photo of a woman. She put it into her pocket and tiptoed back into the hall, past the window with the cracked pane, down the narrow back steps that led to the dark hallway outside the kitchen, almost tripping over the old picnic basket in the mudroom on her way to the back door.

In the hayloft she sat by the window, watching the house and waiting for her mother to come out. The sky over Rose's place was as thick as the quiet in Lance's room. Sylvie strung the locket around her neck, tucking it under her t-shirt, and lay back against the hay, her skin awake but the rest of her tired like she'd run a couple of miles. She waited, listening for the screen door that would signal her mother was headed home. But Nina stayed.

What was she doing in there? Nina needed to get a job—another thing Sylvie had overheard at home. Her mother wanted to go back to school and get a nursing license. She'd wanted to a long time ago, but had gotten pregnant with Sylvie instead. And ever since the lightning strike, her granddad had required extra help. But they needed more money to try her dad's business ideas. It would be expensive at first, he'd said, but after a few years it would pay off. Rose was the key: her land.

Sylvie unfolded the letter from Stella. Maybe her mother was in there looking for something, too, something valuable that she could steal. *Do it*, Sylvie thought. Rose's truck roared up the drive, the engine knocking. It kept knocking even after Rose took the keys out of the ignition and hopped out, Fergus close on her heels. Sylvie could hear it from the barn, so of course her mother heard from inside the house. From the loft window she watched Rose drop out of sight behind the truck. The engine sounded like a cow with digestive problems. After a few minutes she reemerged, went up the front steps and opened the unlocked door, muttering something at Fergus and dropping a plastic bag full of heavy cans on the porch. Then something interesting happened. Sylvie's mother snuck around the side of the house, keeping out of Rose's sight, carrying an empty tote bag and wearing a blue kerchief around her head. Nina went through the brambles and vaulted over the stone wall, hurrying toward home.

Soon after her mother was gone Sylvie followed, descending the ladder and walking into the field, leaving her bike where it was. She peed in her usual spot at the end of a row. The air felt moist like after a storm, but nothing was washed clean. Far off, near the untilled acres, her father slowed his tractor and cut the engine. Sylvie had the feeling that she should leave a trail of breadcrumbs so that she could find her way back to Rose's hayloft. Everything was tangling up, choking itself off. In the distance the whale vane on top of her family's house pointed due east. Stella's letter crinkled in her pocket as she walked. A jangle of dog tags announced that Fergus had followed her. She knelt and reached into her pocket for the last cheese slice. He licked her hands clean and sat with a satisfied look as she ran her fingers through his ruff, letting her whisper love into his ears. "Don't you want to come home with me?" Forget the locket, Fergus was probably Rose's most valuable thing now. He was Lance's dog, anyway, and used to follow him everywhere. Fergus couldn't follow them up the hayloft ladder though; they'd heard dog breaths below them more often than not. Lance would put his fingertips on Sylvie's collarbone, lightly, and say, *Hear your heartbeat?*

*That's the dog!* She'd shove him backward into the hay.

Now Fergus had got what he wanted and was done with her, trotting back to Rose's place. "Bastard," she whispered after him. "Fine, then." As soon as they were spoken, she was sorry for the words. "Come, Fergus! Don't go." He didn't look back.

She kept on, walked right into the green, and wrapped her arms as far as she could around the trunk. The Infamous Elm. She didn't know why the tree was called "infamous." Once, she'd asked Lance and he'd shrugged and run his hands up over her ribcage and got that half smile she'd only just started to recognize. The tree grew crooked but you couldn't tell that from close to it, standing underneath and looking through a curtain of leaves. Light fell in tinted diamond patterns, making everything pretty and quiet. Lots of things could make this tree infamous—she and Lance had tried a few, hidden in the open air.

They'd drunk from a bottle of peach liquor he'd swiped from town, had sat sipping and looking out over the new corn, just the two of them. He talked to her differently when the Bens weren't around. That day, like today, had threatened rain, and the clouds were blue. Lance had stood unsteadily, slapped his hand against the other side of the trunk and said, *Look here*. She'd crawled around to the side that faced the road and there it was: a bumpy scar about three feet high, blackened with tar. *Before your granddad put the tar on*, Lance said, *I could stick my whole hand in*. The scar was old, it had happened years before. *Did he think it would die?* Sylvie asked. *Maybe*, Lance said, *or he just didn't want it to be so ugly*. She'd laughed at that, thinking about her granddad caring whether a tree was ugly or not, with all the other things he had to worry over. Lance didn't laugh. *Whose car was it?* she asked. And he'd misheard her and thought she'd said *fault*.

He must've, because what he said was, *Stella. Stella's fault*.

She pulled the folded letter from her pocket and read it again.

She had watched Stella knock and wait at Rose's door more than once, always holding a foil-wrapped dish—Rose never answered. And a few weeks after he'd died Sylvie had seen Stella limp down Rose's driveway holding her shoes in one hand, looking red-faced and lost.

Lance's olive army surplus coat had been canvasy under her fingers. He wore it even before he'd signed up; it was cheap and warm.

*Are you practicing to be a soldier?* Sylvie had asked, and he'd stuck out his long jean leg and dirty muckboot and said, *No Army here. Pure farmboy.* She couldn't tell whether he was happy or sad. He hadn't mentioned art school in a while, and she was about to ask him but the rain that had been threatening came pattering through the leaves. It was equal distance between his house and hers. When they were kids they would have run off their separate ways, chanting the lightning protection spell all the way home. But he'd grabbed her hand, said, *C'mon*, and they'd run for the hayloft. *Lightning, lightning, go away. Strike us down another day.*

She lay curled around the Elm for as long as it took to remember the exact smell of him that day. Then a wet nose snuffled at her neck. Fergus had come to collect her.

Her granddad's truck pulled into Rose's driveway just as Sylvie returned to the hayloft. The day was turning into a slow parade of her entire family. He slid out of his truck, kicking gravel up the drive as he made his way to Rose. He turned around once, fast—his eyes flashed, visible even from her window, burning with a fire she never used to understand. *Wanting what you can't have.* Sylvie ducked, waited, and then peeked again.

His voice was audible, the roughness of it carrying further than her father's had earlier. "Don't let Perry . . ." Rose slowed her pruning as he spoke, and her head tilted. He thought she wasn't listening because she didn't look directly at him, so he spoke louder. "Rose, you have to hold on . . ."

Granddad didn't look smaller from this angle, just skinnier, his bones as angular as Rose's chopped branches. He knew how to take up space. He turned and Sylvie was afraid he'd spot her again, so she slid down to the hay under the window and rested her head on the wall, listening to his voice hum until Rose's screen door slammed. She looked again, watching him step onto the porch and peer through the door—he'd never enter uninvited, that was a kind of rule-breaking he had no truck with. He pulled something from his pocket and set it on the windowsill. Then he spun around and retreated.

She waited for Rose or Fergus to come back into the yard for what seemed like a long time. The place was too still. She made a list of where to look the next time she snuck into the house—because there would be a next time; today had shown her that it was possible. The fatigue that had overtaken her earlier was gone, and her pulse beat as fast as it had in Lance's forbidden room. But she wasn't afraid anymore. She descended the ladder, not bothering to be quiet. She walked right up the steps and picked up the thing that her granddad had left on the windowsill. An old nickel, looking like it had been run over and then left in a campfire. Sylvie turned it over in her fingers, wondering whether to take this too, but set it back where he'd left it.

*Check on my ma for me.* Lance had asked it of her and so she had done it. But Sylvie didn't owe Rose a thing, not anymore. In the loft, she ate a peanut butter and jelly sandwich, outlined the assignment for Civics class that Ben C. had passed along, and reread the letters from Lance.

She had written him sixty-two letters. Two for every week he was over there. Real paper ones, like women in the old movies wrote to their sweethearts. Lance sent her one paper letter and fifteen emails. She'd printed out all of the emails, except for two. Two she'd held back, not for Rose's eyes. Sylvie kept the papers in a red folder.

Early on, she'd hoped that she and Rose might exchange paper for paper, Lance's drawings in exchange for his emails. Rose would read the messages he'd sent to Sylvie, press them to her chest, and say, *He loved you so much, he told me so. He'd want you to have this.* She'd hand over the well picture, their fingers touching.

That would never happen. Sylvie knew that now. Lots of things she knew now that she hadn't known. She'd never understood all the different ways you could be a stranger to someone until Lance died. There were countless things she didn't know about him, even though she had known him her whole life. She wondered if that was her fault, or his, or maybe nobody's fault at all, just the way things were. It wasn't something she ever wanted to be comfortable with—she never wanted to expect a stranger where there was love. It wasn't like she loved him any less though. Or loved her parents less, or her granddad. But no matter how much she prayed, on the days when she still prayed, she couldn't love Rose. Now, in some weird way, she was grateful for that. Like Rose was the only one who was being honest. Sylvie didn't know her and couldn't love her—Rose's eyes lost focus when they looked at her, and at Rose's place Sylvie could be anyone, or no one. It felt free.

The screen door slammed. Rose was back, clipping away at the bushes and looking like she'd never figure out that two careless trespassers had been in her house. Fergus came onto the front porch and watched. Sylvie's heart skipped, knowing what was coming before her head did.

She crouched by the window and folded each email printout so that the flat paper became three-dimensional. The last page she folded was Stella's stolen letter. When she was done, fourteen airplanes sat in a row on the hay.

She knelt and leaned out the window, not caring, wanting to be seen. "Hey . . ." she started, and her voice was froggy but she kept yelling. "Hey, Rose!"

Fergus thumped his tail, but Rose seemed not to hear at all.

Sylvie had good aim. The first one landed right on the bush in front of Rose. Rose pulled the plane—Lance's plane—from thorny branches and unfolded it. Then she looked up at the gathering clouds.

"Rose," Sylvie yelled. "Rose! He sent those emails to me, but you can have them, too."

"Girl," she called, not even looking in Sylvie's direction, "for the last time, get out of my barn."

Sylvie flew the rest, one after the other, and Rose turned this way and that, picking airplanes out of her shrubs and off the gravel footpath. "One of them is not like the others!" Sylvie called, pointing toward Stella's peach-colored plane. She scrambled down the ladder.

When she got to the yard Rose was leaning way over into the well, like one of the airplanes had flown in and she was hellbent on retrieving it. "Are you okay?" Sylvie pulled on Rose's skirt until she stood.

Rose straightened and pressed the papers against her stomach, moving a greedy palm to smooth the pages flat. They stood face to face, both breathing hard. Rose pulled the pages from her belly and lay them across her forearm like a book, peach stationery on top, scanning the words, her face gummy with concentration.

Sylvie grabbed the stolen locket through her t-shirt. "How could you be so wrong about everything? Why are you always calling me 'Girl'? You know my name."

Rose touched her apron pocket and muttered, "I can't—" She crumpled the papers into a loose ball and tossed it onto the porch.

"Lance is dead." The first time she'd spoken it aloud. Saying it made Sylvie stumble into a bush, thorns scratching her back. She waited for a response, any kind of acknowledgment or regret. Rose's eyes weren't bleary at all. They were clear as the sky wasn't, but she also looked exhausted. The skin on her cheeks was like parchment. She looked at Sylvie then, actually saw her, and something cold made her eyes bright.

"A storm's coming. Get home." Rose went to the porch and sat down on the steps like she was alone. She pulled a light blue envelope from her apron pocket.

Sylvie might as well be invisible. No matter what she said, Rose would refuse to feel it or share it. Sylvie backed away, cracking branches until her heels hit the stone wall and she had to turn if she didn't want to fall. She grabbed her bike. The wind picked up and fairly pushed her home—firm and moist on her back, working through the shirt like fingers.

The ride home was a path she knew like her own palm, but it felt like a foreign country. Flat stretches and curves and gullies, cawing birds and upturned leaves, the air smelling of ozone, a stitch in her side. The whole land knew a storm was coming, but not what to make of it. Wheeling crows didn't know which of them would be picked up and broken. The dirt was hard with unknowing. *I'll never come this way again*. It seemed the birds and the wind and the whispering leaves confirmed it—then the cawing fell silent and the sky went dark.

The storm broke just as she reached her mother's garden, screens knocked out already. She rounded the side of the house to the front door, grit blowing into her eyes and a stitch gripping under her heart. Her mother strode up the hill, shirt whipping up to show her pale stomach, and at the bottom two blue shirts danced together by the storm cellar door; her father was helping Granddad. Nina yelled something and pointed down the hill. Hail bounced off the eaves of their house and onto the ground. Her father hooked his arm at them, beckoning, and disappeared.

Nina pulled her toward the cellar. Panting, she told her mother what she should have told Rose. "I need to find everything he ever gave me and put it in an album because otherwise he's lost. If I forget—"

The sky roared. Sylvie yanked herself free and ran to the house, pulling the door hard against the screaming wind, locket banging against her chest as she took the stairs to her room two at a time, cataloging things in her mind's eye: the photo of him under the Infamous Elm, that silly yearbook note, the empty liquor bottle, a daisy keychain—feeling the flimsiness of a life. Shutters banged and the roof groaned. She stopped in the center of her bedroom, seeing nothing. *What am I, measured in things?* Her back hurt and the side stitch moved over her whole chest. Then the roof buckled and she dropped to her knees.

Hands grasped her shoulders. "Sill—" her mother said, her voice big as the howling stopped and they were cupped in the eye of the storm. "*Sylvie*."

*

If all warnings fail, here is what to look for: the sky turns green, greenish black, brackish. Hail falls. There is a sound that some liken to a freight train, a jet engine, a thousand souped-up Buicks drag racing across the sky. Debris falls from on high—frogs, playing cards, plywood, mud, rock. You may see green sheets of rain. The funnel cloud appears, which at this point should be no surprise. Take shelter. Do not try to outrun a twister in your car, no matter what you've seen in the movies. Get to a basement or a cellar if possible. Alternately: closets, bathtubs, interior rooms. Cover yourself with a blanket or some cushions. Stay away from crumbling walls.

If you are unlucky enough to be caught outside, ask yourself, Why? Why me? If there is no rain, find a ditch and press yourself into it. If there *is* rain, the ditch might fill in an instant: flash flooding. In that case, hunker down on flat land, make yourself small. Stay away from trees, power lines, the exteriors of buildings.

Listen for an electric crackle—this does not bode well. Listen for quiet, a pressure that builds in the ears.

Are you listening, Stella?

Ask yourself, what could I do differently next time? There has to be a next time.

Crouch. Grasp yourself tightly. Remind yourself you are as likely to be killed by a shark as to be hit by a tornado.

Yet, here you are.

# Stella

Before Mondragon's opened for business that morning, perched on a low stool at the back of the store, Stella checked in twelve small blue boxes of paperclips and stacked them neatly on a freshly dusted bottom shelf. She was irritable—she had woken to the same terrible song that had roused her for the past month: *Camptown Races*, played in a cacophonous escalation of electronic beeps. Her old alarm had been a standard clock radio, clicking on each morning at 6:05, and no matter where it was tuned on the dial she heard something about the war, jolting awake with corpses in front of her eyes. She'd thrown it across the room. Ward had run up from the kitchen, staring at the dent in the plaster and the clockface shattered on the floor. "Okay, Stella honey," he'd murmured in that soothing tone of his, which was the way he always spoke to her now. "It'll be okay, I'll get you a better one." The next week the pink clock had arrived, peppy song stored in its plastic bowels. *Camptown ladies sing this song—doo-dah! Doo-dah!*

Stella arranged the staples so that the thin lines between the boxes made neat plus signs, and then considered the next task. She spaced her projects carefully, so that she was never left without something to occupy her. It was important to keep moving, to have a sense of purpose no matter how inane the chore.

"There could be weather," Ward said, and she looked up, startled. Her husband was so quiet these days she sometimes forgot his presence. Ward pointed at the shelf that held the store radio. She'd been tuning out the familiar voice of the weatherman. Ted Waite's voice was smoother now than when she'd been married to him—his round, deep tones spoke of storm conditions; just a heads up, a possibility. *Don't take chances.* Ted's voice faded into a jingle for a fast food chain.

She sighed. "That dumb song is stuck in my head again."

Ward went to the radio and turned the dial, not understanding which song she meant. The tuner settled onto his favorite a.m. talk station, a sign to Stella to make herself scarce. She hated the pundit who held court on the airwaves, but everything she loathed about the man—the bile and half-truths, the oily nastiness and the whiny tone—Ward found bracing, even funny. It was as if every outrageous rant released a bit of steam so that Ward could continue to be unfailingly polite in his dealings with his customers, and with Stella herself.

"I'll head out, I guess," she said. "Do some errands."

"And get the house ready?"

"What?" Stella gave the paperclips one last straighten. "Oh, yes."

"All righty," Ward said. His face was drawn; he hadn't been sleeping well either. The skin under his eyes was puffy and slack.

"Anything you need help with before I go?" she asked, rubbing her temple.

"No. Scottie will help with the windows if I need it."

She turned to the back room to collect her coat and purse. It smelled of the coffee they'd brewed on arrival, and the shifting layers of the store itself. New scents took precedence on any given day, brought to the fore by mood and weather and the settling boards. Today the place had faint underpinnings of birdseed and dried apricots, manure and licorice.

"Stella," Ward said when she met him at the cash register. "Will you call me when you're home?" Her husband was a master of delivering simple statements freighted with meaning. She had given up trying to get him to unpack them, and her new strategy was to respond to everything he said at face value. "Of course."

"Let me know you're all right," he called to her back as the door shut behind her. She raised a hand without turning and fluttered her fingers in acknowledgement, fighting the urge to flip him off.

The sky was clear as a bell, and it felt like she'd pulled a day of hooky; the weather would likely come to nothing. Her car's engine started like a charm, and she patted the dash and whispered, *Good girl!* Without really thinking, she turned left instead of right, heading onto the highway toward the big box store, twenty miles zipping past in a blur.

She'd been to the Discount SuperStore dozens of times, assessing the rock bottom price points and vast selection. Ward hadn't gone; it was a point of pride for him—he assumed anyone could walk in and wander through the aisles. But here, as in most places, you needed proof of belonging. Stella had paid a fee and had her photo laminated onto a white membership card.

The store's parking lot was only half-full, probably due to the time of day. Her double-wide cart had one sticky wheel and a plastic flap where the child, if she'd had one, would sit. She walked past enormous cans of tuna fish and pickles in gallon jars, displayed with outsized bottles of mayonnaise and mustard. Stella tightened her grip on the cart handle, wheeled over to a display shelf stacked with colorful bottles and selected an oversized jug of dandruff control shampoo for Ward. Some quick calculations: it would save them almost ten dollars over the next six months, and she could carefully refill the normal-sized bottle in the bathroom. The shampoo slid back and forth like a cue ball in her otherwise empty cart. Next the perishables. Three pounds of butter, some cream, and two large-breasted, shockingly inexpensive chickens.

In spite of its corpulence, the wealth measured out in acres of batteries and tundras of frozen beef, this place was no more solid at the bone than Mondragon's Emporium. Even with the shelves stacked two stories high, she had a feeling it was fragile, and that if she looked carefully she might see the cracks. Stella selected a few more items, exerting a little too much effort pushing the sticky-wheeled cart, glad for the strain in her forearms and biceps. There was something about being here, saving money, planning ahead, that gave her the exact opposite feeling of the one she was supposed to have. *Virtue*. She felt virtuous. She threw a new fuchsia v-neck sweater into the cart to reward herself.

Outside, the sky was a little more solid, as if she might be able to push against it and feel a resistance—but the sun still shone. She turned on the car radio to catch Ted Waite making noncommittal mentions of weather conditions. Stella hadn't seen her ex-husband in almost fifteen years, and yet she'd know him anywhere. Eddie had been a snake-charming, chain-smoking rake, a salesman whose biggest product was himself, and even young as she was, she'd known exactly what she was getting when she married him. Now, as Ted, he'd be silvery at the temples, maybe a little less muscle on his bones, still that wolfish gleam in his deep-set eyes. So different from Ward, whom she'd married at thirty-five, drawn to his kind eyes and steady ways, his heft and respectability. Early in their marriage she had asked Ward if he minded listening to her ex-husband read the weather on the radio, if he ever got jealous. His eyes had widened in surprise and he'd said, "Well, honey, I never thought about it, but I will if you think I should." And she'd smiled and kissed him and thanked her lucky stars for secure, middle-aged love.

With the exception of one particular shopping trip, her husband had no idea she made purchases at the SuperStore. But what she didn't tell Ward paled in comparison to what he hadn't told her. He had left a message on her cell phone, she noted, but she didn't listen to it. She drove back the way she'd come, purple flowers in the ditch by the side of the highway bobbing in her car's wake.

At Lance's burial Stella had stood at the gravesite, Ward solid at her side, and dozens of people stepped up to shake her hand and offer condolences. Rose wasn't there, and as the only next of kin present, Stella asked for and was given the folded triangle flag from his coffin. Jim Culp had held it to his uniformed chest, point down, smoothing the edges. Then he said something about the "symbol of the grateful appreciation this nation feels . . ." and she lost him, refocusing only to watch clumps of black dirt smack against the coffin. She tried to put the flag into her pocketbook and then thought better of it, carrying it gingerly to the car, arms out stiffly, as she would carry a tray of over-full cocktails. "Where the hell is Rose?" she railed at Ward once they were inside with the car doors firmly shut. "How could she not come to his funeral? His *funeral*?" She had told him to drive straight out to the farm, but he'd refused, had said she was overwrought and had to cool down, and all the way home he spoke in tortuous sentences, saying nothing in that droning tone that increasingly plucked her nerves.

Today the cemetery parking lot was almost empty—her sedan was one of only two cars. Her high heels clicked along the cement then sank into manicured grass as she veered off the path in a straight line to his grave. She never brought flowers; she didn't bring a book and sit, reading; she didn't speak to Lance, or trace the chiseled letters of his name. She kneeled, pushed her fingers just outside the bridge of her nose into the bony hollows of her eye socket and cried in short, hard bursts. The constant pressure that squeezed her sinuses and pricked her eyes eased temporarily, and she leaned her forehead against the stone, feeling the grooves of the dates under his name. She couldn't get over that final date, the close of the dash.

After some time she straightened, wiped off the headstone with her handkerchief and brushed a few dead leaves away. Somebody had left a chain of yellow dandelions on top of the stone. They were still alive, so she let them be, arranging them so that they draped nicely. The sky was a bit heavier. Eddie—Ted, rather—might be right about the weather.

At home, she put the food in the refrigerator and opened the windows. Then she stood at the front window, looking out at the lawn. A three-foot fountain was placed in the middle: a stone girl holding a stone bird, perhaps a chickadee, in her palm. This house wasn't palatial by any means, but that little fountain, chosen and installed by Mrs. Eunice Mondragon before the Second World War, made Stella feel like a lady of the manse. This house was her jewel. Though she had redecorated after she'd moved in, it was perhaps too spare. She might tell Ward she wanted to adopt a cat.

She went to sit at the computer in the study. Ward used it for spreadsheet calculations and some business-related ordering. Stella checked her email—three new messages, all of them junk, promotionals from online retail stores. She clicked over to the weather page that Ward had bookmarked to look at the radar. Miles away a gathering, represented on screen in sluggish swirls of gem-like red, blue, and green; a vivid brilliance that, if found in nature, on the back of a frog, for example, might connote poison. The answering machine on the desk was blinking—several messages from Ward, wondering where she was and updating her on the weather alert. She stood, leaving her shoes under the desk, and went to the kitchen.

Stella was an indifferent cook. Yet once again she found herself sitting at her vintage yellow Formica kitchen table, poring over a dog-eared casserole recipe in a magazine that celebrated an artful fantasy of domesticity. Chicken Tetrazzini this time. She had bought all the ingredients at the SuperStore. The list had been in her head, bumping around innocuously: carrots, onions, egg noodles, cream, chicken. Not joining together in any sort of marriage until now.

She had delivered the first dish to Rose soon after news broke about Lance's death. It had served primarily as a gloopy vehicle for the note she'd labored over: *Dear Rose—I am brokenhearted and I know you are too. I need to see you. Please understand me, Rose—We need to talk. Stella*. Written out on the kitchen table, on her best peach stationery. That first note, like all that followed, went unanswered.

Stella hadn't really expected to be acknowledged. It wasn't all goodwill that sent her speeding down the old county road each week with a redolent casserole. *Understand me, Rose*. The dish was inevitably still warm when she set it on the passenger seat, little beads of condensation forming under the tightly wrapped foil. She zoomed down the road, pointedly not watching the Infamous Elm grow larger as she approached Old Man Brown's land. Stella had a feeling that Rose, and that damn tree, were actually hurtling toward her while she froze in place, leaden foot on the gas, waiting for impact.

As new brides, town girls marooned on a farm, she and Rose had sat out back on summer evenings and drank cheap gin, talking about their parents and how nuts they were, and their neighbors too, including Old Man Brown. Stella slung stubbly calves across Rose's lap and sang, "We've seen it, we've done it, now we can just shun it . . . Denial, baby! Call me Cleopatra, queen of." And for some reason this nonsense never failed to make Rose snort the drink out her nose and all over the grass. They'd called it therapy hour.

*Therapy hour*. Stella never had the illusion that she'd known all there was to know about anyone. But maybe the real crux of the matter wasn't that she didn't know others, but, worse to contemplate, that no one had ever known *her*—that all along, she'd been a stranger to Rose, a stranger to herself. She wasn't going to go sit in the basement with a battery-operated radio and a pack of illicit cigarettes. She was going to make another casserole and deliver it. The realization of her intent, and the fact that her intent had been operating off to the side, on its own, without consulting the rest of her, made her stare blankly into her mug of instant coffee. She ignored the ringing phone and focused on the way her head seemed slightly off her body—literally off, as if it were hovering above, watching from a high angle as her fingers smoothed the magazine spine until it split and fell flat open to the page with the recipe she needed.

*Understand me, Rose.*

She has no right to ask and yet she does, and she'll keep asking. *Understand me. I was young. Nobody expected much of me, remember? No, that's not entirely right—you didn't expect me to be anything but true—but what I knew as true was all mixed up, maybe it still is. Who can say the truth about a person? I've been wondering lately, what was the truth of Lance? I don't presume to know it and I don't love him any less.*

Once he reached sixteen Lance could drive to town on his own, and he'd stop at Mondragon's at least once each week, often with the mousy Brown girl who followed him around like a puppy. Stella always paused before saying her unfortunate nickname—*Sill? Sillie?* Ward didn't trust him. He was on edge when Lance was in the store because, he claimed, once he'd seen the boy sidle up to a box of fancy pens and pocket them. Stella brushed off the idea that her husband would see and do nothing to stop it just as she waved aside the thought that her nephew would steal from them. In either case, she had told Ward not to make a fuss, she'd reminded her husband that Lance was his family now.

She boiled the casserole noodles first and then ran cold water over them, setting the colander aside. Her hands were full of chopped onions when she thought of turning on the stereo, and it seemed too much effort to wash them and walk out to the living room to select a CD. So she worked in silence. Cutting up raw chicken made her queasy, but she did it anyway. Then carrots and celery. The phone rang again. She exhaled slowly, waiting for the silence to resume.

When she thought of Lance now, the boy jumbled together with the young man, the baby morphed into a small hand in hers, pulling for attention and asking, *What's for lunch, Anstel?* He was fluid and she, static. She had loved asking teenage Lance questions, listening to him talk. Not so much for what he said, though she remembered most of it (he used "like" and "um" prolifically, and once or twice he called her "man"), but to see his face move as he spoke: the crinkles around his mouth, and the way one familiar eyebrow raised to emphasize a point.

Stella browned the chicken cubes on all sides, and pulled a big bowl out of the cupboard to mix the whole mess together. By two o'clock a Pyrex pan full of gooey, serviceable sustenance sat on the stovetop. While it cooled she took a quick shower. Then she went back downstairs in her robe, picked up the phone, and dialed Ward.

He answered on the third ring, sounding harried and out of breath as he told her that Rose had come into the store. Stella knew what this meant—her attempts were working, her instincts were right. Rose needed her. With shaking hands, she bent to remove her slippers. Ward was telling her to stay put and wait. He said some things about the weather and she hung up as soon as she could, leaving the robe on his office chair and walking upstairs naked, quickly throwing on a t-shirt, painter pants, and her single pair of flat shoes, old blue sneakers. She could walk fine in heels—actually, she could *stride* in heels, and most days she needed to feel encased in something hard, something that meant business. But this was different. She descended the stairs, silent on rubber soles, and went back to the study to collect her purse.

The casserole she left on the stove, forgotten, patient, and heavy with cream.

A faint green tinged the sky; no rain clouds, just a hint of foreboding. As the car rolled down the driveway she leaned over to open the glovebox, fumbled for her CD and inserted it into the stereo. *Brilliant Works of the Western Canon*. She had listened to audio classes for the past few years—history, literature, philosophy—consuming them as if they could make up for the inattentiveness of youth. This series was called Transformative Literature, and it focused on great books that changed history and could, if read correctly, change your life. The teacher had a courtly southern accent and alternated between lofty proclamations and down-home paraphrases. "In the middle of my life," he began, "I found myself in a dark wood, where the very path was lost . . ." She pictured him in a white linen suit, rumpled, with cheeks as smooth as a baby's.

Once Ward had asked if she wanted to take night classes and work toward a degree. She didn't see the point. Stella tried not to dwell on what might have been. Her mother had given her that advice. Before Glennie had met and married Rose's father, launching them on the trajectory that led from the city to Anderson's B&B, she had gone on a date with a new guy most every Saturday. Glennie had called it "kissing frogs." Lately, when Stella thought of her mother it was of the time when they were alone together, the smallest unit. When Glennie was, in fact, younger than Stella now. And perhaps more understandable for that. Perhaps even forgivable.

"We could argue, could we not," the courtly professor said, "that the desire for some pleasures is entirely justified . . ." She pressed a button and the CD stopped. Time to check the weather. But the radio only offered advertisements, chipper voices talking too loud.

The sky still had that sickly tint, and few cars passed. Stella turned on her cell phone to find four missed calls from Ward. She half-listened to the last message. "I've been thinking about Rose and I think that she . . . just sit tight. We'll work it out, we'll . . ."

Maybe they would work it out. Her mother had known how to surmount the insurmountable—and though Glennie had been a neglectful mother and a clingy wife, she'd been devoted to Rose's father. She'd stuck with him to the bitter end. It was only now that Stella saw any value in that, in muddling love and loving anyway, damn the torpedoes, full steam ahead.

She flipped the phone shut, turned up the stereo volume, and there was Eddie's voice, as smooth as ever, reading the list of counties affected by the warning. *A wide swath*, he said, and she wondered whether he'd remarried, and whether he ever thought of her. Or rather, of that girl he'd known—the troublemaker, the one destined to break hearts, not least of which was her own. *Get ready for it, folks. Don't take chances*, Eddie-now-Ted said. *Once again, these are the counties . . .* She hit the CD button, wanting him gone.

No other cars on the road. The view reminded her of the drawings she'd made in middle school art class to learn perspective: the "V" of the road disappearing into a vanishing point, telephone poles shortening toward the horizon. She let herself drift into the opposite lane, keeping one hand loose on the wheel and dialing Rose with the other. The line was busy. Telephone wires danced overhead.

"They are the hypocrites, the flatterers, the sowers of discord . . ." the CD droned. Where was the professor now? Still speaking about Dante's *Inferno*, or onto something else?

The phone rang again. It was Ward and she didn't pick up. He would figure out where she was going. Her husband had always trod carefully when her past surfaced. In recent years it had been in the form of Lance, though now it was Rose and the damn casseroles . . . *Shit*. Stella looked at the empty passenger seat. So much for the Chicken Tetrazzini. *Well, so be it*. The unanswered ring was shrill, and she turned up the volume on the stereo, the courtly professor now quoting something in Italian. A musical cadence filled the car and she felt as if he were finally getting somewhere. This was what they meant by transformative. When he switched back to English she was disappointed, and made a mental note to try language tapes next.

At the intersection for the county road she saw a pickup and a hand out the window palmed her to a stop. She rolled down the window. Tom Muldoon. He pulled abreast and said, "You heard the news? You know what's coming?"

"Yes, yes, thanks. I'm going to check on my . . . on Rose."

"You probably want to just turn around and call her." His eyebrows were spectacular—white plumes that flew up like wings over his outer eye sockets. The rest of his face was so weathered she couldn't have said whether he was fifty or seventy. He wouldn't look her directly in the eye.

"She's not answering my calls." Stella didn't see the point of not leveling. She watched for his surprise to manifest and caught it: a faint twitch in one cheek.

He rubbed his nose with a thick finger. "My wife and son went down to the cellar, that's probably what she did, too."

"I doubt it. She's not answering. She won't talk to me. We have a complicated history, you know . . . I guess everybody knows that." Her laugh sounded fake even to her. "I've got to go there." Just below his left ear there was an ominous looking mole.

"A car doesn't mean anything to a funnel cloud. Ward know you're out here?"

"Ward? Also complicated, wouldn't you know? I thought it would be simple this time, for a change, but—"

He shook his head to shut her up, irritated. To him, she was just a hysterical woman who wouldn't know a windsock from a twister.

"Thank you kindly, but I'd better run," she trilled. "Say hello to the family. I never see Sue in the store anymore." He squinted in the general direction of her cleavage. Stella gave a sugary smile and pressed the gas. "Ta-ta!"

She flicked on the radio. Eddie's voice crackled in and out—telling her something useful, finally?—then he was gone, cut out by white noise. Warnings all around: Eddie, Tom Muldoon, Ward. She was tired of men's voices.

Her phone rang again, flashing an area code that she didn't recognize.

"Hello?"

A delay and then a click. "Hello."

"Hello?"

"Hello." he said again. "I'm calling for Mrs. Mondergun."

"Mondragon. Speaking."

"Ah, hello, Mrs. Mondergun . . . gone. My name is James. I'm calling today with just one question for you." He paused as if she might eagerly urge him on. She pulled the phone away from her ear and looked again at his number. It meant nothing to her. "How would you like to reduce your family's insurance payments by up to twenty-five percent?"

"I don't—"

"We can provide you with an estimate of savings up to a thousand dollars a year. Some families reduce their bills by one third."

"No, I don't think so."

"Okay, Mrs. Monderson, Mondegun . . . What would you spend two hundred a month on, if you had all that extra money?"

"I'd . . . James, how old are you?"

"I'm twenty-two."

"Do you have any idea where you're calling? Do you know what we're in the middle of here? Where are you, James?"

"Ah—"

"You're in the ether. And I don't have time for this."

"Doesn't your family need—"

"My family? Oh, James, you have no idea. I'm trying to get my sister to forgive me for something that I . . . her son just died. Killed! In the war. Younger than you, James. I can't even—"

"I'm sorry, Ma'am. I'll—"

"She hates me, maybe for good reason. But I have to try, you know . . . it's my life's work to be her family. It's not a matter of love or hate, I'm just trying to show up."

"Okay, Mrs. Monderson, I can see—"

"What can you see? Because I'd love somebody with vision to give me some insights. Believe me, I would. What would you do, James, if you found out your husband, who is very kind to you in every way, was getting his rocks off with a massage therapist who—"

"All right, Mrs. . . . Ma'am, I get that this is an inconvenient time to buy insurance, but . . ."

Her sneaker felt oddly flat on the gas pedal, and the sky was brackish. "James?"

"Huh?"

"James, all kinds of things can do damage, but not all of them are the things you might think."

"Okay, Mrs. Mondeson, I'm going to make a little note here to call you back at a more convenient time."

"No."

"We can—"

"No. *Never.* You got that? Write it down."

In the pause she could hear other voices beyond his, hundreds of bodies in a room, pitching their marks. Then a whispered *Bitch*, and a click, and he was gone.

White noise crackled from the speakers. Eddie's voice was overtaken. She was a few miles from Rose's place. Old Man Brown's house perched high on a slope in the distance. Out past it the sky was darker.

*Going to run all night,* Stella hummed, *going to run all day* . . . Something yellow in the field—a shirt, she thought, a person moving through the green with an animal swiftness. She twirled the radio dial to get rid of the white noise; a pop song came on strong but soon faded out. Chances were slim that Rose would talk, let alone make an appearance. Stella listened to herself crying as if it were another station on the radio.

The tree loomed, surprising her as it always did. She blinked, swerved, and screeched to a stop. Stella flung her arm over the seat back and reversed ten feet, pulling the car to an idle by the drooping leaves of the Infamous Elm. Years ago Dutch Elm disease had infected some branches. Old Man Brown had cut off the afflicted limbs to save the roots, and now the trimmed branches, which faced the road, were healthy and high. But on the other side the untrimmed tree had grown so full and heavy that it bowed low, and most branches touched down and then arced again upward. One had snaked itself into the earth and emerged a few feet later to sprout new leaves. A person could walk under the limbs on the west side and feel enveloped, as if what happened within that green scrim belonged in another world entirely.

In the fields, cornstalks stood stiff as sentinels. They started to sway and then bent in unison, flattening toward the earth. Her knuckles were white. She uncurled her fingers from the steering wheel and shuddered, sliding across the seat and reaching for the door handle, keeping her eyes on the tree; looking only at the green, not past it, not up. Stepping out of the car, she walked over to touch the ugly scar on the trunk—gouged by Theo's bumper all those years ago and repaired by Old Man Brown, who filled in the gash with black tar, sealing the wound. She was the reason people called the tree Infamous. The puppydog Brown girl had mentioned it one day in the store with Lance, and Stella had known exactly which tree she meant: this scar, the gnarled branches, the beckoning seclusion.

A persistent beeping came from her car—she'd left the keys in the ignition and the door open. She crouched and pressed her cheek against the black scar. "Please forgive me," she whispered. "I didn't know. Lance." The tree gave off a hum, a vibration felt in her belly and hands, all the way down to her soles. This Elm: one hundred fifty years spent watching over the prairie, the crops, swaying under the weathered sky, offering shade to trotting horses, wagons, tractors, cars; offering itself to Stella as she sped past, not understanding.

She had to find Rose, call Ward, angle her car someplace and end its beeping. But she held tighter, caught by the rough fact of the trunk. Her eyes screwed shut against the gathering wind and her breath snagged in the bark. Heavy branches hid the sky's dark folds. Hail clicked through the leaves in a quickening tempo and twigs snapped overhead. The tree groaned. *Get a grip, Stella, get to the car.* Then a great rushing sound—a freight train, a stampede of horses—and something sharp jabbed the crown of her head. Metal cracked and she unscrewed her eyes to see a funnel flick down and pluck up her Buick, suspending it some six feet off the road, rocking it upright with the wheels spinning gently. The car pointed toward Rose's land, passenger door hanging open as if waiting for her to leap in. It flung down with a metallic crunch and rose again to flip end over end, up the road and into the corn, chips of greenish-blue glass spraying in its wake.

The tree trunk tightened like a bow. She sank lower, lips pressed against the bark, fingers digging in. *I didn't know.* Air snapped and roared. Glass and branches tore through the green, the trunk was rent. Wetness at the base of her skull, a trickle down her leg. Her heart banged against the wood and it wasn't saying *please*, it wasn't asking for anything. It was pure in its rhythm, so clear she could hear it through the din: *This*, it pulsed. *This, this, this.*

# Part II

Where are we moored?
What are the bindings?
What behooves us?

—Adrienne Rich

# 1.

One night when Stella was ten, she woke from sleep assuming she was in the apartment alone. Her mother had gone out dancing and her prim twin bed was still empty; no sounds came from the kitchen. Stella wandered down the dim hall to the bathroom. A single red eye glowed from the corner by the tub, but before she could unfreeze to scream she saw it was only Glennie, smoking. Her mother sat on the toilet in the dark, bare-assed and lost in thought, holding the cigarette in one hand and a clump of toilet paper in the other. Their tiny bathroom was unventilated, and Stella caught a whiff of sour body odor under the familiar cigarette smoke, a layered musk that struck her as more adult even than the smell of rye whiskey. As her eyes adjusted further, Stella could see Glennie's panties and stockings pulled down around her ankles.

Glennie spoke first. "You're like a ghost standing there."

Stella looked down at her pale nightgown, past her flat chest to the skinny shins and bare toes peeking from under the loose hem. "You're like a scary monster," she whispered back.

Her mother lifted one cheek to pat herself dry with the toilet paper, and then kicked the stockings and panties off toward the baseboards. "We're a regular cabinet of horrors." She flushed the toilet and stood, and her silky party skirt, which had been bunched around her hips, slithered down her thighs into place. Glennie bent over the sink and splashed her face. Then she leaned and nuzzled her cool damp cheek into Stella's hair. "I met a really, really nice guy. He says he has a daughter your age. I want you to meet him." They went to the kitchen and made grilled cheese sandwiches.

Stella never asked where Glennie met Rose's father, Gordon. She imagined that wherever they had found each other, it was dark and smoky: couples dancing with their arms locked around each other's necks and sweatstains showing, probably a bar with a name like Sully's. In the crush at the bar Glennie jostled the elbow of a tall, ruddy, well-dressed man, spilling Scotch onto his shirt and over her arm. A thread was plucked from the spool and laid in a line that led Glennie and Gordon out the door, through the dark rainy city and into a whirlwind romance, leading, about a month later, to a "special dinner" for four at the apartment Gordon shared with his daughter.

In the apartment, Stella sat on the strange couch and stared at the blank television. Glennie laughed in the kitchen—she'd clearly spent some time here. Gordon sang a song to Glennie that Stella didn't recognize, in a put-on Irish accent. She felt like she'd been sitting alone for hours by the time the front door opened.

The red hair was the first thing Stella noticed. "I'm Rose." She'd just come from some sort of after-school activity. Her knee socks didn't hide a large scab. Rose reached down to scratch it.

"I know your name," Stella said curtly. "Your father is nuts for my mother." In the kitchen, Gordon's voice had a pleasing lilt over the clinking ice cubes.

Rose was unimpressed. "My father is nuts about everything."

It shocked Stella, hearing the truth spoken like that. For as soon as the words were out she counted them true. Rose had that effect.

When they all sat down to steak and green beans Stella's mother announced, "Girls, Gordie and I are getting married. We'll be a faaaamily." The word stretched out to envelop a foursome where there had been only pairs.

"Why?" Stella asked.

Gordie guffawed and raised his glass. "To love!" he toasted, "To us!" sweeping his free palm toward the ceiling. He held forth about his big plan to restore an old hotel in some little town off the interstate that none of them had ever heard of and turn it into a fancy bed & breakfast, where he'd ensconce them all like Queens of the May. The whole idea left Stella's brain smooth. She thought about her favorite TV dinner: a piece of chicken, buttered corn, a brownie square. Her mind felt like the emptied tray—small, compartmentalized, and easily perforated.

"What are they thinking," she asked as soon as she and Rose were alone, sent to Rose's room with a plate of sugar cookies, "getting married at their age?"

"You think they do much thinking?" Rose's freckles stood out on her pale face like constellations. Later, Stella would recognize this as a sign that Rose was angry. Now she just found her oddly calm.

Stella's chest trembled, but she couldn't tell whether it was from tears or laughter so she tamped it down. "Can I have a Coke or something?"

They spent the rest of the evening looking through Rose's family photo albums, making up stories about long-dead people in stiff collars. It wasn't the kind of thing Stella normally found fun. And yet. She followed Rose's lead until Glennie called from the living room that it was time to go.

As Stella stood, Rose reached out and grabbed her wrist, hard. "We'll have to stick together." Her eyes burned into Stella's. "It will be awful otherwise."

"That went great!" Glennie trilled on the way home. "You girls will get on like a house on fire, just you wait."

In the weeks afterward, as Glennie and Gordie spent too much money on scratchy wedding clothes for the four of them and made an appointment at City Hall, celebrating in advance the night before and almost missing the cab they'd ordered for ten o'clock sharp, yelling behind them for the girls to hurry and grab the corsage from the fridge, Rose and Stella *did* stick together. Stella found her mother's forgotten purse, Rose had the corsage in hand and locked the door behind them. Then Rose looked down, sat on the stair landing, and took off her shoes.

"What are you doing?" Stella asked.

"Take off your socks," Rose said. "We'll switch."

Stella wore pale pink taffeta and Rose was in pale blue, stiff, with too many bows, and socks to match the dresses.

It was a small protest, but Stella was up for it. "One each?" she suggested.

Rose smiled grimly. "Yes, that's better."

Gordie called from below. The taxi honked. They sat side by side on the first step of the landing, Rose's scratchy skirt brushing Stella's leg. She handed Rose her pink sock. The blue one was still warm from Rose's skin as she slipped it onto her right foot and buckled the white Mary Jane.

"We look perrrrrrrrfect," Rose said, standing, pulling her newly acquired Glennie face.

"To! Love!" said Stella, voice rising to capture Gordie's ever-present exclamation points. Glennie's nervous voice rose up the stairwell.

They grabbed hands and ran. They ran down the stairs and into the cab, and that feeling of lightness and speed, of descent, carried them to City Hall and the restaurant lounge afterward, through the toasts of Gordie's buddies and Glennie's tiny meltdown in the bar bathroom when she discovered a cigarette burn in the back of her dress, a wedding gift from a careless partygoer. It pulled them with startling velocity back to their respective apartments, through packing and labeling and saying goodbye to school friends and neighbors and lives already past. It launched them upstairs and down, running errands for cartons of milk, and cigarettes, and requests to the super, and letters to the utility company, the bank; through phone calls from dumb bosses and bill collectors and irate estranged grandparents; to watching the moving men haul and load two apartments full of furniture, dishes, tchotchkes and dubious antiques—*We'll have space!* Gordie boomed, *All the space in the world!*—until the moving men, panting, rolled the truck door closed and double-checked the address—*What town? Never heard of it.*—and Gordie and Glennie slipped the keys under their respective doors a final time, turning to look down at their daughters, starry-eyed and terrified, announcing, *Now the adventure begins.*

Then they were all in the car together: Gordie driving, Glennie riding shotgun, the girls in the back, wind-blasted, dry-eyed, tank full of gas and trunk full of suitcases and last-minute items that hadn't been boxed up—band-aids from the bathroom cabinet, a set of cat-shaped pillows, a sea green wall clock—all chucked in with no rhyme or reason. Like them. Father, mother, stepsisters . . . "Step. What a strange way to put it," Stella said, marveling, because it was sitting on the step at the top of the landing and pulling on that warm blue sock that she had begun to feel a sense of kinship, as if she might for the first time in her life have a cohort, a co-witness.

"One more letter and it's steep," said Rose.

"Or stop," Stella said, and Rose grinned, wind pushing red hair into her eyes.

Rose reached a palm up to pull her hair back and said, "*Stick* sisters," and the rightness of it made them shriek with laughter, until Glennie, hungover and testy, clicked on the radio, twirling to find the most glee-dampening music possible, which turned out to be country ballads. The car barreled down the interstate, speeding further and further from the city, on a blue mapped line that stretched and thinned, past abandoned and working factories, suburbs and exurbs, shopping centers and palatial summer homes, towns with populations in the thousands, in the hundreds; past fields and farms and dwindling prairie, until the spool unspooled completely, thunking them onto the porch of the former Anderson's Boarding House, which Gordie said he had won in a card game and rechristened as a B&B.

The B&B. Two-story, white peeling paint, a rickety porch swing; half a block off the main street in a town that looked ready-made for a movie about the once mighty Midwest. And though they didn't know it that day, they would soon enough: in spite of the new owners, the town would forever call the place "Anderson's." The name was so firmly stuck that eventually even Glennie and Gordie and Rose and Stella would call it that, and the girls became the Anderson Girls, named for the place instead of the other way round.

That first day, after they'd walked all through the empty boarding house and the parents had closed their new bedroom door, giggling, for a "quick nap," Rose and Stella returned to the front porch. Their suitcases sat by the door. No TV to watch, nothing to read. Glennie had given them a book titled *When Your Mommy or Daddy Falls in Love Again*. Rose had left it in the bathroom at a truck stop diner. They looked at each other. Stella's stomach grumbled; nobody had mentioned dinner. Upstairs, Gordie sang *Fly Me to the Moon*. Rose bunched her hair in one hand and held it up. "It's hot," she said. Stella reached into her overnight bag, took out two hairbands and handed one to Rose. They pulled sticky hair off their necks and shoulders and into ponytails. Stella kicked off her sneakers and sat on the porch swing; the chains shrieked, immediately echoed upstairs as Glennie gave a muffled yelp. "They're so dumb," Stella whispered, rolling her eyes. Rose snorted, sat down next to her, kissed the back of her own hand all the way up to the elbow, and slumped against the seatback in a fake swoon. They swung their legs out and flew for a moment over the porch and above the sleepy street. But the swing was in no shape to hold weight—corroded chains jerked hard on the loose hooks above and they fell in a clatter, seat cracking under them and rusty chains slapping the wood. The racket drew the parents down from on high, and rotted planks snapped as the girls rolled among them, laughing, acquiring a few wood splinters but in every other way unhurt.

*

The father breezed into town like an old-time carny man, gladhanding everyone, extracting money from a few unworldly people and then frittering it away on a handful of ill-advised investments and under-the-table gaming. He sat himself in his one asset, the outmoded boarding house that he'd fleeced from a lonely old widow, rumor had it, and drank. There had been big talk of renovations initially, a return to old grandeur. But the money had run out or never materialized, and mostly the B&B customers were as sorry a lot as those in the boarding house's final era of the '60s—alcoholics and fly-by-nights. No one approved of them, of course.

Louise could remember the first time she saw Rose and Stella. She wasn't Louise Logan yet; it was years before she married, and she still had a surname from a father she scarcely knew. She and her mother, Sharon, were in the supermarket, working their way up and down the aisles, when the texture of Sharon's silence changed. Louise looked up to see what had happened. Her mother was holding a jar of peanut butter and watching a wispy woman with a purple silk scarf around her head and two sullen girls in tow, pushing a clackety cart. There weren't curlers under the scarf, it wasn't like that. Glennie was wearing it like a movie star, and sunglasses too. If Ava Gardner had passed by with a shopping list in hand, wobbling on too-high heels, Sharon wouldn't have gaped any more.

Louise was a few years ahead of the girls in school, but they were noticeable. Stella was friendly and would talk to anyone. Rose wasn't *un*friendly, but was more reserved. Like her father, she had a capacity to bamboozle people, a charm that exerted a magnetic pull. Louise, Secretary of the Student Council, could feel this, and pondered its potential use in the political machinations of student government. A pointless observation, because it turned out Rose wasn't interested in student government. She and Stella skirted the edges of groups, clubs, and cliques, accepted by most, belonging to none. It was a neat trick, an outsider triumph. Friendliness without closeness.

Her mother sat at the kitchen table with three girlfriends every Saturday afternoon, playing cards and dissecting their neighbors' lives. With the arrival of this new family, there was more to discuss. Louise hung around the edges while the women played, arranging finger sandwiches on the good china. Sharon usually mentioned "My Seth" at least once during these afternoons, referring to Louise's absent father's political, fiscal, and religious opinions, and noting how those opinions would be affronted by the flaws exhibited so publicly. With each mention his memory was coated in another layer of lacquer so that the real Seth became as unknowable as a pearl. Rose and Stella dressed well, the card players noted, in spite of the family's financial troubles; the girls shared clothes, even shoes, giving the false impression of a varied wardrobe. The mother's influence, Sharon asserted—misspeaking, Louise noted—calling it *illusions of grandeur.*

Within a few years, boys followed them around like puppies. They followed Stella mostly, with her bright lip gloss and flouncy skirts, and the girls were always together so they followed Rose by default. Truth be told, Louise couldn't say exactly why the Anderson girls, and Rose especially, made her uncomfortable. When they strolled through the school corridors arm in arm, Rose had a way of looking through people who mattered. *Uppity* was the word that sprang to mind, though that sounded racial and of course Louise was no racist, because Rose was white.

One day, Louise climbed the steps of Anderson's B&B. Rose answered almost immediately, wearing jeans and a flannel shirt and carrying a spray bottle of cleaner. She was a junior that year, and Louise had just graduated from high school. Sharon had cashed in a favor from a friend in her card club and arranged for Louise to interview for a job at the bank. They couldn't afford college, though that went unspoken.

"Hello," Rose said, her voice neutral.

"I'm here to see a guest." Louise used her best adult voice. Rose didn't ask who, just swung open the door to let her in.

The place smelled of peppermint tea and mildew. Louise often had the feeling that other people's houses were fundamentally sturdier than her own—the walls thicker, the floorboards even, and windows held tight in their sills. Not so at Anderson's B&B, with its shabby rugs and peeling wallpaper. Rose told her a room number and pointed up the stairs. Louise tripped over a buckle in the rug at the top of the landing and pitched forward into the dark hallway so as not to fall back.

The banister under her hand shook as she righted herself. "Be careful," Rose said from below. In her embarrassment, Louise heard rebuke in the tone. She straightened her shoulders and smoothed her skirt, glancing down at Rose. The picture on the wall above the landing was crooked and Louise reached out to straighten it, wanting Rose to read in the gesture, *I'm still better than you.*

She would cringe, years later, thinking of it. But it took that many years to get past what came next: a reunion with her estranged father in his tiny room at the end of the hall. The ceiling sloped low over the bed and they stood in front of the walnut dresser. Even there her head felt too close to the ceiling. "Sit down," he offered, but she declined. His suit seams shone with wear and tiny red veins blotted his cheeks. Louise knew at once that all the tales her mother had spun were face-saving lies.

He exclaimed over how much she'd grown. "I can't believe you're in twelfth grade already." She didn't correct him. He tried to explain why he'd left, a disjointed story about a job offer rescinded and a friend who'd begged his help starting a business. Beads of sweat appeared on his upper lip, and in a way that she'd never felt with her mother, she felt powerful. He was desperate for something only she could give—maybe forgiveness, maybe understanding. She examined his face and found it wanting. Next she looked to his dresser: a half empty bottle of cheap blue cologne, a few coins next to a battered leather wallet. A newspaper folded for the crossword puzzle set off a faint ripple of recognition, a childhood memory of him at the kitchen table.

"Mother wouldn't like it that you called me behind her back," Louise said. "She wouldn't like it that I'm here." Sharon would be home from her shift as a grocery store checker by now, a job they both knew was beneath her.

Her father talked for a while longer, and Louise's heartbeat slowed, as if she was lying down and on the verge of sleep. She surveyed the rest of the room. Two dark ugly oil paintings of boats on a lake, and a rather beautiful walnut armoire. She supposed his suitcase was under the bed. In the end he gave her a phone number in the city—"Irene is a friend. You can reach me there."—and forty dollars that she would spend on a stiff pair of pumps at Dunleavy's. She would never see him again.

Descending the stairs she became aware of her limbs, and was surprised that she was shaking. The front door gleamed. Before it, the foyer opened into the dining room on the left, and on the right into an old-fashioned sitting room, where somebody had left a magazine on a hard-looking little settee. Rose stood by the cold fireplace, running a duster over an assortment of figurines. Afternoon light slanted through the window and Louise could see all the dust that Rose had disturbed collide in the air, a slow motion dance. Her face was shiny, and there was a hole in one knee of her jeans. Still, her expression had an equanimity that Louise had to take as indifference, or worse, superiority.

"You're just moving the dust around if you don't use polish, you know."

Rose set the duster on the mantel and Louise's tremble lessened a bit. A wide ribbon of air moved through her chest. "That's my uncle," Louise said.

Rose glanced at the ceiling as if they might be overheard.

"He's traveling for work, but he won't be staying long."

Rose nodded. "That's what he said."

Louise stepped a few feet into the room. "I've always wondered what this place looked like on the inside."

Rose's fingers dug stiffly into her jeans pockets and her elbows bowed as if she were trying to make space in a crowd. "Now you know."

"It must have been really nice a long time ago."

Rose shrugged.

Louise tried another tack. "Do you have to clean it all by yourself?"

"My dad and Glennie had to go to the city," Rose said. "And Stella's out."

Louise reached toward the nearest furniture—the top of a wingback chair—and drew her finger along it.

"My mother wouldn't like me coming here." She took a breath. "Because of the class of customer. Even though my uncle . . . So do me a favor and don't mention it to anyone, okay?" A long way at the back of Rose's eyes something flickered, but otherwise she didn't move. Louise turned to go and came face to face with her father, waiting at the bottom of the stairs. He'd come after her with car keys in hand, wanting to give her a ride home.

"Honey," he said, his skin clammy, "My car is—"

"Oh, no, that's all right. I have to run some errands."

"I could wait. Your mother—"

"No!" she yelled, and stomped her foot. "Leave me alone already!"

He stepped back in shock, heels knocking into the bottom stair, and shrank, ill-cut suit jacket flapping open. Louise spun to Rose, wanting to sound confident but her voice forked into a higher octave: "Remember what I said!" She slammed out the door, leaving her long-lost father still lost on the stairs and Rose standing watch.

It couldn't have been the first unpleasant customer-related drama that played out at Anderson's, or even the most dramatic. Still, it was *her* drama, and for that Louise felt forever disadvantaged in her dealings with Rose. It deforested something in her, left some small piece bald and raw.

*

Early in his life, before he had learned to slip into confidence like a suit, Ward Mondragon was too easy to single out. His fingernails were always scrubbed and his plumpness indicated a soft life where other boys' was tough. The Mondragons were among the few prosperous families during hard times—blight and recession and the so-called death of the family farm. They were not wealthy, but the warm comfort everyone felt on entering the Emporium clung to the Mondragons as they moved about town. Ward felt it like his own skin—something alien yet inextricable, carried wrongly, by mistake. He envied his schoolmates their sharp knees and sinewy arms. Later, in high school, he grew into his bulk and proved a halfway decent second-string linebacker. He practiced shooting tin cans so as to be ready for the day one of the boys invited him hunting. Through careful attention and practice, Ward became a man's man.

Part of this grew from an understanding of what advantages his lot could bring: attention from girls, whom he found much kinder than boys, less nerve-wracking and relatively easy to impress. He drove his father's clean sedan on the weekends instead of a smelly family truck, and had no worries about paying for a malt and burgers after a movie at the Royale. Ward married the most easygoing girl he knew, Karena Bystrom, a week after he graduated from State with a business degree.

In the first decade after he took over managing the store, a group of farmers would sit on the Emporium porch on Saturday afternoons and watch the town pass by. Though they clogged up the entrance and left the smell of tobacco, they were good for business. Their presence marked Mondragon's Emporium as established, necessary. Late in the afternoon, Karena would take out a tray of lemonade and they'd lift their hats and give her bashful smiles. She'd chatter at them a bit, just enough to make them feel welcome.

One Saturday afternoon in spring the usual bunch chatted on the porch. The skies had opened up half-heartedly that morning, just enough to tamp down the dust and muddy the gullies by the road. A waste as a real rain, the farmers said. Karena called it a sky scrubbing, dustless and sweet. A clean mineral scent rose up off the ground. Someone had brought a box of kittens, trying to get rid of a barn cat's litter, and it sat near the edge of the porch, shifting as the weight inside squirmed one way then another. Kids stopped and squealed, thronged around the box and then dispersed. A few kittens were taken for mousers. The store doors were swung wide to let in the air, and from where he stood at the register, Ward could see northward down the street and insert the occasional comment into the porch club's conversation. Then Rose and Stella arrived.

It couldn't have happened this way, but it's how he remembered it: They walked down the center of the road, linked arm in arm, skirts brushing against each other. Cars parted like a forked river, drifted to the curb and idled. The sun fell on their bare heads and the shine preceded them onto the porch. All the rest of it—sudden curves where there'd been skinny girl flesh, cheeky lipstick, the cloying smell of gardenias—this he noted later. The sway of their skirts announced to Ward and Karena and the porch club that something new was coming. And suddenly, briefly, the whole town was entranced. As if the girls had sprung up from the fields, a product of that fleeting, misty rain.

*The Anderson Girls. Roseandstella.* Whispered, nodded, noted by a raised eyebrow and a prickle at the back of the neck. The Anderson girls had arrived, some six years after they'd first set foot in town. When they stepped up the porch to Mondragon's, conversation faltered and Ward could sense but not see the tipping of hat brims. They were about sixteen, Ward would guess. *Too young for the porch club,* Karena enjoyed pointing out later. If someone had told Ward that two decades later he'd be married to Stella, he would have shaken his head and tried to imagine what could make him a widower at such a young age, because there was no other way he'd be without Karena.

Karena was always good with kids, giving little pieces of candy, and asking nicely after their parents whether they were paid up or not. Ward's favorite college professor—who had gray streaks in the hair at his temples and wore a jacket with leather elbow patches—had said, *Goodwill is one of the great intangible assets of any business.* Karena knew that in her bones. Strange that Ward, born into it, had to learn it.

He watched the girls from a safe distance. Rose had a certain uprightness in her walk. When she turned to look at something her upper body rotated fluidly—no neck snapping or hunching or giggling. Stella seemed to take two steps for every one of Rose's—checkers jumped across a board and back again. "H'lo, Mr. and Mrs. Mondragon," she chimed as they entered the store. That day, they bought the bag of rice they'd been sent for, plus some hairpins and a celebrity gossip magazine. As Rose paid he started to ask after their parents, but thought better of it. They were learning, too, he supposed, to present themselves in a way that made life bearable.

"Best thing in the world," he told Karena later, "is if those girls went away to college."

"Not likely," Karena replied. And she was right.

*

"Look at them," Scottie Dunleavy's mother commanded.

Mrs. Dunleavy stood by the window at the front of the shoestore, watching Rose walk by with her new boyfriend, Theo, and with Stella—the three of them abreast, hand in hand, Rose in the center. They were heading toward The Bluebird, probably to meet Stella's date, one of a rotating number, though lately it had most often been a slick, overly confident water filter salesman named Eddie. Stella chattered away and tugged on Rose's hand, making a face. Rose laughed, and Theo, who was tall, glanced down at her with such helpless adoration even Scottie felt the pang of it.

"Lucky guy," his father said, turning back to the register.

*He knows he is*, thought Scottie, impatient with the obvious. He picked up a display shoe, studying it, watching the stitches loosen and tighten as if the leather were breathing, and gripped hard to steady himself.

What his parents cared for and talked about was so far from Scottie's experience that it was almost foreign. Fashion and good books and the latest movies. Scottie's father gave up on him early, but his mother never had. In her presence, he was both a devastating failure and an astounding genius. The force of her need sent him stumbling into shoe displays. She loved the label of "son," she cared for the symbol of him, her perfection and her failure . . .

"Godawful boots," she interrupted his thoughts, watching the trio walk out of view. "Such a farm boy." She put a hand on Scottie's shoulder, drawing his attention back to the street, outside the gullies of his own mind. A new doctor had just diagnosed an anxiety disorder and pushed a prescription at him, though he had yet to down a pill.

"And there goes Karena Mondragon," his mother noted, carefully laying a trail of breadcrumbs. "She's in a better mood today. Those pants are a nice shade of blue, don't you think?"

"Here is the town," he whispered. "Here are the people." She dropped her hand.

Just then, Ward stepped onto the porch of Mondragon's Emporium to greet his wife. His eyes scanned the street as they always did, and he smiled and waved at Scottie and Mrs. Dunleavy. Scottie and Ward were the same age, and Ward had already taken over from his parents, who had retired to Florida at the earliest opportunity. His mother waved back at Ward enthusiastically. Though he was the closest thing Scottie had to a friend, the sight of Ward depressed him: the desperation, the kindness, the familiarity and contempt. Things happened to his neighbors and he noted it briefly and moved on. What he cared about was:

*seams*
*shoe glue*
*birds*
*the smell of coffee crystals in a fresh-opened jar*

This list had come to him in the early hours of the morning and he'd written the items on an index card in perfect, tiny block print.

"Life's rich pageant," his mother said wearily. "Why don't you go help your father with the new inventory."

*

Rose liked to walk down Main Street after midnight, testing out her night vision, seeing who was where. Storefronts were shuttered and televisions flickered through thin muslin curtains. The town, even in sleep, had a faint electrical dome and outside it the land murmured, velvety and dense. She startled a coyote once, and stopped and tilted her head and listened for the breath and the darkness. Day or night, it was out there.

She never worried about running into anyone she didn't want to see. One night Rose bumped—literally bumped—into two boys from her high school. They shared half a bottle of Wild Turkey and then wandered off, as if all night dwellers were bound by a contract of cordiality. She kept walking, only the slightest weave betraying her alcohol buzz. The Bluebird was silent. Emma Templeton would turn on the lights at 5:00 a.m., Rose knew, an hour before the first shift began. Out behind The Bluebird was the town's most down-and-out business, faring even worse than Dunleavy's Fine Shoes: The Tip Top Launderette. It was a bad business idea to start with, since most people had their own washing machines, and at the very least a clothesline for drying. Gordie had launched the Tip Top with great fanfare soon after they'd moved to town. When migrant labor put down some roots there was a slight upswing in business, and women too poor to own washers came with duffel bags full of muddy work clothes, threadbare sheets and, almost inevitably, kids in tow. During shift breaks, Rose would sit with Stella on the back step of The Bluebird to smoke two cigarettes and watch the women in the Tip Top with their shiny hair and tired eyes and overpriced orange boxes of soap. Seeing people in a private domestic moment, sorting underwear and treating stains, reminded her in some ways of life at Anderson's B&B. Now she passed it by.

A shadow skulked around the next corner. Not the coyote. The red dog that lived with Mr. Rikker walked with her sometimes. Tonight he waited, ears pricked up, until she drew closer. Then the ears flicked and he wagged his tail. She leaned over and ran a hand across his neck, feeling for the collar. "Did you jump the fence again?" He didn't have a nametag. "What's your name tonight?" She usually called him Bingo, and he appeared to understand, though his listening skills were selective. He was content to follow her as she passed the bank and left Main Street to wander through smaller side streets with genteel old houses, most in need of paint. Something small and rodent-like rustled across a lawn and Bingo went after it, silent, faster than he looked. As his tail receded she kept walking, past driveways and dark windows. Tree limbs arced overhead. On this street, the town's doctor and mayor had built homes a hundred years ago. Near the end of the block was Mr. and Mrs. Mondragon's place. It was the kind of neighborhood, Rose thought, where nobody had trouble sleeping. A set of eyes blinked at her from a telephone wire. "Are you an owl?" she whispered. She was momentarily chagrined at how little she knew. What kind of bird, what type of elm, why the grass here grew so soft in summer, who else lived in these houses and how they came to this place.

At First Methodist Church on the corner, Rose took a small cobbled footpath that ran along the old brick building and into the graveyard behind it. A motion-sensor security light blinked on as she passed the church's back corner and she let herself in, leaving the gate open behind her. The light was new. The kids who regularly hung out here on full moons must have left evidence. *Dumb,* she thought, *ruining it for the rest of us.* Rose stood in the darkness near a row of headstones until the light clicked off. She'd been one of those kids. That was how she knew about the Doorway of Destiny.

The story was passed down through the high school ranks to each incoming class: walk through the stone arch in the old cemetery during the apex of the full moon and you'll see your future. Also, the kids laughed, you may get lucky. She and Stella had come when they were freshmen and walked through the Doorway holding hands. Stella had proclaimed it boring and left with a boy. But Rose, though she hadn't seen anything amounting to a destiny, had felt a frisson of excitement—a cloud had passed over the moon and in the dark, bumping into things and righting herself, her other senses heightened. Hearing sharpened, center of gravity lowered, she could find her way to the farthest corner of the graveyard just from the scent of the honeysuckle that spilled over the back fence.

Rose avoided the graveyard on full moons now, only coming when she was sure to be alone. This cemetery had run out of room long ago, in the early 1900s. Now all the dead were laid to rest in a clinical, sprawling expanse out by the interstate. These headstones were old, crumbling, and there was a pleasing decrepitude; the suggestion that death is what happened in the past, death is done. A few of the wealthier old families had built ostentatious stone mausoleums and statues, and she would find the occasional fresh bouquet placed by a dutiful descendant. The Doorway of Destiny was not tended by descendants. She grabbed the stone in each hand and leaned forward over the threshold just as someone brushed through the gate, pushing it further open with a clank. The security light clicked on. Rose ducked and stumbled, losing her grip and falling forward through the arch onto her hands—something jabbed her right palm. She crawled into the shadow of a large headstone, pulling her legs into her chest. The light clicked off. She waited. The darkness in front of her eyes grew darker, and Rose smelled something rancid. Then Bingo poked his snout into her neck, snuffling hard. She reached for his soft chest fur and he settled to a seat, yawning wide to share his horrid breath. "Did you catch that squirrel?" she asked. "Okay, you're right. Let's go."

Walking back along the wide sidewalk the dog kept close to her heels, only darting away when headlights approached. Rose kept walking. A man rolled down a window and leaned his head out. "What are you doing out at this hour?" It was Mr. Dunleavy, Scottie's father, in a suit jacket and no tie. She'd forgotten that the Dunleavys lived on this block too; she had once seen Scottie draping his father's car in a cloth cover out in front of a brick house one block down.

"Oh," she said, "nothing, really. Just walking." Mr. Dunleavy's car was nice, a white, old-style Cadillac. She watched him look her up and down, noting the grass stains on her knees, and had a feeling of power and discomfort that had grown familiar in recent years. "How about you?"

"Business meeting," he said, and left it at that. He peered over his steering wheel and she had the feeling that he was thinking about driving away without another word. "Get in. I'll take you home."

She considered it. For a heartbeat she felt that she had actually fallen through the Doorway of Destiny into a new life and that this was her destiny. Rose stepped back and Bingo came out of the bushes. He put his paws on the car door, stretching himself on hind legs to look in the window. Mr. Dunleavy raised an eyebrow. "He's my escort," Rose said.

"Is that Rikker's dog?"

"Yes." Under the streetlight they could see what looked like blood on Bingo's mouth. She added, dumbly, "He's cute."

Mr. Dunleavy's approval was not forthcoming. "I can't have the dog in my car. Are you going to get in? It's really late . . ."

Rose felt her destiny ripple and fade. "I have to walk him home," she pointed at Bingo, who had given up on Mr. Dunleavy and wandered over to poop on a neatly trimmed lawn. "Thanks anyway."

Mr. Dunleavy still didn't leave. "What's his name?"

"I don't know, actually, it's not on his tags. I call him Bingo."

"Huh. You should know his name." He pressed the gas and drove on, engine purring.

She made good time the rest of the way home. Rounding the corner by the Rikkers' backyard she leaned over, grabbed Bingo by the collar and held onto him until she could open the gate of the chain link fence and shut him inside. She crouched and stuck her fingers through the links, wanting to say *thank you* and *goodbye* and *be careful*—but he trotted away too fast. As she stood she saw someone peering out the window, so she hurried on. The trick was getting to the B&B before daybreak. Not because the parents were awake by then; they slept 'til almost nine o'clock, leaving the girls to start the coffee and set out pastries for paying guests, when they had them. But she and Stella had their own rules, and Rose followed them to the letter.

In some ways, the walking was just a prelude to coming home. She climbed the fire escape at the back of the house and crawled through their bedroom window just as dawn lit the sky's edge. Stella, who had arrived home after her date not long before, was still awake and rolled over in bed, hair dark on the pillow, eyes bloodshot. Rose shucked her clothes quickly and dove under Stella's blankets. The worn cotton sheets printed with tiny blue flowers, Stella's pale arms, their legs twining together—all of it pushed the darkness back for another day as warmth moved from Stella's skin into Rose's and the boundary between them blurred. She shivered.

"You're home," Stella murmured, "tell me all," and Rose whispered her night across the pillow.

Eventually word got out about their nighttime adventures. People said a lot of things, each story as true as a dime left on a railroad track—twisted and stretched out of proportion, but recognizable.

*

In the final year of her illness, Perry's mother, Mae Ford Brown, took to dabbing handkerchiefs in lavender oil and wearing them over her face like a domestic bandit. The house was cold and too quiet, medicinal smells lingering in her sickroom. Perry would come home from school and see her standing in the front parlor windows—apron wrapped twice around her skinny frame, white kerchief over her nose and mouth and another covering her hair. Visitors jumped, startled. Some days, most days, he'd start, too. A faint jump of the pulse, seeing his mother swathed in white at the window looking like a ghost already.

His Old Man cried like a boy at her funeral, the preacher sat and muttered, church ladies scurried in the kitchen. Perry didn't cry. He felt like he was alone in a field, dirt pressed firmly against his back, cloudless sky blank overhead, voices along the edges too soft to hear, him too empty for tears—nothing but the flat line of horizon. Until a month or so later when all the ladies' casseroles ran out and they turned back to their own pantry for supper. The fruits and vegetables Mae had preserved lined the shelves in neat rows: tomatoes, zucchini, peppers, pickles, a dark purply currant jam, his own snot salty and slick on the roof of his mouth.

It helped, then, to have Theo on the neighboring farm. But it had always helped. Perry had known Theo his whole life: a neighbor, a wished-for big brother. Theo's family and the Browns had been neighborly for generations, a relationship built out of shared hardship, favors, and side-by-side pews at church. His Old Man had had respect for Theo's grandfather, but Theo's dad was another story. "No grit," the Old Man said, "No guts, no instinct for it. A dreamer is worthless out here. The son's the same. " Lazy about crop rotation, late to the game with pest control, and haphazard about his equipment—the family tractor was always breaking down. The neighborliness had gone through a rough patch some years back when the Old Man had refused Theo Sr.'s request to borrow a working tractor, right in the middle of the harvest. No money, was the problem. They had less land than the Browns, and Perry knew that when his Old Man looked east he was contemplating an annex, calculating how much he could increase his profits. Calculating, above all, how his action or inaction might speed the acquisition along. Theo's parents died too young, in a horrible accident on the highway after visiting a cousin across state lines, and Theo had scrabbled it out in the years since. The Old Man had been more helpful after, but just helpful enough. He was biding his time.

When Theo started dating Rose, the Browns weren't sure what to make of her. Perry had seen her in town, standing with Stella on the porch of their parents' B&B. They were like butterflies stuck to a dusty window screen—so colorful the rest of the street looked drab. The girls stood close together, whispering secrets, skirts blowing into each other's legs. Red and black, hot and cool, that was Rose and Stella. He thought the whole place was in for change: klieg lights, a brass band, angels singing.

The first time he spent any real time with Rose was after his Old Man tried to teach him how to drive, getting mad every time the gears ground together, yelling until Perry couldn't hear directions anymore—only gravel and grinding. "Clutch *then* gas, boy! Listen! Are you listening?"

Perry wound up on the side of the road three miles from home, watching the Old Man's taillights disappear. It was twilight, Perry's thirteenth summer. The horizon glowed in front of him, earth darkening and sky a uniform pale. He came out of himself then, the way he always did after spending any stretch of time with his father—flexed his hands, heard knuckles crack, tilted his head back.

It was quiet in that way that lets you hear each individual sound. The wind rustling across the corn tops, gravel knocking against itself underfoot, birds calling to each other, *too-wee, too-wee,* his slowing heartbeat, the receding engine. No thoughts in his head but naming the sounds, placing them, hanging little labels on the scene like the illustrated reading primer his mother had once given him. Truck, horizon, road, farmer, bird, corn. *Boy.*

Theo came into view against the eastern sky. They walked parallel tracks, calling to each other, nothing of importance.

"You walk here?"

"No."

"Drive?" Theo asked. Perry had told him that he wanted to learn.

"Yeah." The dust was only just settling from the Old Man's retreat.

"I can show you some on my truck."

"All right."

"You got beetles?"

"Some."

"We just dusted again."

Perry knew that. He'd seen the whole production. "Guess they moved right over to our acres." Something his Old Man would've said.

"Well, you can dust, send 'em back my way." It was impossible to anger Theo.

Perry nodded, feeling the land flat underfoot.

"I'd like it if you came for supper. Rose is going to cook a chicken. You can drive home, after, in my truck. Get a little practice." They walked along, not abreast, more than four feet between them. Perry on the road, Theo weaving along the edges of the field, raising one hand palm down to run along the tops of the corn.

He ate with them. Theo and his girlfriend, Rose, who charred the bird and undercooked the potatoes. They were like the newest family that ever was, talking softly, opening the circle to let him in. Rose gave him some tinfoil-wrapped biscuits to take home, touching him between the shoulder blades as she walked them into the driveway past her father's rusty LeBaron. Perry drove Theo's truck home—gears grinding only once, his belly full of chicken and coffee. Theo sat in the passenger seat, and for a time there was no sound at all but for the engine and the wind over the fields. Two farmers driving up a road.

He stiffened as soon as he set foot inside his father's house that night, the creaky floorboards echoing the unnatural flat of the land he'd felt earlier. So he went out to the barn and slept on a blanket in the hay, the cats' eyes gleaming round him with what he told himself was steady devotion.

After that, on as many afternoons as he could get away, Perry would head over to Theo's place, preparing some trumped-up excuse that they never asked him for.

He could almost always count on Rose being there, and Stella was sometimes with her. The girls came as a pair, Perry thought, filling Theo's house with music and fresh cut flowers, and treating Perry like a little brother. "Perry, honey," Stella would say, touching his shoulder, "run and pull some mint from that shady spot by the creek and I'll make us all some crushed mint lemonade." Or "Honey, be a sweetheart and run and ask your daddy if he can loan us the big pickup for the afternoon. Theo needs it to clear a felled oak."

He never talked much, by custom and from natural shyness. They knew if they wanted to hear a peep from him they'd have to ask questions. After he'd done some chore they'd sit him on the porch and give him a lemonade. *What'd you learn today in school, Perry? Are you still sweet on that girl, what's her name—Nina? You know any songs on the harmonica to play for us?* And he'd blush or nod or shuffle. But he always listened.

Rose was probably going to marry Theo. Perry knew this because Stella told him, in that breathy, half-mocking tone of hers. "I never thought we'd stay in this godforsaken town, is the thing. We're city people! But Rose isn't listening to reason."

"Stella, shut it," Rose said.

A long sip of mint lemonade for everyone. "The point is," Stella went on after a while, "Theo is trying to figure out how to keep more money coming in, he might get into sales and travel with my boyfriend Eddie, so we'll need a man around the place. Maybe you—how'd you like that?"

He shrugged, blushing.

"Stella, *enough*," Rose said. They always bickered like that, harmless, Stella sassy and Rose sharp.

It was too tart, but he'd have died before telling Stella her homemade mint lemonade gave him a sour belly. He picked up his harmonica to play "Javelina." Rose was shelling peas so fast they pinged into the pan like rain. Stella paused to repin her dark hair. As she raised her arms his eyes followed the curve of her shoulders and lingered on her neckline and the curving flesh underneath. Then he felt Rose's gaze—she was staring, a tiny smile on her face. She cocked a reddish eyebrow and gave her head a faint shake: *Don't think you're smooth, kid*. His whole body went hot. The music jangled wetly and flatlined. Perry dropped the harmonica to his lap along with a string of spit.

"Well!" Rose said.

"You okay, honey?" Stella asked. "Overheated?"

"Sounded like dead cats there at the end."

"Don't make fun of him, Rose . . . you okay, Perry?" He nodded mutely, took a sip of lemonade and promptly farted, quick and hard. Rose pressed her lips together, trying not to smile. Stella put a hand back up to her hair. "Well, I sure liked that first part. Really pretty."

"Gotta go," he muttered, and ran home, their soft laughter at his back. He knew full well, and so did they, that he'd be back the next day.

The problem with knowing people forever is that your image gets stuck. They stop seeing you grow or change and instead see you frozen in some moment that makes sense to them. And you can't pick the moment. He knew Rose and Stella would forever see him as that awkward boy: skinny, bug-eyed, harmonica-sucking. And what could he do with that?

*

Rose didn't expect to be good at growing things. "You have a green thumb," Glennie told her, surveying the small patch in the yard behind the B&B where Rose had planted summer squash, tomatoes, basil, cucumbers, a flowering vine she'd forgotten the name of—all from seed packets purchased at Mondragon's. Rose stood at the kitchen window, wanting more space to garden. Her stepmother, having bestowed this compliment like a jewel, wandered off to ask Gordie where she'd left her reading glasses. Glennie and Rose's father spent their days quarreling and drinking and strategizing new ways to "break out of the slump," as Gordie put it. In true Gordie and Glennie fashion, they were keeping up appearances and only stepped out perfectly dressed, smiling brilliantly. They went out much less often now. Glennie's smoker's cough hadn't quite morphed into the cancer that would kill her.

Rose stepped into the backyard to fill her lungs with fresh air, attention caught by the colors that she'd coaxed from the dirt. In spite of the size of Anderson's, Rose felt more and more as if they lived in a rabbit warren—dark cluttered rooms, long narrow corridors. When Stella was out she slept badly, tossing and turning, the temperature of the pillowcase never right. Her night walks became more frequent. It was Stella who kept the walls expanded with her stories, her capacity to meet new people, their double dates. Rose knew her job, in part, was to keep Stella from making impulsive mistakes. Anyone could see that. Only Gordie seemed to notice that she needed Stella just as badly. The self-absorbed force field that had powered her father blindly through half a century had surprising moments of clarity that allowed him to comment on her life with an insight that took her off guard. "You need a woman around, my girl," he had told her years before, when she'd complained about his marriage to Glennie. "Lord knows you need more than me." Right he had been, right he was.

With Stella's encouragement, she took on some shifts at The Bluebird Café, at first just opening the register and getting the morning pastries ready for the steady stream of customers who came in for Emma Templeton's espresso and homemade pie. Emma had worked as a waitress for decades before scraping together the money to buy out the original owners, the Dunbar family. The Dunbars had named the place The Bluebird of Happiness. Ironic, since Dill Dunbar had terrible gout and spent his final years in the kitchen reclining like a pasha on a plastic lawn chair and hurling insults at his wife and their two unlucky kids. When Dill finally died, one of the children sullenly scraped "of Happiness" off the two front windows, and by the time Emma bought them out, everyone just called it "The Bluebird." "And who am I to change it?" Emma asked Rose during one crack-of-dawn workshift, the coffee maker hissing as it heated up. Like most of Emma's questions, it did not require an answer.

The "of Happiness" was gone but if you knew where to look, a faint outline was still visible on the window. Every evening in early summer between 6:42 and 6:51, the setting sun hit the glass in just the right place and a shadow slanted across the floor: *ssenippaH fo*.

Rose watched for it.

She met Theo at The Bluebird. He first registered as a presence during a Saturday afternoon shift. Stella was working too—they split tips and tables down the middle—and when he walked in he looked from one blue polyester uniform to another, torn between them. "Have a seat!" Stella beamed, shooing him to a booth in Rose's section. He was lanky and agreeably nice-looking, but not unsettlingly handsome like Stella's on-again-off-again boyfriend, Eddie. Theo was several years older than Rose and Stella, with a broad face and clear brown eyes. He ordered a slice of apple pie and a root beer. When Rose took it to him he said *thankyou* and then cleared his throat and she paused a moment, wondering if he was preparing to say something else, but rushed off when no words came.

It wasn't an instant meld—no soul spark, no meeting of the minds. But he came back the following Saturday, and the one after that. Gradually he took root in Rose's section. He seemed to trust her implicitly, which struck her as odd, though he seemed to trust most people. There was a certain not-of-this-world-ness about Theo, and she and Stella discussed it, studying his life once they came to know him. "It's that farm," Stella said. "It's a different world out there. Slower, salty earth, and that sort of thing."

"Salt *of* the earth," Rose reminded her.

"Exactly."

Unlike Gordie, Theo was a hard worker. He barely drank and didn't smoke—he helped Rose to quit cigarettes, in fact. The first time he took her out to his land it wasn't the quiet that struck her, or the green corn, or the wide expanse of sky. Late afternoon, in Theo's blue truck they crunched up the gravel drive in front of his empty house. He had no family left. "Home sweet home," he said, voice free of irony. Against the land and sky, sun dropping in the west, the small farmhouse was outlined like a paper cutout: strong edges, solid and solitary, a clarity of purpose. That feeling of clarity stayed with her. Yet the light also made his place indistinct and thin. "What color was the door and trim? How many windows?" Stella asked her later, and Rose had no idea.

She handed over her body that day like a slice of apple pie at The Bluebird, matter of fact and polite. His gentleness didn't surprise her because that was Theo to a T. "Can I call you T?" she asked him, after, lying in the brass bed that had belonged to his parents.

"Just so long as you call me," he replied. She laughed. A fine sheen of sweat covered them both, and the skin of her breasts and belly was pink from stubble burns. "Let's go again," he said. "It'll be better for you from here on out." She pressed herself against his warm chest, understanding that it went both ways now, that she also trusted him.

"How'd that happen?" she whispered into his skin, so soft he couldn't make it out.

Some time after that she brought the leftover seeds from her packets and casually scattered them in the fallow garden plot that ran along the side of his house. She took the subsequent bounty as a sign. How could she not? Cherry tomatoes, zucchini, cucumber, and a luxuriant length of vine that produced three large, perfect cantaloupes. All with barely a glance, just the occasional watering. "So damn *easy*!" she told Stella. "So much more space!"

"Don't you think he might be helping it along?" Stella asked. "You know, when you're not there."

"He doesn't have time," she told Stella. It was likely true. He pushed his shoulder against the endless work like it was a heavy oak door he had to break through. That entranced her, too.

"Rose and the beanstalk," her father said, eyeing her pole beans as he stood at the kitchen sink before dinner one Tuesday night at the B&B, running the water until it was cold enough for his drink. Gordie wouldn't eat what she grew. Food had lost its appeal for her father; he was in an early stage of heart disease, beginning to grow gaunt.

"How was your meeting?" This was the question they all asked Gordie when he came home, the meaning of *meeting* broad and vague in the family vocabulary. A drink, of course, with a friend, an "angel investor," a card sharp, or his own reflection in a dim mirror.

"Magnificent!" He cleared his throat, phlegm rumbling in his chest. "Promising. Chet Featherstone may have found a buyer for the Tip Top."

"Really?" Rose no longer watched her tone when talking with her father. It had been too long; she'd been doing his laundry since she was eight.

"Don't mention it to Glennie yet. I don't want to . . ."

"Right." She took a breath and told him then that she was moving out to go live with Theo, that they were talking about marriage in a couple of years. "I've graduated now, I'm ready. Stella will come stay too, for a while."

Gordie set down his glass and looked at her. She did not rush in to fill the silence. His shoulders were still wide, his suit jacket impeccable, and his lined brow had a reassuring gravitas. She could see why people, certain kinds of people, were given to loaning him money.

"I thought you girls would run like hell for the city," he finally said.

"I know," she agreed. "But we can have a good life on the farm."

He took a long sip, ice clinking. His hand was steady and his face sober when he clicked the glass back onto the counter. "I hope so."

It wasn't often that Gordie held back an opinion. He was not drunk, though he played at it so well it was hard even for her to tell. She gazed at him, trying to see through his watery eyes straight into the brainpan behind them. She'd never understand him, why he was the way he was, so prone to folly, running off the edge of the world with a treasure map clutched in hand.

"I hope so, too," Rose said. The front door slammed and Stella's quick tread came toward the kitchen. Glennie called from the sitting room and Stella veered off path to answer her mother. They'd sit down to dinner together at 6:30, a tradition held tight, one that Rose had every intention of continuing with her own, better, family. She turned to the stove, lighting the burner under a pot of water.

Gordie put his hands on her shoulders and pulled her to face him. Of all the words he ever said to her—and God knows her father talked a blue streak—it was these words she remembered. Scotch on his hot breath as he whispered into her ear: "We live from hope to hope, my darlin' lass."

# 2.

Scottie was running the shoe store on his own now. Before she'd died, his mother had listed what he had to improve in his dealings with people: "Son, pay attention!" she'd said. "I'm talking here about people skills . . ." While she'd droned on, he'd watched a bumblebee crawl around the window frame in his mother's bedroom. Every once in a while it had summoned the energy to buzz and push itself at the pockmarked glass. *No dice, bee,* Scottie had thought, just as his mother said, ". . . and I know it's not something you always notice, but believe me, other people do. Do you understand?"

"Yes," he'd said firmly, his attention caught by movement out in the yard. A raccoon, foraging around the trash can. He still heard the cadence of her voice in his head. "Dressing well murmurmurmur . . . eye contact murmurmurmur . . . ironed shirts murmurmurmur . . . smile, Scottie, smile."

"I think you're the best mother in the whole world," he'd interrupted, mostly to get her to shut up, and was terribly embarrassed when she'd burst into tears and held out her arms. For what seemed like an hour, she'd sniffled into his hair.

Now he remembered her tears more than her actual words, and not unpleasantly, though it was all mixed up with the sounds from the street and the tireless effort of that dying bumblebee. Though countless others appeared, he never saw his mother's ghost standing at intersections. She stayed right behind his shoulder, in his blind spot, near him but forever out of sight.

From the store window, he watched Stella walk up the street. She was coming from a shift at The Bluebird, and still wearing her powder blue uniform. She'd switched out of work shoes, he noticed, and wore a pair of perilous looking slingbacks. A man was with her, not one that Scottie recognized. Stella pushed her hair out of her eyes and laughed a bit too enthusiastically at something he said. The man held the door of Rikker's Liquors open with a flourish.

When they returned to the street, each held a bottle in a paper bag. The man leaned in, whispering something into Stella's dark hair, and she took a step back. Scottie could see restlessness in the grip of her fist on the bottle, and in the way she took a quick sidestep toward the open door of Mondragon's. She looked inside and called something to Ward, waving, and then shook her head at the man. *Maybe next time*, her lips moved.

*Maybe*, Scottie thought.

"Buzz, Mama," he said aloud to his empty store, as if speaking in bee language would make a difference, would cross over and she'd hear him, somehow, and not need translation.

*

In the earliest days of her marriage to Perry, Nina Brown expended so much energy trying to please, to slow the arrows her new husband and father-in-law aimed at each other, that she barely noticed when some of them grazed her. She was seventeen, trying to finish her senior year of high school, and up all night with a fussy baby. They ate breakfast together when the sky was still dark, silent because the Old Man didn't like morning chatter. Perry was gone in the afternoons, working at Logan's Oil & Lube to learn about engine diagnostics and repair. He was taking classes at the Vo-Tech too. When the baby was old enough, Nina was going to become a certified nursing assistant, and eventually a nurse. They called it their escape plan.

One day after lunch with her father-in-law, who broke his silence only to tell her that she used too much mayonnaise, she strapped the baby into the car seat and headed toward town, no clear idea where she was headed—the empty church? her mother's? the grocery store?—listening to the strange little whimpering sounds that were not, could not, be coming from her. "Shhh," she said to Sill, big-eyed in the back seat.

On the county road, she saw Theo's truck, with Rose's red head behind the wheel. Rather than just waving past, Rose slowed, leaning out the window to call across to Nina. "How's it going?"

Nina took a breath and let it go. "The baby won't stop fussing," she sobbed.

Rose peered into the backseat at Sill, who was quietly sucking on a stuffed monkey. "Come for lunch tomorrow," she said.

"My . . . Mr. Brown needs . . ."

"Sherwin Brown can make his own sandwich. Come on over any time before noon."

Nina showed up promptly at 11:45, Sill hoisted on her hip. Stella swung the door open, holding Lance's hand as he pushed at the screen. Nina had spoken to them only briefly before this, though she'd listened to Perry go on about how great Theo was, and how it was so nice at Theo's house after he married Rose. She knew that Stella had been divorced not long before and that she worked at The Bluebird and helped out with childcare. She knew that Rose had a brisk competent air. But that was all Nina knew, which, it suddenly occurred to her, was not enough at all—and now here she was standing on the porch expecting a free lunch.

"Good, you're here," Stella said, pulling her in as if they'd done this forever. "You can help peel the eggs."

They made egg salad, with plenty of mayonnaise. The next week, Nina went back again, and the week after, until it became a regular Wednesday lunch, sometimes Saturdays too. Nina wasn't sure what they had done to make her so comfortable. It had to do with Stella—she seemed bored, and was looking for someone new to talk to. She was used to getting attention, Nina thought, and filled the hours Nina and Sill spent there with chitchat and stories about her high school adventures. There was something infectious in the way she tossed her hair and raised an eyebrow to punctuate a sentence, hungry for approval but self-deprecating about it. Rose, too, made Nina feel at home—she was quieter and less overt, but always welcoming. They took pains not to let her act grateful, and gave her things to do. Nina would sit in the kitchen with them, peeling potatoes or sifting flour, watching Lance stamp around and Sill, on a square blanket by the table, pushing herself up to follow the boy with her eyes. Her baby knew it too—here they could be happy.

"Hand me the colander, would you, Nina?" Rose asked that first day, pointing at the cabinet. Soon enough, Nina knew her way around their kitchen as well as her own. They went on picnics at Johnson's Creek, and though it was technically on a neighbor's property, they called it "our swimming hole."

She hadn't expected Rose to be so steady, so certain of things, coming from the people she came from. And yet she was, or seemed to be. Nina paid attention to that—studied it, even.

Their swimming hole. Oaks ringed the water at Johnson's Creek, and inevitably dead branches fell in and lay rotting on the muddy bottom, giving off a rich murky sediment. It wasn't the pristine, clear lake from some picture on a calendar but it was theirs, surprisingly deep, and cool. Rose and Stella loved it, and because they did, Nina did too. Stella would call over and they'd make a picnic lunch, gather the children, and meet there on the banks. They dipped the kids in the water like tea bags, there was a hum of conversation and laughter, and the constrictions around Nina's heart loosened for a time.

One day in particular, she and Stella and Rose sat on the banks keeping flies off the food. Theo was in the water with the kids and a couple of inflated plastic rings. Perry was due to show up later; the Old Man wanted him to finish some chore. Rose and Stella were arguing about something—they often squabbled, those two, and it sounded, if you didn't listen to the words, like old women on a park bench, speaking in a foreign tongue and saying things that were rueful and meandering, never urgent—as if they had all the time in the world. Nina lay on her back against the checked blanket, watching dappled leaves move against the sky and listening to the trees. Her muscles softened and light pulsed warmly through her eyelids. She drifted off until Theo's yell and a rushing of air woke her. Then splashing and a wave of something not yet fear, but rumbling toward it. Rose and Stella weren't on the blanket anymore.

"Sylvie," she said, hinging bolt upright. There her girl was, in orange water wings and purple bathing suit, her face contorted in a wail, her little potbelly straining with the effort. Nina plucked her out of Stella's arms, holding her daughter to her chest and bouncing, still not knowing what was happening. Nina's calves were wet—she'd waded in without noticing. Stella stood at her side, eyes scanning the water. Two heads surfaced at the same time—Theo's slick as an otter, Rose a dark red. They were in the shady overhang of a dead tree, and Theo's voice bounced off it and across the water so that Nina heard it as clear as if he'd whispered in her ear: "Where is he—Rose, I just turned around for two seconds to take Sill back to—" Rose sucked a deep breath and went under.

"No," said Stella, at Nina's side. She took three steps and dove, fully clothed. Theo went down again too. Suddenly Nina was alone with Sill, water lapping her shins, clutching her quieting baby and looking at the ripples where her three neighbors had been. No, four. Four neighbors. Lance's rubber ring floated a few feet downstream, empty. It was impossible that a boy could disappear surrounded by adults in a swimming hole no more than thirteen feet across. *It wasn't—he couldn't—*A red-breasted robin swooped across the water and arced upward to rest on a forked tree branch.

Theo and Stella broke the surface, clutching each other's wrists, each briefly hoping that they had the boy in hand. Theo flung Stella's arm away. "Where?" he panted. "Nothing—" Stella said. "There's his floaty!" Nina screeched, pointing to the shallows. Sill was asking for something—juice, she wanted juice, and she was hungry too. Flies circled the blanket, buzzing over their forgotten potato salad and lemonade. Theo tried to swim right to the floating circle, but it was too shallow. Stella dove under, resurfacing almost immediately because she'd sucked in water with a jerky sob. *This is not happening,* Nina thought. *This is another person on another blanket somewhere else and I'm dreaming it.* The birds sang happily.

"Applejoos!" Sill demanded. "Wait," Nina said, and misspoke: "We have to wake for—" meaning, *we have to wait for*—but in either case she never finished because Rose broke the surface, holding the body of her son. She walked out of the water in a straight line, purposeful, almost unhurried, rising fast and straight but barely moving—as if by force of will, not muscle. Her wet blouse and shorts clung to her strong limbs. Did she walk on water? No. Well, Nina couldn't say. She glided, as no one can in wet clothes, carrying a limp boy. No splashing or struggle. Her hair as red as that robin and her path as smooth.

Lance's skinny shoulders were fragile against Rose's right arm, his knobby gray knees slung over her left. On the soft bank, Rose knelt and pushed on his chest. She rolled him to his side. A spurt of water trickled from his mouth. His lips were blue, and his eyes half-open and sightless. Then Rose pressed her lips to his and breathed and breathed again, and Nina slowly became aware of a great commotion all around them. Theo and Stella struggling out of the water, Perry and for some reason the Old Man too, arriving late to the scene, sliding around the muddy banks and yelling advice, yelling about a doctor. But Nina felt as still as Rose, as if they alone, and their children, were outside time. The hubbub went on around them, but what really happened that day, the impossible act that Rose pulled off, that happened under the calm eye of God. All the rest was invention.

After the twelfth breath Rose paused and looked up, lighting on Nina. "Come on," she said, "come on." Nina stepped heavily toward Rose, but Stella brushed past, knelt on the other side of the boy and put her hand on his throat. *Come on*, Nina heard again, though it wasn't Rose who said it. Then Lance opened his eyes, coughed, rolled to his side, and vomited into Rose's cupped waiting palms.

After Rose brought Lance back from the dead, there was a long blank space. Nina didn't remember what they said, or who gathered up the picnic things. She didn't remember how they got from the creek to Rose and Theo's house. Nina snapped-to in the kitchen. The front door slammed. The Old Man had called the doc and he'd come, proclaimed the boy fine, and left. Stella stood by the stove, holding Sill. Lance was standing there (standing! breathing!) saying he wanted toast and jam. None of them had eaten. Perry and Theo and the Old Man weren't in this part of her memory at all, though surely they had been there, perhaps seeing the doctor off.

Nina touched Sill's face and saw the pulse beating in her daughter's chubby neck. She could barely look at Lance. He made her eyes hurt. Some strange incandescence had overtaken him. Images came before sound, and when the sound came back the kitchen was unbearably noisy, the lingering food smells overwhelming. Nina wandered away, leaving Stella to cope with the kids, and walked down the hall into the bathroom. She turned the key in the lock, pressed her back against the oak door, and sank to the floor. "What is your life?" she whispered. "It is even a vapour, that appeareth for a little time, and then vanisheth away." The daisies on the wallpaper trembled. Her hands rested on her knees, and she noticed there was a perfect half moon of dirt under each fingernail.

Another sound intruded, a steady clacking, and at first she thought her own teeth were chattering. Then she saw Rose, sitting sopping wet and fully clothed in the dry, claw-footed tub, half hidden by the shower curtain. Rose was looking at Nina, had been watching her, and for the first time ever in her dealings with another human (she was young, after all, and sheltered), Nina felt such a deep, vast chasm between them, it made her hackles rise. The whites of Rose's eyes were too white.

"Rose," she finally choked, "you'll catch your death."

Rose started laughing. Hysterical laughter, but near enough to the old Rose that Nina was able to stand and walk forward, and say appropriately soothing things, and help Rose out of the wet clothes, and draw a warm bath, and smooth her forehead—all the while feeling that they were walking, each of them now, on a grave.

Nina was young then, yes. Impressionable. She looked up to Rose and Stella. But that didn't account for it. Afterwards, she said to Perry, "It was a miracle. Did you see what Rose did? A miracle." And he told her she was reading too much into it, that she'd been so shocked she'd missed most of the action and that it was fully explainable; Rose wasn't superhuman, none of them were. But Nina knew a naysayer when she heard one. She was raised on a farm, she'd seen plenty of death. Lance had been dead. And Rose brought him back.

Then he was standing in the kitchen, asking for food, and all of them acting like nothing had happened.

*

Eddie started the game. He was very good at fun. In the early days of her brief marriage, it surprised Stella to see the gold band on her finger; but even more than that, it surprised her to see her husband's face when he looked at her. When she opened the door to greet him he would pause as if caught in a spotlight, a honeyed grin lighting his black Irish features. He had asked her to marry him out of the blue, walking up to her at The Bluebird during a month-long trial separation, ignoring the man sitting at her table as if he were just another bottle of ketchup and dropping to one knee right there in the middle of the café. Even Emma Templeton had been a bit dazzled.

One Friday he arrived at the farm after a two-week sales trip, shirtsleeves already rolled up and tie long gone, sweeping Stella off her feet in the middle of the driveway. Rose and Theo came onto the porch to greet him. "Where's your softball?" he asked Theo as soon as he set Stella down, and they went, the four of them, past the corn, gold as wheat in late September, crossing into Old Man Brown's fallow field to play a kind of tag-base-dodge-ball, Eddie starting first, winding up and tossing to Stella, who caught the ball neatly and chased down Theo to tag him. Through some unclear made-up-on-the-spot rule she ceded the ball to Rose, who passed it to Theo so that he could run full force at Eddie, letting off a war whoop. Stella fell to her knees she was laughing so hard, and somehow Rose had the ball again and tagged her out, but the weight of Rose's pregnant belly tipped her forward as she leaned down so she grabbed Stella's shoulders and swung herself to a seat with a grunt. Stella threw the ball to Eddie and leaned back into the scratchy weeds. They watched the men wrestle.

"They're like—" Stella and Rose spoke in unison. Then stopped.

*No jinx,* thought Stella.

"Children," Rose finished.

"True. But I was going to say maniacs."

Rose rested a hand on her belly. Stella leaned her head over to press an ear against it and then her mouth. "Hello baby, this is your Auntie Stella. Don't be alarmed, we just seem crazy sometimes. We're all waiting to meet you."

"Don't encourage, not too early," Rose chided.

"Hey kid, don't piss off your mom first thing, that's my advice. Don't come out yet. See you in a couple months."

Rose nodded, satisfied. "Who's winning?" she asked.

"We won," said Stella. "Of course."

Theo struggled to his feet, holding the ball aloft. "This brave victory is for him," he called over to Rose. "He'll be a good athlete, wait and see."

"*Him*?" Stella asked.

"He's convinced."

"What do you think?"

Rose shook her head. "Who knows. But Theo's picked out a name already."

"Tell!"

"I want to hold off."

"Okay. But I can't wait to meet little Irwin."

"Hmmm."

"Humbert? Algonquin? Damien? Reginald?"

"How'd you know?" Rose's skin was luminous.

Eddie rolled to a seat, grabbed Theo behind the knees and pulled him over. He wiped an arm across his sweaty face, and a piece of grass in his hair speared Stella's heart. Her husband called across the weeds, "What's it take to get a cocktail waitress around here?"

After the first year, Eddie's trips got longer, the spaces between his homecomings further apart. Stella told Rose, "I'm a salesman's widow." Then, "Does he think I won't notice he's gone?" And finally, "That bastard had better call." The marriage dissolved as quickly as it had begun.

She and Rose needed each other more than ever, and the depth of it, the extent of their stuckness was only just dawning on them. Glennie and Gordie became seriously ill within months of each other, and Rose and Stella shuttled between the farm and the B&B with food and prescriptions, taking turns sleeping over and providing care as best they could, until it became clear that their parents needed a nursing home. They declined and died so quickly—over the course of six months—that if Stella hadn't known better she'd think Glennie and Gordie were being graceful, not lingering, taking care not to be a burden. "But of course they never were that considerate," she told Rose, who snapped back that she'd better can it and stopped speaking to her for two days. They made up in Rose's kitchen, crying into each other's shoulders with exhaustion. Theo walked in and then turned right around and left them to it. An hour later they stumbled into the backyard, red-eyed and calm, to watch Theo and Lance splash in the boy's little wading pool.

Afterward, they couldn't find a buyer for Anderson's and the bank threatened to repossess it. "Let them," Rose said, but Stella knew she was putting on a brave face. They needed money. Theo's house had it in for them. The roof leaked, the stove ate half a box of matches just to start a flame, and their hairpins disappeared only to turn up months later, bent and rusty, spat out half-digested from between the floorboards. A fever had overtaken Rose and Theo—make more money, keep the land, save the legacy, work harder. *More keep save work.*

Outside of her shifts at The Bluebird, Stella's days had structure only because of the boy. Lance was often at her side, small hand in hers as they walked to the creek or down the drive to get the mail, underfoot in the kitchen when she made him crustless peanut butter sandwiches, "helping" her set the table or pulling her into the backyard to see his latest mud creation. He called her Aunt Stella, but his high eager voice ran the words together: *Anstel*, he would call. *Anstel, come see*. She'd put down whatever she was doing and go to him. "We need you here," Rose said when Stella offered to move out and find her own way. "You know how much Lance loves you."

Lying alone in bed at night Stella pondered her value in the family unit.

"Let me take a picture of the three of you," Stella said to Rose one Sunday afternoon. She balanced her sweating old-fashioned glass on her thigh, the lime wedge shocking green against pale skin.

Theo was just home from a sales trip. Eddie had signed him on enthusiastically, in a commission agreement that Rose said sounded like a con. They were peddling expensive reverse osmosis water filtration systems to office parks and apartment buildings, though Theo told them Eddie had a hodge-podge of other deals in the works, one of which was a green alfalfa powder that wealthy suburbanites bought to make into antioxidant smoothies. It wasn't going well for Theo; he didn't have her ex's killer instinct for aggressive pursuit and closing deals.

"C'mon." Stella waved a hand at Lance, who tore around the yard kicking a foam football that she'd bought for him at Mondragon's. "How'd he get to be four already? We need photographic evidence."

Rose frowned and smoothed her shirt. "I'm not . . ." Everything she wore seemed tattered. Lately, she'd been talking about cutting her hair, one less thing to fuss with. Stella knew the tiny blue veins in Rose's eyelids as well as she knew her own face, and considered them as Rose pressed her eyes shut for more than a normal blink.

She'd been doing that lately, claiming fatigue, but Stella knew that Rose was depressed, not yet come to terms with their parents' deaths, or maybe just worn down by the work of the past few years. The fact that she herself had sailed over that sea of grief almost unscathed worried Stella. Shouldn't she have wrestled more with the end of her marriage, and with the ultimate finality of death? Sometimes she suspected that she was just less sensitive than Rose, less deep. But for long periods, she didn't think of it at all.

"You're gorgeous. Come on." Stella swirled her glass, ice clinking. She stood and called to Theo, who was tinkering with something in the barn. Avoiding them, Stella thought. She found Eddie's forgotten camera and took a few snaps of Lance. When Theo appeared she bossed them all into place in a row on the back porch. Rose on one side of Lance, Theo on the other. They hadn't yet had time to get used to each other again, she could tell. Rose still felt the distance from his trip.

"Lean in," Stella said. "Cheese!"

Theo's arm draped around their son and he rested his palm on the small of Rose's back. Rose sat up straighter.

"For God's sake, Rose. Smile!" Stella snapped. Theo leaned back, bracing himself for a spat.

*Cheeeeeeeeeeeeeeez!* Lance squealed. Rose widened her eyes and joined him, and Stella took her shot.

"There." She handed the camera to Theo, running her fingers through her hair. "Now get one with me."

He obliged, dropping to one knee so he wouldn't block the light. Stella tilted her head in the way she'd learned from the magazines and Lance hammed it up, yelling *Cheez Whiz* and making faces until they were all laughing and the roll was used up. Theo stood to go into the kitchen for an iced tea, pausing to kiss Rose on the top of her head, and Lance ran into the yard.

"They'll look great, you'll be glad we did it," Stella said.

"I know." Rose took a sip of her drink. A smile fleeted across her face, and her shoulders relaxed. The endless list of chores could wait.

*Look!* said Lance. *Look!* He was back to his solo game, throwing the ball high, catching it, tossing it again.

"We see you," they said in unison.

The first time Stella noticed Theo in a new way, she was putting on a record for dinner. He'd arrived home late Friday afternoon, and wandered into the parlor to tell her Rose had supper on the table. "Welcome, stranger," she smiled. She stayed at the dim end of the room by the old turntable, flipping through albums.

"Howdy, Stel," he replied, and wandered over to the side table, switching on a lamp so she could better see the titles. Theo's white shirt was rolled up to his elbows and in the pink light of the faux Tiffany lamp the hairs on his forearms were spun gold.

She looked away. "Any requests?"

"Whatever you like," he said. She glanced up to see if she'd misheard his tone. Something covert slipped between them then, and everything changed. His golden armhairs shifted under the faint breeze of the flipping record sleeves, which her fingers kept turning, blindly. Rose called from the kitchen and he left. Stella pulled an old Fleetwood Mac record from its sleeve, feeling the keen edge of the vinyl on her fingerpads—not as sharp as a knife, but sharp enough.

Over the months to come she tapped into that undercurrent as a phlebotomist taps a vein—gingerly, but with great attention and focus. It was always there, sometimes fainter than others. And almost unconsciously she began to summon it—*tap tap*: a flicker in her eyes, slanting up then darting away; stopping in front of the lamp in a sheer skirt; an arm brushed against a cotton sleeve—*tappity tap tap*.

They were in the habit of riding into town together on Saturday afternoons—Theo to pick up a few things at Mondragon's, Stella to get the groceries—so there was plenty of time to relish the tension. It had nothing to do with money or work or her failed marriage. It had nothing to do with Rose. It was a diversion, that's all, and she was caught up in the fun of it. Until one day on the way to town he sputtered a confession, eyes flying off the road and locking onto her face for so long that she clutched the door handle, thinking they'd surely run into a ditch. "Stella, you're so beautiful, I can't stop thinking about you . . ." It wasn't the first time a man had said that to her; she shouldn't have been swayed by the weak stupid words. But it wasn't the words that did it. Her nipples hardened at the scent of his panicky sweat and the nervy flush on his cheeks, and she grabbed his hand, raised his palm to her left breast and pressed it there, wanting wordlessness and absorption, wanting to feel consumed.

But there was no release. She couldn't come with Theo, and it wasn't because they were in the awkward confines of the truck. That first day Theo drifted off the road into a little clearing on the edge of Old Man Brown's land and parked underneath the old elm tree. Elbows and knees smacked against the dash and they rocked the cab with their eager rutting. She came to the brink again and again, only to be yanked back with a jolt. It wasn't a matter of focus or clumsiness, but some wrongness of ownership—putting on the opposite shoe by mistake—and she'd feel a shiver of revulsion, a sliver of shame, only to be overtaken by excitement as he moved within her and moaned into her open mouth.

Still she didn't think of Rose. When they weren't together, her desire for Theo stilled to the barest prick. She was just Stella, Rose's right hand, the one putting on the music for dinner each night and bringing flowers to the table. Then Saturday would come and they'd be in the truck again together. Her brother-in-law's hands grew rougher as his guilt compounded and at first she liked it, careful to let him bruise her only where Rose wouldn't see. But even that grew wearying as she twisted and thrashed and bumped her head on the metal door handle, exhausted by her frustrating anti-climaxes. So she began to service him—why waste time? She'd bat his hands away, lean over to undo his zipper, slip onto the floor of the truck cab, hold her hair back and suck his salty penis into her mouth even before they reached Old Man Brown's ancient elm. The floorboards vibrated under her knees as the engine slowed and idled and his bitter spunk darted into her mouth. He'd wait until she smoothed her hair and slipped back into her seat. Then he'd shift gears and they'd keep driving—climaxed, anti-climaxed, and morose, her tongue gummy on the roof of her mouth.

They flogged a month's worth of lust and adrenaline over the course of a season, and as it sputtered to a close they both felt it. Theo was as taciturn after sex as Eddie had been a talker. She'd spend the second half of the ride into town thinking of how to start the next sentence:

*We're both unhappy with how this is—*

*We can pretend it never—*

*I could never come between you and—*

But she couldn't finish the thought, let alone say the words.

On their final day together in the truck, she sank to her knees even as Theo said, "No, Stella, let's not keep—" because she couldn't not by then, she was compelled. As he grabbed her shoulder to pull her back up to the seat, she fell onto his right leg and the truck sped and jerked and she succeeded at last in a memorable climax: she jettisoned them right into the elm, fracturing her collarbone and a rib and knocking Theo's lights out. No time to untangle themselves and agree on a story. Old Man Brown and a rat-faced junior deputy arrived on the scene, swimming into her blurry line of vision, reading the clues even as they asked if she could hear them, and if she knew how many fingers they held in the air. "One," she blurted. "That's a single finger, and I guess I know which."

The men looked at each other over her head as she giggled, throat thick with tears and chest splintered in pain.

After she left the farm, communication with Rose and Theo and Lance was severed. Rarely, she'd see them from a distance, angling the old blue truck through town. Stella never ducked or looked away; she didn't have to, they never came near. She thought about moving away, calling Eddie and asking for a loan to make her way to the city. And yet, she stayed.

Emma Templeton rented her a little efficiency apartment above The Bluebird. The clattering kitchen woke her each morning, and she'd slip into her uniform and head down to ready the place for breakfast. She worked almost as many hours as Emma herself. Stella bantered well enough with her customers and with Emma, but inside was a stillness that she could pull around herself at will. In this way, a full year passed almost without registering.

She tried not to dwell in the past. But when her mind wandered she would find herself outlining arguments in her head in a kind of reflexive impulse, an attempt to explain what had happened, if only to herself. Stella had never resented Rose. They'd accepted each other with such fullness that there was no room for dreck. They were who they were, together. Rose was sturdier, sensible, the one who got things done—but she prized what strengths Stella had. Her strengths! Picking music and flowers and the perfect shade of lipstick for any complexion. Stella was very good at brightening up a room or keeping a conversation moving, but that didn't mean she enjoyed it. She was almost thirty before she realized that, working a busy lunch shift at The Bluebird and banished by the only family she had left. She sat on a stool and put her head down, curving her shoulders inward as the realization worked its way from her stomach to her head.

*

Rose found herself, at the strangest times, thinking of her father. Thinking of him outside the narrative that she and Stella had created to understand their parents in retrospect: *deluded, ditzy, doomed.* Gordie had brought them here through force of will. He was the engine—and they'd stayed! That had surprised even him. For that fact alone, she owed him something. What had he seen about this place that the rest of them missed until almost a decade had passed? Had he known then that the town and the land would answer a question she hadn't yet posed: *Where will I be rooted?*

She'd pluck one of the runner beans that thrived in her kitchen garden, or drive past the spot where he'd taught her how to change a flat tire, or catch a whiff of Ward Mondragon's woodsy cologne, and her father's name would spring into her head. *Gordie. Where are you? We're still here.*

She had tried to talk to Stella about it, when she still had Stella to talk with, but her stepsister had been and likely always would be angry. "Come off it! They were losers, Rose, that was it. They had no inkling of anything beyond their own noses, least of all our future needs. What we have that's good, *we* made. *We* did it. Not them." A large part of Rose agreed with that sentiment, and she didn't judge Stella for it. But having Lance had swung open a door in her heart and sometimes she called through it to a father who would never answer.

She pulled a bean from the vine, sniffed it, and tossed it into the basket. Lance ran around the side of the house. Perry and Nina's girl, Sylvie, following close behind. "Mom, Mom, can we have cheese sandwiches?"

"All right," she told him, waving them toward the kitchen. "But dinner's in an hour and a half. Split one." He would make it himself. Lance was self-sufficient, she prided herself on that.

She had been in the front yard when they brought Theo home after the accident, mulching her just-pruned rose bushes.

"Rose," Theo had said to her. "Rosie." His forehead was bloody and his white shirt stained, the sleeves rolled up over his strong arms. He wouldn't walk up the porch steps with her, just stood there, the police car behind him. A young deputy in a blue uniform stood by. Old Man Brown was there too, and in her confusion she watched him walk as if in slow motion to the deputy, muttering words into his ear, something harsh in his manner.

"Where's Stella?" she asked. "What happened?" Theo's face swam before her. She rubbed her eyes, her vision blurry.

"*Rosie.*" His voice cracked and then she knew. She knew exactly.

He told her that they'd called for another cop car to take Stella to the clinic with a broken collarbone. Then Theo packed a small suitcase and hovered by the door, saying that he'd call from the road, he'd be back for her, he'd give anything for another chance. She sat in a corner of the parlor as darkness moved across the house and did not turn on the lights. Her eyes were still blurry, but bone dry. After a while, icy tendrils of self-doubt filtered through: *It's my fault. I should have known. I could have stopped it.* Then anger reasserted itself and she knew it was anything but her fault. Lance had made plans to sleep overnight at Benji Logan's, a lucky thing because she could not imagine functioning. At some point the phone rang and she counted up to sixty before it went silent.

At 3:00 a.m. she got up to use the bathroom and made herself a cup of tea. She sat at the kitchen table and considered her two hands resting on the wood—calloused, hangnailed, in need of a good scrubbing. She had to form some sort of plan, some coherent response that would help her explain things to Lance. *What should I do?* The people she would normally ask were gone. Even then, before the shock dulled, she understood which betrayal was greater. Stella was her sister, blood-without-blood, and she had to have known what she was doing. *No, that's not right,* Rose shook her head. She couldn't let Theo off so easily, he had an equal measure of responsibility.

*You girls keep looking after each other,* Gordie had said to them a month before he'd died, his face gray and his hair greasy on the pillow. They'd agreed effortlessly, because he was on his deathbed, and because of course they would—it went without saying. Rose and Stella had always looked after each other, certainly better than the parents had. Nothing Rose could imagine would change that. Her kettle whistled and shook on the stove, almost empty. She'd forgotten to switch off the gas. A cup of strong English Breakfast, leaves steeped to a full-throated bitterness, had cleared her head. She stood to turn off the burner.

As she stared out the window, a face appeared in the glass. Not her own reflection, no face she recognized. The eyes were large and haunted, and the skin held the gloom of the darkness around it. Rose was incapable of astonishment—she simply stood, staring. In the hall, the cuckoo struck four o'clock. There was no moon. Any light that fell on the visitor came from her kitchen. The face shut one saucer eye in an exaggerated wink and the lips moved. *Stay,* she heard quite clearly, and she blinked and the face was gone. "Gordie?" she whispered, but there was no reply. She saw only her own small shadowed eyes then, in reflection. *Stay.* Rose sat, staring at the sludgy tea leaves in the bottom of her cup. She heard the house's heartbeat: the hall clock ticking, boards shifting, the roof sighing overhead. *Stay,* the house asserted with each beat, and with every breath she felt more sure. She would rely on herself, she would help her son take root and thrive. She could do it without them.

In town word didn't spread as she had feared it might, and she had a belated, grateful feeling that it had something to do with Sherwin Brown clamping the lid on that deputy. Keep farm troubles quiet, let town people gossip about their own selves. That's what Old Man Brown thought; it's what they all thought, if they bothered to think about it. Rose had never bothered. She hadn't considered a lot of things, she realized now, and felt, for the first time in her life, shamefully slow-witted.

Emma Templeton appeared a week after the accident and quietly packed Stella's clothes, books, and toiletries into two suitcases, erasing her presence from the house. Emma took Rose's hand in the driveway and said in her crisp forthright way that she was sorry for what had happened but she was sure they'd sort themselves out sooner or later. Rose let her hand go limp as a fish. She told Lance that his father had been called away on important business, and would be back eventually. It was harder to explain Stella's absence, so she was curt about it, needing to forestall his questions. "She had to go earn more money. Everyone needs to be self-sufficient, even Stella."

Theo appeared one month later to the day, baseball cap in hand. "I'll love you hard, Rose, I'll make it up to you." He thought anything could be forgotten if he said just the right words.

Not Stella, no. Stella didn't even try. Rose struggled not to feel surprise at this. She had expected a tear-stained letter, a groveling phone call, some attempt at an explanation. None was forthcoming. So she felt robbed of resolution, the satisfaction that would come from rejecting Stella's apology. The silence made her consider that Stella was not remorseful—that perhaps she had manufactured the wedge out of some need to divorce herself from Rose's life. But why?

She had no idea what she'd done to make Stella flee. Rose tried to pull herself up from this line of thinking. She hadn't understood Stella at all, that was the long and short of it. What she had thought was a given was not, and never would be, fathomable. Even after more than a year had passed, and she and Theo had regained a semblance of their old ease, she turned over that hard fact at least once a day, every day, and then purposefully set it aside. Rose refocused her energy on creating a stable life on the farm for her son—there was plenty of work to do, it was easy to keep busy. She grew confident that she'd made the right decision.

Now she crouched to pick the low-hanging pole beans and sat back on her heels. Lance's voice bounced off the kitchen walls and through the open window, in the bossy tone he often took with his younger neighbor. "Cheddar cheddar cheddar. Duh. And pickles! Sit there, Sylvie . . ."

*Gordie,* she thought. *Dad, Daddy. Wherever you are, can you see him? He has your eyes.*

*

As Sill began to walk, and then run, Nina, too, found her footing, making herself indispensable to her father-in-law, learning the rhythms of the place and carving out her own space in it. She had less free time for lunches and socializing with the neighbors. Perry cut down his hours at Logan's Garage—there just wasn't enough time in the day—and almost without discussion their escape plan fell by the wayside as their lives grew more firmly rooted on the farm. Nina embraced the church she'd been raised in with renewed dedication, bringing her daughter twice a week and sometimes even her father-in-law. With Rose and Stella, she drifted toward fleeting pleasantries—waving as they passed on the road.

She had no regrets, to speak of.

One day Perry asked her to meet him for lunch out in the east field. It had been a long time since she'd sat under the sky with him at noon, certainly not since Sill had started grade school. She packed two of his favorite ham sandwiches and set out. Taking long strides, thinking of everything and nothing, watching the light play on the young corn and puffy clouds drift past. *I'm lucky*, she thought. She was more certain that he loved her than she'd been eight years before, and less in need of the words. Nina had become a true Brown in that regard.

Her stomach flipped when she saw him standing by his tractor, baseball cap shading his eyes. "Hey, stranger," she grinned, tossing him the paper lunch sack. "How about—"

"Come here for a minute." Perry set their lunch on the tractor seat and walked her over to the elm. "Around here." He showed her where the truck bumper had made impact. Sap ran from the gouge, and fresh wood chips were scattered at the base of the trunk.

"Oh no," she said. "What—"

"Theo," he said. "And Stella." He told her what the Old Man had seen.

Nina shook her head. She felt nothing, not a lick of compassion or distress. "Oh no," she repeated, as if the words themselves could find the feelings.

Perry touched the trunk. "It needs to be tarred up."

"What were they—" she put a hand on his shoulder and pulled him to her, breathing in the clean salty smell of his neck. The feeling of luck and lightness that she'd had on her walk had dissipated. Leaves rustled. She pressed the length of her body against his, but he kept his hands at his sides.

"What a mess." His voice wavered and he stepped back, taking off his cap and running an arm across his forehead. She could see *his* distress. Where was hers? What was wrong with her?

"They'll figure it out," she told him. "Rose is strong, they'll get past it."

"He's my friend." Perry kicked at the wood chips, his eyes dark. He was angry.

She sighed and leaned against the tree. "True. It's not like him." Perry loved Theo, but he wouldn't be able to talk to him directly about this. That's not how the men she knew operated. She looked toward the house, calculating how much time she had before Sill came home from school.

"Theo's not like that. He . . ." Perry stopped.

"He's not dumb," she finished for him.

It was dumb, though. Terribly dumb, and careless. She supposed that if there were a divorce, the Old Man would get the land pretty quickly. This whole fiasco would have confirmed her father-in-law's already low opinion of Theo.

Then it hit her, what Rose was in for. "What a mess," she sighed, echoing Perry. She touched the gouge in the trunk. It would be a shame if the tree died. Not long before, the Old Man had told her that this tree used to have a companion six feet to the east. They grew in concert, rooted so far back into the family memory that he couldn't say when they *weren't* there, leaning toward each other. The companion had been lost to Dutch elm disease, but still the remaining tree's eastward facing branches stretched higher, reaching out to empty space.

She picked up a piece of splintered bark. "You'll seal it up, right?"

He nodded. "I don't know how much Lance knows."

Of course, the boy—that's why Perry was so upset. "They won't let it affect him. They're not going to . . ."

"He's ten. How can he not know?" Perry asked. And for that she had no answer.

She decided there and then not to pity Rose. Rose had done her that favor once, the favor of not pitying, and it was the least Nina could do in return. "I'll try to talk to her," she told Perry. "But it will be her choice, I won't pry."

The next day she went over. It was easy enough to come up with an excuse. She asked to borrow a do-it-yourself plumbing book that she was pretty sure Rose owned—she'd seen it in the old days, propping up a chair leg in the parlor.

"The bathtub spout broke this morning and I'm going to try to replace the faucet handles too . . ." Nina faltered, not committed to her own story. She was a terrible liar. They stood in the yard by the old well, with maybe three paces between them. A bird passed over, its shadow fleeting a dark bruise across Rose's face. Nina felt a nip of adrenaline at the sight.

"Come in," Rose said. "I'm not sure where to find it."

"I'm sorry to be a—"

"Don't," Rose snapped. Nina bit her tongue. Rose took a breath. "I mean, don't worry. It's no bother." Her face was pale; she looked anemic. Her freckles had never seemed so distinct.

"I'm always a bother." Sweat pooled in Nina's armpits. "You must remember that?"

Rose went into the house without answering, and passed quickly through the hall and into the parlor, calling behind her, expecting Nina to follow, "If it's anywhere, it's here . . ."

*Under the wine-colored chair,* Nina thought, following along and watching as Rose scanned the bookshelf behind the record player. The shelf was stuffed with old *Reader's Digest* bound editions, some cookbooks, and on the lower shelf, a small collection of dime-store Westerns.

"I'm sorry, I don't know." Rose shook her head. Her hands rested on her hips, elbows out, feet wide and firmly planted. They were alone. Nina had timed the visit carefully—Lance and Sill wouldn't be home from school for several hours. There was no sign of Stella, of course; she and her things were gone.

"Well," Nina said.

It didn't escape Nina that Rose hadn't offered her a cup of coffee. Rose knew why she was there, or suspected, and wasn't having any of it. She had no intention of discussing her marriage troubles with Nina. If they had been drifting toward that sort of friendship once, they'd bypassed it. Nina had chalked the rift up to busyness, but it also had to do with the Old Man's hunger to acquire more acres—she had felt in recent years that Rose suspected all the Browns were working toward the same end. Beneath that was the feeling of strangeness, of dislocation, that she'd experienced in Rose's bathroom the day Rose had brought Lance back to life. It brought on a stiffness that Nina had preferred to avoid. But now Rose needed someone—or to be more precise, she needed God.

"I wonder," she said, shifting her weight onto her heels and trying to make her voice less squeaky, "I wonder if you know how the Good News has helped me."

Rose cocked an eyebrow.

"I know that you aren't . . . that you haven't been . . . but I want to tell you, Rose, that Jesus Christ has carried me through some very trying times, and if he can do it for me . . . The Lord upholds all that fall, and raises up all those that are bowed down."

Rose walked to the couch and sat. A tiny puff of dust rose up from the upholstery. The family had never much used this room. Rose pulled a pillow into her lap and ran her fingers through faded fringe. This had to be an invitation.

Nina continued, still rocking onto her heels, talking to the side of Rose's face. Rose in profile was less unsettling than Rose head-on. That shadow that she'd seen fleeting over them was still in the room, she sensed, and her voice rattled on, a mouse in a cage, telling Rose about how she'd doubted for a time as a young girl, her life so clearly off the track she'd planned. What *was* the plan? What if no one was in charge and it was all completely random? Of course she'd never stopped going to church, but her heart wasn't in it. Rose knew this, she'd known Nina pretty well back then, she must have seen how lost she was, and full of doubt, and lonely, and . . . And then. Then the spirit came. Jesus lifted her up. One frigid January morning as she pulled towels out of the washing machine. She felt a touch on the crown of her head, gentle but firm, and a feeling of blessed warmth and joy suffused her right there in the freezing laundry room. A whisper came into her head from the inside, not without. *Nina, have faith in my love.* That's all. That's all He'd said, and all she needed to hear. Have faith. And since then, she'd found new purpose. She was a better mother, and better able to deal with things when Perry and the Old Man went at it. And she was never lonely now, that was the thing. If only Rose could . . . the church is such a welcoming community, the way people—

"Look," Rose said.

Nina stopped, breathing fast, feeling like she'd run a mile. Witnessing was hard work. "Yes?"

"No, look." Rose pointed at the chair by the cold fireplace. One chipped mahogany leg was propped on a battered hardback book, the block print on the spine faded but still readable. *Plumbing 101: A Do-It-Yourself Guide for the Home Handyman.*

"Oh," Nina said.

"You can take it with you."

"I will, thank you. And thank you for listening, Rose. I know you've doubted God but—"

Rose stood and lifted the chair, tapping the book out from under with her foot. She set the wingback down, wobbling now on uneven legs, and bent to retrieve the manual, holding it out to Nina.

"I doubt everything."

The shadow swam up the wall and into a far corner. That adrenaline feeling surged again, and Nina's breath caught. She filled her lungs deeply and walked forward to take the book. Rose's tone didn't strike her as proud or superior, the way she could be sometimes. It felt honest, and sad. She searched for a reply.

Sometimes Nina had a sense that all the humans she knew were on a wide plain, on foot, traveling in the same general proximity but each body facing in a slightly different direction. Strangers and pilgrims on the earth. It was more of a geographical than a spiritual concept—people scattered on a landform, barren vista stretching out—and she had never thought to try to explain it to anyone. At church that feeling sometimes shifted to one of communion and she felt herself moving in concert with others, and seeing the same horizon. It brought so much peace. If she, Nina, or Jesus Himself, could touch Rose's shoulder gently and angle her in the right direction—just a nudge, that's all it would take—then Rose might turn her face toward something better. How to do that, she had no idea.

Rose escorted Nina to the porch, and even as she walked to her station wagon she fumbled for words to convey that feeling—but by then Rose's door had shut.

In the weeks that followed the Browns had Lance over for dinner often, and Nina sent Sill over on errands to check up on them, and to distract the boy. She wondered if Rose could see that Nina was using her eight-year-old daughter as an ambassador because she herself had failed. Theo was gone for about a month—another sales trip, Lance said.

Rose, to Nina's eyes at least—and Nina watched carefully, from a distance—continued on just as before. No mention of any trouble. No outward signs of distress.

*

Ward's wife, Karena, was restless for years before their eventual split. The easygoing girl he'd married had become surly, snapping at him when he asked her whether she'd done the ordering, and once even hurling a can at the wall during a Friday morning restock of the soup aisle. He'd interrupted her in the middle of humming "The Alphabet Song" she told him later, by way of apology.

That afternoon, she set down her clipboard, picked up her handbag, and walked out the door. "Where are you going?" he asked. Her reply was garbled by a passing truck but went something like, *I want to live, I'm sick of the smell.*

He stepped outside to draw a deep breath of new air, and reentered the store with clean lungs to try to catch what she'd found so objectionable. No different than usual: the scent of birdseed and old wood, and a faint sweet smell of the apricot juice he'd opened after lunch. He himself, he was fairly certain, smelled of Irish Spring soap, with underpinnings of wintermint mouthwash.

"How are you?" Rose asked. He'd propped the door open and hadn't heard her coming. She stood near the rack of seed packets by the front window.

"Rose!" he said. "Never better." He was genuinely glad to see her, and not only for the distraction. She had grown into herself in recent years; there was new warmth in her smile and a softer line to her shoulders. Stella was still living with them out at the farm, and everything seemed settled.

"Any luck finding a buyer?" he asked. She and Stella had inherited Anderson's when their parents died. Glennie first and then Gordie, in quick succession. Their parents—the place itself—seemed to crumble without the girls. Some people blamed them for moving out, but Ward never had. He was close enough to see that Rose and Stella took care of their parents as best they could. Karena didn't blame them either—he felt a pang and diverted it, answering his own question. "You will soon enough, soon enough." Repeating a phrase was one of his tics that had begun to set Karena off. He stepped behind the counter, resting his palms on two darker indentations near the register. *Shut up, for once.*

He waited for her to come to him. Some seeds for her kitchen garden, a few bags of dried beans, a bottle of Miracle-Gro. She set her items on the counter like fruit that might bruise.

"Stella's favorite magazine has come in," he said.

Rose picked it up, looked at the price on the corner, and returned it to the rack. She wore a jean skirt that he'd seen a thousand times before, on a multitude of women. Her face was clear and unlined.

"I guess that's it," she said.

He reached into the jar that Karena kept behind the counter. "Candy for the boy?"

"Lance," she said, to remind him.

"That's where all the Miracle-Gro goes?"

She tilted her head, confused.

"He's growing like a sprout!" Ward boomed too heartily. Karena was so much better at this. At remembering the names of people's children, at not reminding customers that their parents had died, and that they were now and maybe forever short of cash.

"He is." She grinned, and he had a feeling that any mention of her boy would elicit that response. "He's across the street with Stella, trying on shoes. School starts next week."

"That's . . ." he lost the thought. He'd caught a whiff of his apricot juice, bottle open on the counter behind him, and felt a twinge of shame, as if the smell were unseemly. "That'll be ten ninety-eight."

She paid and he counted out her change and slipped three foil-wrapped chocolate eggs into the bag. *It'll be okay*, he almost said. This was another tic of his, saying things to people that he himself wanted to hear. She thanked him and turned to go.

"Rose?" She paused, clearly feeling the pull of her son and Stella from across the street. Her red hair was almost Technicolor, lit by the afternoon sun slanting through his windows—the tip of a match, a startling effect. He had the strange sense that it was fading the rest of her, and him, and felt a pang of indefinite dread. "You have a wonderful day, young lady."

Karena bought herself a ticket for a two-week cruise to the Bahamas. "I'm going to get a little space and perspective," she told Ward. "A little me time." She had giggly late night phone conversations with Julie O'Shea, her best friend from high school. Julie was also going on the cruise, he found out when Karena mentioned it in passing, along with two other women from Karena's exercise class. They had all dyed their hair the same streaky blonde—"It's just highlights!" Karena said—and wore similar formfitting yoga pants to show off their newly toned thighs. And now, apparently, they traveled in a pack.

He told himself that if he kept the faith someday Karena would again seem blessedly uncomplicated. "Go. Enjoy yourself," he said benevolently, as if she'd asked his permission.

While she was gone he had no one to spell him, so he had to ask Scottie to watch his store a few times. Just for fifteen minutes, while Ward ran to the bank or to the drugstore for more antacids—his stomach had been bothering him. He tried not to ask too much of Scottie, who had recently lost his parents' house and was adapting to a lonely, odd life there in the back of Dunleavy's. *Caving in*, Ward thought, determined not to do the same.

"Sure, Ward," Scottie said over the phone. "I'll watch your door and if anybody goes in, I'll run right across the street." As Ward started his car, he watched Scottie in the rearview mirror, almost spectral: tall and skinny, standing with one thin hand pressed into his doorframe, peering out into the world but not quite of it. Ward pushed his foot into the gas pedal and sped to the bank, where he rushed Louise Logan through her usual chatty routine.

Scottie wasn't in the doorway of Dunleavy's when Ward returned. Stepping inside Mondragon's, he saw Scottie behind the register and

Theo with his wallet folded open, head bowed like a choirboy before a hymnal. Ward felt a sudden lightness, the knot in his stomach loosening. Here they were, reassuringly known, Scottie grimacing as he handed Theo change.

Ward had always liked Theo, who had steady brown eyes and a smile that Karena called "goofy but cute." He was a regular customer, as his father had been before him. To Theo, loyalty meant something. Today he slouched a bit, jeans sliding down his hips, his shoulders bowed toward the counter. Ward thought again of a young man praying, from a painting he'd seen somewhere: a solemn pose lit by a glowing stream of light.

"Hello," he said belatedly. "Did you find everything you need?"

Theo raised his bag in answer. "I hear Karena's off seeing the world?" His smile didn't touch his eyes, which were a bit glassy.

"Well, good, good," Ward said as Scottie came out from behind the register. "Yes," he continued, "My better half is gallivanting with some girlfriends . . . she left me a freezer full of food and a list of chores . . ." For a moment the three of them stood awkwardly, a loose triangle in the middle of the store, out of their usual places. "Boy, does she deserve a break . . ." he started, and then stopped himself.

Theo shifted his bag from one hand to another.

"Will you say hi to Rose for me?"

Theo gave the tiniest flinch. Ward wasn't looking for it and wouldn't have predicted it, but there it was. He raised a hand to his stomach. Then dropped it.

"You bet," Theo said. A quick smile darted over his face. "Well, I'd better . . . we have one more stop, there's never enough time."

Ward and Scottie watched Theo climb into his truck. Stella was in the cab, her head leaning against the window, and when she saw them looking she lifted a hand in greeting.

"Thanks," Ward said to Scottie.

The truck pulled away and they watched it go, the two in profile silent, almost stony, though Ward supposed they could be listening to disco music in the cab for all he knew.

"She stole a pair of shoes when she was in high school," Scottie said.

"Stella?"

"Then brought them back the next week, in tears. She said she'd needed them for a dance, and had worn them only once and felt guilty the whole time. She offered to work to pay them off. My mother talked to her for a while, and said she'd learned her lesson and sent her on her way. They weren't sellable after that. Just plain black pumps."

"Huh," Ward said.

"I always thought that maybe she never intended to steal them at all, only wanted to borrow them to wear that once on her date, and she just couldn't figure out how else to return them. They wouldn't fit through the mail slot. We'd have noticed if she'd walked in with them. So she told us she was worse than she actually was, but maybe she also lied about reforming her ways."

"Either way . . ." Ward wasn't quite sure what they were talking about. Did Scottie know how bad it had gotten with Karena?

"Sometimes we teach ourselves our own lessons," Scottie said, not checking for traffic before he stepped into the street.

"Scottie," Ward called to his friend, "I owe you one."

The man Ward saw on his monthly visits to the city was named Michael. Ward liked consistency, and Michael had it—a solid upper body, furry chest, dark hair silvering at the temples. "Who do you want me to be?" Michael had asked on their first meeting, and Ward responded without hesitation: "My professor." Tweed jacket with leather elbow patches. Michael lit a cigarette and asked, "Want a smoke?" Ward did not. He wanted Michael to swat the flesh of his buttocks, part the cheeks, and do his work. Ward was silent, always, mindful of the hotel's thin walls. As was Michael, save for a guttural groan at the end.

Ward savored that groan, mimicked it on the car ride home. It was as if he dropped through space in a capsule—no clear sense of the drive, only aware of arriving. He flicked off the radio, sucked air deep into his belly, and sang, "Uhhhhhhhhhhhhhuh." Then patted the hidden soreness in his thigh. That groan was the reason Michael was his regular, paid city man. The cadences, the animal satisfaction of it, sometimes punctuated by one hard-stop "Fuck," sustained him over the intervening weeks, replayed during the infrequent sex with Karena—rode right over her softer female moans—and became a texture of his interior life as much as those leather patches or the smell of greasy, forbidden potato chips bought at a mid-point rest stop.

Problems arose when he had to do several things at once. For example, when Karena called to ask what he wanted for dinner just as a customer stepped up to the counter, even as he discreetly rubbed the chafed patch on his shoulder left by Michael's stubble. Or when he was withdrawing two hundred in cash for his city trip, calculating the hours until he'd be in the hotel room, and Louise Logan asked how Karena was doing. He felt a tiny tearing in his guts then, a physical pull as he tried to shift gears.

On his last visit, he'd pressed the usual hundred into Michael's hand and Michael said, "I've got something for you too." He gave Ward a new business card. On it, Michael's name, first and last, and a telephone number Ward didn't recognize. In small letters underneath the name, four words: "Massage. Deep Release. Discreet."

"I'm moving," Michael said, "so that's my new answering service. And rates are going up. One twenty-five, for you."

Ward recognized a business reaching for the next level when he saw it. "Sounds like a good move."

Michael's fingers patted his jacket pocket for the next cigarette. As he turned toward the elevator he said, "Throw out the old number, that's no good as of next week. I'll see you next time, Craig."

Ward had assumed that Michael's name wasn't really Michael, though he realized when he saw the card that it was, that Michael was comfortable using his real name, printing it in raised, shiny letters on card stock. Ward thought, as he slipped the card into his pocket, that he should recommend to Michael that he leave off the extraneous words—his name and phone number were enough and the rest defeated the promise of that final word: *Discretion*.

It took years for the marriage to end, and still it took him by surprise.

He stopped going to the city, for a time. They made an effort. Karena found a therapist and they sat on opposite ends of the couch in front of a stranger once a week, discussing their feelings. The discussable feelings. Largely, he listened.

But good behavior has its limits—or maybe he, Ward, was just limited. "Not all there," Karena told the therapist. "He's phoning it in."

One inevitable morning he parked his sedan in the far corner of the bank parking lot. A battered pickup truck blocked him from view of the street, and he took out his new cell phone to dial Michael. The answering service picked up.

As Ward walked toward the bank, Rose came out the door and crossed the lot, clutching a slip of paper. He drew himself up, realizing it was her truck he'd used for cover. She needed cover too—this idea came to him quickly and with no good reason, though just that week Emma Templeton had told him that Stella had moved into the apartment above The Bluebird. Emma hadn't said more, though of course there was more to the story. There was always more.

Rose walked quickly, staring at her shoes, and he had to call out to get her attention. She stopped, and nodded a greeting.

"Rose, it's been a while. How are things? How's your boy?"

"Lance," she reminded him. "He's fine."

"I know, I remember. He must be getting ready for college, right?" He smiled to let her know he was joking.

"He's ten."

"Ten years old! Where does the time go?"

She looked at her watch. Her hair was pulled into a sloppy bun and there were kernels of sleep in the corners of her eyes, as if that morning she'd just rolled out of bed and into the truck.

"Everything okay, young lady?"

The curves of her mouth flattened. She held up the withdrawal slip. "That woman is too much sometimes."

"Louise?"

She waved a hand, dismissing the name. "How are you, Ward?"

"Oh, you know . . ." he paused as a car peeled through the light at the corner. "Karena's divorcing me." He felt faintly nauseous. He hadn't told anyone yet. The only person who wouldn't be shocked, he supposed, was Scottie.

Rose rocked back on her heels, meeting his eyes. "I'm sorry." Her freckles looked like someone had drawn them on with a pen. He wondered if she was eating enough red meat.

"We tried our best," he said, echoing the therapist. "But paths diverge."

She shoved the bank receipt into her pocket. "They do."

"Well," he edged away. "I'm sorry to share bad news. Say hello to your fellas for me, will you?"

"Oh, no, you shouldn't—Ward." Rose reached out to touch his arm, bringing him to a halt, eyes boring into his. She spoke slowly, as if she were willing it, and not just for him. "You'll be fine."

His eyes prickled and he blinked, irritated and grateful. He went straight to Louise Logan's window to withdraw two hundred dollars.

"Back on schedule?" Louise asked, and he laughed. Louise seemed out of sorts too, less talkative than usual, and his forced chuckle didn't raise her eyebrow as it normally might. As he readied to leave, as an afterthought, she asked after Karena.

*Fine, fine.*

The truth was, he didn't know what he'd do without Karena. Now there would be no stop to the spinning that he felt each time he put his hand to the hotel room door and sensed a man standing on the other side. It would be unceasing, the spinning. It would ruin him.

*

Louise thought it was such a shame, and completely unsurprising, that Rose and Stella let Anderson's slip from their fingers.

"An asset like that, with so much potential," she'd said to her husband, Dave.

"Potential for what?" he'd asked.

"That building could be . . . almost anything." Not having any sort of inheritance to look forward to herself, she often imagined how she might spend other people's legacies. She and Dave, they had resolved, would make sure Benji had something when they were gone. Even if it was just their two-bedroom ranch, fully paid off.

She had entered new territory with Rose on Benji's first day of kindergarten. When she'd picked him up he'd announced that he had a new best friend named Lance and another new best friend whose name was also Benjamin.

"What's Lance's last name?" she asked, feeling a slight twitch in her right cheek.

Benji didn't know, but Louise was fairly certain. A Parent-Teacher Meet & Greet at the end of the week confirmed it. She held Rose in her peripheral vision for a full half hour, circling carefully, before they arrived together at the refreshments table.

"Hello, Louise." Rose wore a blue blouse and her hair was pulled back with a tortoise shell barrette. Her face was thinner than Louise remembered, and her neck sunburned. She looked tired, but to Louise's eyes still attractive, even outdoorsy. Louise looked around for Dave and saw him sitting in a row of tiny desks talking to Rose's husband, Theo. Dave said something and Theo laughed, throwing his head back. *Men have it so easy,* she thought.

"I've heard Lance's name about fifty times this week," she blurted. She picked up the largest brownie on the plate and took a bite.

Rose smiled. "Yeah, they've hit it off. There are two Benjamins in the class, you know, so I wasn't sure whether your son was *the* Ben until just yesterday."

"The other is Benjamin Culp." Louise pointed across the room to his parents. "Our guy is called Benji, at least for now."

"Yes," Rose said. "Benji. A nice name."

"He likes dogs but he's allergic." Louise sighed, and leaned across the table to pick up a small bunch of grapes. It would be her responsibility to keep the conversation going for a decently polite yet brief period of time. Rose was no more interested in niceties than she had been as a teen.

"So how did Lance like the first week?" she asked. "Benji practically grew two inches, he was so proud of himself that first day."

Talking about their sons kept them going for a few minutes. But even as she chatted Louise considered how much more of this was to come: awkward conversations at Little League games and bake sales. Rose would always act superior, a reminder to Louise that she had been measured and come up wanting. *I'm not the only one who's wanting,* she thought, and took another brownie, diet be damned.

Rose was talking about a drawing Lance had made and Louise interrupted her to say, "I was very sorry about your parents, by the way. And the B&B."

"Oh," Rose stopped, dropping her hands—she'd been describing a crayoned monster.

Dave interrupted them at just the right time—or the wrong time. Louise told him later, "Next time you see me stuck in a corner with Rose, *please* come rescue me right away. God, that woman."

"Hey," Dave said now to Louise and Rose, waving Theo over, and Benjamin Culp's parents too. "We need to set up a play date. Our kids are the Three Musketeers!"

Just as she'd foreseen, their sons' friendship meant Louise was never rid of Rose. The boys, along with Ben Culp, were inseparable. At least she was able to minimize her contact with Rose, keeping it to brief chats as she picked up and dropped off the kids for play dates and soccer matches. Louise was never anything but exceedingly polite. "Really," she told Dave, "I deserve a medal. If Benji didn't love that kid so much . . ." But she found herself liking Lance too. Though he was unruly, Lance had an effusive, good-natured charm and he knew how to talk to adults—and she truly believed, based on what she observed, that Rose liked Benji. Louise supposed that she and Rose were setting aside their mutual distaste in the interest of the children. She was proud of herself, and in a strange way proud of Rose, too. *We're grownups.*

Though most of the news she received was over the counter at the bank, Louise didn't glean Rose's scandal at work. Dave was a volunteer fireman and, in that capacity, had gotten to know the county sheriff's deputies. One Saturday afternoon he drove her to the mall a few towns over. They agreed to meet at the car in an hour, and went their separate ways. As she'd carried her bag into the parking lot she saw Dave in conversation with the youngest deputy sheriff, John Peabody. John was shaking his head. There was something skittish and coltish about him, almost pretty. He didn't seem capable of wielding a gun. They parted just before she stepped up to the car. Dave didn't say a word while he put the bag into the trunk. She had to work it out of him like a splinter on the ride home: a tawdry lover's triangle.

"Those girls were close as knives in a drawer!" She could almost, she thought in retrospect, have figured it out on her own. The clues were there all along, you just had to know where to look.

Louise made the mistake of tipping her hand to Rose the next time she came into the bank. She swallowed hard before she spoke. "Rose, how are you? How's Theo?"

Rose looked blank. "He's fine."

"You doing okay?"

"Yes." Her eyes narrowed as she handed her deposit slip across the counter.

"I heard about the accident, I'm so glad no one was hurt." Louise kept her voice neutral.

Rose's cheeks paled, emphasizing what Louise's mother Sharon had called "those unfortunate freckles." She picked up the plastic pen on its silver chain, took a square of scrap paper from the stack set out for customers, and wrote, pen chain whispering against the counter. Louise stared out the window, her mistake dawning. When Rose finally slid the paper toward her Louise reached for it too eagerly.

Rose's eyes locked on hers as their fingertips touched. "Read it."

Rose had lovely penmanship, and for a moment it distracted Louise from the content. *Louise*, the note read, heralded by a winsome L with a loop at the top and bottom, script you'd find on a wedding invitation. *I expect you've heard some things. I expect you to hold your tongue. If you ask again or breathe a word to anyone, especially Lance or Benji, I'll make sure you regret it.* Louise's cheek twitched. They looked at each other. Her face felt carved—something hollowed out and sculpted—a jack-o'-lantern or a cabbage, something soft and vegetal. She fumbled in her cash drawer.

"I'll take my receipt," Rose said. She took the cash, plucked both flimsy pieces of paper from Louise's fingers and left, her back straight in a blue shirt.

Louise came to think of it as The Stickup. Rose, the stickup artist, sliding her demands across the counter, Louise shoving something valuable into a burlap sack, not even trying to press the alarm. There were a million ways Louise could have reacted, a million ways to hold onto her dignity and not cede power. None of them had come to her aid.

She followed the instructions on that note to the letter, even with her book club.

*

In the beginning, the Old Man didn't pay them any mind. Why would he? What good could they do him? Theo's father had been worth something, but Theo himself didn't have the guts. The *instinct*, is what he told Perry.

The wife, though. Rose.

He drove over to pick up a wrench that Theo had borrowed and been slow to return. She came around the side of the house and raised a hand, halting him in his tracks. "One sec," she said, and vanished into the backyard. He'd had every intention of scolding her for Theo's lack of responsibility, leaving her unsettled. But she reemerged a few minutes later holding two tall glasses of lemonade, his wrench in the front pocket of her loose trousers. She handed him a glass and the tool and then wiped her hand along her shirt, leaving a faint dark path.

"That manure?" he asked, for lack of anything else to say, nodding at a dirt pile. He got a confirming whiff right after he spoke. She was taking care of the plants that Theo's mother had tended, which had grown puny in the years since her death.

"I'm hoping they'll bloom the way Theo remembers. Eliza had a green thumb, I hear." She needed a sun hat. Pink flushed her cheeks and forehead.

"They should, if you're good to them. It doesn't take all that much." She smiled. "Just a little extra love."

He had no small talk left. She didn't seem to care, just sat on the porch steps and sipped lemonade. Sweat rings bloomed under her arms. He'd interrupted her work.

"I used to look in the windows of flower shops and never thought a second about what it took to grow those bouquets."

A fly buzzed his hat. He pulled it off to wave it away. Not knowing where else to put himself, he sat on the steps, resting the hat on his lap. The lemonade he set down untouched beside him.

"They're thirsty," he said. "Water them good when you're done."

She agreed, and they talked for a while about watering methods and schedules.

"I don't even remember what color they are," he admitted. "The blooms."

"Mostly red and white. They were scrawny last year." Her second year here. This was by far their longest conversation to date. She swatted at the same fly that had been buzzing him. "I'd invite you in but the baby's sleeping."

The porch sloped at an angle, and the yard was alternately dusty and overgrown. But she'd made progress, he noted. Envy settled like a lozenge in the back of his throat. He took a sip of lemonade to clear it, and coughed, surprised. Real lemons.

"Stella made it," she told him. "I did the backyard first. Easier to fit in an hour out there after dinner. This is going to be more work."

She didn't say it with any sort of anxiety or resentment. He wondered how a person came by such contentment.

After the idiocy with the truck and his elm tree, he saw an opportunity to make inroads. He couldn't imagine she'd want to stay with Theo, and with Stella popping up every time she went into town.

She must be planning an exit, he thought, and he could sweeten the pot. They needed money, it was obvious. He went over when Theo was out of town on a sales trip, trying to interest people in useless widgets. "Of all the dumb ideas," he'd told Perry, "Theo as a salesman wins the prize." But it was useful, having Theo out of the way—the Old Man had a deal in mind, and he wanted to deal with Rose.

She was weeding in her kitchen garden while Lance played with friends in the backyard: three boys in jean shorts leapt through sprinkler spray, daring each other to dive across. Rose invited him into the kitchen for a piece of coffee cake, but he declined.

"Sit down, at least." She pointed him to the back steps, and they sat and watched the boys belly flop into the mud for a while. *Too lenient*, he thought.

"Want some iced tea?"

He shook his head and cleared his throat.

"How's Nina?" Rose asked. "She keeps herself busy. We'll have to plan another picnic one of these days."

He saw no point in beating around the bush. "I've been thinking about expanding again. Trying to. And wondering if you'd be interested in selling me those eastern acres."

She crossed her legs and leaned an elbow onto her knee, calling to the boys, "Watch the berry bushes!"

The kids kept going. She recrossed, right leg over left. He waited. He did not say the things out loud that he knew she knew. *Theo clearly can't handle it. You have too much land and not enough at the same time. The only way to survive is to go big, and there's no way in hell you can do that.*

She tilted her head and scratched her scalp, thinking, but still said nothing. He wished that he had agreed to a glass of tea. Something to look at. One of the boys squealed as he slid too far and scratched an outstretched arm on a low-hanging blackberry bramble. "Benji," she called. "Hold up, boys! Lance, Benji, Ben. Come here now."

"His mother's sure as hell going to ask about that scratch," Rose said under her breath, standing and slamming through the door into the kitchen. She came out with a plate of cookies and a tube of antibiotic ointment. "No cookies 'til you're hosed off," she said. The boys stood in front of the hose and let her spray off the mud, and then the one called Benji held out his arm while she squeezed on some salve. They stomped onto the porch with wet feet and dripping hair to attack the cookies. Boys broke around him like water, ignoring him completely until she said, "Say hello to Mr. Brown."

The Old Man looked down at his shirt, spattered with their muddy spray. He nodded at the boys but fixed his eyes on Rose, determined to get her respect. "We've been here for six generations," he said, "and neighbors with Theo's people for five." The boys chattered behind him, voices high from adrenaline and sugar. He decided right then to tell Rose a story that his own family was sick of hearing: His great-great-great uncle Enoch Brown was bitten by a rabid dog, so the story went, and in his madness went hunting for it, believing the hair of the dog could cure him—could cure every wrong that had ever befallen him, all the woes of his hardscrabble life and all the evil in the world. Enoch Brown was gone before anyone knew to stop him, and found three days later with his rifle cocked against a stump and his fingers stiff on the barrel. He'd shot a perfect semicircle in the dirt around him before taking the rifle into his mouth and working the trigger down with a long birch switch. Paw prints marred the dirt around the body, clumps of fur and foam, and a shuddering lack of blood. A civil war militia was dispatched to kill the dog. And after, the family talked about the hair of that dog blowing across the body of Enoch Brown, blowing across the land, bringing them luck and a certain kind of blessing: Brown blood, running in undercurrents across their rich acreage, thick and muddy as oil.

"They buried the dog's body a stone's throw from Enoch's in the field there behind our barn." He stopped talking and rubbed a palm along his shirtsleeve, feeling almost tipsy.

She'd put a hand to her forehead, pushing at the furrow between her eyebrows as if she had a migraine. "Wow."

He stood abruptly. The boys sat, a row of skinny chests, silent and wide-eyed. They damn well noticed him now. "Think about it," he said to Rose. "Talk to Theo. I know this land better than anyone."

"Sherwin," she shook her head, lips set in a grim half-smile. "Cookie for the road?"

*

Sylvie remembered when their two families were friends. Not just her dad and Lance's dad. At the very edges of her memory: Rose and Theo and Stella and Sylvie's parents, all looking down at her, saying, *You can do it*. They encouraged her to sit up, she thought, and then to stand. Lance was there, always, fleeting through kitchens and living rooms, dashing across scratchy grass. She wanted to keep up.

Those days when everyone stopped and sat still and laughed were rare, but they happened. At Johnson's Creek, they carried her most everywhere: over the big boulder and across the boggy parts of the footpath. Lance threw her red ball so it splashed into the dark part of the water and she cried until a man picked her up and walked her out to it. Her toes were in water, and then her knees and belly. She laughed when they reached the ball, and he said, *Grab it, hon*, and then he carried her back and set her down on her mother's blanket. That was her strongest memory of Lance's father, Theo. The smell of woodsmoke in his hair and his tan shoulders and the ball's red reflection on foresty water. And the sounds of the women on shore—

her mother, Rose, Stella—their voices trailed her through the water and then reeled her in. *Come on.*

By the time Sylvie was in kindergarten, her mother was so busy she never went to the creek, or had lunch on Rose and Stella's porch. Sylvie wondered sometimes if Nina had just decided she didn't much like anyone outside the Browns; that's certainly how she acted, though she never said a peep. But Sylvie still liked Lance and his family, and as soon as she was old enough to walk over there by herself, she did.

Stella's ex-husband had left an old trunk behind, and she would let Sylvie and Lance rummage through it: long dresses, uniforms, a sword none of them had seen the likes of. *Memorabilia*, Stella called it, word rolling off the tongue. Stella said the things were more than a hundred years old, stuff from an old war, when skirmishes were fought in the Midwest. Old guns, too, but no bullets, and a tiny tin of gunpowder that they weren't supposed to touch. Lance loved it. And because he did, Sylvie did too.

Rose smiled sometimes in those days, and Lance could always make her laugh. When they tired of the dress-up trunk, there was softball out back, warm bread with jam, and if they were lucky, Stella's fizzy grape drinks served with paper parasols. "What's for dinner?" Lance asked, and there would be chicken and dumplings on the stove, steam pinking cheeks and hair curling around faces. His father was always off working and there were no muddy boots or loud television shows. The house smelled of Stella's honeysuckle soap and Rose's fresh cut roses and sweetpeas, placed in vases near most every window. While Rose finished up in the kitchen, Stella sailed out in her almost-clean apron and waltzed Lance through the sitting room, twirling in three full rotations before stopping in front of the old record player and picking an album from the stack. The sitting room had a sofa and armchairs that shone in the light so that you did not notice the splitting seams. Stella picked something old, sung by a lady Sylvie had never heard of, and then she stretched her hand out to Sylvie and they curtseyed and twirled together, singing along at the chorus: *Perhaps, perhaps, perhaps* . . . Until Rose called from the kitchen, "Food's ready, wash your hands."

As Rose spoke the phone rang. It was Nina. "It's almost dark, Sill, come on home now." Leaving that house felt like the worst punishment in the world.

Then Stella was gone as if she'd never lived there, and Rose was busier than ever, but never mean. As often as she could, Sylvie went over after school and they'd draw or make forts. Other people's mothers had pop and cherry drink mix. Lance's mother stabbed triangles into the lids of partly rusted tins of juice and set them on the counter next to a bowl of sour green apples and a loaf of dark bread. "Help yourself," she'd say. Rose really meant that part about helping themselves. Lance would drag a chair over, pull down fancy glasses from the highest shelf, and pour with his knees still on the counter. Then he handed them down, juice yellow and smeary against the glass. It tasted sweeter than it looked.

Even later, in sixth and seventh grade, if the Bens weren't around Lance would still hang out with her. If the Bens were there, forget about it. Once she went over to see if he wanted to go looking for tadpoles in Johnson's Creek and the boys were standing in the front yard. The armbands on their jackets matched the red in the trees. Lance was going hunting with Ben Culp and his father, and Ben Logan too. Ben C wasn't Tall Ben then; he hadn't had the growth spurt yet. They were just C and L. Ben L saw Sylvie watching them and pulled a face.

"Shove off," Lance told her. "No girls allowed. You can clean our boots when we get back." The boys laughed like they always laughed together, and hoisted metal in the air. They owned shotguns now, had no memory before guns.

She went to the creek herself but found no tadpoles. Fall's first frost had turned everything burnt umber and crisp, and the water was brackish, clogged with dead leaves. Anything alive was buried in the silt and muck. She stuck her hand deep into the slime to prove she was just as brave as them, she wasn't afraid of anything.

*

As Perry grew older, his relationship with the Old Man achieved a direct coldness that was at times exhilarating. When Nina told him she was pregnant—sitting on the high school's empty football field after a Friday night game, her face pale and worried in the dim light filtering over from the parking lot—he felt a strange calm settle over him. Nina's family was devoutly religious; they had only one option. He could, he thought, follow in Theo's footsteps and create his own family. Figure out a way to make extra money and still be a farmer, attend to tradition and also try for something new.

He wanted more credit for doing the right thing than he got. Nina didn't act at all grateful when he asked her to marry him, she simply expected it. The Old Man called him a dipshit who couldn't keep his dick in his pants, but he settled into the idea of having a daughter-in-law around the house—another person to boss around. Rose and Stella held back whatever surprise they felt and hugged him with what he suspected might have been pity. Perry had to wait a while to tell Theo, who had started traveling for his sales work. He could no longer walk across the fields on any given afternoon and find Theo ready to talk.

The thing was, there was no way around it. He grew up, was what he did. Perry didn't need neighbors to boost him anymore. He had a wife and soon enough a daughter. Standing by the tractor one April afternoon, he told the Old Man, "If you ever hit Nina or Sill the way you did me, I will end you." The Old Man laughed it off and walked away. But Perry had said it, and the Old Man heeded the warning. That success emboldened him. He reminded himself that he had twice the amount of land Theo did. When they talked now they were equals. More than anything else, they were busy. Perry found that he loved the rhythm of work: a love, maybe the only love, that he'd inherited from his father.

Months went by, and years, and Perry looked up to see his daughter heading off to second grade, an orange superhero lunchbox clutched in her small hand. Perry waved to Sill, but she didn't see him. She hurried down to the county road to meet up with Lance. They would walk to the bus stop together. He watched Sill stand on one leg and rub her calf with the back of her shoe, patiently waiting. She'd stand there all day, he knew, if she had to. Within a few minutes Lance appeared, a couple of years older and a head taller than Sill. She swung her lunchbox up in greeting, crouched, and hopped into the road—she'd been obsessed, lately, with how far she could jump. Lance put out a hand to steady her once she landed and then gave her a little shove. There was a careless ease in the gesture, and Lance kept walking, certain that his pesky neighbor would keep up, hopping along at his heels.

Later that morning, Perry drove over to Theo's and found him on the back porch. It had been a few months since Theo and Stella's incident at the tree—*The Infamous Elm*, was how Nina had started to refer to it. Perry had been waiting for the dust to settle. They were trying to act normal, he supposed, for the sake of the boy.

"Seen this?" Theo greeted him by holding up a magazine. It was an article about the relentless growth of agribusiness, nothing Perry didn't know already.

He swung himself down to a seat on the steps, looking out over the backyard. Sill had been over to pick berries not long ago. Nina had told him that Sill had asked Lance where Stella was, and Lance said he didn't know. Rose had sent her home with three pints and a purple mouth.

"You could beat them, you know." Theo stretched out his legs and rocked back in the old chair. "You have enough acres . . . you've just got to figure out how to grow whatever the business suits aren't. There's got to be something."

Perry smiled at the compliment, half believing it. Theo could still put him at ease faster than anyone. "You could too."

Theo shook his head. Perry heard someone in the kitchen behind them. Rose was home, though she didn't come out to greet him. As soon as her steps receded into the house, Perry leaned onto one hand, feigning nonchalance. "Work going all right?"

Theo eased his weight forward to click the front legs of his chair onto the floor, and put his elbows on his knees. "Work is . . . going." He looked out over the yard.

"That's better than nothing. That'll do." Perry felt too eager. He thought of Sill, dancing along behind Lance on their way to the school bus.

"Yes." Theo smiled without a trace of humor. He looked at Perry. "Are you happy?"

"Am I . . ."

"Sorry." Theo leaned back. "Never mind."

"No, it's . . . I guess so." Perry rested elbows on his knees, a self-conscious mirror. "Why not?"

"Good. You should be. We should all try to be, right?" Theo set the magazine down and crossed an ankle over his knee, tapping his fingertips along the sole of his boot.

"Right." Perry sat up straighter. It was time to go, he had to help the Old Man do some maintenance on the harrow. He said as much and left, walking around the side of the house. The radio was on in the kitchen and the news announcer's voice drifted out the window, the man talking about how much he liked his new Chevy, which came fully loaded and with more horsepower than a man had a right to ask for. Perry stopped and turned around.

Theo was right where he'd left him, still tapping on his shoe and staring out over the grass. "Are *you* happy?" Perry asked.

Theo smiled for real this time, his eyes lightening. "Trying, yeah. Believe it or not." He shrugged, his face rueful but also familiar, the same Theo that Perry had always known. That steady certainty was in him still. "Yeah," he told Perry again, nodding, firming his resolve as he spoke. "Yeah, thanks. We're hanging in."

Nina took the call from Rose, and her voice when she called Perry was sharper than he had ever heard it, pulling him off his work and spinning him out toward Rose's farthest acres.

Theo had been meaning to fix the sticky steering column on his tractor. Rose found him in the afternoon, his legs crushed under a wheel, internally bleeding from a punctured spleen. She couldn't lift the machine to move him, had to fold up her sweater, place it under his head, and run home for help.

Perry arrived just after Lance, who'd come home from school and seen the note pressed to the kitchen table. Lance was thirteen, a strong kid but not full-grown. Rose was wild—she wore a faded dress and big brown boots and she circled the tractor, kicking and pulling at its metal edges. Lance fell to his knees by his father's head and put his ear to Theo's blue lips. "How long?" Perry asked Rose, but she didn't know. She came around to Lance, dropped herself to the ground, put her feet on the machine and shoved. Lance was quick to add his own weight, and Perry his, until they raised it just enough to pull Theo loose.

One side of Theo's chest was higher than the other. His right arm was flung above his head, the left across his breastbone, fingers twisting the cloth of his shirt. The wide set of his eyes gave him a surprised look, and Theo stared into the bright sky like it had asked a question he was giving his all to answer. His legs were dusty and loose, and his right boot was missing.

Rose reached out and shut the eyelids. "Holy hell." She sat back on her heels. Perry put his hand on Theo's shoulder and felt the cooling under the thin cloth. Then Lance crouched to lift his father.

"Let me," Perry said, but Lance brushed his hand aside and hoisted Theo into the fireman's carry. Blood trickled down Lance's back, shaken loose from his father. The boy stumbled and then found his footing. Perry put his arm around Rose and they walked back slowly, keeping pace with Lance, all three panting like runners. Rose felt wispy under his arm. Perry watched Lance's back, thinking, it was all in the timing. Theo might have lived if Rose had gone looking sooner, or if he'd been thrown an inch or two further.

The kid's knees didn't buckle until they'd almost reached home, and Perry stepped forward to catch Theo as Lance rolled out from under him. "Where?" he asked Rose. She pointed Perry to the downstairs sewing room—Stella's old room—and Perry stretched Theo out on a flowery spread, the coldness of him shocking under his fingers. He looked at Theo's face, the high cheekbones and graying brown hair. It was like seeing someone sleep for the first time.

Rose's voice came from the kitchen—she was making the call to the coroner, and Perry walked out to the back porch to find Lance. He was smoking a cigarette and handed Perry the pack before he could say a word. Perry was glad to have something to look at. Minutes passed before his own cigarette was lit, time slowed.

"A fluke—"

Lance nodded.

"Nobody's fault."

Lance's eyes squinted as he took a drag. Twilight had come and the back of their house was softly lit. Rose's climbing ladybanks and blackberry shrubs, two old lawn chairs, and the brown grassy circle in the center—all of it turned reddish in the light.

"You need to be strong for Rose."

Lance nodded again. "I will."

"And if you need anything, just call us, okay?" He should've left it at that, but he didn't. "And if anything comes up on the land, or anything else you can't handle, you come talk to me, okay?"

"He'll come talk to me." Rose stood at the screen door behind them, her shape a dark outline behind the gray mesh.

"They coming?" Lance asked her.

"Yes." The coroner. The sheriff. They knew the way.

"I'll stay," Perry said, and her head tilted toward him in agreement. He felt the weight of his adulthood then, and hers, and for the first time realized that she'd been almost a child herself when they'd met. He wondered briefly if he should offer to call somebody for her—Stella?—but then thought better of asking. Rose would do what she wanted.

Nina and the Old Man and the coroner arrived all at once, and Perry slipped away from the group, went to his fallow acres and rolled back the stone for Theo. *Jesus God. Of all the men to take*. Theo's had the worst luck of any family he knew. And yet, Theo's wide eyes had seemed astonished at the rightness of the world, even up to the end.

There was scarcely a sign of Rose or Lance for at least a month. Nina and Perry made visits with food, but Rose didn't ask them in, so they never stayed long. Sill said that Lance was never on the school bus. Finally the truancy officer drove out and said something. "Rose should come to church," Nina said one night as the Browns sat around the supper table, "If there's any time you need it . . ."

"They'll sell us the land soon," the Old Man said. "She can't manage alone."

Nina set down her fork. The Old Man thundered on, riding over Nina, directing his lecture at Sill this time, telling her that Theo wouldn't have lasted on the farm as long as he had without Rose. "She's the flinty one," he said. "They would've sold years ago, and taken a loss." There was admiration in his father's voice, and also scorn. The Old Man speared a small potato with his fork, pointing it at his granddaughter as he spoke. "Theo's grandfather—Lance's great-granddad—he was different. He could squeeze seeds out of gravel, and had to some years. Unless you put your guts into it, you've got no business living out here."

Perry brought his iced tea to his lips and took a long sip. Silence fell. Another kind of conversation: forks against plates, everyone working their own thoughts, and the dining room clock ticking. The Browns spent any number of nights this way.

Later that summer, Perry heard a whirr of wheels spinning on gravel. Then screeching gears and a sputtery engine. He walked out to the porch. Down on the county road, Rose sat in the passenger seat, clutching the dashboard. She was teaching Lance to drive. Perry could see the kid's brown hair flipping around his eyes as he looked down to shift. Their old blue Ford lurched up and down the road for almost an hour.

"Poor kid," Nina said. "Talk about the hot seat." She and Sill sat on the porch and drank iced tea, clapping when Lance made it into second without stalling.

Rose should have taught Lance to drive on some road on their land, Perry thought, so he wouldn't have to learn on display. That's what Theo would've done. But Rose never thought like that. The truck lurched and stopped. The kid kept trying.

"He's just like his dad," Nina said after a while. "Even-keeled." She smiled.

The Old Man had stepped onto the porch, drawn to the spectacle. "Plenty of Rose in him too," he said, "just watch."

Perry walked out to the barn and worked oil into an old harness, a useless piece of leather. He thought that Lance looked like Theo and saw like Rose. Meaning, he had Theo's long legs and brown hair and high cheekbones, the hint of Osage in the family tree—and Rose's way of seeing, quick to sum things up. *He'll be all right,* Perry thought. *Better than all right.*

Not long after, Perry caught Lance and two friends—the Bens, Sill called them—setting fire to a bag of manure that Nina had planned to use in her kitchen garden and left out behind the barn. He heard a popping sound like a firecracker. Then Lance's voice: "Aw, man!" Perry rounded the barn and saw Lance holding a can of lighter fluid while the Ben in a blue t-shirt tossed a lit match.

"Hey! What are you doing?"

They scattered. The taller, blue-shirted Ben broke for the road, and the shorter, squat one followed him, longish dirty blond hair flying. Lance tossed the lighter fluid can and spun toward home, his worn sneakers covering yards before Perry recovered to yell, "Get your ass back here, dammit!"

Down by the road, a boy let off a peal of laughter. Perry grabbed an old shovel and tossed dirt over the flames, beating them down, and with each whack of the shovel he smelled manure. He smacked down so hard, the shovel blade snapped off the shaft. When the flames were out he looked up. Lance stood twenty feet into the field, corn up to his waist, panting, his face solemn and unreadable. "That's right," Perry said. "Stay put. I know where you live." Lance gave a hint of a smile, almost a sneer, and took off for real.

The Old Man was livid when he heard and called Rose to give her hell. "A spark on that old wood, that's all it would take," he spat into the phone. She offered to replace the shovel and said Lance could do some work for them to make up for his carelessness. "Carelessness!" the Old Man scoffed. Perry cringed, registering the thin vein of satisfaction running underneath his father's indignation.

"I'll handle it," he said.

That weekend, he drove Lance into town to pick up a replacement shovel at Mondragon's. The boy wore an old Bruce Springsteen t-shirt that Perry was fairly certain had been Theo's, and kept a gob of chewing gum in his cheek. Rose had nipped the cigarette smoking in the bud, Perry hoped. "Shit happens, right?" Perry said, but his attempt at a joke was lost on Lance, who shifted the gum in his mouth and blew a noncommittal bubble. The boy slumped further against the door. "Planning an early exit?" Perry asked. Then he vowed to keep his mouth shut. Theo had made it look easy. He turned on the radio and told the kid to pick his favorite station, and they rode the rest of the way to town on a thumping bass beat.

The aging weekend group was on the porch when they pulled up to Mondragon's. Farmers talking about everything and nothing. Tom Muldoon sat by a cardboard box under a hand-lettered sign: *Puppies Free to Good Home.*

Before Perry cut the engine, the kid opened the door and slid out. Perry watched the men on the porch notice Lance's presence, a tiny ripple acknowledging the family's recent loss. He followed Lance onto the porch, and they stood shoulder to shoulder looking down into the box. Four mutts in varying patterns of black and white squirmed on an old Army blanket.

"My Labrador bitch went on a date with the wrong dog," Tom Muldoon said, greeting Perry. "Some kind of collie, we think. But they'll be good family dogs, probably good hunting dogs too."

"They don't cost anything?" Lance asked. These were more words than he'd strung together all morning.

Perry put a hand on Lance's shoulder, steering him through the door into the store. "Dogs cost a lot," he whispered. "Food and vet bills aren't cheap. Nothing's really free."

Ward called a greeting from behind the counter. Lance pulled away and walked to a rack of magazines while Perry spoke to Ward. He took his time, wanting to give the boy a breather, a chance to look around. Also, he was relieved to be speaking to someone who could hold up the conversation. Ward yammered on as he usually did, in a way that had always struck Perry as a little forced. He mentioned an upcoming trip to the city, asked after Nina and Sill, even evaluated the merits of the frozen dinner he'd eaten for lunch. Perry responded—*sounds fun, they're great, what do you know*—all the while watching the boy circling from the magazines to the tools to the sundries, until finally he couldn't put off paying and raised his voice a notch to ask, "What do we owe you for the shovel?"

That was Lance's cue to come up to the register, peel his allowance out of his pocket, and pay the piper. Lance did not come. Perry turned and saw the boy hanging out of the doorway, looking at the pups again.

"Lance, c'mon now," Perry called.

Ward had a piece of toffee ready. "You're too old for freebies," he said to Lance, sliding the red-wrapped candy across the counter as the boy came to join them. "But what the heck."

"Thanks." Without meeting Ward's eyes, the kid popped the toffee into his mouth right along with the bubble gum.

"It's twenty bucks," Perry said, pointing at the shovel. Being an adult, it struck him, often amounted to being an asshole.

Ward hooked a thumb under one of his suspender straps and shifted his weight, belatedly realizing that a power struggle was unfolding. Lance chewed, working the gum-toffee to the front of his mouth, and tried to blow a bubble without success.

"You look so much like your dad," Ward said quietly, speaking more carefully now. "He was a great guy."

The boy jammed a fist into his jeans pocket, looking down. But he couldn't hide the flush that hit his cheeks, or the tears that rose but did not crest. He pulled out a ten and a five and slapped the bills down next to his empty toffee wrapper.

Ward shot a glance at Perry, perhaps a signal of caution, or regret that he'd mentioned Theo. Perry thought, *If I were a better person and knew how to do these things, I'd know exactly what that look means*. But he wasn't, and couldn't be sure. He paid the difference, thanked Ward, and lifted the shovel over his shoulder.

On the porch, Lance crouched over the box, scratching the hyper pups behind the ears. Perry watched the boy, still hiding his face as he curved a palm under a warm belly.

"He likes you," Tom Muldoon said, and winked at Perry.

The all black one was the fattest; the pup wriggled onto his back for more belly rubs and then stood on unsteady legs to scratch at an ear, falling onto a haunch in the process. He stood, shook himself, walked over a brother and sat in the corner, keeping an eye on Lance.

Perry took a breath. "That's a good one right there," he said to Lance. "The black one."

Later he would tell Nina that yes, he knew it wasn't his place, that Rose probably wouldn't let the boy keep the dog and it would be all his fault, Perry's damn fault, for raising the kid's hopes and then dashing them. He knew better, he did. "But . . . I guess I don't know," he said. "It just seemed like the right thing to do."

Lance held the puppy on his lap the whole ride home. It was watchful, and mostly calm, once trying to climb onto the dashboard to bark at an approaching car. Lance laughed.

"What are you going to call him?" Perry asked.

The boy considered the dog for a while, then looked at the horizon.

"Fergus," he said.

# 3.

When Rose brought her son in to Dunleavy's Fine Shoes (&Shoe Repair), it was Scottie's first sale all week. The blue truck rumbled to a stop in front of his window and Rose sprang out like a girl. Then the kid stepped out, a little slower—he was looking across the street to Mondragon's Emporium. Rose didn't look. She was not looking at Mondragon's with a will that was offhand but no less strong for it. It was about Stella, he knew, and the old trouble between them.

The kid, Lance, had a carelessness with the world that most kids do. Scottie disliked him immediately. He wanted sneakers, asked for a brand and style that Scottie didn't carry, and shrugged when Rose picked up a basic blue and white runner. The boy had grown since he had last seen him, and the kid was almost Scottie's height. Lance slumped in the chair, feet stretched out in dirty work boots, one foot turned in at an angle—a boy in an almost man's body. He wore a black t-shirt faded to gray with lettering that read, *The odds are good, but the goods are odd.* A baseball cap shaded his eyes and longish, silky hair poked underneath it. Scottie couldn't say what his face looked like.

"This one," Rose said.

Scottie went to the back to get Rose's choice, found he didn't have that in the right size, and pulled the one pair of size 11 sneakers he had on hand. The kid winced when he saw them, and asked if he had any other styles. Scottie said, *No.* So the boy tried them on, walking around and staring down at his feet.

"How do they feel?" Rose asked.

"Okay."

"Enough room in the toe? Where's your big toe?"

Scottie dutifully bent to feel and the kid moved away, toward the window, looking at Mondragon's. Stella had been married to Ward for several years at that point.

"They're fine, Ma."

"Extra support for pronators," Scottie muttered, hoping they wouldn't ask him what that meant because he wasn't entirely sure. Rose nodded and otherwise they ignored him. She clutched her bag in the way of proud people with not much money—about to spend and feeling it almost physically.

"Well?" she prodded.

The kid bounced up and down on his toes. His feet looked like white cars, with rounded edges and clunky detailing. "Yep," he said. They were unpopular shoes five seasons ago, even more so now. Each of them knew it. "There's something on the lace," Lance said, pointing. The white cotton was discolored, a brownish patch that could have been a water stain or, if the shoes had ever done time on display, a badly cleaned patch of Dogberry puke.

"I've got spare laces in the back," Scottie said. He held out his hands, waiting, while the kid sat, removed the shoes, and handed them over.

"You're sure they fit?" Rose asked.

"Ma!" Lance said. He put his boots back on and wandered over to the window, checking Mondragon's again. Scottie turned to the back and stepped on Dogberry's tail. The cat let out a low growl that rose to a yelp, and Scottie leapt back, dropping the sneakers.

"Yikes," Rose said.

"Sorry," Scottie said. "Sorry, sorry."

"That your cat?" the kid asked, and Scottie stooped to pick up the shoes without answering. Whose cat would it be? They looked at each other, mother and son, and Rose gave a small shake of the head.

"Ah, anything you want to try on, Rose?"

"No. Thanks." She said each word distinctly, a pause between them.

He felt their eyes all the way to the back. The spare laces were in a box near his hot plate, and he sat on the cot to relace the sneakers. Scottie turned the shoe in his hand. He put on his magnifying visor and pulled a thin-tipped, indelible marker from his pocket. Then he traced his finger along a gulley on the sole and wrote: *I will do anything to belong.* In the corresponding groove on the other side: *I am a fuckwad.* He sat, blowing on the ink until it dried. Even knowing where to look, once he removed his magnifier Scottie had to pull the shoe almost to his nose to see it. "Dunleavy's special," he whispered.

He stood, arranged his penknife inside his pants pocket, and started back to his customers. Dogberry had retreated to his spot in the window, recovered from the indignity that Scottie had inflicted. Glancing at the security mirror hanging overhead in the corner, he watched a reflected Lance walk over to the cat and touch Dogberry gingerly behind one ear, testing before he ran a hand down the cat's back. "He smells Fergus, probably," the boy said to Rose. Scottie couldn't hear what she said in response. Dogberry arched his back with pleasure.

Scottie shifted the sneakers to his other hand and returned to the stockroom, tossing them onto the worktable. He pulled the ladder out and shoved it against the corner above his bed, climbing to reach the furthest stack of shoeboxes, opening and setting aside at least half a dozen before he found what he was looking for, in the correct size. Vintage canvas basketball shoes, about twenty years old, with a large white star on each heel. He put the box under his arm and climbed down. Then he picked up a pen and wrote one word on each sole: *Odd. Good.*

"Want to try these on?" he asked the kid, handing them over and watching the eyes widen in recognition.

"Jeez," Lance said, and looked at his mother. "These are cool."

Rose paid cash. Scottie slipped the box into a shopping bag and handed her the receipt. "Thank you," she said. She set the words on the counter and walked away; that was how Rose did things. He patted his fingers on the edge of the cash register, leaving clammy fingerprints, and then looked to the kid at the front of the store. Lance was standing by the window display, idly turning a dress shoe in his hand and peering out into the street. The boy bent and leaned forward, looking at the glass. Scottie scurried toward them, calling thanks and goodbye and come again. Rose was at the door, her fingers on the handle. But the kid didn't move—he was reading Scottie's tiny lettering backwards, hand on the display shoe, eyes intent on the glass. He had good, young eyes. *You don't see what's right in front of you. The world makes fools of us all*. After a moment he straightened and looked at Scottie.

The only time anyone had noticed one of his secret messages. Scottie stopped, speechless. It felt as though his body still moved, walls receding as his eyes dilated. The kid could do most anything—read it aloud, point and ask bluntly, *What's that?*, smirk conspiratorially, or just look at him nervously. He didn't. His eyes, like Rose's words, were level. Scottie glanced to the bag but Rose was already swinging the shoes toward Lance. The kid took it, his eyes still on Scottie; then he gave a little half-nod, half-shrug, and walked out the door.

"Thank you?" Scottie called feebly.

Lance slid into the passenger seat of the pickup, looking once more at the legitimate sign on the window, and the faint trail of black lettered dust beneath it. He rolled down his window, set his elbow on the sill and hooked his fingers into the roof ledge, tapping his thumb on the worn rubber weather stripping. Everything he did seemed new to Scottie, and vaguely mysterious.

A month went by, and the next time he saw the boy the long hair was gone. Lance sported a buzzcut, and Ward confirmed that the kid had signed up for the Army. In hindsight, Scottie figured that chances were good that Lance had been too preoccupied with his own life to register the message. He had likely blinked and forgotten it on his way to some new dull teenage thought. Or perhaps he hadn't managed to read the backwards lettering after all, hadn't even bothered expending the energy. But Scottie was not convinced of this. The kid had looked that day, and acknowledged Scottie's interior life without judgment or resistance. Rose's palm flat on the counter, pushing bills forward; the boy by the window, eyes level, Scottie's words still pressed upon them; his hand damp in his pocket, heart zooming—and him, Scottie, he was just a body, *being seen*.

*

Louise, for one, could not believe she was the mother of a seventeen-year-old. "It doesn't seem possible," she told Dave when they took their Sunday afternoon walk, looping six times around the high school track. "I don't feel middle-aged."

"You won't feel old, either, when we're eighty," Dave said, linking his fingers through hers as they puffed along. "That's just the kind of girl you are."

Benji—he was still Benji in her head, though mostly she remembered to call him Ben out loud, now that he'd forsaken his old nickname—had announced that he was going to study theater at State, and he had absolutely no intention of ever settling down in some backwater. He had New York in his sights, though at this point he couldn't afford a dorm room in the state capital without their help. Benji had turned into what the school guidance counselor called an "artsy" teen, dying his hair purple and wearing clothes that made him stand out, and not in a good way. Last week she'd stopped him from leaving the house in a shirt that read *Pussy Power*. "It's ironic, Mom," he'd groaned.

"That's not what I'd call it," she said, sending him in to change. She'd turned the shirt inside out and stuck it far into the big trash bin at the corner of the garage, which is where she'd also shoved his copy of *The Communist Manifesto*. Louise supposed she should be grateful that his friends were still his friends. Lance and Ben C looked much more like boys are supposed to look, and dressed as you'd expect, but Benji's experimenting did not seem to faze them.

"I don't want him to be . . . to get too far out there," she said to Dave as they rounded lap three.

"He'll get grateful," Dave said. "Just give him a few years out in the cold world." It surprised her, sometimes, how well she and Dave got along, eighteen years and counting. She took care not to be show-offy about it, her happy marriage.

Benji's friends were nicer to her than he was. Ben Culp had grown into a reedy, quiet kid, a crack shot by all accounts; he wasn't interested in college at all, and everyone expected him to follow his older brother into the service. Ben C had an awkward, old-fashioned politeness, calling her *ma'am* and asking her permission before he took a can of pop from the fridge. And then there was Lance. Rose's son was around several times a week, shooting hoops in the driveway, or helping Benji fix up Dave's old Chevy Impala, and Louise would pause on her way in from work to greet them. She was used to his easy manners by now: "You look nice today, Mrs. Logan. Did they treat you all right at the bank?" Louise recognized the skill set of a certain kind of only child—one comfortable serving as a companion for grown-ups. She'd had it herself at his age, more at ease with her mother and her bridge cronies than with her own peers. Benji had somehow become that other kind of only child, used to center stage, expecting adults to dote and then disappear into the wings when something more interesting to him came along.

"Well, aren't you the flatterer," she'd said to Lance, and tilting her head at Benji, suggested he give her son some tips. Benji rolled his eyes and didn't even bother to wait until she went into the house to laugh.

Now as she and Dave walked, they discussed the news that Lance had joined the Army. Louise wasn't disappointed, exactly, or even completely surprised, but she felt a prickle of distress. "I just thought . . . I wanted him to go to State with Benji," she said. "They'd be perfect roommates. They'd keep each other in line. Benji's got better study habits and Lance would help with . . ." *Social skills. Talking to girls. Being normal.*

"Not every kid's as lucky as Ben," Dave reminded her as they finished lap six. "Wanna take one more spin?"

Later that week, Lance showed up at the house and before sending him down the hall to Benji's room she took the opportunity to ask him about it. She poured him a glass of milk and pulled some sandwich cookies from the cupboard. "So," she said, slicing open the package, "The Army!"

Lance nodded, looking a bit shy, which was out of character. He was still getting used to telling people, she supposed, getting used to managing reactions.

"What decided you? What did the recruiter promise?"

He laughed at her directness. "Oh, I guess the usual. They'll help me out with school eventually."

"Wouldn't you rather go to college now?"

He took a cookie from the plate and ate it slowly, staring into the fish tank burbling on the counter. Louise had sometimes suspected that Lance's manners hid what he really thought about people. Nevertheless, she thought he liked her—he liked all the Logans; he wouldn't be around so much if he didn't. Now Lance seemed as if he were trying to appear contemplative—or maybe he was just stumped by her question. They peered into the tank together. Her favorite angelfish was pecking at the plastic merman's head.

Louise took a bite of cookie, feeling the creamy sugar coat her teeth. "What will . . . what does your mom say?" He was used to her asking questions about his mother, and he usually gave a diplomatic answer, though once in a while he let a good tidbit slip. That was how Louise had come to know that Rose worked all the time to keep the farm going, that she had picked up shifts at The Bluebird as soon as Stella moved on to greener pastures at Mondragon's, and that she called their neighbor, Sherwin Brown, a greedy nutjob.

Lance scratched the back of his neck. "She says that I'm going to have to adjust to being, you know, regimented. But it's only a couple of years. You can get used to anything for a couple of years. I can, anyway."

"That's pretty mature of you." Benji would never say a couple of years didn't amount to much.

"Yeah." He gave a half-hearted smile. Chocolate crumbs were stuck in his teeth. "We'll see how it goes."

She pulled a glass from the strainer by the sink and drank some water, swishing it around her mouth before swallowing, and looked out the window into the backyard. The neighbor's poodle mix was barking at nothing again.

"Well, I guess I'll go find Ben before I eat all these myself . . . thanks, Mrs. Logan."

Her back still to him, she asked, "What would you do if you had all the time and money in the world? What would your choice be then?"

"Wow. I don't know. I guess travel. I'd probably travel. See the world."

"Benji wants to go to New York."

"Yeah, New York would be great. I'd start there. We could share an apartment." She blinked, hearing this echo of her college wish for Benji: roommates looking out for one another. Lance didn't want to stick around any more than her son. *Does Rose know that?* she wondered. *Rose has spent so much energy holding onto that land for him and he might not even want it.*

"That would be great," she said, turning and forcing a smile. "You should aim for that. Who knows what a few years will bring."

"Yeah, who knows."

"But you know what they say, there's no place like home. Remember that."

She put a few more cookies on the plate and shooed him down the hall. The neighbor's dog was still barking. Louise pulled a cardboard box from the top of the fridge and went into the backyard, shaking it. "Mister! Mister—what a dumb name for a dog. Here. Will this bribe you to be good?" His barking escalated as she approached, and then, crunching happily on the biscuit she tossed over the fence, he fell silent. Louise stood in the backyard, looking at her small, tidy brick house.

It was all she had ever used to want. Benji's room faced the yard, and she could see her son and Lance through the window, looking at something on Benji's desk. Her son grabbed a cookie and pulled it apart to reach the icing. Lance said something and Benji stood, punched him in the shoulder and then turned to take a jacket from his closet, the black one that he'd stuck weird patches and pins all over. They were probably going to work on the car. She could predict almost exactly what they might be saying to each other, and with what inflections. But they looked for this moment like strangers, two unknown young men inside her home. Louise wondered if anything she said could alter any decision either of them would make, good or bad. This was how all mothers felt at some point, even Rose . . . she wiped the thought away impatiently, smelling dog treat and cookie on her hand as she ran it across her face. *Gross*. Benji led the way out the door, and they were gone.

"New York, New York," she said. "A helluva town." Mister cocked his head, trying to understand the words, hoping they meant another treat.

*

In the first years of her banishment, Stella worked long hours at The Bluebird—sixty-five a week, she needed the money—and most mornings she trod a path from her daybed to her tea kettle. Then down the stairs to the café counter and kitchen and tables and back again. She worked her life into a fine cocoon. At the end of each shift she walked upstairs, feet numb and lower back throbbing, heated a can of soup to lukewarm and sat on her daybed to eat, the scent of griddle grease rising from her pale blue polyester uniform. Single and seemingly available, she brushed aside date requests, under-the-table gropings, and one drunken marriage proposal.

The news of Theo's death shocked her. Stella wrote a condolence note. Very simple—even, she thought, rather elegant—on cream-colored card stock with one pale purple flower. *Rose and Lance, I am so sorry for your loss. Please accept my deepest condolences*. She put her phone number beneath her name. But she did not hear from them. There was nothing she could offer that Rose would take. She was thoroughly on her own. Which, in a strange way, felt familiar: her original state of being.

One night she sat at her table with a cup of Irish Breakfast tea and made a list of how she wanted her life to be different:

*Nice clothes and car, etc.*

*Someone who doesn't drink. Someone older?*

*Good values*

*Knowledge of the world*

*Travel? (Venice!)*

*Smart about finances*

*Appreciative*

*No farms, town only—City??*

*Family centered*

She set the pencil down, let it roll between her fingers, and then picked it up again.

*I want to meet someone understanding, not stubborn, not prideful, not thinking he's always better—not like you, Rose. How come you never looked me in the eye to curse my name? Why didn't you come have it out with me? We could've gone out in a blaze of glory instead of this godforsaken limbo—it is limbo, Rose, and you're in it too whether you like it or not. But you're the one with the son who's old enough now to come to town on his own and he remembers me and I can get him to love me again. I raised him too. He hasn't forgotten. And whatever he has forgotten I'll remind him of, because what happened happened and I am at fault but that doesn't mean that I'm not allowed to care anymore, it doesn't mean I have no rights. It doesn't mean—*

And here she ran out of paper. Stella folded the page into eighths like a school note and stuck it into a library book about backpacking through Eastern Europe. She set her elbows on the cover to flatten the seams and forgot it there, leaving it in the book for some future traveler to find and unfold and be puzzled by and then refold to use for a bookmark and leave on a table in a noisy little café in Budapest.

Thinking of her list, she bought herself a new lipstick. She began visiting Mondragon's a few times a week, lingering at the counter. And she planned how to best use the opportunity when she ran into Lance—his coach often brought the team to The Bluebird after a game. He was growing taller every week. There was a new, better life in front of her, if she made the right choices.

She got Ward to fall in love and propose so easily it almost wasn't sporting. He was lonely without Karena, that had a lot to do with it. Older men, she noted, seemed no more equipped than younger ones to be comfortable alone. In spite of his bulky size, Ward had a delicate soul. Talking about his parents and their legacy (his mother had passed away down in Orlando only a few years before), his eyes misted with tears. Stella leaned across the counter to softly squeeze his hand.

"Would you like to have dinner with me sometime?" Ward asked abruptly, looking surprised.

Within the year, Stella found herself living in a sturdy brick house on a wide street, with her own sitting room and a large, sunny kitchen with a new fridge. She quit her job at The Bluebird and after some months had passed she heard that Rose had taken on some waitressing shifts—her stepsister was in town regularly, though their paths never crossed. Stella rolled over in bed each morning, flinging an arm across Ward's wide chest, and reaffirmed her decision to make her life better, with or without Rose's forgiveness. It was easy to love Ward—he was kind and thoughtful and eager to teach her all about running Mondragon's. If he seemed distracted at times, or distant, she gave him space. He always came around, hugging and twirling her after his business trips to the city as if he'd been gone a month instead of one night. She would never again, she vowed, pretend to be someone she was not; she would not grab too hard or push away—she would *be*, just herself, and that would be enough. Now after she showered in the mornings Stella dressed in nice skirts and heels and soft sweaters. It was a uniform as much as The Bluebird's blue polyester, but it presented a closer approximation of her new self than anything she could have hoped for. She was determined to be happy.

After he got a driver's license, Lance came into Mondragon's every Friday afternoon, and midweek sometimes too. He often brought the Brown girl with him, following adoringly at his heels. Rose never found out that her son had reclaimed his banished aunt, so far as Stella knew. Sometimes Lance mentioned Rose, something she'd said or done, and Stella felt a little click in her chest, an unlatching—but she was always painstaking with Lance. She never pried; she never tried to justify her past actions to him. They were new together. She was redeemed in his presence and he was the apple of her eye, the son she never had. Rose had nothing to do with it.

One Friday Lance came in and Stella made her usual fuss over how grown-up he was getting and asked what his plans were after graduation. Before he could answer she rushed in: "College, honey. Talk to Ward, he went to State, you know."

Lance looked at her husband and asked, "You liked it?" As he listened to Ward, Stella found herself searching Lance's face, looking for pieces of Rose, of Theo, and finding them. He had Theo's bone structure but Rose's brow shape, and sometimes he shot a look that took her straight back to childhood. She remembered the feel of Rose's warm sock on her foot, and shivered.

From a distance, she tried to convince Rose that college was possible. "Ward and I can help with tuition," she whispered to Lance the following week. "You tell your mother that." He nodded vaguely—he knew better than to be a messenger between them. So she wrote Rose a letter, her first contact since the condolence note. Stella sat at the kitchen table, used her best stationery, wrote and rewrote and cut an entire paragraph. She was still occupied with it one night after dinner when Ward wandered in for some frozen yogurt.

"What's up, honey?" he asked, pulling a bowl from the cupboard.

"How does this sound?" She rattled off the letter.

Ward set down his bowl. "You want to pay for the boy's college?"

She realized too late her mistake. Ward had mentioned once or twice lately that he was worried about cash flow. "Oh, please sweetie, can't we just help? He's such a good kid and getting out of here for school would be so great for him. And State's not that expensive, really. I just feel . . . I want him to have choices, Ward. Like you did."

Ward blinked. The bowl sat empty on the counter behind him. "Choices? I . . . we'd need to tighten our belts, Stella, quite a bit."

She undid the wide red leather belt that cinched her waist, sat up straighter, drew it in two notches and smiled prettily.

"Well," he said. "Let's see what Rose says."

Rose didn't say anything. Not yes or no, not a curse or a lament. She just didn't reply.

And the next thing Stella heard, Lance had called up that recruiter Jim Culp, the bastard, and signed his life away.

Soon after, Lance stopped by the store and casually mentioned that he needed a couple of new jerseys. She pounced at the opportunity. "Well, I just was thinking earlier that I need to run and get some new socks for Ward. How about we head over to the mall? He can close the store just fine on his own—can't you, Ward?" she called to the back. "I'll drop you at your truck afterward and you'll still be home in time for dinner."

Lance grinned. "You got time?" When did she not have time for him? Then they were off, buckled into her champagne-colored sedan, barreling down the road ten miles over the speed limit.

On the way back from the mall Ward called her cell phone and asked her to bring a file from the home office. In a blink Lance was sitting at her kitchen table; the one and only time he'd ever been to their house. He drank milk and shoved chocolate cake into his mouth, and she had the impression that everything about him—his red t-shirt, the glossy brown hair, the white plate he held in place with two fingers as he ate, his young back against the vinyl chair—all of him was vibrant with life, the most spectacular and yet the most natural sight her kitchen had ever seen. Combustible with promise.

His own promise, but also that of Rose and Theo, and Stella herself. *We made you.*

"Another piece?" she asked, as soon as he set the fork down.

He belched. "Scuze me." He covered his mouth in a delayed attempt at etiquette and looked at the clock on the wall. "I guess I'd better get home." Then: "It was nice to see where you and Ward live, Aunt Stella."

"Anytime, Lance. You know that."

He smiled, picking up the plastic shopping bag that held three new cotton jerseys. "You're so nice to me now." She must have blanched, because he corrected himself. "I mean, not that you weren't nice before . . . but, when we didn't see each other."

"I regret that," she said in a rush. "I regret not being there after your dad died and . . . all the rest of it."

He shrugged. "We did all right."

"I know you did. But I wish—"

Later, she replayed this conversation over and over in her head. In each recalled version, she said something beautiful and true and it locked her imprint onto Lance forever: the words took on shape, and the shape took on heft and became tangible, a suit of armor. But she could not remember what she had actually said to him that day. And if she didn't remember, no doubt he forgot as soon as she dropped him at his truck, pecking him on the cheek and asking him to run the file folder in to Ward.

Her sturdy sedan door clicked shut after Lance with a finality that echoed in the car and the street, a repercussion she still heard each time she walked into the kitchen and sat at the bare table: the pitiless sound of his leaving.

*

Rose set Stella's letter onto the kitchen counter and looked at it. Messy handwriting, fussy paper, flowery sentences—what gall.

*Dear Rose,*

*I very much hope this note finds you well. I write because I have heard that Lance is almost ready to graduate (how hard it is to believe that so much time has passed!) and I would like to extend an offer of assistance for college. Ward and I (he's my husband now, as you may have heard) would very much like to help in some way, such as paying for a portion of tuition or room and board.*

*I realize that this offer comes out of the blue, but I hope you'll consider it seriously. I am so fond of Lance, and I want him to have every possible success, as I'm sure you do too. I still consider Lance my godson. We have no children of our own, and are lucky to have resources. Ward went to State and he might be able to help set up a few campus introductions. Please let me know when we could talk further about this. I hope you will respond, for his sake.*

*Very truly yours,*

*Stella Mondragon*

*P.S. He's grown up so well, Rose. You must be extremely proud.*

Rose had unfolded the letter so many times over the past few weeks, the peach-colored paper had started to curl up around the edges. She still couldn't get over it, reading and rereading to make sure her mind wasn't playing tricks. That Stella would have the nerve to try to barge back into their lives—*buy* her way back in! The letter struck Rose as so willfully clueless, she could only assume that the Stella she'd known and this snobby sentence-writing Stella were not the same person. Or, more specifically, that the years had turned Stella into someone even more awful than the duplicitous two-timer she'd known. Rose crumpled the paper and smoothed it out, then crumpled it again, lit the gas burner and touched a corner. Before the flame could take hold completely she pulled it away from the fire, batting it with a dishtowel, and then slid the refolded rectangle into her apron pocket.

"Damn her," she said to the kitchen sink.

The front door slammed and Lance was home, asking about dinner.

"Chicken and rice," she said. "How was school?"

"Pretty good. Chicken and rice! All right!" He flung a cupboard open, looking for a snack. "Hey, why did the chicken cross the road?"

"Because it wanted to get run over. Don't ruin your dinner."

"To lay it on the *line*. Want to drive to the city this weekend and try out at the comedy club? If you bomb they throw tomatoes." He grabbed a loaf of bread from the top of the fridge.

Rose pressed the small of her back against the counter. "Do you ever see Stella when you go to town?"

"Aunt Stella?" he tilted his head, thinking, as if the town were so populated he couldn't quite remember which woman she was. "Aunt Stella, sure. Did you know she's married to Mr. Mondragon now? I was in Mondragon's last year and she walked right up to me and said she barely recognized me, I'm so tall now." His arm stretched to the cupboard behind her head for a new jar of blackberry preserves.

Rose felt his answer creep into the kitchen, tap-dance around her outline, playful and ominous. Her feet were cold. She moved to the stove. "Oh."

He buttered the bread, unscrewed the jam lid and scooped out a goopy knifeful, dripping it on the counter and all over his thick-cut bread. Rose gathered herself and swatted a dishtowel at him. "Ma?" he said, swiveling out of her way. "She was nice. She said she clipped out the article in the paper about me, from when we won regionals."

He looked up, brown eyes like soft deerhide. He knew things better than she gave him credit for.

That night Rose couldn't get comfortable, rolling from one side of the saggy brass bed to the other. She was so restless that Fergus, who usually stayed in Lance's room all night, clicked down the hall to check on her. He snuffled at her pillow and she reached a hand out to scratch under his chin. "It could be," she whispered, "that I am the disingenuous one. What if the offer is just an offer and I should accept it, for his sake?" Fergus yawned against her palm and set one paw on the mattress next to her shoulder. "Pride goeth . . . and blah blah," she continued. "College is college." Fergus yawned again and went back down the hall to Lance. *Go.* That dog was the only one with the right priorities. She would talk to Lance about it—should she?—and see how he reacted.

She threw a cardigan over her pajamas and went into the hall. Halfway to his room, she stubbed her toe on something and stopped, pressing a palm into the wall as she crouched to rub her foot. Rose had a body memory of this walk: she'd done it hundreds of times, when he was a baby and a young boy and cried out for her at night. She'd been better at navigating obstacles then. Rose continued, limping. Lance had left his bedroom door ajar for Fergus and she could hear the dog's tail thump, announcing her approach. She snapped her fingers at him. The room smelled like dirty laundry—Fergus was lying on a pile of it. A half moon shone through the windows, light spilling across her father's old oak dresser and onto the twin bed where Lance lay sleeping, mouth half open. He wasn't yet a snorer, as Theo had been. She sat at the edge of his bed and put a hand on his shoulder.

"Lance? Lance. I have a question."

"Hunh." He rolled over to face the wall.

She shook him lightly.

He groaned. "Already?"

"Afraid so." He was too good at telling her what she wanted to hear. Her best bet was catching him by surprise.

He rolled to his back. "Hey, Ma. It's not . . . What time is it?"

"Night. Just one question."

"Jeez, Ma."

"Do you want to take Stella's offer?"

"Huh?"

"You know what I'm talking about. College."

He hoisted himself to his elbows, peering at her. "What's with the kamikaze raid? *Now*, Ma?"

"Just level with me. Do you want to take her offer?" He flipped onto his stomach and pulled the pillow over his head. She waited. "I won't be upset."

The moon lit the room well enough that she could see his football poster reflected in the mirror over the dresser: a hulking padded man grinned and held up a sports drink. Her baby toe throbbed, and she pulled her foot up to the bed, touching it gingerly. It had already started to swell. She thought of saying, *It's not about me and your Aunt Stella. It's about you*. But she wasn't sure she could make it sound convincing. There would be a pause, however slight, before Stella's name. He would hear it; he always did. Instead she asked, "Hey, what did you leave on the floor in the hall near the bathroom?"

"Ma!" His voice was muffled through the pillow. She resisted the urge to smooth the covers up over his shoulders.

"Just tell me and I'll go."

"Fine. I left my backpack there. So I can flush my homework."

"Very funny. Hey, knock knock."

Silence.

"Knock knock."

"Who's there?"

"Orange."

He drew the pillow onto his chest and rolled to his side, facing her. "You are the worst joke teller ever."

He wasn't wrong. Theo was the one who had been good at this. "I wish I were better at lots of things. Like paying for college."

"You're good at things. You know it."

"Do you remember when you and your dad and I went to the State Fair? He was cracking up the people in line with us for the roller coaster, and he managed to sweet talk the guy into letting you on, even though you were half an inch under the required height."

"We'd waited so long by then, it would have sucked not to get on."

"Right."

Lance didn't respond, and his breathing evened. Fergus stood, circled, and settled himself back into the laundry pile. Her son seemed younger now, and smaller. She had a sense of time slippage—if she walked back down the hall to bed Theo would be there, warm and snoring. And downstairs, Stella would be in her old twin bed, sleeping on her stomach, hair shining across the pillow. Rose sat, knee pulled up to her chest and sore toe in hand, and felt ten years, fifteen years, drop away. The moon slid a few inches further across the windowpane.

"Wherever you go," she whispered, "come back to me." His breathing changed. She knew he was awake. "Tell me what you're thinking."

"I'm thinking I'm kind of hungry."

"Okay," she sighed. "Pancakes?"

"I'm also thinking I don't want Stella to give me money."

The room tilted. She sat straighter. "Are you sure?"

"It would be weird. Plus, I don't think I need it. But I do want . . . I need to go away somewhere. For a while, not forever. Have some adventures." he laughed, a little embarrassed. "And learn things," he added belatedly.

"I know. The world is big. You know what I used to wish for? I used to wish that my dad's luck would come in, or mine would, and I could spend a couple of years on a boat. Not a cruise ship. A big sailboat with a crew and a galley. Sometimes I'd imagine I owned the boat, but other times I was happy imagining just being on the crew. Docking on little islands, navigating by the stars . . . I told my dad once and you know what he said? 'They change their stars but not themselves who journey across the sea.'"

"What's it mean?"

"It's a quote, probably from some—"

"No matter where you go, there you are," Lance said.

"You're pretty smart."

"Don't tell anyone."

"Too late. Word is out." She pulled the covers up around his shoulder.

"Not really." He smiled. "Hey, Ma?"

"Yep."

"Are there more blackberries?"

She'd forgotten he was hungry. "For the pancakes? For you? Let's see." Rose stood, feeling blood sting its way down the leg that had been folded. Time reset itself. She was pushing middle-aged and he would leave her too, for a while at least. Stretching out a hand, she waited for him to throw back the covers and walk with her to the kitchen—taller than her, her hungry son, rubbing sleep from his eyes.

*

The Old Man walked into the living room and the grandkid was crying and carrying on. Nina sat on the couch next to her, rubbing her back and asking what was wrong. Sill said that Lance was going into the Army. Her face screwed into a red crimp of pain and she sobbed, "He told me like it's no big deal. Two years!"

Nina cut him a look, and as the Old Man retreated to the kitchen he heard her say, "One way or another, college or service, you knew he'd leave." Soon after, Sill stomped up the stairs. A door slammed. The females in his family were not prone to wild displays, and this struck him as over the top. He would have said as much to Nina if she'd joined him in the kitchen, but she did not. He went to the barn, thinking about what he'd heard. The Army. This was a good sign. Lance needed discipline—the Old Man had thought so even before the pyromaniac incident—and the military would whip the kid into shape.

Later that week Sill announced that the recruiter had gone out and it was done. She was calm by then, her face pale. Rose had made a plate of cookies like it was a party, Sill said. After she spoke, she bit her lip and looked down at her boots. The Old Man hadn't expected Rose to support something so practical, and he realized that he'd underestimated her, not for the first time. His worst miscall came not long after Theo died. The Old Man had gone over thinking he was doing her a favor and halfway through had made a clumsy play for something beyond his reach. He hadn't stopped to strategize, that was his mistake. But it was her fault—she had a way of unsettling him.

The summer after Theo's accident, Rose had taken to walking to the creek every day, in late afternoon. He was the only person who seemed to notice, and got into the habit of going out once or twice a week for a chat. The lonely widow. She was so young still, in spite of the circles under her eyes and the crow's feet. Going to the creek was her small way of getting out of Dodge. When he asked her about it, she said it was the only thing that made her feel good, floating on her back, ears filled with water so she heard only her heartbeat, staring at the circle of sky. One day he found her sitting on the creek bank on a towel in damp jean shorts, hair dripping down the back of an oversized green t-shirt. She had never been good about remembering to wear a hat, and her freckles had spread. Then she smiled at him, and he sat, confused. He had a reason for talking to her that day, though she didn't seem in a hurry to hear it. Several times in those months she had asked him how he'd handled things after Mae's death—as if he had wisdom about how to feel anything properly. Him!

Soft breeze ruffled the water. He watched one drip fall from a lock of hair, absorbed into green cotton. Mae hadn't known how to swim. The Old Man thought about saying so to Rose, but instead he put a hand on her shoulder and left it there, feeling her gradually stiffen.

He should have dropped it. But instead he said the first words that came to him. "You should let me have those adjacent acres."

She pulled away and looked at him, freckles stark in the dappled light. "I have to get home. Lance will be back from practice soon." She stood, shaking more droplets from her hair.

*That damn kid.* He rose to his feet and reached for her shoulder again, but she stepped back.

"Sherwin." A warning in her voice. She wasn't swayed by him at all, he was nothing to her. Just an old bone to gnaw on and toss aside.

"I need . . . You expect my help. And I'm only—"

She bent to pull on her sneakers. "Gimme a break. I don't expect anything from you. We've just been talking is all, about something we have in common. The one thing we have in common."

His hands dangled useless, so he clenched them. "Leasing, then. That's it. You can't do it alone. We'll see how it goes. I'll have the option to buy you out down the road. If you want it." She rolled her eyes and pulled wet hair to one shoulder. "I'll give you my ideas and increase production—"

Rose leaned forward and traced the tin in his heart-side pocket, mockingly flirtatious. Then she gave it a hard tap. "The last thing I need is your ideas." The same tone he'd heard her take with Lance from time to time—so condescending, clearly meant to derail him.

"The longer you wait, the less I'll offer."

She flicked water off her wrist and stared. "How many ways do I have to say this? You can't have it."

"You think? You can't do it on your own. I'll take it at auction eventually, you know that. Theo knew it, too."

A damp strand of dark red hair was plastered across her forehead, as rich as it had been when she was a girl. Nothing about her had faded. Measured out over the years, they'd spent the equivalent of a day in each other's company.

"It's Theo's land, not yours. I'm keeping it for Lance."

"Are you so sure he can handle it? His daddy wasn't so gung-ho, especially toward the end."

Rose came at him fast, pressing both hands into his shoulders, pushing hard, keeping an arm's length between them. "Ask me why my answer is no. Do you think I need this? Any of it? No. Nothing—" she shook her head, "I don't need *anything* to do with the old attitudes and the same old . . . That's all this is, settling old family bullshit. You're the last person, Old Man. You'll be the last person to get it, no matter what happens."

Since Theo had died she had seemed so alone to him and small in a way that pulled him in. There under the trees she wasn't small at all—she was drying quickly, the heat from her anger evaporating the water from inside out. Steam rose from her hair into the humid air. She turned and left him there.

He'd carried the memory of that indignity for years, telling himself he was biding time. But now a satisfying thought struck him: he'd helped this new outcome along. His warnings had led Rose to steer Lance toward a smart decision like the Army. Toward being a man, someone who has what it takes to tough it out and keep the land. Someone to be proud of.

*

Ward remembered the smell of the student center on the first day of classes: cleaner than clean. And his favorite professor, the only one to wear tweed with actual leather elbow patches and smoke a pipe. Linked somehow with the white tablecloths in an Italian restaurant that he passed countless times but never entered. College memories. Ward didn't remember specific books or dorms. He recalled fragments of things, almost impossible for him to explain. When Stella had asked him to tell Lance about his college days, hoping to convince the boy to set his sights on State, Ward launched into a ten-minute retrospective on the classes, the campus, the pretty coeds, the books. Whose college experience was he telling? Not Ward Mondragon's. Joe College was the star of his story—an opaque, boring young stand-in who went to football games and drank coffee with his frat buddies in the wee hours before exams.

Ward was proud of Lance's decision to join the military and more than a little relieved that he wouldn't be asked to help pay for school. But in his heart he knew that Lance was no more G.I. Joe than he, Ward, had been Joe College. Even after the boy left for basic training Ward couldn't picture him as a soldier—he would always think of Lance in his store, pilfering small items, smiling at his Aunt Stella, and grabbing the hand of the tongue-tied Brown girl on his way out the door.

The talk show host Ward listened to on the radio had things to say—sly, smart things about America's waning influence, declining values, and drift toward limp-wristed foreign policy. *A sleeping giant is awakening,* he crowed. *Are you ready? Can you feel it? We will not forget who we are. We will be great again*. The voice grew stronger, until Ward, who usually found it easy to tune out the pundit as he attended to customers, found himself distracted, asking people to repeat themselves. "Turn it off. Please!" Stella snapped, less patient now. "That man is vile. He'll march us right to war." She switched to the local station and the familiar voice of her ex-husband Eddie, sounding pleased with himself as he recited the day's market prices. Stella smiled and tilted her head fondly at the radio. She caught Ward watching and blew him a kiss.

His wife! It still surprised him, seeing Stella's face on the pillow next to his. For the first year of marriage he'd done a silent double take every morning. She had entwined their lives so carefully, learning every business procedure that he taught her, laying out their work clothes side by side every night, slipping healthy snacks into the store fridge to encourage him to eat less candy during the day. The house was renewed too, with a fresh coat of paint and new rugs in each room. Stella had agonized about color choices that seemed to him bafflingly similar—he still had no clue whether the bedroom walls had been redone in "cattail" or "reed."

They had a careful kindness with each other. Ward knew this was because they shared a determination to have this time be different. Which made it doubly strange that he'd left Michael's business card in his suit pocket for Stella to find when she took an armful of clothes to the cleaners. He could have tucked it away any number of places: behind the mirror on his dresser, under the heavy lamp in his home office, in the back of his tool drawer. Or better yet, memorize the number and leave the card behind in the hotel room along with empty condom wrappers and the heavy animal smell of sex. He'd done it in the past; Ward had always had a head for numbers.

Stella came downstairs with an armful of clothes and said, "I'm going to the cleaners, back in a bit." A prickle at the back of his neck sent him upstairs to the bedroom. His suit was still hanging inside the closet doors, swinging slightly, and the business card—Michael's name and that ridiculous tagline: *Massage. Deep Release. Discreet*—had migrated from the right breast pocket to the left. That was careless of her, he thought, until the fact of his own carelessness pushed him backwards so fast his legs hit the bedframe and he sank to the mattress.

Ward sat in the living room, waiting to see what she would do. What she did was executed with the exactitude of a surgical strike. She didn't return home until after eight o'clock, carrying four plastic bags from the Discount SuperStore. Neither of them had ever set foot inside the place. "I went shopping," she said, meeting his gaze.

"Stella."

"Got all this stuff for less than forty bucks." She had bought cleaning supplies—a gallon of bleach, window wash, scrub brushes. Also a rubber mat for the store, a shower caddy, a box of chocolate-covered coffee beans, and a gallon of full-fat Neapolitan ice cream.

"All right."

"I ran into people there . . ." She rattled off the names of three of his customers. Former customers.

"Stella—" It came out low and craggy. He couldn't continue. She set the bags at her feet, waiting. Michael's moan entered the air of the room. Ward shook his head, mute. Stella picked the bags up and walked to the kitchen. He sat. Two hours later she came down the stairs in a pair of sweatpants, her hair pulled up into a messy bun; she'd scrubbed her face of makeup and looked barely older than a college student.

"Okay," she said. "I get it. I really do get it. You prefer men."

"I'm not—"

"Shut up for a minute. I think I knew this even though I didn't know it, if that makes any sense. Ha! Making sense, isn't that rich?

You're gay but you married me anyway, right? Tell me if I'm wrong. Speak up or forever hold your peace."

Ward studied his shoes.

"Well, that's an interesting choice. That's something you might have mentioned sooner, maybe in the dating stage when we were sharing ourselves with each other, and when I told you *every fucking thing* I ever did that I did not particularly want the world to know and . . . and I suppose I should've figured it out—God, am I dumb—because you were always so *remote,* but I just thought that you were, I don't know, giving me space or being middle-aged or . . ." She paused to catch her breath.

"Stella—"

"Did I say I was done? Did I say, *Go*?" She started pacing. "We made a decision—together, I thought—about our future, but because I was lacking a certain very important piece of information, you know what, Ward? *You* made that decision. You didn't let me in on your little secret, and . . . Do you know . . . do you have any idea how incredibly selfish that is? And mean? I feel so damn foolish." Her face twisted. He was waiting for the tears. Stella would cry and he'd beg forgiveness, he'd get on his knees, tell her he'd never do it again. It could still work out. He could see how it might, just possibly, work out.

"Did you use protection?"

"Yes," he sputtered. "Of course. I'd never—"

"Every time you go to the city, I'm guessing. You can see how I might have trouble believing what you're saying to me right now. We're going to get tested, both of us."

He raised his hands, helpless. "Okay."

"Ward, just tell me. Why? Why didn't you just come clean? I really liked you but I would've . . ."

It felt like he was physically stretching, reaching for something out of his grasp. Finally he said, "I love you, Stella."

She sank to the sofa. "Huh. Really?"

"Yes! You are the most beautiful, wonderful—"

"Oh, for fuck's sake. You are so full of bullshit you've even fooled yourself." She laughed, the warm, round laughter that had first drawn him to her. "Yes, you are, you are, you *are*. Well, there's my answer, I guess."

"What answer?"

"Why it happened. Why me. It's karma. I've got some payback coming." Her face grew very calm. He watched her explaining it to herself, thinking, *You're wrong*—but when he tried to speak she shook him off again. "I have to think. You know this already. When I was younger I did some very careless, very silly things, and I thought that if I just took extreme care and analyzed my choices I could get past it, I could get some sort of, I don't know, hall pass to a better life. I could know myself and understand things, understand people better. But I clearly can't and didn't and here we are." She brushed a forearm across her eyes. "Lance needs me, you know. He needs more family than just Rose pulling for him. And with him gone, Rose might be willing to . . . with stability and a place to . . ." She let out what sounded like a gasp that morphed into a hiccup. "What am I going to do?"

They sat together in silence until the clock over the mantel read a quarter past two. Ward tried to frame sentences in his head, but no words came to rescue him. Her back was straight and she kept her eyes on the clock, scarcely moving as the minutes ticked by. Ward felt as though they were strangers on a bus journey, seated together, with no relationship other than this shared temporary space.

At two-thirty fatigue overtook him and he gave up. He stood and said, "I'll do whatever you want, Stella. I'm sorry. I'm sorry. I wish I could undo it . . . you have no idea how much. Just tell me what you need and I'll do it." He trudged upstairs and fell into an unrestful sleep.

She stayed with him. She moved her things into the second bedroom and slept alone, but in every other way—working together, eating, how they presented themselves to the world—everything was exactly the same. He should have been happy. But Ward still had a panicked feeling that he couldn't shake—that they were on that bus trip together, and that one of them, at some point, would collect their belongings and disembark. She only stayed with him, he knew, because he offered her something she'd never had before. Stella believed that she'd earned her early misfortunes, brought them on through a blend of karmic imprudence and good old-fashioned idiocy. She was waiting for Lance to come home safely, and looking for a chance to reach out again to Rose. Mostly, she was focused on what she called her payback, looking backward at what she'd done instead of forward. But she would look up sooner or later, take stock of where they were. She would. Or he would.

*

Scottie was on his way to the laundromat, which for years had been under new ownership, rechristened as "Carters Clean Clothes." Everyone still called it "The Tip Top," just as the old boarding house, shuttered and crumbling, would always be "Anderson's." He hoisted the black garbage bag that he used for carting laundry from one shoulder to another, feeling his lower back twinge. Someday soon he might be too old to carry it. A wagon would do, he thought. He trudged forward, letting the weight bend but not slow him. As he passed a newspaper box, he noted the large, bold headline: *TROOPS MOBILIZE*.

Several cars passed, pulling drafts that rustled the ghosts along the curb. The usual suspects. A well-dressed man and woman checked the clock over the old town square, waiting for something.

For a moment Scottie thought they were his parents—the fashion was the right era—then drew closer and recognized Gordie and Glennie, a rare sighting. They were translucent in the mid-morning light, the street visible through them. Just then Stella stepped out of The Bluebird, holding a to-go cup of coffee. The ghosts turned their heads to her like sunflowers. *That explains it,* he thought. She had car keys in her hand and was rushing; Stella always seemed to be rushing. Lately she'd been going to the café almost every day, timing it just before or after Rose's shifts, and always buying a single cup of coffee. Never two. Stella looked at him, almost through him in that way she had, and smiled briefly. "Hi, Scottie."

He returned the greeting and paused to watch her set the cup on the roof of her car as she unlocked the door. Glennie looped her arm through Gordie's and stood on her toes. Stella's head was down, so she didn't see Rose's blue truck coming. But she must have sensed something, if only the intensity of the focus from the sidewalk observers, because she fumbled and dropped the keys, ducking down alongside the car to pick them up, hidden from Rose, who pulled in and parked.

Rose opened her door and slid out, dressed for work at The Bluebird—pale blue uniform with white buttons and a nametag over the heart. As her feet hit the ground she leaned in to grab something from the passenger seat, so Rose didn't see Stella stand up, holding the reclaimed car keys. Glennie and Gordie stepped back under the café's awning as if shielding themselves from a blast of wind. Across the hood of her car, Stella took in Rose's truck and then Rose herself. It was a perfect day, one cloud passing across the sky. Stella let go of the car door handle and pressed a hand to her stomach. Something about the way Rose held her head when she stood upright told Scottie that she had belatedly registered the car she had parked beside—she was very straight, even formal, stepping back stiffly to shut the door.

There were about three feet between Rose's truck and Stella's car. Rose slung a canvas tote bag over her shoulder, eyes locked on the café window. Stella swallowed and let go of the keys—they hit the ground with a hard jangle, skidding. Rose swiveled her head and their eyes locked over the hood. Stella took an audible breath. Scottie squinted, surprised. There was no one watching, other than he and two ghosts and one jay, perched on a telephone wire and puffing his chest. Gordie checked his watch and looked at Rose expectantly, appearing to Scottie almost corporeal in the dim light under the awning. Stella opened her mouth as Rose moved into action, stepping swiftly up to the sidewalk, swinging the café door open with a gust that blew Glennie's skirt against her legs.

"Rose, how—" Stella started. Too late. The door shut.

Gordie and Glennie drew closer together, patting each other on the arms and straightening their clothes. They turned toward the town square, fading from view with a swiftness that seemed to Scottie almost like disappointment. Stella crouched to grope for the keys under the car and her cheeks, when she stood and caught him still watching, were splotched bright pink. She looked him up and down.

He clutched the bag closer to his body. "I've got laundry."

"You look like a turtle out of its shell." She slammed into the car and drove away too fast. The forgotten cup of coffee on the roof rolled down the back of the sedan, leaving a milky spray on the black macadam.

Through the café window, he saw Rose already behind the counter, her face implacable. She would not look at the street. She was erasing that moment of almost-connection as if it had never happened. A faint glow came off her, a kind of willed focus. Emma Templeton bustled out from the kitchen holding a tray of pies, and Rose set one on the counter and began slicing it for sale.

Once the boy was deployed and the news got worse, Rose glowed so bright the ghosts fell back, blinded, and some days her feet scarcely touched down. But Scottie knew it couldn't last: all future and no past.

*

He had a ridge of pimples along his entire jawline for the first couple years of high school. Feet too big, arms too long. The school bus dropped Lance and Sylvie at the end of the county road, same as always, and they had to walk a stretch together. He stayed about ten feet ahead and Sylvie watched his shoulders and the brown back of his neck and wondered, *Where did you go?* The old Lance, the boy that liked her and had smooth skin—he was hibernating. Gravel skittered under their feet, back and forth, almost like conversation.

They became friends again because she went over one afternoon and found him by the creek. "Your mother isn't selling, is she? Now that you lost your dad . . . You'll stay here?"

There was a shred of leaf in his hair and he smiled. His eyes were calf color: soft brown, that newborn shade that coarsens with age.

"I've missed you," she blurted.

"Here I am."

And there they were, like they'd been sitting together by the well all that time, chucking in stones and listening.

Not long after, Sylvie went over to deliver some blackberry jam, thinking how much had changed since she'd picked the berries—her and Lance friends again, the sour tartness mellowed by heat and sugar. "I picked them over by Johnson's Creek," she told Rose, handing her the jar. "That's where the sweetest ones are."

Rose took it, an odd look on her face. Then Sylvie remembered what Nina had told her to say. "Is there anything you need? We're happy to help out."

"Sylvie, you tell . . . tell your grandfather . . . tell him thank you." Her voice didn't mean "Thank you." Lance came onto the porch and

Rose turned, holding the jar in front of her like a toxic lab specimen, and went inside.

He said he'd walk her home. On the way she asked, for the first time, "What do you miss most about your dad?"

"What do I miss?" Lance spoke a short list in a singsong, in rhythm with their steps. He grabbed her hand and swung it out with his—pointing to the horizon and then back behind them, horizon, town, horizon, town—faster and higher until it almost hurt.

"Hey." She pulled her hand away, wanting to be serious, to act like grownups.

It was only later that she thought, *He held my hand.*

Lance didn't like school much, but he was good at drawing and geometry. Rose wanted him to go to college—she got on him whenever report cards went out, saying he had to apply himself.

"How are you supposed to do that when you're always working?" Sylvie asked.

He shrugged. "It'd be different if we had help but we don't, do we?"

"I guess you could sell." She thought of her granddad as she said it. "Sell and move to town. You could do better there. Rose could get a job in a store or something—you'd have more time."

"Trying to get rid of us?" he asked.

He was mostly joking but partly not. It was hard to tell, sometimes, how much of them came from their families. Even if they didn't want it to. It was just her and Lance talking and walking down the county road—but it was like Sylvie's granddad stood over her shoulder and Rose stood right behind Lance and they were giving each other the stink eye. Everywhere they walked on the land their elders had walked first, invisible tracks under their feet. Which is partly why she said, "I'll go, too. I'll go with you." Lance just laughed at that and told her that her mom would kill him.

Then they were talking about something else, or not talking at all.

But it stuck in her head, the thought of living in town with Lance in their own house. That night she asked her mother if that's why Stella left—if she fell in love with Mr. Mondragon. Even though it was years between her leaving and her marrying. Nina shook her head and said something about Nosey Parkers. It was hard to imagine Stella falling fast for Ward Mondragon. He was much older than her, and fat, with circles of sweat under his arms in summer.

"Where did Stella live?" Sylvie asked. A little rented room over the Bluebird Café, her mother told her, which is also where Stella worked then. Sylvie thought that wouldn't be so bad—you could walk to the store and to the movies. The grill smells probably didn't seem like much, not after living with all the smells on a farm.

"Rose was brokenhearted when she left," Nina added, with a funny, almost embarrassed look on her face. "In her own way."

*Rose brokenhearted.* It sounded too soft to Sylvie, not like the Rose she knew at all. But maybe she just wasn't a charitable person.

The first time Sylvie kissed Lance they were at the bus stop. He was cranky because he'd wanted to drive the truck to school but Rose wouldn't let him. The Bens lived too far away to pick him up so early and she, Sylvie, had only a learner's permit and no actual car. It was late October, and cold. His breath came in little white puffs and he wore a red down vest over a blue flannel shirt. Lance didn't say a word to make her think it would be a good idea, just shot her a sidelong look as she crunched over the gravel to stand in front of him. There was a tickle in her throat urging her on. She hooked her fingers into the vest armholes and pulled him closer, standing on tiptoes, and then stopped his breath puffs with her mouth. It was not at all like in the movies. Her courage failed and she froze, lips pressed against his, unable to move the action forward or back. She heard him swallow his gum and his hands rose to grip her waist. Then the bus came.

She missed him after school because she had band practice and got a ride home, and he must have taken the bus because he was not waiting for her when she walked past the wall of lockers. The tickle in her throat had tightened into soreness. That night after dinner she went out to the Infamous Elm, their old midpoint meeting spot. It was very cold, but Sylvie wouldn't have noticed if her mother hadn't complained of the temperature. Her skin was on fire: it felt elemental. She had no justification for feeling so powerful, but she knew he would come find her.

She had gone to third base that summer with Ben Culp, at a party out by the reservoir. She'd felt a detachment the whole time, wondering in some tiny corner of her mind how Ben would describe this to Lance, if it would be at all flattering. She'd played on and off for years with her church camp friend, Jessica de Trinidad, savoring the furtive slippery textures of sleeping bags brushing together and small hard nipples and watermelon lip balm. So Sylvie knew, to a certain extent, what to do and what to feel. She breathed in the cold air, exhaled to the count of three, and then he appeared through parted branches: same red vest, his hair now pulled back in a small ponytail that made his face look skinny. Sylvie reached out and touched the nape of his neck, wanting to free the hair from the rubber band but stopped, worried that he would tell her not to.

"Hey there, Sylvie." Lance leaned in, putting his hands where they'd been twelve hours earlier. She crunched on a wintermint Lifesaver, wanting to show him the sparks. Then shards of the candy were on his tongue, his vest zipper pressed cold against her collarbone, and everything felt liquid and brittle at the same time. She was pressed between him and the tree; he grasped the tree; she was in the way and had trouble breathing—the phrase "get wood" popped into her head and she giggled. He kept his mouth on hers, his tongue twining around her tongue. His hands moved over her ribcage and breasts and her leg hooked around his hip. She pushed against the Elm for leverage, trying to make herself higher—she was too short, felt tremendously that she wanted to be taller, and at that moment he dropped to his knees, pulling her down with him. Metal dog tags jangled. Out beyond the scrim of dark branches Fergus kept watch.

Every nerve in her body moved to the surface. She burned so hot she kept him warm too. They spread her coat beneath them, and he fumbled with a condom. Covered only haphazardly by his down vest and shirt, as the temperature dropped and their breath misted a faint fog between their faces, she felt herself spreading out and further out, across the fields and toward some far horizon, and she reached up to pull out his hair band, snapping it around her wrist as he hissed, "*Oh god*," and sank his face into her neck. Cold air rushed in when he rolled off. "Whoa," he said. "That was . . ."

"Yes." Her limbs started shaking. She shook so hard she couldn't stand up to dress herself, and he had to help her, pulling on her shirt, finding her bra belatedly and shoving it into her coat pocket, lifting one leg and then the other to slide back into her jeans. Her body belonged to someone else. Her trembling arms and legs still stretched beyond her own outline, and her known self had shrunk to the small hot spaces in her chest and throat.

"I might be getting a cold," she said.

Lance and Fergus walked her home and she snuck in the back door, tiptoeing past her granddad's bedroom and staggering into bed. It turned out to be the flu. She was sick for seven days, and she'd given it to Lance—he confirmed it when she called once the worst of the fever had subsided. "Oh, no, you too?" she croaked, and he croaked back, "Yeah, Typhoid Mary." That whole week she kept his hair band on her body, occasionally using it to pull her own hair back, but mostly just looking at it on her wrist, proof of what had happened.

Later, prompted by dutiful friends, she would ask the questions that girls are supposed to ask. *What do I mean to you? Will we ever go out for real, like to dinner or a movie?* But in all honesty the answers did not matter as much as she had been led to believe they should. She knew him like no one else. And in her best, most powerful moments—which usually occurred lying with him in Rose's hayloft, fingers running over skin, shuddering, that feeling of being lit, her heart a furnace—she felt how he knew her.

At least once a week after school they went to Mondragon's to buy candy and sodas, pens, paperclips—whatever excuse Lance could come up with. If his Aunt Stella was there, she'd make a fuss over him. Stella wore bright lipstick and low-cut dresses that Sylvie thought looked a little funny on someone that old. She was still pretty, though. Stella would pat Lance's cheek and smooth his hair and tell him how tall he was growing. And she'd always give them something for free: a bar of chocolate, a magnet, a laminated map. She'd put her hands on Sylvie's shoulders and look her in the eyes. "You take care of him, okay?"

On the drive home, he'd pull whatever he had stolen out of his pocket. Nothing big, ever. A handful of nails or a box of pens. A small bottle of alcohol, if he'd had a chance to walk along that shelf. He wasn't mean; that wasn't him. It was the only way he could go see Stella and not feel like he was betraying his mother, that's all.

"They had a feud, those girls," her granddad said.

"Over what?"

"Whatever it is people feud over. Family stuff, bunk."

Her mother was ironing over by the radiator. Nina looked hard at the Old Man and said, "That wasn't bunk." He muttered a reply too low for either of them to hear and went out to the barn.

Sylvie looked at her mother and the steam rising from the iron that didn't quite reach her face.

The dog was always with Lance, so the first thing she thought to say when he told her he was definitely going to enlist was, "But what's Fergus going to do without you?"

They sat on a rock on her dad's fallow field. His sketchbook rested on one knee. She reached out and hugged Fergus, pressing her face into his ruff, but she clutched too hard and he shook her off and went to lie down a few feet away.

"He'll be okay," Lance said, though he didn't sound convinced. "My mom knows what to do."

*No,* she thought. *No, no.* She asked, "What about art school?" even though she knew they didn't have the money for it. That's why Rose supported the idea of him enlisting in the first place, though she said she thought the military was going to be tough for someone creative like Lance, someone used to having space to roam. Sometimes when Rose talked about Lance, Sylvie thought she had no idea what her son was like at all. Other times, it was like she and Rose were in a fan club together, mooning over magazine photos pinned up on a wall.

At Lance's goodbye party she heard him drunk and laughing with the Bens and some other boys. Laughing in that way that isn't nice, the way boys do together. She knew that if she went up and asked, *What's so funny?* They'd say, *Nothing.*

Nothing's funny.

The morning he left, under the Infamous Elm she told Lance something her granddad had said to her once about their inheritance—needing guts to make it on a farm. "Do you think that's true? Are you really sure you'll come back and make a go of it?"

He clutched his stomach and fake threw up and made noises like the victim in a scary movie. Then he dropped his arms to his sides. "There's only so much guts anyone can spare." He pulled her close. One minute they were talking about guts, the next minute lips were pressed soft together.

"I'll write to you," she promised. "Every day. You'll get sick of hearing from me."

He left on the bus, with his duffel bag and his canvas coat and the letter she had given him.

Sylvie walked over to Rose's almost every day after school and often found her on the back porch staring at some distant vanishing point. It seemed that Rose lost herself to some degree—or lost the self she used to be. Her focus was off. Everything she did, practical and purposeful as ever, moved her body forward while her mind drifted, currents always eddying toward Lance. Sylvie understood this. It happened to her, too. When Sylvie arrived, Rose would smile and offer her something to drink or a piece of stale crumb cake. Sylvie had the feeling that if she asked, Rose would have no clear memory of how she, Sylvie, came to be there.

Months passed this way.

Rose left the radio in the kitchen on all the time, tuned to news of the slow-building war—the war none of them had predicted. Far away, men were sitting in rooms at long dark tables, deciding their fate. Time slowed and then sped. *Troops are en route*, the radioman said. She'd had no idea that it could take so long to go to war and then happen in a blink. *Is it inevitable?* the radioman asked some spent diplomat, his tone indicating that he already knew the answer. Further back, in the parlor, Rose's favorite jazzy singer played on repeat.

In addition to the emails that Lance sent to Sylvie, he also sent her some messages to print and give to his mother. Rose didn't have a computer.

Sylvie read them, of course—there was no way not to. Some of the things he wrote to her he also wrote to Rose, word for word. Basic information: *It sure is hot here, except when it's cold. Sand gets in everything. The boys are trying to get more armor. Berettas are dinky. I am okay. Don't you worry about me.*

To Rose he wrote: *How is Fergus? Can you get someone to help you fix the east wall? Don't forget to put the tractor in the shed before winter. Can you send some of those socks that wick sweat? I sure miss your homemade jam. I'll be home soon to eat it. Give Fergus a butt scratch from me.*

To Sylvie: *I miss you like crazy. Have you seen Tall Ben? Make sure he has my unit number so he can find me when he finally gets here. The guys here are mostly tough and nice. Wish I could be sitting in the hayloft right now with you. Will you check on my mom for me? I wish you would. Sometimes I worry about her being alone.*

On Rose's porch, Fergus rested his chin across Sylvie's thigh, sighing heavily. Her mind catapulted across years, when Lance would be home and safe and they would dance through the parlor before heading upstairs. In her imagined future she couldn't say exactly where Rose was, though now she sat right next to Sylvie, heavy newspapers and a world map stacked next to her, staring at the radio.

A never-finished scarf rested in Rose's lap, knitting needles flying, staving off dread.

*Hey there Sylvie—*

*I'm sorry its been so long. The problem is I don't get access much to computers these days. But now I've got some downtime, so lucky you.*

*Ahhhhhhhhhhhh*

*The problem is, I don't know what to say. There's a crazy beetle crawling up the wall. I'm not even gonna smash it.*

*How are you today? Thanks for all the emails. Sounds like everyone's pretty much the same.*

*I read them, but not always all the way through.*

*I don't call my mother that often. Prefer to write when I'm in the mood, which it turns out also isn't often. I'm sorry for that—I'll try to write her a real one and mail it and everything, and maybe even one for you too.*

*The problem is here is the only place that feels real to me, and these guys.*

*The problem is I know thats fucked up. But its also true.*

*We watched a war movie the other night and could not believe how fake they make it look. The movies are bullshit. The colors, the pretty camera angles, watching a bullet go through innards like you're riding the bullet or inside the bullet like its rocketship bullshit, and the gear and how everyone has something to say all the time, the right thing to say even if its the wrong thing. The problem is there's nothing to say.*

*Ee yie ee yie yo, Sylvie.*

*Yo. Sill.*

*xxxxxxxxxxxxxx*

*That stuff above is just me wriring shit. I typed it last week when I was a little high and saved it as a draft but I'll show it to you Sylvie because you deserve to know. That's true. Right now I'm just really tired havent slept. But I am fine. Thats the truth. Will you check on my ma for me? Make up something up about what I said but make it better. She's proud but she could use*

And he'd just stopped there and hit "send," maybe by mistake, or out of fatigue. Sylvie replied right away, and kept replying. But he never did, so those were the last words of his she'd ever have.

*

It was early, just past seven o'clock. Nina was mulching the flowerbeds at the front of the house, and Sill was on the porch finishing up some homework and eating toast before she set off for the bus stop. They both heard the car on the county road and looked up, not recognizing the engine. The Army recruiter, Jim Culp, drove too slowly toward Rose's place with another uniformed person in the passenger seat. Sill launched off the porch, grabbed her bike, and was off riding toward Rose's before Nina could call out. Some time later, Nina saw the car coming back down the road, faster, but still kicking up no dust. There was no sign of life from Rose's land, no sign of Sill—just a great, deep stillness.

*

Sylvie rode directly through the field. The Infamous Elm rose up like a church steeple. She vaulted the wall, stumbled over a forgotten hoe and went down hard. She pushed through the thicket, thorns crawling in every direction, rosehips like pebbles, forearms bleeding. She saw his face clearly in her mind's eye.

Rose stood in the doorway and the uniforms were on the porch, talking. Sylvie waited three yards back, panting so loud she couldn't hear the words.

Her shirt was torn and sticky with sweat. Rose looked over at Sylvie once. Then she slammed the door.

Ben C's brother wore a black armband. His face when he turned was moony with confusion. He hadn't done it before. Lance was the first in the county. When he saw Sylvie, he shook his head—not like saying, *No*, but like someone shaking off cobwebs.

"Need a ride home?" he asked, resting his fingers on bright buttons.

"How?" she said, and then there was more cobweb shaking and he told her.

She backed into a bush and broke a few branches. She stood there, shoulder blades bleeding a little—the thorns were big—until he drove away. Then she went and climbed the wooden ladder and curled into the hay.

*

They were watching TV when Stella grabbed his knee and wouldn't let go.

Ward and Stella had a routine—a scoop of ice cream after dinner while they watched the late news. It was really frozen yogurt, but Stella called it ice cream. She had switched back to the low-fat dessert once they'd made it through the full-fat gallon she'd bought at the SuperStore. Ward took this as a good sign. She was working toward forgiveness, helping him watch his cholesterol. Most nights, after the weather girl gave the forecast, he'd flick off the TV and she would rise to her feet, an empty bowl in each hand. "I don't know why we watch," she'd say. "What a waste of time." Just local news—car crashes and crimes of passion and sad drug stories.

Save for that night. A picture of Lance flashed onscreen: brown eyes, cropped hair, wide cheekbones, and that stony expression that young men assumed for their uniformed portraits.

"No," Stella said. "*No.*"

She wouldn't leave the couch that night. The ice cream bowls sat untouched. Ward smoothed her hair back from her face to kiss her brow, and her eyes when she looked at him were like the bruises her fingers had left in the soft flesh on each side of his knee.

*

At the funeral, Perry stood between Nina and Sill. His daughter's shoulder shook under his arm. Nina reached into his jacket pocket looking for a tissue—then she went still, as if she had lost the thought, and left her hand there. They watched the sergeant give the folded flag to Stella, who was a pale, yellowish color, sharp bones in her face making her unpleasant to look at for the first time in Perry's memory. Rose wasn't there. He'd noticed that earlier, he supposed, in the church, but it only now sunk in.

Several hundred people were there, most of whom he recognized. The preacher spoke platitudes, his voice wobbling when he said "youth." Perry flinched. He flinched again when a clod of dirt hit the coffin. Who were all these people, and how did they know Lance? They didn't, was the answer. They didn't know anything.

At home, Sill disappeared. Nina reheated leftover stuffed green peppers for dinner, and he sat at the table, not waiting for his father and wife to join him before he cut a forkful and shoved it into his mouth. He chewed the slimy mouthful a good minute before he could swallow.

Across from him, the Old Man settled in and cleared his throat. "I think we can—"

Perry slammed his fist into the table. The salt shaker teetered. He slammed it again, just to watch it move. Nina walked in from the kitchen.

"Shut up," he told his father. "*Shut. Up.*"

*

The Old Man took the Almanac from his nightstand. He never actually read it anymore—it served almost as a scrapbook, holding articles that seemed important to keep, mostly about local land politics, and some snapshots. Tucked into the back cover was the folded newspaper article memorializing Lance. The reporter who had written it, Will Snead, had included the requisite photo—the boy in his uniform, his eyes looking just past the camera. He'd talked to the Army rep, who was quoted saying the expected things about honor and sacrifice. He had filled in details the Old Man didn't quite know what to make of: a truck moving supplies from point A to point B, an improvised roadside bomb planted by a nameless enemy. And this one fact: the kid had had a nickname—Loogie—bestowed by his platoon-mates for some reason that Will Snead did not know or bother to mention. Loogie. He had been over there just shy of a year. The second part of the article had the local quotes. Lance was high-spirited, according to Donovan Mead at the high school, which the Old Man knew was code for hell-raiser. He played football. He was survived by his mother, Rose.

The Old Man hadn't held on to the clipping for any specific reason. More because of a strange unease, a lack of reason. It bugged him. The story could have been written about almost any kid over there. What did he know now, about Lance, that he hadn't known before? Not a goddamn thing, except the nickname: *Loogie*.

He took another sip of juice and pressed his fingers into his left shoulder. He turned off the television, put the Almanac back where it belonged, lay down and pulled the red handkerchief from his pocket to cover his eyes. He watched the blackness behind his eyelids.

*

Louise slid two hundred dollars over the counter and her eyes searched Ward's. "How is everyone doing?" she asked. Ward started to answer and exhaled a single dry sob.

The walls receded, and she fumbled for his receipt, shocked, trying to focus. He pressed his thumb and index fingers into the corners of his eyes, and when his hand dropped, they were pink and inflamed. Ward gathered himself and his money and walked blindly to the parking lot. She followed, a few paces back, trying and failing to think of something to say. He'd left the keys in the ignition and the engine running.

*

Everyone shrank. Scottie watched it happen.

There was the faintest trembling under his feet. Not right away. It was after Ward told him the news, a week or so later—as if the earth expelled a breath. He looked at the street, the ghosts milling, the birds chattering on the wires. Does this happen for each of us? Will it happen for me? A piece missing. A kaleidoscope clicked once to the right, rearranging.

*Get over yourself, Scottie.*

*

Gone. It was all gone, all of it.

Except it was all still there, more than before—house, garden, fields, trees, gravel. All Rose had, there and gone, all at the same time. Thistles, thorns, shiny leaves, cottony seedpod skeletons, sharp rocks, black ants, rocky earth, dung beetles. Even inside the house: broken glass, red-bellied spiders, snails, aphids, silverfish, termites. Things underneath pushing out what she'd thought was hers.

*

Stella knocked at the front door and then walked around the house, peering in the windows. Nothing. So she backtracked to the car, exited the driveway, drove a bit down the road and cut the engine. She retraced her steps, sat on the back porch, and waited. An hour passed. She raised a hand to push at the hair above her temple, flattening it, and then ran fingers along the edge of the casserole dish until the tinfoil threatened to tear.

Rose came through the thickets. She was carrying a picnic basket with a broken lid and wearing clothes in need of a good scrubbing. Freckles stood out against her pale skin. Worst of all was Rose's hair—the shock of rich red was now white. It was gathered in a bun. Wiry tendrils framed her face. "Your hair!" Stella blurted.

Rose stopped a few feet away and cocked her head. The flat planes of her cheeks moved for long seconds. "Go away," she finally said.

Stella clutched the dish, half lifted it in offering. Then she dropped it to her lap. "Rose, don't send me away. I loved him too."

Rose drop-kicked the empty basket onto the porch and walked past Stella into the house. She watched the basket clatter to a standstill before she followed. No sign of Rose in the kitchen, so she put the casserole on the top shelf in the refrigerator and, clutching her shoulder bag, walked further into the house.

Theo's place had been troublesome back when she'd lived there, but now . . . The whole place tilted southward, a sinking ship. Grooves between the floorboards could snap a toe, and dark stains seeped from the ceiling. In the parlor, patches of faded upholstery shone thinly. A cassette of Johnny Cash's greatest hits was placed on the end table under a forgotten cup of tea. It smelled of old potpourri and creeping mold. Stella went to the record player and lifted the arm; a clump of lint stuck to the needle and she picked it off, wiping her fingers on her skirt. Dust hit her throat, and she coughed.

Upstairs, Rose's bed was made, a quilt pulled tight over the pillows. There were no jars or bottles on the dresser, no books on the nightstand. Water dripped into the bathroom sink, trailing a rusty stain down the porcelain bowl. The door to Lance's room was shut, and Stella pressed her fingertips and the heel of her palm against the wood. Then quickly pulled away. "Rose! Where are you? Please talk to me."

She found her downstairs in the smallest room, the dark little sewing room at the end of the hall that had been Stella's room and still held the twin bed that she'd slept in years before. Now it was an extended pantry. Stacks of yellow newspapers and canned vegetables lined one wall, and a sack of potatoes slumped in a corner. Rose stretched out on the bed, eyes closed. Her arms were folded into an X across her chest, fingertips touching the shoulders of her ratty blue sweater.

"Please, Rose," Stella whispered.

She didn't move.

"I brought the flag, Lance's flag. It's yours now." She reached into her shoulder bag and held it out. "Take it."

Rose yanked the sweater away from her body, set the cloth triangle against her chest and refolded her arms, flag hidden and eyes closed tight. The bedsprings trembled.

"Stella," Rose rasped—and these were the words that Stella wouldn't be able to shake. Later, they snagged in her gut and reeled her back again and again to Rose's porch. "I can't do this."

"You can. You will." Her voice was thin. "I'll help you."

Rose seemed to sleep then; her face slackened. Stella returned to the kitchen and wiped down the counters. She loosened the foil and set the casserole in the oven at 375. Then she dusted the parlor and put soft music on the old record player—Peggy Lee singing about murderous card sharps and surreys with fringe on top—as if sounds and smells could shore Rose up.

Stella was rummaging in the refrigerator crisper when the screen door's rusty hinges screeched. Rose had passed wordlessly behind her and out the door. Stella pulled a dishtowel off the oak table and followed. The sun was fading and a soft noise carried through the late afternoon air—a faint keening.

Rose turned to look at her, and Stella saw that the white hair wasn't the worst of it. Rose's eyes were fossils. Stella's hands worked the dishtowel, wringing and twisting. Still, there was nothing to do but keep moving—she followed Rose into the far corner of the yard.

Rose dropped to her knees; the sound stopped. Her shoulders pulled forward, and she didn't pause or look up—just bent, traced a triangle in the dirt under a blackberry bush and began to dig, clawing at the ground.

Fergus crawled from his refuge under the back porch and sat on the steps. Stella looked at the knot she'd made of the towel and dropped it. She knelt alongside Rose and dug too. When they had a hole about two feet deep, Rose raised her shirt, pulled the folded flag away from her belly, and placed it into the earth. They threw fistfuls of dirt after it until the hole was filled. Rose shifted her weight and sat with her legs tucked to one side, a pose so rooted in Stella's memory, so identifiably *Rose*, that she sat back herself, mirroring the position. Stella leaned forward, smoothing and patting the grave, working dirt further into her fingerprints and palms.

The air glowed on the porch and on Fergus but it fell short of where they were. "God," Stella said, stretching dirty hands to clutch Rose's forearm. "Rose." She dug her fingers in and wept. Inside the house, the breadcrumbs on the tuna noodle casserole began to burn, giving off an acrid smoke. Stella leaned forward to peer into Rose's face. The white head was bowed. Stella didn't think before she did it—she reached out and put her hand under Rose's chin, tilting her face up. From a great distance, and slowly, Rose focused, taking in Stella's wet cheeks and runny nose and her need.

There was a crackle, an electric shock of recognition. Stella caught a whiff of the burning casserole and mistook it for singed hair. Rose pulled from Stella's grip, crouched onto her haunches, swung an arm wide, and cracked Stella across the face. The force of it flung them out from under the brambles. Rose rode the momentum, rolling and scrambling to her feet. "Get out."

She turned into her smoky kitchen. A minute later the door screamed and Stella's handbag arced through the air.

Stella lay sprawled, feeling the blood pulse on its journey until her eyes were as dry as Rose's had been. She heaved herself up, not even bothering to straighten her clothes, retrieved her bag, and skulked along the side of the house. Fergus impassively watched her go. Her knees were brownish purple. She kicked off her high heels and limped down the driveway and up the road to her car, dirt and snot-stained, twigs in her hair. No one drove by, but if they had they'd have assumed the worst. *Let 'em,* Stella thought. *It'd be nothing new.*

In her sedan, the smell of her new middle-class life—leather upholstery and tasteful perfume and her sneaky cigarettes—mingled with the animal scent of sweat and blood. She checked the rearview mirror. Her lower lip was red and puffy. She licked the blood and sat in silence, listening to the cottony pulse beat in her veins.

The idea that people manifested their own good and bad luck—Ward believed that. Comfort was a matter of being deserving. Catastrophe, on the other hand, was for the weak-willed and the unprepared. The notion must filter through the water fountain at the Chamber of Commerce, that bastion of heartland prosperity. Those who have inevitably feel entitled to it. And if we merit good fortune, the flip side of the coin is the bad, which must also be deserved. But luck and karma theories didn't work when considering Rose—they exposed the small-heartedness, Stella's stinginess toward her own younger self and her disregard for Rose, the one person she'd never dreamed would turn a stranger.

She grimaced, the tight skin of her lip throbbing. A slew of events—human folly, hand of God, ruthless chaos—whatever was to blame, Lance was gone. *Who deserves this?* She slipped on her shoes, got out of the car, and strode back to Rose, slamming the kitchen door open. Rose stood at the sink, running water into the percolator.

Stella drew herself up. "Fuck karma and fuck old mistakes and fuck war."

Rose didn't turn, just set the coffee maker on the counter.

"I loved Lance too." Stella waited, breath rushing in and out of her lungs. Rose was silent, her head bent; immovable.

Stella stalked back to the car, face stinging. She pumped the gas too hard, feeling the engine thrum like a ventricle of her own heart, and swung a U-turn toward town. Orange light smeared the horizon. *And fuck you too, Rose.*

*

*Stella:*

*I'm cold all the time. My hands are cold, my feet are cold. There's a weight on my shoulders—an actual thing sitting up there, a slab of marble, or, no, a chest full of rusty lug wrenches. It interferes with how I hear things and see things, so if I didn't respond when you said you loved—I'm sorry. Time is strange. When were you here? It could be last week, or longer. It takes a while for words to work their way in.*

*I know you did. I know you do.*

*I've drunk pots of coffee, which explains this messy writing. I don't sleep any more. Dreaming isn't—Last night, Gordie walked right through the wall and stood at the foot of my bed. He looked so young! His hands moved in big swoops like a concert conductor, but there was no music. I felt that I wasn't listening as I should, that there was some important sense missing—His eyes were alive with questions. I fell out of bed and scared the hell out of Fergus.*

*Do you remember in junior high when Nat Bernson wrote "Stella its a whore" in giant letters on the side of the water tower? He was mad, I think, because—well, you know why. The gnat couldn't spell "is." Stella is a whore. You and me and Glennie and Gordie went out that very night with white paint and covered up your name—just your name, remember? Not the "its a whore" part. Our sense of civic responsibility didn't extend very far and it was late. Afterward, every time we drove past that leftover graffiti I would repeat it to myself, over and over—its a whore, its a whore, its a whore . . . its a war.*

*A weird litany of aggression. That was as real as war was, to me. When we were kids, the men in suits who read the news said things that slid right off the screen—children killed, what's for dinner; soldiers maimed, time for bed. That should not be possible. It should* <u>*not*</u> *be allowed. For every soul killed in conflict we should each flay one square inch of skin from our complacent asses. We'd all be assless before a day is out. Stella, I'm an assless wonder. It's not lug wrenches I feel, it's bones.*

*Do you hear what I'm saying? The news never meant anything to me. That nice gray-haired man in the suit stared into the camera and said what was happening elsewhere. Then elsewhere became here, without warning, my house.*

*I'm elsewhere, Stella.*

*Of course you know that everything I have to say is worthless. I have nothing left of worth. Play some violins (is that all there is, Peggy Lee?).* <u>*Everything*</u>*, Stella—The doctor gave me a bunch of pills that make my mouth bitter and dry. I have no spit. They aren't working, no matter how many I swallow. Though maybe the fact that I'm writing to you means they're turning me unrecognizable. What a relief that would be.*

*Stella, I can't believe I let him—*

[This one, unsent, went into the compost pile.]

# Part III

It was over for maybe minutes
then it was never over.

—Heather McHugh, *Acts of God*

*

The storm advances across towns and farms, spraying wreckage. A churning force eats the air and grows bigger, weighty with destruction. And yet the way it moves at times has the wild lightness of dance—feet on the earth, head in the clouds, darting and turning on a whim. Of course, how you see this depends entirely on where you are.

A strange, sleepy calm. The far-off flicker of green lightning.

*Inside.*

Why did the chicken cross the road?

Because he had to get supplies to a Strategic Border Town.

We were not at war when I signed up. Then you know the rest.

Before I see them, I hear them. Like listening to a faraway station on the radio in your truck at night: snatches of voices, music, a preacher saying how to live. Then turn a bend or pass a cluster of wires and they're gone—white noise, a faint buzzing, snow on the air, the land stretching out in darkness and mountains in the distance. So you keep driving and for no apparent reason they're back like they were never gone—the sounds of life, trying to sell you oil changes and hamburgers, singing about love and betrayal and giving up and trying again.

Why did the chicken go to war?

Because a Strategic Border Town needed supplies and somebody had to drive there and back again. I did it dozens of times. It was simple, in a way. It was also very hard.

Why does the chicken cross the road?

Because they pull me across again and again.

The radio crackles in, each voice a tug. I stop the truck and step out onto the side of a dark road looking at the mountains. Then a bird skims over the water, leaves murmur, their voices carry to me and I'm tunneling toward the surface, pulled by the voices. I'm spinning through trees by Johnson's Creek and into my own yard, the sounds still fading in and out.

Even when they're quiet, people give off a kind of hum. I listen. Some of what they tell me happened a long time ago, some of it is happening now. The mountains, the road, Johnson's Creek, my mother's yard, Sylvie in the hayloft. Beyond that, further afield: Perry's rocky acres, the intersection by Mondragon's, Stella's kitchen table. I step from one to another like they're rooms in the house that made me. Stepping through, I remake them.

Come back to the yard and my mother. She stares into space. Fergus barks in greeting but not his glad, chesty bark. He knows what I am and what I'm not. They appear most clearly in dim light. Shadows move across the wall. I'm in the hayloft watching the light glow. Blink and I'm gone, moving toward those mountains; they're getting closer. Snatches of voices, old stories, my mother's work boots scuffing across the threshold. Leaves rustle at the side of the swimming hole, something pulsing green at the bottom—I'll never grasp it.

Whisper through the wind over my mother's shoulder, to Fergus on the porch, to Sylvie with her hair gleaming and Stella kneeling on the grass, to Scottie in his window—the whole outline of this place holds me. It's still my place. I'll always be crossing that dusty road but I'll be here too, in the yard and the creek and the old rocky acres—

I'm driving at night. The mountains are textured now, individual shapes instead of one big mass. Sounds on the radio aren't as familiar but I listen for voices and sometimes hear them. And if I can hear them, what do they hear of me? When my mother drives down the county road can she hear me gunning the engine? An old Johnny Cash song, an ad for an auto chain, a big-voiced girl singing about memories and gunpowder—and me asking, *Why does the chicken cross the road? To see you.*

Mother, listen. Head on home, keep the radio on—talk to Fergus, sit with Stella. Keep going, keep listening. Turn the radio on, I'm not gone.

*Here I am.*

The twister gathers force as it proceeds, until it doesn't.

Warm air rushes ecstatic through the center, pulling and turning, forcing cold air out and down in waves, feeding the dance. Cold coils, pulling inward, more of it and stronger until the warm air snuffs out, the funnel choked, thinning and lifting away. It stretches into a long ribbon, harmless now, twirling across the sky.

Pull back the eye. Unseen by almost everyone below: heads bowed, hands clenched into fists and clasped in prayer, hands reaching—

*

*Mother.*

Green light. Green light and stillness.

Slowly, carefully, Rose rolled to one side. She thought about sitting up for a long time before she pushed her hands underneath her and did it. Porch boards creaked. Vines and branches covered the house. She parted a tangle and looked at the garden. A piece of chimney sat in the yard, pointing west toward old Route 9. Crumbling bricks littered the brambles, and an abandoned wasp nest lay near the bent screen door. Fergus was gone.

She rubbed a sore spot on her hip. The porch planks must hold grooves where she'd dug in. Rose crawled to her hands and knees and hoisted herself to her feet. A sudden weight on her bladder, and no time to find the bathroom. She yanked down her underwear, hiked up her skirt and crouched into an unsteady squat over the edge of the porch to pee. Relieved, she stood and stumbled through the door.

The parlor was smaller, chunks of plaster crumbled near the mantel. In the kitchen, tins and flour covered the floor, and the stove had gone missing. She opened a can of tuna fish and put a bowl out on the porch for Fergus—if he smelled it, he'd come. Then she mixed a half-full jar of instant coffee into a tin of pineapple juice and drank it down.

In the upstairs bedroom, she pushed tree branches aside and searched in the closet for the thick olive canvas duffel. She tied a scarf around her head and put on her old wool coat, and gathered a few more clothes. Then she found her knitting needles, wedding band, the picture of the three of them together, plus a bag of bobby pins, and threw everything in.

Rose knew even before her hand touched the doorknob that his room would be intact. She could feel the house's bones as she made her way down the hall, where it was brittle and where it had held. His room had held. The door swung open to that same bright silence. She had a tremendous urge to stretch out on his bed and watch the light move down the walls. Instead, she went to the closet and shoved aside a long coat, reaching for the file box tucked into a far cubby. From the box she took the thick folder of his artwork, a few letters, printouts of messages that Sylvie had given her, and laid them carefully in the duffel. Downstairs the cuckoo released its latch, but no subsequent chime sounded. Gears whirred, more clicking, and then quiet.

As she returned to the porch Fergus raced into the yard from the direction of the pasture, a wet, oily patch on his hip. His nails scrabbled on the porch planks, the panicked scrape trying to convey what he'd seen. "Come here." He was panting, his eyes dilated. She ran her fingers through his damp fur, but could feel no punctures. He sniffed at the bowl of tuna but wouldn't eat, so she brought him water from one of the canteens in the pantry. While he drank, Rose grabbed her shears and cut the branches that clogged the porch steps.

A cricket chirped, stopped as if surprised, and chirruped again. Nothing was where it should be. A wingback chair—not hers—sat wedged in a ditch. Disembodied blooms and thorns from her rose bushes littered the yard, reaching out, torn bases stretching dryly into the air. Branches lay around her, her cheeks stinging. An iron skillet waited upside down at the base of the porch steps. She used it as a steppingstone, expecting it to sink, but her weight didn't register. A cherry wood rolltop sat in the east field, looking like it hadn't a scratch. Torn books, dresser drawers; broken, flinty wood everywhere, and rusty nails. The truck was where she'd left it, but she had no idea where to find the keys.

The air smelled clean. If she didn't know better, she'd think it was morning. Rose shook her head, tried to breathe evenly and stop the shuddering. From the middle of her yard she could see the house collapsed to the left, though perhaps the perspective was skewed by the tree sticking out of her bedroom window. The house teetered, she was sure of it, and had the sense that the world was folding in one step behind her. "Let's go," she called to Fergus. He dragged himself to his feet, moving slowly, and now she could see that he was limping, favoring his right back paw.

Lance's wheelbarrow was wedged against the base of a fallen oak. She pulled it upright, her palms moving over the rubber grip ridges, sinking into where his hands had left indentations. Maybe she was the one teetering. Her stomach rumbled. She set her duffel in first and then wheeled over to Fergus, coaxing his front legs up and heaving in the rest of him when he didn't complain. Rose lifted the handles, took a cautious step, and paused to pick up something that glinted—an old, scarred nickel. She slipped it into her pocket. Fergus curled into the wheelbarrow, his back pressed against her duffel bag.

"There are a hundred ways that this can end, and I know almost all of them." She hoisted the handles and pushed forward.

Fergus barked, like always, at something Rose couldn't see.

"Okay," she said. "Oh boy."

*

*Cross the road.*

Stella had glass shards in her hair, small green chips from the shattered windshield. Something had hit the back of her head and when she reached up to touch her skull the damp mass felt alien, like the pelt of an animal. Her vision was fine. The car was upended yards into Old Man Brown's cornfield, and from this distance the champagne-colored metal looked impossibly clean and shiny. There was her car, here was her body.

She brushed glass crumbs from her hair and shoulders. Her purse was somewhere; with it, her phone with its tiny digital heart. She stepped back from the Infamous Elm to survey the damage. The trunk was pulled open like a wishbone, fresh wood exposed from the top branches through the thick core, ending about five feet above the roots. Branches and wood chips littered the road, and it occurred to Stella that the tree wouldn't survive this. The knowledge came slowly, like swimming upward from a dream state into the alarm clock morning: *Going to run all night, going to run all day . . . I'll bet my money on the bobtail nag, somebody bet on the bay*. A red-winged blackbird flew from a bare top branch into the wrecked field then back again, the only color in a cloudless sky. Stella took a breath, which turned into a burpy hiccup, and before the shaking could overtake her she started walking, not toward town but where she'd been going all along, to Rose.

Of all the times she'd traveled the road, this was the first she'd walked. Each individual stalk and pebble vied for attention, but everything was out of place, and instead of crops and weeds and cigarette butts there were planks of wood, clothing, scrap metal—things that had no business being there. She saw what looked like a kitchen cabinet door, complete with a worn blue pastille knob, and paper of varying sorts. Up on its hill the Brown house was missing a rooftop corner—the shape she was used to had reconfigured like a chipped tooth.

Stella blinked and realized she was terrifically thirsty. The tongue in her mouth felt mealy and she swallowed hard. Her head hurt, but she didn't want to touch it. Would Rose's old splinter of a farmhouse be standing? Her chest trembled, and she couldn't tell whether it was from tears or laughter. When they'd met, as girls, Stella had asked, "Can I have a Coke?" And Rose had given her one. Stella imagined that carbonation now, popping into the cottony corners of her mouth. She touched her cheek, which felt a little gritty, and refrained from licking her lips. Her walking pace did not match the urgency that she felt—and the urgency itself was dulling, as if it were in a hermetic corner of her mind, or maybe it was in the Browns' missing attic room. She giggled at that thought, and hiccupped again. Color filled the sky. She breathed in blueness with each step.

And then there was Rose, walking up the road, pushing a wheelbarrow. Lance's dog sat in it, patiently watching the world wheel past. Stella's feet kept their pace—fast or slow, she didn't know. The road smelled of wet stone. She waited until they were within a yard of each other and said, "I've lost my purse."

Rose's chin and cheek were bruised, and her hands were a mess, covered in scratches. She looked on the verge of saying something.

Stella waited. A starling hopped along the ditch beside them, searching for supper in the tamped dirt.

"Do you remember when we first met?" Stella asked.

Rose didn't answer, but she was there. Rose stood before her!

"Ever since then . . ." Stella stopped, stretching out her hand. "Where are you hurt?" The starling found a grub and snatched it up.

Rose took a breath. "I can't tell."

The words were thin: shale from the side of a mountain. Rose bent to touch Fergus, making sure he was still there. Stella kept her hand outstretched and when Rose straightened she placed hers lightly against it, palm to palm, fingertips against wrists.

Stella felt another hiccup coming, a bubble of long-held air working its way up her chest. She coughed, pulling her shoulders straighter, pressing her feet into the road as she filled her lungs. "Come with me."

Rose let her take the wheelbarrow handles and they walked together, passing the Infamous Elm without comment. They turned up the long driveway to Old Man Brown's place.

*

*Sit together.*

The Old Man had yelled something about being an idiot when Perry left the shelter—no argument there. Perry had crawled through the storm toward the house those last few yards, searching for Nina and Sill with eyes clamped shut, hail pounding, and only found the porch steps by the angle of the slope under his knees. Inside, he scrambled to the first floor bathroom, holding onto the sides of the claw-footed bathtub and screaming for Nina. He couldn't hear his own voice. In those minutes their loss became palpable, stalking around his outline in the tub. When the roof cracked he felt everything he knew recede from view—and yet he still clung to the porcelain. His body wanted life.

He unfolded himself when the noise stopped and staggered through the house, silent, too spooked to shout. At the top of the stairs he looked right and the open wall showed a green field. His stomach dropped out of his body. He ran into Sill's room, ears roaring, and flung open the closet door. They were twined around each other, sniffling. "My God," he said. "What the—" He fell to his knees as Nina and Sill crawled out, air flowing from the new gap above them. Perry embraced them fiercely and let go just as fast, and they helped each other to their feet.

Sill pulled her shirttail up to wipe tears and dirt off her face. "Mom?"

Nina rested a shaky hand on Sill's shoulder. "Later."

He took them out onto the landing to see the missing roof and exposed beams, and looked at Nina. "If you'd been in our room—"

Nina covered her eyes with her hand. Then she set to work, directing Sill to help her find the items they'd need: blankets, clothes, and other necessities. Even if they'd wanted to talk about it, there was no time to moon around.

"I have to go get him," he told Nina. "He's still down there." Perry could hear his wife and daughter whispering as he descended the stairs, almost as if they were in church.

From the front of the house the damage was stark, almost clean. He backed away from it, turning only when he was halfway down the hill. Perry focused on his hands; here, solid, pulling back the storm cellar door.

"Dad, it's done." No answer. He called again as he descended the ladder. "Dad?"

The Old Man lay on the cot, toes pointing straight at the ceiling, left hand in a fist at his side, right hand touching his chest. His eyes were open, blue irises dull. Perry knelt, moved his father's hand, and put an ear to his heart. He caught the usual smell—Ivory soap, bay leaves, tobacco—and something else now, faintly sweet. Perry closed his father's eyelids and bile rose quickly in his throat—he tasted the ham sandwich he'd had for lunch, on its way back up, and the apple. He swallowed hard and considered the ladder. The Old Man had lost muscle mass in recent years, his bones hollowing. Perry hoisted the body over his shoulder and slowly pulled him up the wood slats.

At the bottom of the hill he called to Nina and she came running. She didn't ask what was wrong, just leaned over and felt for herself. Nina took the Old Man's feet and Perry grabbed him under the arms. They hauled him up the hill and directly into the parlor, death requiring the best room in the house. Sill watched from the door as they laid him on the sofa. His daughter's face was dirt-streaked and very calm; the perforated edge of paper ripped from a three-ring binder was stuck in her hair like confetti. She stepped in to touch her grandfather's cheek.

"Probably a heart attack," Perry said. "He—" he lifted a hand to his chest and stopped. Overhead, a chunk of roof clattered through to the second floor. Perry spun on his heel and walked out to the barn.

The sky was scrubbed clean. A fresh mineral scent came off the ground. It occurred to him that he had no idea how to act in this situation; he felt nothing—numb, sore knees, that's it. Even his lower back, which he'd have bet money would give him trouble after lifting the Old Man, was uncomplaining. The barn seemed fine, more or less, and the tractor. A swath of corn lay flattened. The late afternoon sun caught something shiny out in the field that bordered the road—it might be a car, but from this distance he couldn't be sure.

His Old Man. He was old, but he'd never seemed mortal. When Perry had considered his father's death, it had always been about logistics, not about the body. The fact of the wiry corpse was something else altogether—unnatural but familiar, akin to the way flying dreams mimicked swimming. "This is something else," he said aloud, and put his hand to the back of his neck. Perry looked again at the house. The first floor seemed fine, certainly salvageable; maybe they could pick it up and move off the hill.

He was thinking about the skeleton of his house so he wouldn't have to think of the skeleton of his father—he knew enough to know this. Perry bent and took a handful of dirt from the same spot his father had scooped up earlier. All he tasted was minerals and ozone; dirt washed clean. "God." He wanted to lie down right there on the ground, but just then Nina and Sill came onto the front porch, and Nina called that they would get some food ready. She was clenching her jaw, he could tell from the way she moved; keeping it together for Sill. Then she looked past him toward the road, and a dog barked.

Rose and Stella were walking up his driveway, Stella pushing a wheelbarrow, Fergus riding in it like royalty, his ears pricked. The dog gave another bark to announce their arrival. "It's something else," he whispered into the dirt in his hand, letting it scatter out of his loose fist as he went to greet them.

Rose wore the same thing he'd seen her in that morning, an old cotton dress and boots, but she'd added a coat and a red handkerchief around her head. Her eyes scanned the Brown house, and then his face. Stella wore pants and sneakers and had what looked like blood on the side of her neck. They looked as battered as he felt. Rose held tight to Stella's arm, elbow linking through and fingertips resting across the forearm.

"One for the history books," he said, and ducked his head. "You all right?"

Rose moved her head slightly, acknowledging his words. Stella watched Rose's face intently. Rose cleared her throat and whispered hoarsely, "Look." The weathervane on his roof was leaning akimbo, rocking back and forth—the whale's face bobbed down, and the motion gave the impression that it was diving into the depths.

"Got to fix that," Perry said. The understatement of the year. He had to fix everything: the weathervane, the roof, the house on the hill, the hill itself. Rose's eyes went quiet, as if in speaking she'd startled herself. They were all in shock, he supposed, though it seemed to be doing Rose some good.

"Come on up. There's food." Something told him not to ask about Rose's house. Stella let him take the wheelbarrow, and as they walked up the hill she said that it was her car out in his corn. It would have to be hitched to a truck and pulled out.

That they were here and talking at all was the most extraordinary thing, and yet he felt that nothing would astonish him ever again. He wondered if he could find the Old Man's bottle of whiskey. "I have to tell you about my father."

Nina and Sill came onto the porch holding plates and several jars of canned peppers and pickles. "You're here," Nina said flatly, setting plates onto a chair. Stella moved closer to Rose and looked out at her car in the field.

"He . . ." Perry started, sucked air in a dry cough and tried again. "It was peaceful, as far as we can tell." He guided them into the parlor. Rose went to the Old Man and crouched, peering at his profile. He did look peaceful. With his eyes closed and his jaw slack, the Old Man could have been sleeping. Nina must have moved him, because his hands met across his torso. Rose touched them. Then she curved her fingers over his forehead to his hairline.

"A heart attack," Perry said, though no one had asked. Stella hovered just inside the door, touching the back of her head.

"Or a stroke," Nina spoke from the corner, her eyes dark.

"I'm going to look for whiskey."

"Should you call someone?" Stella asked.

"Phone's dead."

"And the cell service was just busy signals. Come eat." Nina clearly wanted everyone out of the parlor.

"What happened to Fergus?" Sill asked once they returned to the porch, glaring at Rose. She'd helped the dog out of the wheelbarrow and onto a blanket, where he lay with his legs curled under him, licking one paw.

Rose lifted her hands. "I don't know."

Perry remembered how she'd seemed when Theo died, that wispiness, and felt his gut twist. "I'll check him out. I just need to find—" He stumbled blindly away from them, down the hall to his father's room, where he crumpled onto the bed, knees curved into his chest. A word came slowly to the surface of his mind like a fish rising through a murky pool, taking shape whitely: *orphan*.

Nina needed more food and two extra chairs. There was ground beef in the fridge that would only go bad if the power stayed out, so she put it in a bowl pulled at random from the dish drainer and told Sill to give it to the dog. Through the screen door, she watched as Fergus got to his feet and sucked in the meat without chewing, licking the bowl clean. Too late, she realized it was the Old Man's oatmeal bowl, with the blue band around the rim that matched his eyes. Nina went to the sink, surprised when water came out of the tap. She could hear Stella out on the porch, talking to Sill or Rose or the dog. Whoever it was, Stella didn't get an answer.

Nina pressed a fist into her stomach, reliving that long fall down the hill on the way to the storm cellar—shaking the Old Man when she should have held him steady, letting her emotions get the better of her. She'd have to hold it, that knowledge, and contain it somehow, what she'd done and hadn't done.

She hurried out to the porch, snatching the empty bowl from between Fergus's paws. "That's enough—" Her voice was too loud, they were all looking at her. "Stella, come into the bathroom. I'll look at that cut on your head. And Sill, can you make up another plate of crackers?"

In the bathroom, Stella sat on the toilet seat and bent her head forward. Nina took a bottle of liquid castile soap from under the sink, worked some into a washcloth with water, and patted it against the gash. "It's not too deep. I think you're fine. Scalps bleed a lot."

"It's cold." Stella reached up and touched Nina's wrist. "Do you have anything for Rose to put on her hands? The cuts . . ."

Nina stepped back, wondering where Perry had gone. She wasn't up to playing host alone. "There's extra towels under the sink, if you both want to clean up a bit. And ointment in the medicine cabinet for her hands." She hadn't even looked closely enough at Rose to notice. "And Tylenol's in there too, take some of that."

Stella stood, her face a shade paler than usual. "Don't be too nice to me, Nina. I'm trying not to freak out."

Nina gave a harsh laugh, a bark that echoed off the bathroom tiles. "I'm sorry," she sputtered. "I'm not—the dog was in Sherwin's oatmeal bowl and I—I'm sorry. I'm sorry. We're all just—" she stopped. Now would be the time to exit the bathroom, but she stood looking at the bottle of soap in her hands.

Stella stepped to the bathroom sink, giving a little yelp when she saw herself in the mirror. "Jesus, I look like the cat's ass."

Nina cringed. Stella wasn't as charming as she liked to think she was. That thought galvanized her. "I'll leave you to it."

Down the hall to the porch: still no Perry. Rose sat on the front steps, Fergus at her side, looking down over the county road. They seemed content, as if they'd sit there all night if she let them. Nina put a hand to the doorframe and then retreated to the kitchen.

"The world is topsy-turvy," she announced to Sill, who jumped nervously and dropped a cracker. A white line of anger was grooved around her daughter's lips. "What's wrong?" Nina asked without thinking, and leaped without even a pang of guilt to the hope that Sill wouldn't tell her, not right now.

"She can't even take care of a *dog*," Sill hissed. "His paw is—"

"I know. Let's feed them, and then—"

"Then they'll go," Sill whispered, and Nina felt her daughter's vein of anger deflate, become something more familiar, a choking sadness.

"They might have to spend the night. We'll see." She realized she was still holding the bottle of soap, and set it on the counter next to a plate of peanut butter crackers. "You are entitled to be upset. You are." The roaring suction in the closet was overhead still, where they'd left it. Nina gripped the counter's edge and shuddered. "Come on. I'm going to put more chairs out. You make up one or two more plates. The sooner we eat . . ." She had to move, she *was* moving, picking up the full plate and heading for the kitchen door, pitching her voice higher so it might reach him, wherever he was, ". . . have you seen your father?"

Sylvie leaned her head against a pantry shelf, picked up a small bottle of peach jam and rolled it across her temple. Her mother's canning projects neatly lined two shelves. The rest were stuffed haphazardly with grocery store staples: soup and beans and boxed macaroni. Out on the porch, her mother's voice, too shrill, and the sound of chair legs scraping over the wood. Sylvie crouched and found the big box of salty crackers buried under bags of dried pasta. The storm wouldn't have found them in here, the kitchen's nucleus, carefully curated by Nina to supply the Browns with weekday sustenance and an emergency stockpile that could, if necessary, keep them alive for months. She set the peach jam where the crackers had been and stood up, her legs still rubbery from that bike ride through the fields. She touched a jar of pickles with a forefinger, pulled her jeans away from her waist and gingerly tapped the bruise on her pelvic bone. Her hips would be sore for a while.

Before the storm hit, her mother had followed her upstairs: *Sylvie*. As soon as Nina spoke, the house cracked so hard she'd thought her eardrums would pop. They'd rolled to the floor, her mother's body covering her. All noise and thick dangerous air. Nina grabbed her wrist and they crawled to the closet, the only place without a window, and somehow got the door shut. It wasn't any quieter inside, just darker. The ceiling buckled—a piece of roof ripped away. Then the walls shook like paper and there was an incredible feeling of suction, as if it would turn her skin inside out. Sylvie's hair flew straight up. Her clothes flew off hangers and up and out, and her shoes, old photo albums, letters that she'd started but never sent. Sylvie was pulled up off the floor, and Nina too, but her mother hooked her legs under the built-in shelf against the closet wall and locked her arms around Sylvie's waist. Whatever screams they made were lost. Hangers flew past, and pieces of wood. She was two, three feet off the floor, her head yanked back, Nina beneath her, her mother holding her around the hipbones so hard Sylvie felt herself tearing in two. Then the noise snapped off. It was quiet inside the eye, dusty and dark and peaceful, but she had a sense that it was teeming with life. Her bones felt spongy and her heartbeat slowed. A flash of green lightning, and a hiss, and it was gone—just gone. Along with her clothes and shoes and mementoes of who she used to be.

She grabbed the jar of pickles, sweaty fingers slipping a little. Slow steps came down the hall from Granddad's room. He could still be here, a part of him, walking the halls, looking for someone to talk to. The thing her mom and dad hadn't understood was that he was just lonely, her granddad. In the middle of the family he'd felt extraneous. You could see it when he wasn't talking: sighing and whistling and rapping his fingers on the kitchen table to remind himself that he was still there. He talked tough to them, trying to get attention.

"Granddad," she whispered, lips moving against the pickle jar lid, "talking never got anybody anywhere in this family."

"What?" Her father stood at the door, eyes bloodshot, clutching a bottle of whiskey. Perry held it up like a trophy. "Found it." The Old Man had received it years before, a gift from a friend in the

Veterans of Foreign Wars, and opened it rarely. Sylvie moved to the counter, put more crackers on a plate and began adding toppings: sliced cheese to half, peanut butter to the rest.

"Looks good," her dad said, hunting in the cabinet for a glass. He pulled one down, filled it half an inch, and drank the amber liquid. Then he poured a quarter as much and held it out to her. "Want to try?" She wrinkled her nose and knocked it back, letting it sear her throat, swallowing hard, waiting for the heat to creep up her belly. "Bracing," Perry said, "But only when you really need it. Don't tell your mom."

Nina called from the porch, tired of waiting. He reached into the cupboard, hooked his fingers into the lips of three more glasses, and then picked up the bottle. "Best come on out."

"I'll be there in a minute. I have to finish . . . Daddy, will you make sure his dog is okay?"

Perry stopped, standing on one leg, foot angled up to push through the door without using hands. "Honey." The end had been so close in that closet—he couldn't know how close.

Sylvie looked down, blinking. "In a minute," she repeated. "I'll be . . ." She bent to pull a segmented platter from the lower cabinet and when she stood, he'd gone.

She spooned a different condiment from Nina's special shelves into each plate segment: gherkins, cherry chutney, spicy baby carrots. As she unscrewed lids her granddad's liquor did its work and her ribcage softened, bruises receding from the front of her mind. She sliced apples into a bowl and the rhythmic movement shook loose something her granddad had said to her soon after Lance died, words she'd rejected almost as he'd spoken them. "You'll think of him, and you should. But give yourself a break from thinking too."

Sylvie arranged the apple cores end to end in a straight line on the counter. She lifted a bread and butter pickle slice and set it on her tongue, succumbing to the tangy sweetness. Her mother's voice, Stella's voice, the clinking of glasses. It sounded almost like a party out there on the porch. Almost.

Nina had arranged five chairs in a half circle and they sat, looking out over the fields and the road below.

Fergus lapped for a long time at a bowl of water and then settled at Rose's feet. Perry shook off his daze, put the bottle on one of the old TV trays Nina had set up, and went to sit next to the dog, carefully examining his leg and hip.

"There's part of a nail missing, and what could be a puncture in between these toes," he said. "It may be fractured." Rose bent over to look, running her fingers down Fergus's back. The way he thumped his tail made Sylvie look away, out over the barn and past the old school bus stop.

Nina hated the smell of liquor. She thought about saying a prayer but didn't. "Eat," she commanded.

They ate like starving people, leaning in, clearing the platters of crackers, the sliced apples, praising Nina's spicy pickles and peppers. Nina ran the back of her hand over her mouth, feeling a warm tingle of cayenne. Even if she'd failed the Old Man, her confidant, the thorn in Perry's side, Sill was safe. Nina pressed a hand under her ribs, a sore spot where Sill's kneebone had dug in—if her betrayal manifested in her body, would it be here, in cracks and bruises?

She looked at Sill, who'd slid off the chair to sit cross-legged next to Fergus. He devotedly tracked her daughter's peanut butter cracker, drooling as it slowly disappeared. Nina took another pepper from the plate and dabbed it onto her paper napkin. It wasn't a betrayal, it was a choice: her own flesh and blood. She patted at the still-tingling skin around her lips and wondered how it would feel to have Rose and Stella spend the night—of course she would invite them. It was expected.

Stella drank three glasses of juice in quick succession. The Tylenol was finally kicking in. Their meal was strangely casual, an ease among them that had no right to exist. Even so, she thought, I'll never fit in and that's just how it is. She picked up a cheese slice, rolled it up and popped it in her mouth.

Perry regarded the dog, so focused on his daughter's food but perfectly content to watch what he wanted disappear from reach. "That's a good one," he had told Lance, pointing to the puppy in the cardboard box. "That black one right there."

Twilight seemed suspended. The sun moved slowly to the horizon, reluctant to leave. Rose saw the first tentative flicker of a lightning bug, shining too early out over the corn, another creature confused by the storm. Sylvie leaned forward, pressing her cheek against Fergus's wide head; a gold locket swung out of her t-shirt and rested on the dog's ruff. She felt Rose's gaze and straightened, her brows high and eyes round, slipping the necklace back under her shirt.

"You'll sleep over," Nina announced, thinking about how they'd have to maneuver extra mattresses down the stairs. None of them could sleep in the parlor with the body, and she wondered who would take the Old Man's bed.

"Oh, no. We can't—" Stella started.

"Of course you will. Don't be silly," Nina said, more sharply than she intended.

"Well, thank you, Nina, but—"

"We can't have you out at Rose's place by yourselves."

Why, wondered Sylvie. Was it really any safer here? Or was it just that her mother didn't want anyone outside the lines she'd drawn in her head? Nina's decree sounded like something her granddad would have said, and Sylvie marveled at how alike her mother and grandfather were, and not even related by blood. She reached up and pressed the stolen locket into her sternum. Rose had seen what she had, and Sylvie didn't care.

Stella shook her head. "I need to get to town to see that Ward's all right. And the store."

"And I'd better—" Perry paused. "I'd better stop by the sheriff's anyway and ask them to send the coroner as soon as possible. I'll drive you."

It wasn't spoken—Rose herself had scarcely said a peep—but they all understood that she would go with Stella. Now that Sylvie was done eating, the dog returned his gaze to Rose. So did Sylvie, Nina noted; her daughter stared at Rose with a stark challenge in her eyes, clutching at something over her heart. Rose gazed over the porch rail, a blank expression on her face. It wasn't Stella who bothered her so much. Nina didn't want Rose in her house, and Rose knew it. The sooner she followed Stella to town, the better. Nina pressed her knuckles into her side, pushing against the uncharitableness like it was a bone. Rose saw the gesture and for a moment their eyes locked.

Nina leaned forward and grasped Rose's hand too firmly. "I pray for you," she said. Rose dropped her eyes to the dog. Nina meant it—she prayed for Rose every night, and for Lance. She prayed for the Old Man too, for everyone she'd failed. She prayed for herself, riddled with faults, praying even as she fell short. Then she turned her prayers to the ones she held close, the only ones who, when she invited in, she meant it. Sylvie brushed crumbs from her lap, slipping a reserved cracker to Fergus. Nina let go of Rose's hand, her lips still warm from the peppers. "Will you please take some food with you? I have—or had—a pantry full of preserves."

"Have," Sylvie said. It was all still there.

Stella looked at her, a little surprised that the girl had spoken.

"Yes, *have*," Nina said. "Will you, please?" She leaned back in her chair, exhausted.

Stella's head throbbed dully. She had never thought too much about what had turned Nina chilly toward them all those years ago. Now, she looked at Nina watching Rose and saw fear shadowing her face. She sighed, and pressed a hand to her head. Nothing they could do about that. Nina would have to wrestle it herself, if she were inclined, and Stella doubted that she was. Rose had returned her gaze to the fields. Stella wondered what she was looking for, and cleared her throat. It was up to her to move things along. "Well," she began, "we're so grateful."

Perry took the cue, scraping his chair along the porch boards as he stood. Sylvie jumped up and gathered the plates. "Thank you," Stella said to her. The girl smiled wanly before she went to the kitchen.

"She's such a good girl," Stella said to Nina.

Tears filled Nina's eyes and she bent over to rub her hands along the bruised shins under her jeans, hiding her face. Perry cleared his throat and Stella sat perfectly still, listening to her head pound.

"Lightning bugs," Rose said. A few more winked on over the fields, flitting around the barn's edges.

The weathervane gave in to its own weight at last, and clattered through the open roof to the landing below. Fergus leapt to his feet, barking. As they readied to go the casual feeling stiffened, became almost formal. Perry gave Stella extra Tylenol for her aching head. Nina called Sylvie back onto the porch to say goodbye, and they stood in front of the house, thanking each other, beginning sentences and letting them peter out midway.

"Better go while there's light," Perry said. They climbed into the Old Man's truck—Rose in the middle, Stella by the window, with Fergus in the half-seat in back. Perry very carefully set Rose's bag and the wheelbarrow into the truck bed. As they pulled away, Sylvie ran down the porch steps and leaned in the passenger window, handing Rose a tiny oval black and white photo of a woman. Stella recognized it as one of Theo's grandmothers; how the girl had come by it, she couldn't say. Rose examined it as if she'd never seen it before, and slipped it into her pocket.

They drove with the windows down. It was slow going. Perry had to weave like a drunk around downed power lines and random junk in the road, and at points they stopped and moved debris so they could pass. Fergus hung his head out the window, tongue flapping whenever they picked up speed. Perry stopped at the intersection of the county road, no other cars in sight. *North, south, east, west, who's the one that you love best.* He supposed he had loved the Old Man, though the nature of that love might never make itself clear.

Wedged next to him, Rose held tight to a jar of Nina's pickles. He took a deep breath, keeping his eyes on the dash. "Rose, I hope—"

She unlaced her fingers, reached over and touched his arm.

Perry tapped the gas and switched on the radio as they rolled through the intersection. The Governor was talking about sending help and prayers. The storm had given them a great shake, he said, and yet they would prevail, there could be no question; they always had and always would.

Ted Waite came on with the latest. A trailer park on the south edge of town had been hard hit. "I'm thinking of you," Ted said, to everyone and no one. Stella snorted.

Main Street was a wreck. The twister had hit a bit before three-thirty, and after it passed birds and frogs fell from the sky. Their corpses littered the pavement, tiny blobs of flesh dotting the debris from buildings and power lines. Perry could only drive as far as the bank, which looked square and airless, untouched except for a telephone pole stretched halfway across the parking lot. Rose and Stella would continue on foot to Mondragon's, and Perry would have to walk the rest of the way to the Sheriff's office. He lifted the dog down first and then the wheelbarrow and duffel, setting them in a row at his neighbors' feet, thinking, this is how they'll remember me now.

He looked at Rose. "We'll be in touch."

"Thank you so much," Stella said, clasping his hands.

Louise watched it all from the bank window. Dayana and Bill were in the back. They'd been occupied following post-emergency protocols, and now the two of them were looking for the missing emergency supplies box so they could check it off the list. Louise had tried several times to reach Dave by phone. The lines were still down, but she wasn't really worried. Her vault, his cement garage—two of the safest places anyone could be.

She was taken by the sight of Rose and Stella together, each holding one handle of a wheelbarrow as they started toward the town square. So they had found each other. They walked slowly, Rose's dog limping and peeing on a new scent every few steps. Stella touched her head with her free hand and then looked at her fingers to check for blood as if she'd been knocked around a bit. Louise thought of the emergency kit with its gauze bandages and antibacterial cream. She went to pull the kit from under the kitchen sink, tossing cleaning supplies to the side, leaning into the far reaches of the cupboard, already framing questions. *Do you need a bandage, Stella? Or aspirin? Rose, how can I—*

"Louise found the kit!" Dayana called to Bill, and they crowded into the small kitchen, laughing about how silly they were to have missed such an obvious place.

"Heyyyy, where's that cake I've been hearing about?" Bill asked, and Dayana started pulling plates from the cupboard.

"A celebration birthday, for sure," Dayana sang. "We survived! Louise got the best cake, didn't you, Louise? Only the finest for us. Is it in the fridge? Where did you put it?"

"I have to—" Louise sputtered and grabbed the kit, hurrying out to the street. But Rose and Stella were moving more quickly than she'd thought and were too far ahead, she couldn't catch up now. She stood, clutching the kit to her chest and smelling the emptied air.

Ward took a shovel to everything he could, working over the front window panel that hadn't broken and the expensive liquor bottles, shoving over the few shelves still standing. He tried to be quick, before the street came back to life, though he had the sense of moving in a dream, limbs still heavy from the Valium. But his size served him well, and he smashed everything the storm might have reasonably reached, until the storm's wreckage and his self-inflicted damage were, he hoped, indistinguishable. He stopped, panting, to survey his work. Go too far and there would be questions. But would this be enough? He had to believe so.

He walked to the front, looking through the empty window frame to Scottie's place across the street. The boards were still in place at Dunleavy's. Ward picked his way carefully around the small economy car that had somehow landed on his porch, nose facing inward, collapsing the left side of the porch into a cracked bow. He crossed the street, turning once to look at his storefront. A camera, he thought. He'd have to find one, they would want pictures.

Ward knocked and entered, and hearing no sounds went to the back room and found it empty of Scottie but full of his strange reconfigured skeletons, wings and tails poised for flight. Ward stood in confusion and a growing awe until Scottie, hearing footsteps overhead, flung back the trap door and broke the spell.

"You made these?" Ward asked.

Scottie, being Scottie, didn't answer.

Ward looked at the creatures, and Scottie's cot, and the towering stacks of shoeboxes, and if he'd had a fleeting thought of raising the issue of vandalism—his own and Scottie's—it fled with the wing-shaped shadows up the wall. Scottie rubbed sleep from his eyes, and Ward had the sense that he'd woken his friend from a hundred year nap.

He stepped back a bit, giving Scottie space. "There's a car on my porch, a Japanese model . . . someday it'll make a good story. Do you happen to have a camera handy, so I can take photos for the insurance company? They'll send an inspector out for sure, but I need to make a record of the damage."

Scottie pulled an old point-and-shoot from a shoebox on the shelf above his cot and said, "I'll come and look in a few minutes. I need to . . ."

I need to collect my *self*, he thought. The very presence of Ward in their private room sent Dogberry leaping straight back into the cellar, and Ward hadn't even noticed. As soon as Ward left, Scottie drank the dregs of the coffee he'd brewed that afternoon and considered his space. The boards had held, and the darkness was unchanged. He thought he might move his bed down to the cellar. It would leave more room for his projects here. Below, he'd slept better than he had in months, dreaming of his creatures flying overhead, a dovecote come to life. Cooing sounds, the whisper of feathers gradually burying him. Ward's bigness and noise had chased the feeling away but he knew he could get it back.

He heard raised voices on the street and went to open the front door. *Here is the town, here are the people*. Ward called to Emma Templeton, who was walking in the direction of her café holding what looked like a potted ficus. Emma turned, pointed at the Tercel on Ward's porch, and smacked a palm to her forehead. "It's already becoming a joke," Scottie said to the cat at his feet. "We'll move through it so quickly."

"Easy come . . ." Ward yelled. Ward seemed so light and giddy, Scottie wondered if he'd opened one of his liquor bottles. Emma didn't answer; she'd paused about a block down to talk to two women, and as they parted the figures continued toward Mondragon's. A dog limped alongside them. He and Ward identified them at the same time—he could feel Ward's momentary confusion, adjusting what he'd hoped about Stella being safe at home. Then Ward stepped into the street, waving his arms and calling as if they had to find him in a crowd. "Stella! Rose!"

As they approached Ward went to meet them, hooking one arm over Stella's shoulders and kissing her on the temple. Then he put his other arm around Rose, pecking her on the cheek, looking for all the world like the leader of men the town had always wanted him to be. Ward said something Scottie couldn't hear. A ghost slipped around the corner, a tall figure in a baseball cap, watching, leaning into the shadows. Rose put a hand to the back of her neck.

Stella handed Ward a duffel bag, pulled herself out from under his arm and started up the steps. Ward whispered something to Rose, and she let him set her wheelbarrow against the porch and steer her around the car and into Mondragon's. Through the empty window frame, Scottie could see Stella move toward the back, taking stock of the damage. Ward followed his wife into the store, but Rose and her black dog hung by the door, itching to beat a retreat. Streaky pink clouds splashed across the sky to the west.

The power would be out for days and fireflies were the only streetlights. In the dimming light of dusk Rose seemed permeable, part of the threshold, as likely to dissolve into the street as to enter. *Join me*, Scottie thought to call, but just then Stella stepped out from the back room, clacking a spoon against a can of dog food and calling to Fergus. The dog went to Stella as she bent to fill an empty bowl, and Rose gathered herself and followed them in.

*

*Listen.*

An air current buckles. The voice on the radio crackles in and out.

It's gone. Creation gives way to dissolution, clearing the way for more life. More gardens and hopes and failures, more cold fronts and squalls—more war. Which is to say, with as much rhyme and reason as it began, it ends. Whoever professes to explain it is selling snake oil.

The voice on the radio: Ted Waite. He will be fired in a station consolidation not long after the storm; but he'll reinvent himself, land on his feet, new worlds to conquer. And all of them, for the rest of their natural lives, will long for *his* voice when they turn the dial. *Talk us through it. Tell us what happens next.*

*

First there is Ward: older, wiser, a tinge less sad. He sits in a café on a Tuesday afternoon, waiting for his lunch date. This café is called Suzanne's, and includes a Leonard Cohen quote about tea and oranges at the top of every menu. He likes the place. It reminds him of The Bluebird, except twice as expensive and with inferior pie. The waitresses all know him. Suzanne's is only a block from the office where he has taken a job as, of all things, an insurance adjustor. Each afternoon as he stands at the register to pay for his cup of soup and half turkey sandwich, he taps the toothpick dispenser and thinks of his Emporium. Then he stands taller, glancing sidelong into the mirror hanging above the counter as he lifts a toothpick to his mouth. Sometimes, here, he catches a glimpse of himself as a stranger would. A brief recognition delay and he has time to assess: not bad looking, older and slimmer than expected.

"You look tired," Karena says, leaning over to kiss him before she slides into the seat across the table. Her cheeks are pink and she's draped a long red scarf around her neck. She looks happy, leaning back into the booth and unwrapping her scarf as they give their orders to the waitress.

"You look fabulous," he tells her, and means it. Her face and body are softer; she is dating the owner of a Ford dealership and has let her once-frosted hair go gray. They meet for lunch every few weeks, always at Suzanne's, talking about their jobs, their hopes, interesting movies. No rehashing their old married life. They just pick up the thread midstream.

Ward has lived in the city for most of the five years since the storm. He didn't move right away—it took months to iron out the insurance. When the agent came to photograph the sinking porch and damaged stock at the Emporium, she had noted that the boards were splintered evenly; and both windowpanes were broken as if they'd been hit directly in the center. But Ward stood his ground, and the photos of the car on the porch helped his case. Interestingly, as someone who would say he cares quite a bit about personal responsibility and business scruples, he had no qualms about being entitled to the insurance payout. He had paid his dues.

In that strange holding pattern, he often went home to find Rose standing at the window in his living room, staring into the yard at the bird girl statue. A heavy composure had settled on Rose. Her spastic energy had given way, helped, no doubt, by the new prescription from Dr. Willis. Stella was calmer too, very focused, striving to provide a stability that wasn't really in her nature. She insisted that all of their conversations about the divorce be held in the bathroom, afraid that Rose would overhear and care enough to spiral downward. In whispers, they agreed that she would take the house and he would get the insurance payout. The only time Stella cried was when he told her, finally, that he'd found an apartment in the city. She set down her toothbrush on the bathroom sink and embraced him, toothpaste and tears wetting his shoulder. And then he left. He left so easily, he wondered if he'd ever really been moored at all. Ward read periodically about the town's revitalization efforts and felt a vague gladness, like hearing that an old school friend has achieved some minor professional award. He received an occasional update from Stella—and, once or twice, a rambling phone call from Scottie—but mention of people and things he had lost track of made him feel no better than a stranger.

The waitress brings their drinks—coffee for him, herbal tea for Karena—and tells them the food will be up in five minutes before moving on to the next table.

"I'm completely stumped by this work thing I have to tell you about," Karena says. "But first, how are you?" She raises the cup to her mouth, puckering her lips and blowing to cool the hot liquid.

"I'm estranged." A confession. He's gotten a little better at this, saying what he's feeling.

Ward means it as a general statement, but she thinks he refers to Stella and rolls her eyes. "You were a terrible husband but you're a great ex. If Stella has any sense she'll come around eventually."

"Am I?" A great ex. What else is he? All of his energy now goes into finding out.

"So," Karena takes a sip of tea. "Why so tired? Are you seeing someone new?"

Ward picks up the salt shaker, passing it hand to hand and pondering the answer.

*

It has been too long since Scottie Dunleavy has made art. In an effort to remedy this he drove out to Johnson's Creek with his bird net. He sits now at the edge of the water, net folded at his side, thinking about stringing it between two trees. Fall has arrived early, and red leaves clump along the banks. A longspur sings from the tree, signaling to its mate. The flocks have arrived from Nunavut for the winter, and he might be able to catch one by nightfall.

A social worker had come sniffing around the shoe store that morning. She wore a cheap blue suit and chewed spearmint gum. She said, "Your friend Emma Templeton is worried that you might be not taking care of yourself. Are you?" She peered toward the back room and then looked searchingly at him. "Are you having trouble keeping track of things? What have you been eating?" She waited two heartbeats for an answer. "Who else is a friend to you? Who do you care for? Do you ever get out to see family?"

He's out now, isn't he? Wearing an almost clean orange hunting vest with licorice in the pocket, and jeans with the cuffs rolled up three times. "Ward was my friend," Scottie told the social worker. "But he declared bankruptcy and went to the city." A light glinted off the back wall of her eyes when he spoke. She belatedly handed him a business card: Ramona Alvarez, County Human Services. He knew she would click her pen before she did it.

The town is as readable to him as it has always been, though there is less to watch from his front door now that Mondragon's has closed. He walks to The Bluebird once a week and listens to conversations hum around him. If Rose is there on one of her backup shifts, she'll give him a grilled cheese sandwich and only charge for coffee. Rose doesn't work at The Bluebird as often now that she has a job as a teacher's aide. She has a knack for terrifying the kids so they don't get out of line, she'd told him, sliding a sandwich and fries onto the counter.

He should not have taken the food. It made Emma see him as a charity case, and food is not the reason he goes to The Bluebird. His end of Main Street is oppressively quiet: shuttered storefronts and ghostly figures lining the sidewalks, watching for people that never arrive. The newspaper referred to a *malaise* that hit the town after the storm, as if the twister was to blame for every abandoned memory. It was a handy excuse for Ward, but in the scheme of things had the storm changed anything? Scottie thinks about this whenever he walks to Emma's end of the street, with its still-active café and bank and drugstore, ghosts trailing curiously behind him. There is a sense that he is moving from a withered limb into healthy flesh and blood. Yet still part of the whole, much as people like to pretend otherwise. He knows this; the ghosts know. Rose does too. The social worker hasn't a clue.

"You know nothing," he whispers to the water's edge.

Still, he recognizes a predator when he sees one, he knows who has the upper hand. "I'll be back," the social worker had warned, jotting something into a small spiral notebook and jamming it into her suit pocket. He feels sorry for her, this grown-up Ramona the

Spy—Ramona the Raptor. No one, living or dead, looked up when she walked into the street, got into a black Oldsmobile and drove off toward the interstate. But she got to him—she must have, because he's here with his net and hasn't strung it. It has been at least a year since he collected materials, though he thinks about it often enough. He makes beautiful sculptures in his head and then takes a nap.

*Who do you care for?*

He can think of an answer now that she isn't staring him down.

"My cat." His voice is loud and startling, pleasing in the crisp afternoon air. "That bird, this log, that stone, this water, those trees, that sky. All the people, seen and unseen—"

He stops himself, pulls out a strand of licorice, and chews, feeling awake. After he eats, he'll set the net.

*

Louise Logan stands in a checkout line at the Discount SuperStore, waiting to purchase adult diapers for her husband. The checker is new, and the line moves slowly. The smell of barbeque wafts over from a sample table on Aisle 24. Behind her someone sighs audibly. Louise doesn't turn around to commiserate. She has to be home by three o'clock to relieve Dave's home-care nurse. The checkout girl waves to a manager, asking for help, and the woman behind Louise vibrates with displeasure.

For the first time in her life, Louise is not working in customer service. After she was laid off from the bank she struggled for more than a year to find something, fearful for a while that she would have to go work at that dirty Crown Co. meatpacking plant, which was being sued by its employees for unpaid wages and overtime. Finally she had landed a job at the Discount SuperStore, keeping the books in the back office; part time and no benefits, but better than nothing. And they were good to her two years ago, when Dave had a massive stroke—one minute joking with his assistant at the garage, the other listing and slumping, pushing a finger into his temple and saying before he lost the words completely that his head hurt like hell. After much rehabilitation some words have returned, but he spends his days in a wheelchair. Benji moved back home to run the garage, and between his help and the help of the part-time nurse aide, she has Dave home where he should be.

To the left of the long line of registers they have rebuilt the walls to match perfectly. Other storms have followed every year, in patterns the weathermen no longer call *unprecedented*. The woman behind her sighs again. Louise checks her watch. She was risking lateness, trying to wedge in this purchase after her half-day shift; but she hadn't had time to do it during her lunch break.

A voice comes over the intercom, directing shoppers to a special deal in firearms. Louise suppresses a giggle. *Not so smart, fellas.* She has a brief wish that the man in front of her would turn around, or the new girl would look up from her register and they could share a moment of humor to break the monotony. Louise misses working with customers; now she sits in a back office with only an assistant manager for company.

Of course, she sees people she knows in the aisles. Just that morning, rushing in a few minutes late, she'd caught a glimpse of Stella over in the dairy section, placing a dozen single serving cups of yogurt into a mostly empty basket. Louise shifts her purse from one shoulder to another. A sugary smell drifts from the opposite end of the store—cinnamon buns?—wrapping under the scent of barbeque. That morning she'd been in such a rush to clock in, she hadn't stopped to greet Stella. Seeing her always makes Louise think of that moment on the street with the emergency kit. She had re-imagined it again and again until, not right away, but over years of careful accretion, it became more real to her than what had actually happened, remembered even after she'd forgotten the names of the ones who died that day. Her offer, their acceptance. Would you like a bandage, or some aspirin? A memory fixed: her hand pressing the white square of gauze against Stella's dark head. *You're a godsend, Louise.*

She smiles now, remembering. The line inches forward. A man ahead of her unloads gallon jugs of industrial soap and, apparently succumbing to the free sample in Aisle 24, two packages of frozen barbeque wings. The hapless checkout girl reaches for a bag and searches without success for a bar code on the slippery plastic. The woman behind cannot contain herself. "Oh, come *on*." Louise turns to look. A stranger: dishwater blonde, wearing an unflattering horizontal striped sweater. The woman shakes her head and rolls her eyes, and when Louise doesn't respond, peers rudely at the contents of her cart.

Louise faces the register. The girl has figured it out and is picking up speed, gaining confidence—Louise will make it home on time. She readies herself to smile and say something encouraging.

*

Nina scans the sky for telling clouds no matter the season. Today, grays and browns are the dominant color, and the horizon stretches out in a faded blue. She is making the day-long drive to visit Sylvie in Ann Arbor. Perry had planned to come with her, but the young man they'd hired to help with the livestock, an old high school friend of Sylvie's, quit unexpectedly and Perry had to stay and work. Nina is glad for this time in the car alone. She is inexplicably nervous, and the lag between destinations will give her a chance to sort herself out. A pop tune shimmies onto the radio. The strip mall, the cemetery, and the Discount SuperStore stream past in a blur. A highway sign flashes an update: five hundred miles to go.

This past spring, Sylvie graduated with a double major in nursing and ecology, but Nina and Perry hadn't been able to make it to Ann Arbor for the ceremony because the hogs were farrowing. Nina wanted to go anyway, but Sylvie convinced her to wait: "Don't worry. It's not a big deal. Grad school starts in a few months and you can come later." When she tells people that Sylvie has begun a two-year program to become a certified nurse midwife, Nina feels a thrill of pride at her daughter's sense of purpose.

"Oh, babe . . ." the radio singer whines. It's not a good song, but it makes her feel young, as if she's going to Ann Arbor for her freshman year. "I'm going to have to study a lot," Sylvie had warned her, as guarded about her availability now as she'd been all through college.

"Don't worry about me, I'll be studying too." Nina's bag holds a book that professes to be an easy introduction to designing and maintaining websites. She's determined to make an online presence for their business, so restaurants that want heritage pork can place orders directly. A cooler in the trunk holds half a dozen frozen chops for Sylvie.

She shifts and adjusts the seatbelt across her midsection. Nina has gained weight, a significant amount. Dr. Willis warned her to watch it. "Oh, I'm watching," she'd told him. She has cravings she never used to—gooey snack cakes and spoonfuls of sugar in her coffee. But Nina feels fine; and Perry, being no fool, hasn't said a peep about her increased girth.

When she and Sylvie were in that closet, lifted up, almost carried off, Nina felt her lightness as a curse. Only her bulk, puny as it was, kept them anchored. Lying in bed at night, curled against Perry and matching her breath to his, as her mind slows and empties she often has no specific thought but just a feeling of fragility, an animal terror washing over her. To calm herself she'll swing her legs off the bed, plant bare feet on the floor and concentrate on the density of her self, the space she inhabits, bones pressing into the earth. She leans over to touch her toes, bending her knees, resting her soft belly against her thighs, and sways, breathing, feeling herself grow solid. A quick whispered prayer against her knees: "Remember how brief is my life, how frail the race you created! Lord, help me be better, help me be true." Then she climbs back into bed and sleeps like the dead.

The whiny singer fades and she turns the dial, looking for another song that suits her. If there is downtime in Ann Arbor, she'll find ways to fill it. She can always find something that needs doing. Nina's foot is heavy on the gas. Though she's given herself plenty of time, more than enough, she'll speed the whole way.

*

Perry sits in his truck bed, parked on the acreage he has leased from Rose, eating an apple and planning a fence for the new pasture. There's an extra chill in the wind this afternoon. Across the fields the bare limbs of young black maples run alongside his house on the hill, the absence of green somehow making it look more remote. He has become used to seeing his place from this vantage point—has come to feel, rightly or wrongly, that all of it is his.

He slides out of the truck bed with the half-eaten apple in his mouth and presses his hands against the small of his back to stretch. It bothers him that he'd had to fire Ben Culp, the boy they had hired to help out on the farm. Nina thinks Ben quit, but in fact Perry told him to go. After he came back from his second tour of duty Ben was eager for work. Hiring him was the right thing to do on paper: a local kid, a veteran. But the reality of it was bumpy from the get-go. He'd lost weight and shown up late or not at all. The once-quiet boy had become touchy and unpredictable, given to paint-peeling obscenities. Perry never knew how to respond. He didn't want to hear about the inside of the kid's head, he just wanted a worker he could count on. There were rumors that Ben was on meth, and it was easy to believe it. Perry feels torn about letting him go regardless, and in no rush to hire someone new, even though he won't be able to start the fence without help. A swirling flock of longspurs wheels overhead, looking for a spot to rest. He takes the apple from his mouth and considers it, white flesh already browning at the edges.

"I had no choice. What was I supposed to do?" He still forms arguments with his father—I deserve this, I earned this, hear me. Perry had thought his life would be simpler without the Old Man in it. It isn't. There's just one more thing to account for every day: the fact of an absence.

Of course he had a choice about firing Ben. He doesn't need to gin up an argument with his dead father to know this. But how much is he responsible—how much is any one person responsible? Does it stop at Ben or extend to every tragedy on the evening news? Should he bleed a little every time he fills the tank with gas? There is the problem of knowing too much. There is the problem of not knowing. How can both of these problems, all of them, be his at once? His house is unmoved on its hill. At least he knows what the hogs need, and how to grow the corn that still pays the bills. Perry doesn't know where his father would have come down on the Ben question. The Old Man wouldn't have been whipsawed, that's all Perry knows—he wouldn't have spent five seconds bemoaning his choice, he just would've made one.

Perry finishes the apple and throws the core far into the field. Then he slides into the truck and starts the engine. Cold air blasts in as he picks up speed, but he doesn't roll up the window. Perry will lose track of his usual schedule with Nina out of town. He will eat irregularly and fall asleep on the couch. He'll feel the house less and the land more, the reclaimed pasture waiting for him. He'll talk out loud to his father, and he'll convince himself to delay for another month hiring someone to replace Ben. Sylvie won't want to take over—Perry has been preparing for that eventuality since she declared her college major. He and Nina will keep the farm going until their bodies give out and then sell to the highest bidder. But not yet. He'll work as hard as he can for as long as he can, and he'll try to make the right decisions, even when his responsibilities outpace his capacity to answer for them.

Because what else can you do?

*

Stella is in the break room at work, eating a cup of blueberry yogurt and reading a merchandising magazine. She glances at the clock: ten minutes before she has to head back onto the floor. Stella worked her way up from a job at the jewelry counter, and is now the department store's associate manager of women's fashion, a domain that sits squarely between teens and plus sizes. They are pleased with her here. Her boss, Elaine, talked recently about sending her to a special management class and told her that if she wanted she could train to become a buyer.

"What do you think?" Stella had asked Rose over dinner in their usual booth near the window at The Bluebird. "Should I go for it? It might be great. Lots of travel, though." Rose had listened carefully and suggested that Stella discuss it again with Elaine, prudently ask for more details as she also let it be known that she is eager to move up in the company's ranks. It was the kind of conversation that, five years ago, Stella never would have imagined having with anyone, let alone Rose.

After Rose had spoken she'd gone quiet, that familiar faraway look in her eyes, staring out the window. On the street in front of the café, Scottie Dunleavy, skinnier than ever, slipped past carrying a tattered grocery bag; he looked up, sensing Rose's eyes, and they nodded to each other. Scottie seemed to dissolve into the shadows.

"Did you see that? See what I mean?" Emma called from behind the counter. She had been talking to them about Scottie's condition with increasing concern.

Rose shook her head. "He's not losing it. He just doesn't care about the same things you do."

"Like what—bathing? Eating?"

Rose had just kept watching the empty street. Stella thought she might be composing in her head. Rose wrote letters. For a few years she mailed a stack every week—to the White House, the state capital, newspapers, think tanks, every elected representative she could lay claim to, multiple times. At first she'd received polite replies—*thank you for your thoughts . . . our deepest condolences for your sacrifice*. Now, only silence. But Rose keeps writing. An endless line of inquiry without the end stop of an answer.

The break room clock reads 2:56. Almost time to get back to work. Stella dog-ears a page about the return of the pencil skirt and shuts the magazine.

"Tell me what you're thinking." She has asked it of Rose a hundred ways, getting different versions of the same answer: I'm thinking of him. What else?

Stella no longer offers up her own memories as solace. That's not what Rose wants. Rose holds herself apart, holds her grief apart, and Stella, no matter how much she talks, can't reach the core. She strives to be patient. Perhaps Rose had always kept herself in cautious reserve, and Stella's memories of intimacy in their youth were colored by nostalgia and need. Some part of Rose had always been beyond her reach.

And so what if it was? Who's to say closeness has just one way of being? Stella hasn't dated anyone in a while. All of her energy goes into Rose, into figuring out how to keep her listening, delaying the return of the faraway look. The truth is, there's no one she'd rather spend the effort on.

Raquel from the perfume counter breezes into the break room, greeting Stella warmly. She's young and distractible and very likable, very familiar, with brown skin and a cloud of dark hair and the faint mark of a lip ring recently removed. Raquel has decided that Stella, in spite of her advanced age, is a cool confidante. She's excited now, talking about a flirty conversation she had with a cute guy who manages the cell phone shop at the other end of the mall. Stella smiles and listens and gives the merest hint of advice. He'd be crazy not to like you, but don't rush headlong. Be careful with your heart, but not too careful.

Then she tosses the empty yogurt cup into the trash and heads onto the floor.

*

In the kitchen of her Ann Arbor apartment, Sylvie is trying to shake off a dream. Her mother is due in about two hours, and the kitchen and bathroom still need cleaning. Her roommate, Christa, who spends most nights at her girlfriend's place, has offered to let Nina sleep in her room, and she should throw Christa's flannel sheets into the washing machine. She will make dinner for Nina tonight, a vegetable stir-fry, the first time she's cooked for her mother in her own place. Sylvie hasn't yet mentioned to her parents that she has become a vegetarian. The kettle whistles on the stove, and she gets up to pour herself a cup of tea. Strong and black, with honey. She sets her fingers on the edge of the counter and considers them.

She dreamt of him again last night.

When she was younger, in her first lost and lonely years at college, thoughts of him flooded her in that half-awake state late at night or early in the morning, more fantasy than anything else, about the life they could have had together if he hadn't died. Like the movies. He comes home from the war unscathed and they break up and go their separate ways to different schools and on to other boyfriends and girlfriends; though years blur past they still have fond memories, and one day she's home for Christmas and walks into Mondragon's wearing a blue coat and with snowflakes in her hair. It's warm and it smells of pine and fertilizer and sweet liquor and there's Ward Mondragon behind the counter, wearing suspenders and smiling in his shy way. And Stella, humming to herself, standing on a ladder over by the stockroom. Even Rose is there, her hair a deep red, smiling at a tall man in a brown coat. He turns around, holding a roll of wrapping paper. "It's me, Sylvie," she announces, and he laughs because of course he already knows. He holds out a hand, music swells and they walk out of Mondragon's arm in arm, out into the snow and the clear cold air.

She looks at her fingers on the counter, embarrassed at the memory of her teenage yearnings. Plucking the teabag from the mug, she tosses it into the compost pail, trying to be patient with that younger self. Now years *have* blurred past. She's got a career path that she loves and a boyfriend, Matt, who wants her to come to Belize with him for winter break, and very definite opinions on the nature of the war that killed Lance, opinions in conflict with half the people who knew him, including perhaps her own parents.

Sylvie wonders if she can tell her mother something of this, if it's the kind of thing Nina might now be able to hear. She takes a sip of tea, her eyes on the ugly floral pattern on the backsplash above the stove. When she dreams of him now there's no movie music, no plot. They're in the fields or under the Infamous Elm or in the hayloft or just under a vast, cavernous sky and she doesn't know how old they are because their faces don't matter. Time telescopes and they grab hold of each other. This morning when she woke she could still feel his hand on her breast and had the absolute physical certainty that he was still out there—driving to school, swimming in the creek, getting drunk under the Elm—it was all happening right now, and if she paid attention and concentrated she'd keep feeling him. Even now she feels him.

*Here I am.*

*

Tell us what happens next.

Something pulses green in the water, leaves rustle around the swimming hole.

This is how we'll leave her: standing at a window at dawn. She could be in the kitchen of her rickety repaired farmhouse. Or the old Mondragon place, a home shared with Stella, red brick on a wide street. Or in a rented in-law garden apartment in town. But she's here, here she is. Every morning she takes her coffee mug and stands at the window, looking at the yard and the sky beyond it. At her side, Fergus shakes sleep from his old bones, his white muzzle luminous. The light is blue and thin and casts no shadow. Everything, for a few minutes, is lit with an evenness that brings out solid, two-dimensional edges: the trees' wayward branches and a tangle of shrubs. A longspur stops to perch on a branch. Soon the machinations of the day will envelop her—the click of shoes on sidewalks, phone calls and greetings and the humdrum patter of daily life. This moment is what she lives for, this is when she feels him most. *Lance*. The quiet lets her peer across again, and she feels the void, waiting, always there for her—coldness and clarity where there had been tumult.

The bird flies off, breaking the spell, and Rose bends to touch Fergus, pressing a palm to his wide warm head.

# Acknowledgments

Grateful acknowledgment to the editors of *Puerto del Sol*, *Blackbird*, and *Red Earth Review*, where portions of this work appeared in earlier form. And also to the Ragdale Foundation for providing essential time and space.

The image of hot coins before the lightning strike in the Old Man's section is borrowed from Heather McHugh's poem "Acts of God." Camille Seaman's Big Cloud photos provided visual inspiration.

Peg Alford Pursell, Robert Thomas, and Rebecca Winterer generously shared their wisdom across several drafts. In many ways along the road, these friends offered solidarity and insights: Michael Alenyikov, Krissy Cababa, Mari Coates, Peg Cronin, Audrey Ferber, Joan Frank, Judy French, Amy Halloran, Mimi Herman, George Higgins, Faith Holsaert, Rachel Howard, Janeen Jang, Scott Landers, Richard May, Kate Nitze, Lori Ostlund, Cass Pursell, Anne Raeff, Nadia Scholnick, Lisa Gluskin Stonestreet, Alice Templeton, Janet Thornburg, Tracy Winn, and Olga Zilberbourg.

Much appreciation for the community of writers in the Warren Wilson MFA Program, especially these teachers: Adria Bernardi, Lan Samantha Chang, Judith Grossman, Laura Kasischke, Kevin McIlvoy, and Chuck Wachtel.

I'm lucky this book found a home at Black Lawrence Press. Thank you, Diane Goettel, for believing in it. Thanks also to Yvonne Garrett and Gina Keicher for helping to bring it into the world.

At the beginning, and in the end, my family. I'm grateful to my parents for loving books and teaching me to do the same. Most necessary of all is Lauren Whittemore, whose steadfast love and support are true gifts.

Photo: Laura Duldner

Genanne Walsh lives in San Francisco and holds an MFA from Warren Wilson College. Her work has appeared in *Puerto del Sol*, *Blackbird*, *Red Earth Review*, *Spry*, *BLOOM*, *Swink*, and elsewhere. *Twister* is her first book.